Dear Heart, How Like You This?

Dear Heart, How Like You This?

WENDY J. DUNN

METROPOLIS INK

METROPOLIS INK
USA / Australia

web: www.metropolisink.com

email: inquiries@metropolisink.com

"Many things do not happen as they ought;
most things do not happen at all. It is for the
conscientious historian to correct these defects."
—*Herodotus*

*Inspired by a poem of Sir Thomas Wyatt, this resulting novel
is a work of fiction. Historical characters, incidents and
locations are either used fictitiously or conjured purely from the
writer's imagination.*

*Dedicated to the man who made possibilities possible,
my beloved husband Peter.*

Acknowledgments

I have decided to take a rest from the book's final touches to begin to write—at long last—the promised acknowledgment page. Virginia Wolf said that for a woman to write fiction she needs money and a room of her own—two things I lack. Even so, I still manage to write. How? Well, read on and discover how the seemingly impossible became possible.

This book resulted from a daydream stalking my imagination for years—from the moment I first thought that I would like to use Sir Thomas Wyatt's poem as basis for a novel, until I finally put my nose down and did something about it. On this score, I thank my friend Paul Staff who gave so much encouragement during the initial stages of the book.

I owe a debt of gratitude to my brother-in-law Stephen Corneille and dear friend Christina for being willing, and brave enough, to proofread this baby as the novel began to take its final shape.

I also gratefully acknowledge another treasured friend: Cindy Vallar, author of *The Scottish Thistle*, who took time out from her own, important historical writing to critique the book from first page to last, writing a minor thesis of notes in the process. Dear Cindy, you have a noble and generous heart. Thank you!

Ian Fraser, CEO of Indra Publishing, Australia, I must also sincerely thank for his help in keeping alive my belief that this novel would one day find its publisher.

Another group important in my development as a writer is the Montmorency Writers Group: Elisabeth Bromley, Keren Heenan, J. Victoria Michael and Sue Lockwood—such an immensely talented group of writers. Thank you all! I'm so proud to be a part of our "writing kin"!

In my life, I have been truly blessed. Not only do I have a precious family (my husband Peter, and children James, Timothy, Elisabeth and David—the rest know who they are!) but also supportive friends. Ingrid, Glenice, Elizabeth and Vikki—my sister in-law—I must mention especially. The many times Vikki fed my hungry, neglected family I will never forget. My dear friends Glenice Whitting and Elizabeth Batt have both given me constant support and encouragement whenever needed. Nor can I ever forget Ingrid's unfailing belief—during a friendship stretching over twenty-five years—in my abilities as a writer.

I must express my thankfulness to Marilee (Webmaster of englishhistory.net) and her friendship and support, as well as all my good friends at "Tudor Talk" e-list.

I also owe such an immeasurable debt to Kurt Florman, Partner and Editorial Manager of Metropolis Ink. Thank you so much for having faith in this novel!

There is one final acknowledgement. Throughout my novel, I have made use of the poetry of Sir Thomas Wyatt. I wish here to gratefully acknowledge the book used for this purpose: *Sir Thomas Wyatt, the complete Poems*; General Editor: Christopher Ricks.

Lastly, I will say dreams do come true, but often their realisation takes a lot of hard work and perseverance. But the harder the work, the greater the perseverance, then the more joy there is when you hold the dream—tangible—in your hands. I know! Thank God for small miracles!

WJD

Book One

They flee from me that sometime did me seek
with naked foot stalking in my chamber.
I have seen them gentle, tame, and meek
That now are wild and do not remember
That sometime they put themselves in danger
To take bread at my hand; and now they range
Busily seeking with a continual change.
Thanked be fortune, it hath been otherwise
Twenty times better; but once in special,
In thin array after a pleasant guise,
When her loose gown from her shoulders did fall,
And she me caught in her arms long and small;
Therewith all sweetly did me kiss,
And softly said, "Dear heart, how like you this?"
It was no dream: I lay broad waking.
But all is turned, thorough my gentleness,
Into a strange fashion of forsaking;
And I have leave to go of her goodness,
And she also to use newfangleness.
But since that I so kindly am served,
I would fain know what she deserved.

Sir Thomas Wyatt

Prologue

Written at Allington, May, 1536.

My Anna was dark and lovely—full of life's burning light. How strongly my love's fire did blaze. Too strong, yea, too strong for this world. For her bright, burning light has forever been put out; aye, put out, and my life is eternally dark. Too dark *tout de suite* for me to ever see the end of my despair.

I knew my Anna and loved her from the beginning of my life. We grew up together as children, for we were also blood kin—being cousins—and lived our early lives as close neighbours. Then a day came when almost every moment of my childhood became a time to be shared with her. Gentle and sweet my Anna was in those early days, overflowing with laughter and the joy of living life.

I learnt to love her as I learnt to live, and loving Anna made her as much a part of me as the blood flowing in my veins. Anna grew to love me too. Not as much as I wanted her to love me. Not as I desired her to love me. But, for me, enough with to make do and take all my life's joy.

Only once were we true lovers. If our *merciful* and *gentle* King Harry finally decides to allow me to live, then the memory of that one wet, summer's day, those few short hours of bliss when my burning desires were at last led by her to a brief fulfilment will be all which remain of joy. No more. Nothing. All is so empty.

What is now my future but a stark, dark void in which to fall?

Oh, Anna! My burning light. My lovely girl. Dearest of hearts. My only beloved. To know that you lie dead. Oh, how dark has become my world! I cannot help but feel that the best of me is gone. It vanished instantly when your life was taken.

I curse the fates, cursing all the disappointments that caused you to first set your feet upon the road leading to such a terrible, bloody end. But most of all I curse the despot we call King. He so willingly and selfishly defiled your name and honour so to destroy all that was precious to me.

The King never knew you as I did. How could he? He never saw you as I did: growing up untouched by the world at Hever. So innocent. So in love with life. So believing in all life's goodness.

From almost the beginning of our lives, you were always my good and constant playmate, even though more than three years separated our births. Aye—how I remember us: lying on our bellies in the meadows of your Kentish home, breathing in the sweet aurora of the wet spring grass, trying, with so much pure enjoyment, to outdo the other's childish poetry. I think it was with you, my Anna, that I first became aware of the beauty one can create with words. I know it was with you, dearest of hearts, that I first became aware of all that love could mean: its joys that had you ascending near to Heaven, and its heartbreaks that left you sore and bleeding but, yet, painfully and utterly alive.

How could we have known then what life held in store for us? Never could we have imagined that the English Caesar would one day desire you. Indeed, desire you so much that he would cause the breakup of your first youthful love—when you gave your heart to Hal Percy—with the result that you, angry and torn apart, would plan to use the King's lust as a way to gain revenge.

Oh, my lovely Anna! If only you could have known then the danger your scheme would lead you to. If only you had listened to me that dark day (when the cloudless sky served only to mock) so long ago, when we fought in the gardens!

I wish I could wake to find I have been dreaming all these desolate, hateful happenings. Even more, I wish I could wake and find that we could go back. Yea, go back to Hever and the green, rolling meadows of our childhoods, and begin our lives yet again. Oh, dear God—please, dear God—can we not begin our lives again?

4

Aye, begin our lives again but this time, aye, this time fulfil the sunshine that once was?

Of all the thoughts which keep me company in this lonely room in my father's castle, as much my dark dungeon as the cell in the Tower, the ones haunting me most are: *If only your father had not seen fit to send you to France. If only he had seen his children as other than chattels to add to his worldly wealth. If only he could have seen that we two were soul mates and thus, in the best of loving wisdom, suited to be betrothed to one another.*

If only! It would have saved both of us so much grief and agony. It would have saved you from dying on a scaffold. And I believe—yea I believe with all my heart—that you could have grown to love me as I have always loved you. Even now, when your earthly, headless body lies rotting in a disused box meant only for arrow shafts, do I profess my love; I will always love you until my last breath is drawn.

More unending tears roll down my cheeks. Grief imprisons my heart just as my love for you once did. How can my heart still thud in my chest when I am forced to live my life without you?

Yet you are such a part of me that I need but close my eyes to see you at almost every stage of your life. As a child you were a slight and tiny girl who loved to run and ride, but especially you loved to dance. Even when there was no music but what you alone could hear—music vibrating with every beat of your heart. I close my eyes and still see you, my Anna. A fairy child with long, loose ebony hair, wearing a heavy golden dress, spinning this way, spinning that way, always, always spinning. That is how I first became truly aware of you. One day I, a child of five, saw you, a child of two, with eyes shut tight and arms outstretched, dancing to your private and silent melody in a sun-drenched corridor. Full grown you were of middling height—so slight and graceful, with a swan-like neck, made even more bewitching and sensual by an upraised, brownish mole placed where one could feel the echo of your heartbeat. Hair so black it shone with vivid blue lights. Hair which, when loosened, flowed past your tiny waist. Bewitching brown eyes, beautiful eyes—drawing me into deep inside of you. Oh, Anna, how many, many times I thought I would drown into your eyes.

Aye—'tis true—many people said you had little true beauty, except for your eyes and wide, sensual mouth. (A mouth made for kisses. My kisses! Your mouth once so moist and soft, so hot and eager for my hungry lips.) Yea, so many people said that you had little of true beauty—rather there was something about your whole being that captivated. An aura surrounded you making you unforgettable; an aura that led you to such a dreadful death.

No, I am not blind nor am I deaf. I know living with fear on one side and the threat of death on the other made your temper fiendish at times. Indeed, many called you a shrew, therefore believed it was not surprising that the King became sick enough of you to seek any means he had to escape the savaging of your tongue.

Many also called you witch, taking as proof a slight deformity on your right hand, a hand that even so was beautiful. What use is it now, when you lie murdered, to say to them that they speak of what they know not.

You were no witch. Rather you had the gift of living deeply, touching people's lives in one way or another. Most people never knew you; they only saw an exterior created by the King and his selfish lust. Inside you were still my lovely Anna; my Anna so terrified of the Pandora's box she had opened.

As I sit here in my father's home, not knowing for certain if I am to live or die, I slowly and painfully turn over the pages of my life. I find the only pages I desire to dwell upon at all are those emblazoned by your presence, Anna... my dark Lady. Even when you and I were separated, I carried the thought of you in my heart and took solace that my beloved walked on the same earth as I. And I... I cannot help wondering if the King decides I am to live, when he has brought death to so many others (so many others for no cause, yet 'tis I alone he ought to have slain) how am I to live without you—without you, my Anna? Aye my life... a life where I will no longer hear your voice or laughter. A life that will no longer contain the joy of watching you dance so gaily to a song of your own creation. A life where my Anna no longer listens closely to my words, considering deeply what I say. Aye—you—Anna, my dear friend as well as my beloved. What has life now to offer me? These bloody days have broke my heart. By all the wounds of Jesus, I cannot yet think myself forward. Better that I go back to the time of our childhoods at Hever Castle. Hever Castle: more home to me than my father's manor and heritage at Allington. Your Boleyn grandfather had it rebuilt as a statement of his improved status and wealth. Originally falling down with neglect and age, it had been lovingly converted into a fine home for his family and dependents. Surrounded by a moat and green, lush meadows, it was a perfect place for the children we once were. Aye—for the children we once were.

Chapter 1

"Therewith all sweetly did me kiss."

Despite the tenth hour of morning, darkness deluges the room. Even so, at the room's far end, a little light emits from a dying fire in the hearth and a tall, narrow window—at the back of an embrasure constructed in the grey stone wall—gives out some more. In the embrasure, a small boy kneels on the confined window-seat—seemingly gazing out at a dull day as rain beats its rhythm upon the thick lattice glass. Upon the veil of condensation formed onto the glass surface, the boy begins doodling his name: T-h-o-m-a-s W-

The sound of an opening door turns the boy from the window to see—silhouetted against the light in the next room—a man's shape fill the doorway.

Somewhere near, there is the weak mewing sound of a newborn infant.

"Father!"

The boy swings his body away from the window, but he hesitates and sits on the edge of the seat, watching.

The man comes in the room and walks over to the hearth, removing a rush from beside it. Taking a flame from the fire, he lights the candle in the sconce fixed high in the wall, then tosses a log of wood into the fire, stirring the embers back to life. His gaze turns toward the boy.

"Have you been forgotten, Tom? You shouldn't be in the dark."

With his head drooping, face unshaven and eyes red-rimmed, the man sits beside the boy. Glancing at the boy, he looks very sick.

"Tom, my boy, I must leave soon to return to court. Soothly, when I go, I believe it would be best if you leave Allington too. But

8

not to court, Tom; you're too young for that yet. I plan to place you in care of our Boleyn kin. Would you like that, my son? I know you like your three cousins and they are closer in age to you than your sister and brother. They'll be good companions for you, and I would be happier knowing you were not so alone here."

Wordless, the boy moves closer to his father, until he nestles into him. With tears running down both their faces, the father enfolds his small son tightly in his arms.

★

"Anna! Wait, I beg of you!"

The taller boy sped towards the little girl, pausing in her skipping to look back at him and her brother. Her feet barely keep still on the ground. The elder of the two boys reaches her side first.

"Is there call to be always so fast? You must stay with us, Anna."

The other boy, shaking his head as if in repressed laughter, stands beside him.

"Simonette is right, coz. My sister has quicksilver pumping in her veins, rather than the usual red blood." He places a finger under the girl's chin, lifting her face so she looks at him. She gives him an impish grin. "Please listen, Nan If you wish to be with us you must do as mother expects. She would get very cross if she saw you running, and I don't dare think what would happen if she catches you skipping. Remember, sister, who you are."

The little girl bobs a brief curtsey.

"Simonette says one day I shall be a great lady."

The boys look at each other, and laugh. Her cousin drops to his knee before her, with her brother quickly following suit.

"And we shall be your noble knights!" her cousin proclaims in his deepest voice.

Anna laughs and, picking up her skirts, she starts to run, calling over her shoulder, "My knights! Catch me then, I dare you!"

Glancing at one another again, the boys laugh before racing after her.

★

Two boys climb an old oak tree, the older one helping the other up. They climb up until they find a branch on which they both can safely sit; when they do, they settle their backsides, swing their legs, and look out towards the castle.

"Shall we have a wager on how long it will take for them to find us, Tom?"

The darker boy turns to the fair one, considering him.

"What sort of wager, coz?"

"Father gave me a new dagger for my name day; if I am wrong, you may have it. If I'm right, I get to keep it."

"Show me this dagger of yours, George."

The younger boy takes a dagger from his belt, and hands it to the other who inspects it carefully. He looks back to George.

"All right—shall we spit on it?"

Lavishly, they spit on their right palms before clasping each other's hand. Still holding hands, they pause and look at one another. The darker boy clasps tighter his cousin's hand.

"Friends forevermore."

The other boy lays his free hand over those clasped.

"Aye—friends forevermore, Thomas Wyatt."

Hands released, they look back towards the castle.

"So what say you, Tom? How long before we hear the girls bay at the bottom of this tree?"

"I say but only a short time—when the sun reaches where we sit."

"Coz, I say more. My sisters were in no hurry. Indeed, they were more intent to fill their baskets up with flowers to take back for Simonette than seek us amongst the oak grove."

"No matter—we can occupy ourselves while we wait to see who outdoes the other with rhyme. Shall I begin?"

"Aye, Tom. Why not."

★

In my fifth year my father made the decision to send me to my mother's kinsman, Sir Thomas Boleyn, so I could begin my education alongside my cousin George. I find it surpassingly easy to recall my feeling at this time, my feeling of confusion as to why my nurse was not coming with me, and the emotion seemingly stifling the beating of my heart whenever I remembered my mother. Verily, I remember being confused and unhappy for so many, many different reasons. Only as I grew older did I understand that families of our status customarily sent their offspring to homes of relatives or friends to gain the beginnings of their education and strengthen attachments already formed. Yea, that knowledge came to me much later. When it happened that my life was altered for the first time, I was but a small lad, very, very wrenched from all that was loved and familiar.

I already knew my cousins well, for there always had been constant goings to and from one household to the other, as our family estates were situated close to one another and, thus, made us near neighbours in our county of Kent.

My cousin George and I were of similar ages. More importantly, we possessed similar interests and fast became good friends. Add that deep friendship to our kinship, and you have a strong tie, one enduring until savagely cut—cut by bloodthirsty events to befall us as grown men. Aye, George and I had, from the beginnings of our lives, a strong bond of companionship. Verily, even more than that, this bond seemed like a stalwart thread of constant affinity running through the fabric of both our lives.

Like me, he had sisters. But where my sister Margaret seemed a necessary bane, a person I knew little but was committed to for duty sake, George was more fortunate. To be more truthful, fortunate with one sister at least. This sister was named Anne, the youngest of the Boleyn children. George's other sister Mary being the eldest, while he, the only boy, born in the middle.

I felt fondness for my cousin Mary. She was a sweet girl, pretty with fair hair, interested in female pursuits and largely disinterested in anything too intellectual. Anne, even though possessing the most beautiful and expressive eyes I have ever beheld, seemed less pretty than her sister did. Yet, Anna's body, with its fragile bones, promised enduring beauty. If that promise seemed not enough, Anne, even as an *enfant,* was already turned towards a world of learning. So much so I truly believe even Sir Thomas More—who educated so well his own daughters—would have been captivated with, and approving of, the girl child who was Anne Boleyn.

Aye—even when she was a very little girl I adored her. There is a clear memory of George, Anna, and myself as small children. George and I were wrestling, testing our boyish strengths against one another, while Anna—not quite three—sat close by, cross-legged, making flower chains from the assortment of wildflowers in her lap. Soon the time came when George and I had enough of the rough and tumble of our game. We shook ourselves free of dirt and grass adhering to our persons, and walked, with our arms flung over each other's shoulder, to be with Anne. Her face lit up as we came nearer to her and she held out to us the flower chains she had made. I found myself laughing at Anna's obvious enjoyment of her innocent craft, and broke away from George to take the proffered chain of flowers from her smaller hands.

I went down on one knee, while George stood behind his sister—it seemed always so when we were children. George made the decision at Anne's cradle he would seek to be where he could protect her. He simply regarded it as his right and privilege. Thus, as George stood behind her, I carefully placed the flowers upon her head, arranging them to be as if a crown. Then Anna shook her head, causing the flowers to become lopsided. She giggled, and some of her loose hair blew into her mouth, two fingers following after.

"My lady," I said, in my best grown-up voice. I took her hand and hair away from her now smiling mouth, and smiled back at her.

"Anna, if you are to be my Queen, you must learn how to behave!" Anna laughed at me, reaching out both her hands to hold my face.

"Funny Tommy! Give Anna a kiss!" She puckered up her lips to me, and I joined mine to hers in a childish kiss.

I see this scene unfold within my mind and I cannot but help wondering if the events of our past sometimes give us hints, even omens, of what would one day be. But, who is to say which is a brief glimpse to the time before us, and which is but another moment that soon passes into oblivion. If only we could see the omens for what they really are; if only we could see them and arm ourselves, so to protect those whom we love.

★

In our childhoods, George and I—with Anne forever tagging along after us—would find every excuse imaginable to enter my uncle's library—a place none of us children were supposed to enter unless accompanied by our tutor, Father Stephen. It was a wonderful library, possessing one of the most extensive ranges of books in the whole of England. For us three, the library seemed as if some kind of Eden full with forbidden fruit. But, like Adam and Eve of time long passed, we could not resist the temptation of sampling the fruits held within the library's four walls...

Three children—boys of ten and nine and a small girl of seven— sat huddled together on a bench, their three heads bent over a thick and open tome resting upon the middle child's lap. All at once, the closed library door swung open, and a young girl of eleven rushed into room.

"George! Tom!"

The children looked up guiltily at the elder girl's entrance. Then one boy stirred angrily on the bench where he and his companions were sitting.

"Mary!" he cried in a pained voice. A fair, tousled-haired lad, his face specked with freckles, he gazed at the girl as if just recovering from a major fright.

"Why can you never knock, or give some kind of warning, before barging in on us?"

The younger girl, her body gently leaning on the boy who had just spoken as if drawing her security from being thus close to him, gazed up at Mary with huge, dark eyes.

"Please, Mary, do not tell! I begged George and Tom to take down from the shelves father's *Tales of Canterbury*. It was my idea truly," the girl pleaded in a soft, melodic voice.

Mary, hands on hips, glanced briefly at the book.

"Oh, that—as if I care whether you three desire to get into trouble and gain a hard beating for taking father's best books from their proper places! Listen! I've just heard the most enthralling news from Simonette. Father has at last persuaded mother to allow me to be sent to the Continent. I am to go to the court of Brussels next month!"

She began dancing around the room in excitement.

"I can hardly believe it, but I am to be a Maid to Margaret, Duchess of Austria!" Mary stopped in front of the bench, giving a slight curtsy in the general direction of the other three children.

Anne and George stared long at Mary. Then they looked at each other, unaware that, beside them, the older boy gazed at them both. He knew, without questioning them, why they looked at each other with such fear. He feared the same thing: that Mary's departure would soon be followed by other departures, the three of them separated too.

Mary, becoming aware of the silence and mistaking its meaning, stamped her foot.

"You two are just jealous! I am glad to be going. Glad, I tell you! Verily, so very glad to be getting away from both of you!"

She spun around, her blonde, untidy loose hair twirling around her head as if wind-whipped by her anger, and was out the door as quickly as she had entered.

*

I had lived with the Boleyns for about five years when Mary was sent to the court of Brussels. Mary rarely appeared as cross as she was that day. Verily, of all the Boleyn children, I would have said that Mary was the one to have the sweetest temper.

Nonetheless, it was extremely difficult for my cousins to grow up as children of my uncle. Uncle Boleyn was an uncommonly handsome man, with a well-shaped face bedecked by a glorious red beard and possessing piercing blue eyes that reminded you of an eagle surveying the world in which it lived. He was also an extremely ambitious man, a man who planned to step higher in the society in which he lived via the use of his three young children. And they were intelligent enough to realise, from an early age, what his purposes and ambitions were. His children also knew that they had to strive very hard indeed to be able to give to him his pound of flesh, and thus gain their father's hard won approval.

I had not much liking for my uncle and felt very thankful his duties at court meant that he was rarely in residence at Hever Castle. Verily, his visits were never welcomed. Rather we knew when we heard his heavy step approaching the nursery that one of us was likely to be violently punished for some minor transgression. No, I did not much like my uncle. Even when I was a child, he struck me as a heartless and unrelenting man. A man who calculated every move he made. A man only interested in what best served the achievement of his own desires. Verily—I speak only but the truth—my uncle was a selfish man who heartlessly ignored his children's need for a father's love and approval.

I believe it was especially hard for Mary. My cousin never did have the inner strength needed to meet any of Uncle Boleyn's hard demands. Nor was Mary—at least, not until a woman full-grown—able to stand up to her father in any way.

I felt grateful my own father was very much different. He too was a busy official of the Crown, so was also much away from our family estate at Allington. But when home, he would always ride his horse over to come visit me or send for me to return home for a short visit so to see my sister. My father is a godly man, wise, gentle and always even-tempered. His greatest desire, in contrast to my uncle, was to do good and be the loyal friend of all who sought for his friendship. Indeed, in the life ahead of me, never was I to meet a man more faithful to his friends. My father valued truth and honour above all things. Thus, I always looked forward to his visits, and to my visits to Allington.

My mother? What of her? Why do I remain so silent?

Yea, I remember her. Aye, how do I remember my sweet mother—she who I loved and then lost forever. Something in my life that once was a tangible substance, and then altogether too swiftly, like an arrow in flight finding its target, became a black vacuum. I remember, and yet do not want to remember… If I delve too deeply into myself in search of memories of her I begin to tremble and ache, as if inflicted with some unresolved torment. If I delve, I begin to bleed. Therefore, it is best to leave my feelings of dark despair locked inside of me forever. Aye, my loving and beloved mother died in childbirth before I left for Hever, which was one of the many reasons why this arrangement for my upbringing came to be.

As well as my sister, I also had a younger brother, Henry, the child my mother bore into the world as her own life was taken, whom I had left as but an infant when I departed from home. My infant brother died before I had a chance to grow to know or love him, thus being brought up with my cousin George seemed like gaining a brother in his stead. Perchance, even if Henry had lived, George would have taken his place in my heart. The friendship George and I shared comes only once in a fortunate lifetime.

Aye. My cousins became easily and quickly the objects of my boyhood affections. They were also the people I enjoyed squabbling with. And, being children, we had many, many squabbles, but they all ended as they began—in friendship.

Aye. 'Tis so easy to recall my cousins from those early years. Mary, all blonde and always pretty—even if often untidy. A gentle, sweet girl who seemed to never think deeply about anything too important, who grew into a woman easily persuaded and, just as easily, hurt and cast aside.

George. My very good and dear friend George. Tousled hair, lanky, very freckled George, with the brightest blue eyes I have ever seen, always so completely loyal to those he loved. My cousin George was such an important part of my life.

Then there was Anne. My sweet Anna. Anna, who sometimes seemed like a fairy child left in place of a mortal child. Forever darting here and there, as if a spell had been cast upon her; a spell that forbade her to stand still for more than a moment. Anne. Anna. My beloved. Reader, you must realise by now what I thought of her. For this present moment, I will speak no more of that.

My cousins Anne and George possessed a special brother and sister relationship. Forever together in childhood as if God had meant them to be cast out into the world as twins and then decided otherwise. Both George and Anne were musical. Verily, poetry and melody flowed through their veins as well as the usual red blood.

Even when they were very small children, Anne would often write the lyrics to George's musical compositions, while George would do the same for her creations. To me, it came as no surprise to learn that their last night upon this earth was spent composing sonnets for their much-loved lutes. From little children, I know they took to music, just like swans take to gliding upon lakes of crystal waters.

Yea, George and Anne were more to one another than ordinary siblings, but it was evil and vicious of the King and his ministers to suggest that their relationship was ever incestuous. Rather, I say they were like two separate pieces of the same soul.

We three—Anne, George, and I—always formed such a happy and contented trio. The three of us enjoyed playing with words and music, and would often have contests to see who could outdo the other two. Even as young children we were always completely honest with each other about our work. While we were growing up, Anne would constantly tell me, to my great delight, that she believed me to be a great poet.

I can still see her to this day: pixie face, chin upon fist, sitting cross-legged on the thick, green grass looking at me frankly with those big, darkly hazel and delectable eyes. Eyes, seemingly, often taking over her entire face.

"Tommy," she would say in utter seriousness, "you do know how to write such lovely rhymes. Your poems are like keys opening doors inside of you. Some open the doors to your mind, while others are keys that open the secret doors to your heart."

I would laugh at her when she said things to me like this. Here she was, such a little girl, always trying to perceive things in a way that was beyond the reasoning of childhood, but which often appeared even beyond the reasoning of most adults.

Like me, George and Anne loved poetry, and often tried their hand at composing verse. But music, as I have already mentioned, formed the major passion of their lives. Verily, George and Anne both seemed to live just to be able to sing and dance, especially so when the music and the dance were of their own invention and design.

Many an afternoon, when we were children, we would gain permission from Father Stephen to escape from our ordinary lessons so to take our lutes to a tiny chamber in the castle that we regarded as our private music room. Often our good Father, who came to be our attentive and appreciative audience, joined us there. In this room we would sing, dance and play our lutes until our fingers were red and sore, and our voices hoarse, thus could sing no more that day.

My sweet Anna possessed a lovely singing and speaking voice. Indeed, more than lovely, her voice simply enchanted. But, I tell you true, she was no witch, as the King would one day claim. I swear that on my eternal soul. There was true magic in our childhoods, but the magic came out of love, not evil.

Yea, all in all, I know this time of our childhoods was an enchanting time. We three children—close in age and temperament—aided each other's development, helping to form each other's being and, just by being together, constantly enhanced and enriched each other's life.

Furthermore, we were blessed to spend these early years in an enchanting place. Hever. Just that one word will conjure up images in my mind of a small, moated castle. A castle set within tall, yew hedges, amidst green, lush meadows adorned with a thousand and one different flowers. Hever. Amber-coloured stone walls forming the background for climbing plants of all descriptions. Hever. A drawbridge that took me through a gateway—protected by four stone saints set high above in niches—and, once through the gateway, into a timbered courtyard. Even the large, latticed windows, set amongst the castle's stone walls—windows that allowed me look out on the glorious, deer-rich woodlands and the picturesque meadows surrounding Hever—were to me, as a young boy, a thing of immense beauty. Yea, even though very tiny in comparison to many other manor houses, Hever appeared beautiful in every way, decorated within and without in the finest taste and with little care for cost.

Aye, Hever: the magical kingdom of our childhoods.

But Hever was more than that. That one word conjures in my mind the image of a very young girl—bright-eyed, delicate-boned, with tendrils of ebony hair flowing loose—constantly running or skipping ahead of two lanky, growing boys, slowly taking their time getting to their destination whilst engaged in serious talk.

Yea, I hear you say, I speak as if I was a child lost in love. I tell you soothly. I can mark the time and place when my childhood ended. I stood with George upon a barren shore, watching an English galleon become smaller and smaller and yet smaller in the distance—a galleon, ever so swift, leaving the port of Dover. A galleon taking within it a royal bride and a close-to-eight-year-old girl—my cousin, who—unknowingly, and so innocently—took with her such an irretrievable part of me. Verily, though I did not realise it then, Anne had taken in her keeping my heart forever.

I stood on that barren shore, with my feet astride upon those slippery rocks, shivering with violence in the cold. Aye—so cold my tears froze upon my face. I wondered then if it was possible to feel any worse than how I felt at that moment (never knowing that the day I did would be the day she went out of my life and world forever).

I suppose there are many, many people who would deny a child of such tender years the ability to know of love. But I know otherwise. Eros' arrows struck me early in my life: when I was a small boy of five and she was an even smaller girl of two, in a sun-drenched corridor where music hung in the air unheard.

Chapter 2

"I have seen them gentle, tame and meek."

As I have already pointed out at the beginning of my story, I had been five, soon to be six, when my father sent me to Hever so to be educated with our much richer cousins. Anne was then two, the baby of the family but already the dominating personality in the nursery. George was nearly five and Mary his elder just by over a year.

My uncle—still but a knight in those early days of our childhoods—was of the belief that children should begin their education at the earliest opportunity, thus at four, five and six, George, Mary and myself found ourselves busy with being tutored by Father Stephen. Mary, though, seemed always to me a very disinterested scholar, constantly making use of her female sex as an excuse to avoid the library where our lessons usually began. The girls also had a French governess, Simonette. Left widowed, childless, and with little protection in the city of Paris where she served in some lowly position at the French court, this young woman was discovered by Sir Thomas on one of his many trips abroad. Simonette was bilingual, having had an English mother, and obviously very well educated. So, in one of the few acts of kindness in his life, my uncle offered her the post of governess to his two daughters.

This turned out to be an act of greater wisdom than he ever could have realised. Aunt Boleyn possessed little interest in the goings-on in the nursery. To me, she always seemed more concerned with the social manoeuvres taking place at court than the children who were her own flesh and blood. My aunt was a very beautiful woman, even when age took a firm grip on her. My father told me her beauty once caused the family considerable concern, when, newly wed to Uncle Boleyn, it had aroused the strong interest of a near-to-seventeen boy—a boy very soon to be Henry, King of England. But my aunt's beauty only went as deeply as her skin. Elizabeth Boleyn was a shallow woman—a woman who appeared only to be happy when she felt herself to be the centre of attention.

I firmly believe that if it were not for the devotion Simonette gave to her charges, Anne and Mary would have grown up more wild and unmanageable than what they were. As it was, we all seemed—most of the time that is—to be fairly well civilised children.

And then there was the other much loved personage from my past, Father Stephen, who was the household priest as well as our tutor. Grey haired with thick, bushy, dark eyebrows and a huge Roman nose, our priest may have had a body like a barrel, but his soul and mind were those of a Titan.

Father Stephen's first lessons to us were based around the poetry of Homer. How we all—Mary too would suddenly appear out of nowhere to join us—loved the tales of the Trojan wars. It seemed to us children—watching in immense fascination while our Priest and teacher practically acted out the story as he told it—that Father Stephen became more carried away and excited about the exploits of the Greek gods than he did about his own God.

Verily, it was obvious to the four of us that Father Stephen loved everything to do with the Greeks, even more so if they were Greeks of ancient times. I suppose his love could have grown out of his personal experiences. Father Stephen would often tell us how, as a young priest, he had been sent by his order to an order of monks. Monks living their lives on a Greek island, cut off from the rest of civilisation. Father Stephen had been sent there to learn the Greek language, so that he could return home and help his brothers translate ancient Christian writings. Travelling to and from the monastery gave him an opportunity to see many, many wondrous things, the memories of which excited him—and through him us—to the end of his days.

Thanks to Father Stephen's inspired rendering of those wonderful ancient Greek poems, we all became devoted admirers of Homer's *Iliad* and *Odyssey*. Many times the three of us—George, Anna, and I—sometimes persuading Mary and Simonette to join with us too, would act out the parts of those great and engrossing stories. During those afternoons when we acted out the *Iliad*, I well remember that Anne could never decide if she wanted to play the part of a man or a woman, though she did have a liking and portrayed very well the mad and vision-tormented Kassandra. It still makes me smile, remembering Anna, with her black hair flying loosely around face and shoulders, running hither and thither, clothed in some long, old piece of blue cloth, crying out, "Flee! Flee! Flee! The Greeks are coming! The Greeks are coming!"

These tales of long ago fuelled my imagination, keeping it ablaze and eternally hungry for more fuel to feed this fire well and truly alight. Probably because of these stories I became more and more aware of what I truly wanted to accomplish in my life. Yea, even as a tiny boy, my greatest desire was to shape, when I reached manhood, a magnificent work such as Homer's, and thus be remembered forever and a day. Aye—how high do aim the young!

Our good priest was very much my mentor in my firm decision to take up the mantle of a bard. One day he and I talked about my longing to become a poet of note. Walking back together towards Hever Castle, Father Stephen said, "I'm not surprised to hear that you want to be a poet, Tom. You are always scribbling when you should be attending to your other studies. Indeed, you have a condition known in Latin as *cacoethes di scribendi*. My boy, can you remember your lessons and tell me what that means?"

I thought hard for a moment before crying in triumph, "A mania for scribbling, Father!"

"Yea, lad. That you have, that you have! Young Thomas, I am glad you desire to be a poet. Plato thought very highly of them—as do I. But do try to write good poetry, Tom. Nothing upsets my digestion more, my dear boy, than reading bad poetry!"

I started to speed up my pace as his huge bulk began to descend expeditiously down the hill before us.

"Father Stephen, what is good poetry?"

"What questions you children ask me!" He paused to catch his rasping breath, and looked at me with a wide grin.

"My boy," the priest replied, beginning the descent once more, "I believe strongly that any worthwhile poetry will always strike a responsive chord in the person hearing it. Whether as if soft breaths on a standing-harp, or a shiver running up and down your backbone. Perhaps, Tom," he now said, looking straight at me as he stopped at the bottom of the hill to wait for me to catch up to him, "the poem could even be a compelling call—something you cannot avoid—calling you to some kind of action. Aye, my boy. There are poems that to me have been as if battle cries. My lad, always remember this:" he continued, as we walked side by side along the narrow lanes taking us back to the castle. "Plato's overall message in his discussions regarding poetry is that true poetry, like music, comes from the evolved soul, and the evolvement of the soul depends entirely on the growth of a person's inner being. Remember, Tom," the Priest asked then, "how Jesus told us that 'Man does not live by bread alone' but requires spiritual nourishment to truly live?"

"Yea, Father," I said, trying hard to keep up with him, physically as well as intellectually.

"Tom, also remember true poetry comes from what is inside of you, something that is drawn out from the deep springs of your very soul. Furthermore, I believe with all my heart that the composition of poetry is simply one of the many ways we have to be true children of God. The rendering of a true poem, my dear boy, is man doing as his God did when he created us."

Father Stephen stopped. All I seemed to hear was his loud breathing as he leant his body upon a huge oak tree. He looked up at the unclouded sky, smiling as if reflecting upon something truly beautiful. His attention, just as quickly, returned to me.

"I feel so strongly that while we are all bound to this earthly existence, 'tis necessary—no, no, more than that, Tom. My boy, 'tis essential we seek out ways to be creative, for creativity keeps alive our souls and keeps us in constant touch with God and the marvellous creation that we have all around us."

Whenever Father Stephen said something like this, I always knew to take three swift steps away from him. Our dear Priest tended, without warning, to fling out his arms as if he was attempting to embrace all the world around him, but what really would happen is the good Father tended to knock over anyone or anything standing in his way.

★

It struck me many times during my growing years that Father Stephen's talents were such that he was capable of being many different things. Not long after reaching my eighth year, during a pause in one of our outside lessons when curiosity outweighed caution, I asked why he had become a priest. For a long time after my question, he just sat there, resting against one of his cherished oak trees, with his eyes half-shut, seemingly lost amongst almost forgotten memories. I thought my question would go unanswered, which was very unsettling—our priest was always one for answers. But at length, he began to speak.

"Why am I a priest? Why, Tom... I remember my mother... Yea, Tom, I remember my mother..."

"Your mother?" I felt confused, unsure how this could be in any way an explanation.

"Aye, my mother. Upon her, God bestowed so many, wonderful gifts. I was her firstborn. For the first years of my life, she and I were the only people in our world. My father was a merchant and had left us for the Continent shortly after my birth, so for the first years of my childhood there was no other child, no other person to intrude upon our idyll. Yea, my mother and I were very close and I

25

was immensely proud to have this beautiful, poetic, and artistic human being as the woman who had bore me into the world. During those first years, she took such joy to be able to include me in the world she created through her imagination. A private world that only she and I shared; a truly ethereal world full of enriched sights and sounds."

Father Stephen became silent for a moment, and then looked at me with eyes that told me clearly that memories haunted and tormented him still.

"But at the end of the third year, my father returned. By the fourth year there was another child. And another at the end of the fifth. And another at the end of the sixth; after the birth of that baby, my mother lay dead. Gone forever from this world—all the beauty of my childhood buried deep, deep beneath the cold earth. I watched my mother during those last three years of her life, Tom."

Father Stephen paused and breathed deeply, rubbing his forehead with the back of his hand, as if his head ached. He looked at me with his old, blue eyes, bleary and bloodshot. Yet it seemed to me that I could easily see within this elderly man a small boy—almost the same age as I was now—heartbroken, made suddenly alone, so full of sorrow. And the memory of having lost my own, dear mother made my eyes fill with tears—tears I quickly brushed away. Father Stephen looked abruptly away from me, and rubbed his hands together.

"I saw my mother's light grow dim through sickness and childbirth, Tom, until it was at last doused forever. I was close to eight when she died. My father placed me in an Order. I suppose I could not hide the fact that I blamed him and wished he had never returned from his long journey. By the Blessed Virgin, I swore at eight that I would never cause the death of any woman, especially a woman I loved. I suppose becoming a priest was a way of keeping that vow. Perhaps, lad, I am too selfish a person to live completely in the world. Being a priest is a good life. It gives you the choice of thinking only of yourself and God. I do not think I would have made a good husband and father. I like too much sitting underneath a tree and just thinking."

★

After the works of Homer, Father Stephen introduced us to the teachings of Socrates, as related by his former student Plato, which then led on to Plato's own philosophies. I reflected in later years that a great part of the reason he was so drawn to the study of Greek was that he was very much a devotee of Socrates from ancient times. Sometimes, I am even tempted to think—knowing full well I sin most mightily in allowing myself such thoughts—that Father Stephen would have been hard pressed to say whose teachings were greater: Socrates or Jesus Christ. Though Father Stephen's priestly calling would no doubt win out in the end, to declare the teachings of the Son of God as being the greater.

Father Stephen was a wonderful teacher who forever thought of different ways to aid us four on the paths of learning. On many an occasion he wrote a brief play that all of us would then act out in order to help us to grasp some of the reasonings of Plato and Socrates.

Within a dark wood-panel chamber, bright sunlight beams through a high lattice window, showering diamond shapes over the forms of four children. Sitting together on a low bench, the two boys and two girls fidget, holding lutes upon their laps. From a stool near the hearth, where a low fire burns, Father Stephen arises, straightening the folds of his grey cassock.

"So, my young players, we all know well our parts. Shall we make a start, do you think?"

The children look at one another, then back at the priest; one boy gives him a quick nod. Gazing at them with a serious glint, Father Stephen lifts his chin.

"All right then, I shall leave the chamber. But when I return, remember 'tis not Father Stephen you see, but Socrates from times

27

long gone."

The priest strides over to the nearby door. Without a backward glance, he closes the door behind him. The room now emptied of Father Stephen's presence, the children sneak glances at one another, straightening their forms. George begins to strum a song on his lute, humming under-breath. Tom lays a hand on the chords of his cousin's instrument.

"No more, coz. He's coming back."

Pushing open the door, Father Stephen enters the room, but his stance and walk has changed, and gives an air of a more ancient man. He comes and sits amongst the children, picking up a spare lute from the floor and begins to tune it.

George clears his throat.

"Good morrow, Grandfather."

Mary and Anne nudge one another and laugh, Mary biting her lower lip when her giggles threaten to become uncontrollable. With a quick frown at the girls, Tom, sitting beside Father Stephen, strikes up a more serious pose, peering at the man in a puzzled fashion.

Appearing to notice, Father Stephen gives Tom a broad smile.

"My name is Socrates. Could you give me the pleasure, young man, of knowing yours?"

George nudges Tom in the ribs, and Tom squirms with embarrassment, but he still manages to sputters out: "Phaidros, sir."

"Oh, please, please, Phaidros! Not Sir! We are all students here. I am here to learn. Just as you are here to learn."

Tom looks more boldly at his teacher.

"But, you are a grown man, master! Why do you come here, Socrates?"

"Oh, because of a dream, Phaidros."

"A dream?" The boy speaks as if bewildered.

The priest plays three notes upon his lute before looking again at Tom.

"Yes, I dreamt that my God came to me and told me to make

music. But I do not know if the God meant me to make music with my soul or my hands. So here I am!"

The girls giggle again; Tom ignores them and pretends to be confused.

"How can you make music with your soul, Socrates?"

"What a good question, my boy, and I have always thirsted for knowledge and answers to good questions. But I tell you, Phaidros, the longer I have lived, the more I have realised simply this: the more I have sought to know, the less I am able to answer. Nonetheless, Phaidros, let me try for you an answer; you can tell me if you think the answer is good or bad. Close your eyes, Phaidros."

Tom closes his eyes. Anne, gesturing with a finger to her lips to George and Mary, swings herself around on the bench, crouching upon her knees. She places her hands across Tom's eyes, grinning over his shoulder at Father Stephen. The priest grins at her, but then returns his gaze to Tom.

"What do you see, boy?"

"Nothing but darkness."

"Can you see a beginning or end to the darkness?"

Aware of Anne balanced behind him, Tom grins and gives a slight shake of the head.

"No. Not really."

Anne takes away her hands from Tom's eyes, lowering them to rest on his shoulders.

Father Stephen lets out a contented sigh.

"I feel 'tis likewise with the soul. The soul is the unseen part of us, which is infinite compared to our seen part. I believe the only true part of us is the soul; thus the only true music is that which is made by the soul. Does this help, Phaidros?"

"No. I do not understand."

"Nor do I, but at least knowing that we do not understand leaves us free to gain understanding."

29

Aye—this was the type of bait our wise old priest put before our young noses; firstly in English, then gradually adding Greek words. Eventually we were reciting our plays entirely in Greek. Regarding my memory of this particular play, I felt at the time that Father Stephen made use of the word *infinity* deliberately—as a little girl, Anna was always fascinated with the concept of something going on forever and ever.

One of the loveliest memories of my childhood (and there are so many to remember) is of Anna sitting on Father Stephen's lap, under a favourite spreading oak tree, trying to determine what sort of things could be described as infinitudes and the kind of things that were not.

"Father Stephen, do you think there are an infinite number of people?"

"Little one, infinity means that the number has no end. I think it should be possible to count all the people in the world." Father Stephen appeared to be in a half-doze as he sat there shaded from the sun.

Anne stayed silent for a moment, clearly pondering what he had said. Then she looked back up at him, and shook him hard to gain his full attention.

"But, Father, people keep on having babies. So the number keeps on going on and on. Would that not mean there are an infinite number of people?"

Wide-awake now, he looked long at Anne, then laughed his great, deep rumble of a laugh.

"Anne! You are a clever girl! That's a very interesting concept. But when people die, surely…"

Anne broke excitedly into his reasonings.

"But, Father, there will always be more people to replace a person who has died. When father and mother die, there is George, Mary and I to take their places. And my children will take my place when I die—I want lots and lots. So the number keeps on going on and on and on…"

"What a philosopher I have in you, my child." Father Stephen smiled broadly at her. "Just keep asking your questions, my dear, and I will run out of answers... which is how it should be... yea, how it should be." And he leaned his body against the trunk of the oak, and looked at the sky. I looked too, my gaze following the branches that reached up for the sky, a sky sliced into blue daedal shapes by verdant leaves.

★

George, Anne, and I were all swept away by the idealism of Socrates. Especially the romance of this noble man dying for his ideals, and often we wondered aloud to each other if any of us would ever be brave enough to do likewise if the opportunity arose.

Even though, for other reasons than Socrates, I know now how Anne and George proved their bravery to the world. Anne, on the day before her death, joked with her attendants about how her slender neck would give the executioner an easy job, saying also she foresaw how history would see her: Anne Lack-a-head.

And George. How could George ever be forgotten after his day in court, defying death and all by reading out loud a document claiming that Anne spoke and jested to his wife about the grave matter of the King's impotence. Thus, showing to England how the King's bruised pride could lead one straight to the executioner's block.

I believe his action was calculated to be suicidal. George had no desire to live in a world where his beloved sister had been murdered. Yea—murdered with such vicious and bloody intent.

No! No! No!

Why am I remembering this?

I want to stay in a time where all was still golden with the promise of the future. When all seemed good and nothing evil. I want to remember a time when pain was easily kissed aside. Yea, when pain was simply kissed aside.

★

If Uncle Boleyn considered five the age to begin our education, it was also the age he considered us old enough to receive our first riding lessons. Thus, we all acquired our own ponies. Mine was a grey gelding with black markings on its legs that seemed to have never forgiven the fates for rendering him less of a horse than he should have been. Toby was a challenge to ride, but ultimately loyal when the going became rough.

Anne's first horse was a chestnut mare with a white star upon its forehead, which led Anne to naming it Astra. Anna never so much reminded me of a wild gypsy as when she was astride her mare. Her long hair would always be loose and flowing, with the hint of silver earrings gleaming through her blue-black tresses. And was she clothed in feminine attire? Oh no! Not my girl, not my Anna! She always wore one of her brother's outgrown hose and tunic that she had hunted out in the clothes chest kept for our cast-offs in Simonette's room.

On our rides together we always had a loyal and faithful guardian, since forever in grave pursuit of Anna and her horse was the Boleyn's huge Irish wolfhound, a dog that answered to the name of Pluto. It may have originally been Uncle Boleyn's hunting dog—given to him by his kinsman, the Irish Earl of Ormond—but the dog had long ago decided the little girl—who took her first riding lessons on its back—was its true mistress. Verily, Anna always had a strong affinity with animals, especially those of a canine persuasion. All throughout her life she possessed one dog or another, all of which followed her around devotedly. And she was not just close to animals. Anne also possessed a deep awareness of the natural world around her.

One time, just before she departed from my everyday life for that first and dreadful time, we spent the afternoon together when suddenly there was a burst of incessant rain, even though the sun still brightly shone in a sky with only a scattering of dark clouds. Getting off our horses, we led them quickly to shelter underneath some nearby trees.

"Oh look, Tom!" Anne said, pointing upwards to the sky. "Look over there at that beautiful rainbow."

My gaze followed to where she pointed. I saw a magnificent arch of violet, red, yellow, and blue in the sky. Indeed, the whole scene around us was just full of the beauties of nature. The shower that had forced us to find shelter seemed to create before our eyes a veil of crystal droplets—droplets embraced by dancing rays of sunlight as they shone through the leaves of the trees.

It made me feel as if there was nothing better to do than to join this magical dance of rain and sun. This feeling, I know, was also transmitted to Anna, who stood by my side.

She turned, beaming at me, and said, "The world is such a beautiful place, Tommy. I just so love everything about it. How the sun rises and how the sun sets. The full silver moon on a summer's night, and a winter's sky after a heavy snowfall. How the larks sing in the spring to welcome the new morning. The way the wind smells after rain falls on a hot day.

"Blue skies... cloudy skies. Look over there where the sky is blue. Can you see those clouds, Tom? Do you not think they look like cloudy steps leading into the heavens? You know, Tommy, when I die I will go up a staircase just like that, and maybe when all earthly breath has gone out from me, God will let me become a small part of the air all around us. I feel so akin to the wind, Tommy. I almost feel as if the wind is my brother, and, if I wanted to, I could call it to do my bidding."

Anna then rushed out from beneath the trees, back into the rain, to the clearing close by. I followed and saw her raise her arms, and spin around and around.

"Brother wind, brother wind," she sang as she spun.

I laughed at her, and came close to teasing her, but lo and behold the wind did begin to increase its tempo.

To the children we once were, magic seemed to be just underneath the surface of everyday life. Scratch and we would find. It did not completely surprise me then (nor does it now) that the wind appeared to answer Anne's call. But it was no witchcraft. We three as children felt so deeply about so many things that it was as if all these invisible cords connected us securely to what we loved.

★

Often, when we were out riding, Anna would frighten me, especially since we, her elders and male protectors, were supposed to ensure her safe return. She frequently rode as if the devil himself was on Astra's tail. However, I took great heart from the knowledge that Anne was a born rider, a girl who grew up to be a woman who immensely enjoyed the chase. Unfortunately this appeared as one of the many things the King would later find compellingly attractive about her. I believe the King had never before met a woman willing to match, even excel, him in any of his own pursuits as Anne often did.

Without any doubt, Anne and the King had a love of music in common. Many, many years later, when our lives began to be deeply shadowed by what the fates had in store for us, Anne told me this. The King first became interested in her when he stood outside Queen Catherine's door and heard a lovely voice accompanied by a skilful lute player. Opening the door, he found to his great surprise that the voice, and the lute, belonged to the same person. It was at this exact moment—the King himself would one day tell Anna— he made his decision to begin his wooing.

By the Good Lord's Holy Passion! Why am I tormenting myself with what I know will be? It is the long-ago past I want to look back on; the beginnings of our tragedies can wait for a later time. For the present moment I wish only to stay with the boy I once was. Yea, stay with the boy who possessed such simple, complete faith that only good would befall us in the future.

★

If Father Stephen was mentor to our developing minds, then Simonette, the girls' governess who also cast a loving, motherly

34

eye in George's and my direction, was like the guiding star of our hearts. She must have been married and widowed while yet a very young girl because I can never remember her striking anything but that of an exceedingly youthful note—especially compared to the mature auras surrounding our priest and the other adults of our childhoods.

Simonette, in those early years of our childhoods, was a very comely young woman endowed with deep auburn hair, a lovely, soft, porcelain skin, and clear blue eyes. She was a laughing girl who spoke with a pretty, lilting accent. She also played and taught us how to play various musical instruments. Verily, we all received our first lessons on the lute from Simonette.

She always seemed one of those individuals who took great delight in just being alive. Therefore, I remember her as an extremely happy person, with a smile that would dimple both cheeks and light up her eyes.

When not busy attending to her other duties, Simonette did not hesitate to sit with the good Father and the three of us. Her hands were kept busy completing yet another one of her delicate and exquisite embroideries, while we children sat under the green shade of oak trees in the midst of some lesson.

At eventide often we gathered into the girls' nursery to hear yet another one of Simonette's stories. As well as true stories from our country's recent past, she knew so many fables. Indeed, Simonette seemed, to us children, to know by heart a multitude of different stories. What we especially enjoyed was Simonette telling us one of the legends from *Le Morte D'Arthur*. The chivalry of these legends inspired us but I must be truthful and say that the bloodier and bolder the story, the better the four of us appreciated it.

As I grew to manhood I could not help but be curious as to why Simonette never saw fit to remarry. There were suitors aplenty, as I recall, but Simonette was content to stay a part of our lives even when her role of governess had fulfilled its purpose. Sometimes I think she too at first was caught up in the magic of our childhoods—

magic, I believed that stemmed greatly from Simonette's own joyful nature. But later I came to believe that Simonette did not leave because she loved Anne too dearly to depart forever from her, which would have likely been the situation if she chose to marry. It seemed to me that Anna was more precious to Simonette than a daughter.

Yea, we were very happy in our childhoods. As long our Priest was there, for us to tag after and ask endless questions of, and Simonette to lay beside us on our beds at night, soothing us when plagued with childish fears, we had no desire or need for those other more complicated, evasive adults. Adults who sometimes also chose to reside at Hever.

Later in her life, Anne's enemies accused her of being more French than English. In a way this was true. Simonette was more mother to her than her true mother. Indeed, Anna's first words were French and, as she grew up, she went easily from one language to the other. This ability made her later transition to the French court at such an early age so much easier than one would naturally expect.

Of course, learning languages was a very important part of our education. Along with French, we were expected to learn Greek— taught to us via Homer's epic tales—and of course Latin. My cousin Mary easily managed the French because she had Simonette to help her from the early years of her life, but would often have her ears teasingly boxed by our frustrated priest because of her backwardness in regard to learning the other required languages. Eventually, she managed sufficient Latin to be able to say her Psalter well enough, but that was the end of that.

I reflect as I write that Mary must have felt completely left out in the cold while we had our lessons, because she found it all beyond her uncomplicated intellect. As I have mentioned before, Mary, during her parents' long absences, frequently sought out every excuse to avoid the time we spent in the library where the harder lessons were taught. It was so different for George, Anna, and myself. We savoured every moment of Father Stephen's tutelage. He jokingly called us the three muses, and often said that we all would have been dedicated to and followers of Apollo if we had been born in the time of ancient Greece.

Father Stephen, when the day promised to be warm and dry, would take the four of us out of doors for our lessons. Aristotle, Father Stephen frequently said, would no doubt have taken his young charges out of doors when the weather beckoned. He then reminded us that one of these charges grew up to be Alexander the Great, proving implicitly that customary education away from books and the quill did not prevent satisfactory learning. Indeed, it often proved the greater benefit.

On these days Father Stephen would take us on long walks in the woods near Hever, and encourage us to discover for ourselves the many different species of plants that grew there. His knowledge of this subject was absolutely amazing. It appeared to us that Father Stephen knew the name of every living plant found within the borders of our Kentish home. I remember these long walks with so much joy and simple exhilaration.

If I shut my eyes for a moment I can still see us: four children rushing around the towering trees while Father Stephen stood steadfast, his great body overshadowed by the tall oaks, with sunlight filtering through the green leaves, dappling their design on him.

Aye. There, deeply engraved in the memories of my childhood in his long, grey cassock, our Priest will eternally stand. Father Stephen was the centre of our universe, and we (yea, I believe even Mary!) were his four unstable and very energetic planets, forever seeking out ways to rotate around him.

★

I think it now must be obvious that, to us these two people—our aging priest and our gay, young French belle—were a greater influence on our lives than were those other two elusive figures, the seemingly forever-absent lord and lady of the manor.

Having been fortunate in my own father, I could not but help wondering how the fates could have bestowed Anne and George on such an unimaginative and cold man as the Lord Thomas Boleyn. Perhaps he too was bewildered by the offspring that he had begot. I wonder about this because I often caught my uncle gazing on these two of his offspring with a look that could only be described as deep dislike and utter contempt. This attention seemed to be fixed especially on poor George. George, who was sensitive, artistic, gentle, brave—all the things which his father was not.

And there is one more thing I will write down now. Something I have kept deeply repressed in my memory; something only now I remember.... Was Uncle Boleyn really the father to these two amazingly talented youngsters? George told me, when we were children, how he had once heard his parents having a violent argument, and George heard his father accuse his mother of trying to fob her bastards onto him. Knowing now what time held for all of us, knowing how Uncle Boleyn cold-heartedly offered to sit on the judgements of both his children, judgements certain to condemn them both to violent deaths. I remember now that narrow-eyed look he sometimes gave to both of them. And I cannot help but wonder.

Chapter 3

"And I have leave to go of her goodness."

ur lives began to change drastically after Mary's departure to Brussels. It was obvious Uncle Boleyn's interest in his other offspring was now increased, as if debating with himself the best course to take concerning their futures.

This was the time when the betrothal between our Princess Mary Rose to Charles of Castile, later elected the Holy Roman Emperor, was broken off after Ferdinand—Charles' grandfather—betrayed our King—his son-in-law—by signing a treaty for peace with Maximilian, Charles' other grandfather. Thus, Cardinal Wolsey brought into being a new political alliance more to his own liking. The young Princess Mary of York was wed to King *Louis* XII of France.

Even at nearly twelve I was aware of the uproar this marriage caused. How could I not be? Simonette and the other women of the household buzzed here, there and everywhere their deep disapproval of this spring-to-winter marriage. Furthermore, my father told me their feelings of disgust were likewise echoed throughout England to those people living beyond our shores. Mary was just eighteen, and said to be a true paragon of beauty. Verily, many called her "The Rose of all England." Aye, England's budding Rose married to *Louis* of France—a tottering, toothless old man. No wonder all of us at Hever Castle were less than delighted at the news—our feelings of sympathy going out to the young Tudor Princess. However, Mary was no less than a Tudor and it was known she had obtained from her brother the promise that, after this forced diplomatic marriage, she alone would have the choice of who her next husband would be.

Thus, after a proxy marriage had been performed at Westminster in October of 1514, preparations were swiftly put under way for the beauteous new Queen's departure to her husband's kingdom.

Part of the preparations was deciding which attendants would accompany Queen Mary to the French court. Because of her own youth, it was decided several of the Queen's attendants would be some nubile girls—children who would greatly benefit from being educated at the French court.

It happened so swiftly. Aye, so swiftly did we move from innocent childhood to somewhere and sometime that demanded of us defences we had not. One October day George, Anna, and I were enjoying some moments freed from serious study, partaking in a beautiful, splendid autumn day by climbing trees and shaking down leaves on one another. The next day, Simonette and Anne were frantically packing all their personal belongings into travelling chests.

That morning we had received a brief message from Uncle Boleyn telling us Anna had been summoned to form part of the assemblage to accompany Mary Tudor.

George, Anna, and I were in a state of shock. Indeed, I know for certain that everyone at Hever felt completely broken up at the prospect of losing the child Anne forever more. Even Father Stephen seemed to lose his usual calm composure when he came into the library to find only George and I there, both of us subdued and close to tears, with Anne's usual place forlornly and so obviously empty.

By the end of the day Anne and Simonette had finished packing. Aye, because of Anne's extreme youth Simonette was also leaving to attend her in France, and also my cousin Mary, who had been summoned from the court of Brussels to be also an attendant to the new Queen. Anna felt comforted she would soon see her sister, as well as having the tender care of Simonette. But for George and

I, it was not only Anna who we were losing, but also the foster mother of our childhoods. I felt as if all my young blood had frozen somewhere in my heart. Looking at George's sick face, I could easily see he felt the same.

Then the time came when we three children sat around a table, in a small room connected to the nursery, eating our final childhood meal together.

"At least Father Stephen has told me that Tom and I can come with you to Dover," George said.

Anne looked up at that and smiled sweetly at her brother.

"Aye, George. That will give us a few more days together, perhaps even a week," Anne replied.

"Thank the good Lord for small favours," I sarcastically injected.

Anne suddenly lifted her head, as if she had just thought of something.

"Speaking of favours, coz... you've reminded me of something I wished to ask of you. Tommy, will you please look after Aster and Pluto for me? Oh, I wish I could... do you think that if I took Pluto with me to Dover they would allow me take him to France?"

George and I both looked at one another, probably with the same vision in our mind: an enormous Irish wolfhound, almost the height of a small horse, causing complete pandemonium aboard a small English galleon. George raised his hand to the right side of his face, and shook his head slightly in my direction.

"No," I answered quietly for both of us, looking down at a trencher of food I possessed no hunger for. We all then became silent, with me lost in thoughts of what time could now hold in store for us three.

That night lives in my memory as one of the worst of my childhood. For hours I lay upon my bed, restless and in tears. Never had I thought that I would be separated from Anne so soon. Never had I realised how much I had bound myself—heart and soul—to my younger cousin. At long last, I sank into a fretful and unrestful slumber; tormented by ugly dreams.

Father Stephen awoke us for our journey before the break of day. George and I had spent the night before filling our saddlebags with the things we thought we would need for our journey to Dover. Thus, with our gear already prepared, we went down to kitchen to be given, by the cook, meat, and some newly-baked bread with which to break our fast. Anne and Simonette, the servants told us, were busy doing a last minute check to ensure they had packed everything that they might need. However, before we had finished our bread, Anna came flying down the spiral staircase leading from the bedchamber she now slept in with Simonette.

"Simonette has shooed me away," Anna said when she reached us. "She says I am just in the way… You know, I do believe she is in a bad mood this morning. I do not think she wants to return to France."

Anna danced around the room, as if her feet would not let her stay still. I could understand Simonette's reason for sending her away; you could almost breathe in the feeling of Anne's nervous, unspent energy.

"Here," said George and passed her half a loaf of bread from the inside of his doublet, "I saved you some food."

"Thanking you most kindly, sweet brother!" Anne responded with a slight curtsey.

"Good lord," I said in disgust. "You two act as if nothing out of the ordinary is happening."

Both George and Anne looked at me in surprise.

"Is there anything we can do about it, Tom?" George asked, lifting an eyebrow at me.

No. There was nothing we three could do to stop the sands of time changing the pattern of our lives. Indeed, the journey to Dover soon became a memory of the past. As too the memory of our heart-broken farewells. And there is an image, frozen somewhere in my heart, of a priest's huge figure over-shadowing two lanky boys. I know—*aye, how I do know*—one of those boys stood on that rocky shore, watching, in unspoken anguish, as a galleon vanished forever over a grey horizon.

Thus, my childhood ended.

★

Soon I entered fully into my thirteenth year and my father summoned me home to Allington so to inform me of my entry into St. John's, of Cambridge University. It was not my father's plan for me to obtain a degree—which I did not, as I was called home just before the close of my fourth year and the attainment of my Bachelor of Arts. Rather, my father hoped my time at Cambridge would set my feet upon the road he wished for me to take: verily, to be in the future as he was now, a valued court official.

I was very thankful for the time I had spent with Father Stephen. Verily, it was his tutoring which had first opened up the windows of my mind, building sound foundations for all that I studied at Cambridge: philosophy, theology, expanding my knowledge of classical languages, beginning too my grounding in civil law. This last my father regarded immensely important, as it prepared me for my expected role at court. But I never forgot my dream of spending my life with Anne, and I promised myself one day I would turn it into a reality.

At the University, we lived a very simple life. Verily, I could easily imagine life in a monastery similar to how we were expected to conduct ourselves while students at Cambridge. Divided into three camps—the first, of which I was a part, nobility and gentlemen living their lives close to the crown, as well as respected academics— the university mixed together nobility, gentlemen, scholars and esteemed persons, and a sprinkling of persons possessing very little status in our commonwealth.

As similar were our lives to that lived by monks, so was our garb, almost twin to the black robes worn by the Jesuit priests, though our hats were square rather than round like the ones they wore. I enjoyed my time as a scholar at Cambridge, feeling fortunate to be born in this time where all seemed turned to the enrichment of knowledge. Thus, it appeared to me all doors—verily, everything underneath the heavens—were open to us scholars.

★

The narrow bed groaned under my weight as I flicked a roving flea off my wrist, knowing full well that another and yet another would soon replace it. Grabbing my book from off my pillow, I became aware that light flowed all around me; my pillow—part of it now shadowed by my head and shoulders—gone from a dirty, dull yellow to hint at its former duck-feathers' colour of a year past. I turned to see Harry Durham returned from his morning lecture, holding in one hand his square shaped student hat and in the other, book-marked by finger, a thin Greek manuscript.

"Tom! 'Tis long time for you to be gone, my friend! Anon, if you do not go this very moment you'll discover the door locked to your entrance."

I took out from the pages of my book several pages of folded parchment, and again opened them on my lap.

"This letter from my kinsman came while you were gone, Harry. I wanted time alone to read it and make a beginning of a reply. Civil law can do without my company this morn."

"Be it upon your own head, Thomas Wyatt!" Harry said, flinging the hat upon his own cot before pulling the long gown over his head.

Now with tousled hair and dressed in small clothes, he frowned at me, but I saw the merry glint in his gaze.

I smiled in response, thinking how fortunate I had been to find Harry to share my university abode with, meaning one other beside myself also needed to provide furniture and tableware for the room's comfort, not forgetting provision of fuel for the chamber's small fireplace. Not only did it reduce the cost of our board, but Harry and I also appreciated the fact that we had formed an advantageous friendship, which ensured both his kin and mine could well afford our stay at Cambridge. Indeed, it cost my father upwards of twenty pounds a year to ensure that my time of study at Cambridge was lived in a way our family's station required.

Harry went to the one and only chair in the room and began to read his book. I likewise returned my attention to Anne's letter, one of the many that had come my way via George, the same route I used to send her letters. During her first months in France, and because of her extreme youth, Anna was quickly made a part of the royal nursery. Verily, in the letter I held in my hand, Anna relayed how she had become fast friend of a princess of royal blood. Indeed, like her previous letters, her latest communication spoke of her growing love for all things French, but also of her continuing affection for all she had left behind. For safekeeping, I placed the letter again between the pages of my book, and sighed, knowing full well the words I wanted to write to her in reply. But I knew it was useless to write and ask her when she expected to return to England. The decision was not in her hands. Anna would return when her father decided it was time for her to return.

Book Two

1520–1528

The joy so short, alas, the pain so near,
The way so long, the departure so smart!
The first sight, alas, I brought too dear
That suddenly now from hence must part.
The body gone, yet remain shall the heart
With her, which for me salt tears did rain,
And shall not change till that we meet again.

Chapter 1

"But since that I so kindly am served."

ot long after I reached my seventeenth year a groomsman from my family's estate at Allington arrived at Cambridge with a message from my father demanding my instant return home. Anxious and yet curious about the reason my father would have me suddenly withdraw from my studies, I promptly informed the Dean of St. John's of my father's command. Having done this, I then immediately returned to my rooms to pack my saddlebags. Thus, with my father's servant as my only company, I began the long and arduous journey to Allington. Arriving there, I found my father's home in a state of turmoil—almost as if someone had upturned an ant nest, and its former inhabitants were scurrying here, there and everywhere in utter confusion. I spent some minutes questioning my father's servants as to his whereabouts; thinking as I did how strange it was that many of them looked at me with an inquisitive, amused glint in their eyes. I then went to seek him out in the library.

I felt not surprised to hear from our servants that this was where my father was to be found. Since my mother's death, my father took more and more consolation in making study of the classics. He especially admired ancient works of a stoic nature, and it was in these books he would seek to immerse himself, whenever freed of court duties. Yea, for many long hours, my father made a serious study of these works so their philosophies began to be mirrored in his every action.

When I entered into the chamber, my father stood by a bookstand near a large window at the far end of the room, dressed in a simple black doublet, unadorned by any jewel other than my mother's large Celtic cross. Ever since her death, my father had taken to wearing this around his neck. The black garments, it seemed to me, greatly increased the impact of the silver of his hair. In recent years, my father had begun to age rapidly, but he still held himself erect and tall, and to my impressionable eyes, struck an extremely imposing figure. He looked up from the book he was reading.

"Tom," he said, closing the book on the stand with a resounding bang.

With a swift stride, he walked over to embrace me.

"You arrived sooner than I expected. I suppose you're wondering what is ado?"

"Yea, father," I replied, as he released me. I felt very mystified as to the reason for my urgent summons home.

Reassuringly he smiled, walking back towards the window. He then turned back to face me, saying: "My son, 'tis good to see you looking so hale and grown. Sit down, Tom… I have some important news for you."

I found a stool near where my father stood, and hastily sat, feeling glad to give my aching legs a rest. We had ridden very hard the last three hours, knowing that we were close to sleeping in our own beds, and I had yet to get my land legs back. I looked up at my father, who stood there silently, still with his hands behind his back, and waited patiently for him to speak. His previous delight at seeing me now seemed to have completely disappeared. In fact, he appeared abashed and ill at ease—two conditions, I would have said, that were totally unlike my father's usual character.

At last his figure stirred, and he looked me straight in the eye.

"Tom. Recently the King gave me the wardship of a thirteen-year old girl, a girl who has been dowered, by her family, with an estate near here. Not a great estate, I must admit, but her lands would greatly add to our own holdings in Kent… This girl comes from a very good family, Tom. Indeed, my dear boy, the girl has more noble blood running through her veins than we Wyatts can ever lay claim to."

My father paused, glancing quickly at me. He then took a hand from behind his back, and tugged at his ear.

"Thomas, I have made the decision you will wed Elizabeth, and have made arrangements for the marriage to take place immediately."

I sat there stunned. Never in my wildest dreams had I imagined that the reason for my recall from Cambridge could be plans to make me a husband. The room was again silent, but my head was splitting with my need to cry out: *Nay! Nay! Nay!*

My father's voice broke into my consciousness.

"Boy—surely you've something to say?"

Now it was my turn to look my father in the eye. I had always loved and admired him deeply. Surely he would understand why this marriage could not, must not, take place.

"Father. I cannot," I at last said.

My father moved slightly and straightened his form, saying gruffly, "What do you mean you cannot?"

"I simply cannot, father," I replied, this time in a far more tentative voice.

My father then darkly frowned at me.

"That is not a good enough answer, Thomas. Surely you must realise that we Wyatts are not as wealthy as our needs require. You are my firstborn son, indeed, my only living son. 'Tis important your marriage builds on what has already been erected. Elizabeth not only fulfils that need, she is also young enough to be shaped to her husband's requirements. I married your mother when she was close to Elizabeth's years and I close to yours. I also felt not pleased at the prospect of becoming a husband. But, I tell you soothly, my son. My marriage was the best thing, Tom, to ever happen in my life. Furthermore, this girl shows much promise of becoming a very desirable woman. I believe you will not be disappointed in the wife I have chosen for you… I have given this matter a great deal of thought, my boy. Indeed, Thomas, I am very determined this marriage will take place as soon as possible."

I got up from my stool so I could be on the same level as my father.

"But father, I have already decided on another."

My father stared at me from underneath bushy, dark brows. I thought, crazily, *Why is his hair so silver yet his eyebrows so dark?*

"So, Tom, has she got a name? Or is she some trollop you have been making calf eyes at whilst you should have been busily studying your books?" he roared in irritation.

I took a deep breath; my heart beat so fast that I feared my chest would burst.

"I desire to marry the Mistress Anne Boleyn," I blurted out.

My father stared at me again, looking at me as if I had lost my senses, then erupted with laughter. Groping around, he found a stool to sit upon and put his knuckles to mouth. Glancing at me, his head shook slightly, as if he still did not quite believe what I had said.

"Oh, Tom. I am sorry my boy, but I had to laugh. I always knew you were a romantic lad, as well as a dreamer, but even so I could never imagine that your head was so much up in the clouds you could even begin to believe Boleyn would agree to match either of his two daughters on you. Surely you must realise how high his ambitions for his offspring are?"

Without waiting for an answer, my father leaned forward and began to speak even more earnestly. "Anne, I believe, Tom, is promised to the Butlers of Ireland. She is the only sure way Tom Boleyn has to gain what he sees as his rights in Ireland. Especially now that his elder girl has entirely ruined her reputation by jumping from a King's bed to that of his groomsman… I hear the French King has even given your poor cousin Mary a new nickname; he calls her his 'hackney.' Broken in by the King only to give service to others in his court. I feel very sorry for the girl. 'Tis what I would have half-expected myself if I had sent such a young daughter away from her family to a licentious court—such which is found in the court of the French King. Not the best way, I would have thought, to ensure a respectable match. 'Tis a good thing too that your uncle decided to bring Mary home. I believe Boleyn's fortunate both his girls' reputations were not ruined. Aye, Tom, Boleyn is very fortuitous indeed. Anne was so young when she was first sent abroad, she was sent to Queen Claude's court, which, I have been told by those who should know, is just as good as being sent to a strict nunnery."

"Yea, father. I realise all this already, but…"

"Tom, I am not finished. I want you to listen and try hard to understand. I am sorry, my boy, but you must begin to face the truth. When Boleyn and I began our careers at court we were on a par, but I knew even then that his ambition would lead him far. Especially when I saw for myself how Boleyn encouraged his own new bride to play at love games with the King, when the King was a prince and no more than your age—nay, even younger. My son, his ambition has led him far. Much higher than my lack of ambition has led me. But I rest easy in my bed. I have a reputation with the King for being an honest man, Tom. There are not many men at court that can boast that, but I am afraid Boleyn wants more for his daughter than just a son of an honest man.

"In any case, Anne has been in France for the last four years or more. I cannot understand you, Tom. How can you say that you desire to wed a girl who you last saw years ago? Surely you must realise that Anne is no longer the child you once knew? Tom, my lad, you would no longer know her!"

I tried now to speak in earnest to the man before me, even though feeling that all the doors of escape were fast being closed to me.

"But my good sire, I do know her. I have always known her. We have written to one another over the years. Not much, I admit, but enough to tell me that she becomes with every passing year more and more the Lady of my heart's desire…"

"Thomas!" my father roared again. "Have you not heard a word I have said? Boleyn does not think a Wyatt's good enough to kiss his feet, despite our kinship to his wife. Why do you insist in believing he would even begin to listen to a suggestion of joining our bloodlines with his? He has his sights set higher than what he can see at Allington. Tom! Tom! Tom! Wake up boy! We do not live in some romantic fable, but in the real world. Mistake me not and heed me well, Tom, when I say to you that you have as much chance of gaining Anne Boleyn as a dog has of gaining the moon. Furthermore—and I should not have to remind you of this, Thomas—you have a duty to your family, and part of that duty is to marry whom I deem best."

My father, as he has said, is an honest man and I have always believed whole-heartedly in his honesty. His words then were like being plunged into cold water, of being savagely woken up from my dreams of what could and would be. I felt sick at heart and defeated in spirit, and listened in silence as my father informed me of the plans already undertaken to get my wedding swiftly underway.

So, what of the other party? What of the girl I was to marry? How do I begin to describe Elizabeth? Yea, Elizabeth... I first met her the night I arrived home, seated next to me and eating supper amongst other family members at the dais. At near fourteen, Elizabeth appeared to me to be fully grown, made to look even more mature by the black mourning clothes she wore. My father was right about her promise of desirability. Elizabeth not only possessed lovely silver-blonde hair, but also large blue eyes lighting up a perfect oval face, unblemished by any imperfection. She was a little taller than average. Verily, in height she almost reached to my ear, and her figure seemed to me very statuesque.

My father had explained to me the reason for the great hurry to make me a wedded man. That is, he feared that her wealth, status, and developing beauty would tempt a more powerful family than ours and, before we knew what happened, her wardship would be given over to some other man. The King had strongly hinted to my father that the girl would make a very suitable match for me, but the King was fickle in his favours so my father had moved fast when he decided to take the King at his word.

Thus, here I was, sitting near a strange girl soon to be my bride. What could I do but try to talk to her? And that I found very hard. In all my life, I do not think I have ever found it so difficult to begin a conversation as the one I tried to begin that night. First I looked at her with half a smile, but even though she saw my gaze and smile upon her, she remained silent. So silent the heaviness of this silence surrounded us, threatening to submerge us both. So, I forced myself to speak.

"Lady, my father tells me that you and I will soon be man and wife."

She quickly looked back at me and then just as quickly looked back down at her wooden trencher.

Dear God, I thought. *What do I do now? What do I say now?* Taking a long and steadying breath, I tried again.

"Lady, surely you can speak?"

By all the wounds of Jesus—how clumsy and pompous that sounded, I thought.

The girl again glanced at me, her dark, blue eyes narrowed, looking at me with deep suspicion.

"Yea, I can speak, Master. But I find that no one listens when I do so. Sir, I would rather be left alone to think my own thoughts and keep them to myself."

And with those words she turned herself away from me and went back to eating. I stared at her—stunned. Obviously she was not pleased with the forthcoming wedding either. But who was she to speak to me like that? Especially since I felt exactly the same way, but at least I had made some effort to forget my own pain, and make some attempt at friendliness.

★

Thus, two days after my arrival from Cambridge, I married Elizabeth. In many, many ways she was just a child then. But I, at seventeen, was also a child. My dreams of Anne had kept me innocent, imprisoned me in a time long gone. Marriage to Elizabeth savagely tore me from all my dreams—made me deal with a flesh and blood female where for so long I had dealt with only the memory and the conjuring of my dream. I was as much a virgin on my wedding night as my girl bride. I suppose on reflection that may have been the beginning of all our troubles. I knew what I was supposed to do, but was clumsy in the doing of it. Elizabeth was still a whole month away from her fourteenth birthday. I know the experience scared and hurt her. But I, too, was scared and hurt. I know also that I took a lot of anger to our wedding bed. Anger at the world and my life that seemed to treat with me so ill. Anger that made me survive the day and able to perform the man's part for the first time that terrible, loveless night. It was not the best way to begin a marriage.

Chapter 2

"They flee from me that sometime did me seek."

n 1522, France and England were once again at loggerheads with one another, with the grim result of war being declared yet again. It also had another result: Anne's father felt it best she return from France before the crisis worsened. For a short time after her return, Anne—now fifteen— stayed at Hever Castle, but only long enough for Uncle Boleyn to arrange a post for her as a Maid to the Dowager Queen of France, now the Duke of Suffolk's wife.

Despite a short note from George, written from his studies at Oxford telling me Anne had safely arrived home, I did not realise she had arrived at court until a day I walked down the corridors of Greenwich Palace. At once, I espied a very thin girl walking with a long-legged stride amongst a group of older ladies. As we passed one another, the girl lifted her face and we both stopped still, staring at one another with astonishment. Indeed, to me it seemed as if time froze in its tracks, only beginning its march again with her cry of "Tom," followed by my cry of "Anna." Without further words, we ran into each other's arms. I swung her up and around, kissing her joyously, to the obvious great disapproval and dismay of Anne's companions.

It was such a wonderful feeling to have my girl in my arms again. The last time we had seen one another was when we had done our farewells as children at Dover. Now we were no longer children, but two young adults trying to stake out our own claims and lives within the seesaw world making up the English court.

But even these innocent moments of such utter happiness can

be threatened and marred by that which surrounds this world. We both became aware of Anne's companions, gazing at us both in shocked and disapproving silence.

"'Tis my cousin Tom," she said to them, in way of explanation after we released one another from our public embrace. Still the women gazed at us with grim and hard faces. We looked at one another, and knew, without saying, the uselessness of trying to make any further explanations. Anne's eyes illuminated with quick decision, and she curtsied in their general direction.

"Please excuse us, but my cousin and I have seven long years to catch up on."

With those words she grabbed my hand, and fled with me to the gardens just outside the palace's doors. Once out of sight of the palace, and hidden from view by a tall and long hedge, Anna flung herself on the grass, pulling me abruptly alongside.

I laughed. I could not help but laugh. I felt so entirely happy. Anne was back with me, and apparently still the Anna I remembered with such love and happiness from my childhood. She sat there upon the abundant grass and gazed down at me, as I laid balanced on my side looking up at her.

"Oh, Tommy! 'Tis so good to see you again!"

I noticed then that Anne spoke with an enchanting French accent; an accent she was to keep until the very end of her life. Anne reached to gently stroke the side of my face.

"You have grown into a man, Tommy, but your eyes are still the eyes of the boy I once knew."

"And you have turned from a charming little girl to a charming young woman," I replied, resting my hand briefly upon hers.

Anne smiled.

"Dear Tommy! I am so glad we have met. George told me you had gained a post with Cardinal Wolsey, but father gave me so little time before I came here that I had no opportunity to write and tell you of my appointment to the Dowager Queen Mary."

"George also wrote to tell me that you were at long last home from France."

I took possession of her hand, marvelling how small boned it still was. I looked up at her, and asked, "Tell me, Anna, did you really enjoy your time in France?"

Anne's face suddenly lit, her eyes focusing as if looking upon all her recent memories.

"France is so very beautiful, coz, and some of their palaces truly defy anything your imagination could conjure up... but I am so glad to be back in England. I had so little freedom while I served Queen Claude. I could hardly ever get on a horse and ride to my heart's content... I think that is why father sent me so quick to be Maid to Queen Mary. He got sick of all his groomsmen being tired out from following me when I was in the saddle."

We laughed together. Then Anne reached out with her free hand, and gently touched my face again.

"Now tell me, Tom, is your life everything you ever wanted?"

I snorted, sitting upright. I put my arms around my knees, and looked away from her. All I ever truly wanted in this world was sitting right there, next to me.

"Is life ever what you truly want?" I asked her in reply, not daring yet to return my gaze to her.

Anne laughed. A delightful laugh only she possessed. A laugh filling my whole world as if with young gaiety—undisturbed by anything cold or forbidding.

"Oh, Tommy! Still ever so serious Tommy! I am very sorry you feel like that—especially since I know you're an old married man, with a son no lest! Surely that must make you happy?"

"Yea, Anne. 'Tis good to have a son, though he is only a baby as yet and I see him little."

Anne laughed at that too.

"And what of your wife? What is she like? Or do you see her little too?"

"Elizabeth is with child again, coz, so I suppose that means I have seen her recently... What is Elizabeth like? Very pretty, I deem, but… she does not like me writing poetry."

Anne reached out to briefly touch my hand.

"Tom! I am truly sad for you! I would have thought that any woman worth her salt would love to have a poet for a husband."

We were silent together for a moment. Then I took her hand again in mine, and gazed long at her. Anne still sat on the grass, her ebony hair mostly hidden by the fashionable headdress, yet to me her spirit appeared to be as gypsy as ever.

"And you, Anne. What of your own life—is it what you want?"

"Oh, yes, Tom." Anne took away her hand from mine to clasp both of hers together. "Oh, yes! My life is what I want, Tom! I am so very happy, coz. Life is so unbelievably wonderful, so utterly marvellous! I want to sing out aloud with joy. Dear Tom. Dear cousin Tom… I am in love with the best of men, and he with me. Is that simply not miraculous?"

My heart sunk down to my shoes. I'd fantasised for years that Anne would come back home from France to be my love, despite all the hindrances the world could and would put in our way.

Swallowing my true feelings, I asked her, "And who is this best of men?"

Anne laughed softly, lying gracefully and carefully on the grass. Her head rested on a hand as she gazed with eyes full of dreams at the clear blue sky.

"Hal Percy," she said softly. Those two words were said with such a depth of feeling I began to feel sick with jealousy.

"Oh, Tom," she said, rolling on her stomach and looking up at me with cheek leaning against a hand, just as she would do as a young child.

"Hal is all I ever wanted. Gentle, sensitive, full of humour and pranks. He is so very, very beautiful. I just love to sit where he cannot see me and gaze at him and know him to be mine. All mine! I really do not know, Tom, why he loves me. I am so skinny! I do not believe I will ever grow in the places a woman is supposed to grow." Anne placed her hands on her small breasts, shook her head, and laughed. "But Hal doesn't care! He says I am all the woman he has ever wanted. The woman he wants to be his wife and the mother of his sons. Cousin, fortune has been so very good to me."

Inwardly I groaned. From the time of my thirteenth year I had known there was only one girl for me, yet circumstances and fate always saw fit to rob her from me.

Determined not to show Anne any of my true feelings, I calmly (as best that I could) continued talking.

"Hal Percy. Your father will be pleased. The heir to Northumberland no lest. But my father told me years ago that an arrangement for you had been made with the Butlers of Ireland?"

Anna remained silent for a time. When I gazed at her, her face seemed tight with thought.

"Anna?" I asked.

She looked at me, shrugging.

"Yea, cousin, father still hopes to marry me to James Butler. It is the one sure way he knows to make sure that he procures what is his... but I hope he will see that to gain Hal Percy as his son-in-law will be the greater gain. Everything is very secret at the moment. Hal wishes us to wait until he has spoken to his mother, so she can speak for us to his father. I know I am no great prize for the heir of Northumberland, though Hal thinks otherwise. His mother, Hal believes, will be understanding and help us gain our great desire."

Immediately we could hear the loud ringing of bells, telling of a new hour now upon us. Anne got up, thoughtfully shaking off the grass from her dress. I stood too.

"I must go Tom... I have been asked to play my lute and sing to Queen Catherine... I'm so very glad you are here, Tom; it will be so good to practice our music together like we used to as children."

With that she kissed me gently on the lips, and instantly sped off in the direction from which we had come, leaving me standing there alone, looking after her rapidly diminishing form.

★

Anne proved good at her word. Verily, over the next few weeks we did have many opportunities to make music together. But not alone. No, never alone. For at these times a tall, slender, dark-haired singer accompanied us. A young man whose dark blue eyes rarely left the form of Anne. Indeed, Anna's eyes were likewise engaged, forever seeking out his.

Painfully, I admitted the truth to myself: Anne and Hal were both struck by the same arrow. Verily, the Lord Harry and Anne were so much in love that the vibrations of their feelings almost conquered the vibrations of the music we made together. So much in love they were completely absorbed in one another. So much in love they were totally oblivious to the fact I played my lute only through a barrier of bitter pain and jealousy.

But I could not really begrudge Anne her happiness—and she was so happy she brightly shone with its inner glow. Rather, I knew I could not offer her anything she would not rather gain with Hal. So, I took what there was for me to take: an occasional moment in Anne's company, even if this company included that of Percy.

One early morning I went with them out riding—so early in the morning the frost lay heavy on the grass and mist rose in heavy grey swirls before us; so cold our breaths iced as we breathed.

Anne made my heart hurt painfully this day. Yea, more than just hurt when I saw her ride with Percy. Dressed as a boy, with her thick, black hair tumbling out from underneath a feathered cap, so like how she rode with me when we two were children. And I found myself wondering, while I sat astride my horse atop some hill watching Hal and Anna race along some rustic lane, why did I torture myself? Why did I choose to be here at all, unable to be anything else but an observer on their developing love? Then I saw clearly the answer. It was not only because they asked for my company, so to make their outings a trio and thus gain the camouflage of respectability. But also, in truth, I just wanted to see for myself how it could have been if Anna had chosen me.

What means this when I lie alone?
I toss, I turn, I sign, I groan.
My bed to me seems as hard as stone.
What means this?

I sigh, I plain continually.
The clothes that on my bed do lie
Always methink they lie awry.
What means this?

In slumbers oft for fear I quake.
For heat and cold I burn and shake.
For lack of sleep my head doth ache.
What means this?

A morning then when I do rise
I turn unto wonted guise,
All day after muse and devise.
What means this?

And if perchance by me there pass
She unto whom I sue for grace,
The cold blood forsaketh my face.
What means this?

But if I sit near her by
With loud voice my heart doth cry
And yet my heart is dumb and dry.
What means this?

To ask for help no heart I have.
My tongue doth fail what I should crave.
Yet inwardly I rage and rave.
What means this?

Thus have I passed many a year
And many a day, though naught appear
But most of that most I fear.
What means this?

Aye! What means this indeed! I loved Anna from boyhood, and nothing, nothing in our lives, or the time before us, would ever release me from this love. Because of Anna, all my life's joys have been brief and fleeting. But, if I had never loved Anna, I would never have known, nor understood, why the poets and the singers spend so much of their art bemoaning about love. I would have never known what it was to truly love a woman. Love a woman so much it was simply enough to be near her, sitting at her feet—even while she sang her love songs to another.

It is hard to keep anything secret at court, and it was not long before people were talking about Anne and Hal. But it was mostly good-natured talk. All the world seems to take great pleasure in the love of young lovers—all the world that is except the King and Cardinal Wolsey.

Aye. King Henry had taken great notice of the girl who sang and played the lute to his Queen like an angel. Too much notice. For now our King wished to make her his latest quarry, having tired of Mary Boleyn and wanting to replace one sister with another. But Anne and Hal were so caught up in their innocent world of young love both of them were completely unaware of the lustful gleam in the King's eye, and how the hunt was now on. Anna and Hal saw only each other, and were thus protected for the moment from realising that their brief bright day was to turn into darkest night.

Nothing disturbed or annoyed our King so much as to have his attentions not noticed. The King's solution was to have a word in Wolsey's ear. Wolsey's solution was to completely demoralise Hal in front of his fellows for falling "head over heels" in love, and against the wishes of the King. And worst! For falling, stupidly, for a foolish upstart of a girl.

I was still a part of the Cardinal's household at this time, thus, I heard firsthand from those who witnessed this interview between Lord Percy and the Cardinal. Hal, I was told, replied to the Cardinal's abuse in this fashion: "Sir, I had no desire to cause the

King displeasure. If I have done so, I sincerely entreat his forgiveness... But I consider myself old enough to be wise in regard to choosing myself a wife. I also have no doubt that the Earl, my father, could be persuaded to my choice. Even though, I will truly admit, Anne is but a simple maid, she comes from a noble lineage. I pray you, good Sir, to speak on my behalf to the King."

The Cardinal, I was told, arose from his chair, utterly confounded by these brave words of Percy. He stood there, his face reddening with rage, and then gestured angrily to his fascinated attendants.

"Listen to this boy! The wisdom that comes sputtering out of his mouth!"

He then rounded on Percy, yelling: "You foolish, foolish youth! Did you not hear me before, when I told you that the King has other plans for Mistress Boleyn? You forget your place, young Percy! It is not for you to say this or that. It is not for you to say anything at all. Your duty is to submit yourself in obedience to your King and betters."

Hal Percy was crying hard by this stage—braver men than he had quaked before the fury of the Cardinal. Nonetheless, he still attempted to battle hard against the fates.

"Sir, ordinarily I would do my duty," Hal now said, through his tears, to Wolsey. "But this is no easy thing you ask. I have pledged myself to Mistress Boleyn, and have no desire to relieve myself of this pledge. Verily, good Sir, I feel myself honour bound to serve best my conscience and my heart."

Wolsey now fixed upon Percy such a look that those who watched quailed themselves before the red-tide wrath of the Cardinal. But still Henry Percy, though bowed and now silent, refused to speak those words that would have him submit utterly to the wishes of the King and Wolsey.

Thus, this interview having had little of the desired effect, the Cardinal now called for Percy's father to deal with the son. Deal with his son he did. Verily, almost as soon as the Earl of

Northumberland arrived at Hampton, the Earl dragged Harry Percy off to be wed in some hastily arranged marriage. They said it had been pre-contracted, but no one knew of it until Wolsey and Hal's father had been closeted together for over an hour.

So ended Anne's greatest love affair. Thus was sowed the seed to one day flourish into our lives' greatest tragedy. But never did I then imagine the blood-soaked harvest that Anna's heartbreak would lay before us...

It is not surprising Wolsey played such a large part in achieving the desires of his King. Verily, they often said at the English court the King trusted only two men with any great power in his Kingdom: two men who were known throughout the land as Cardinal Wolsey and the Duke of Suffolk.

The Cardinal first came to the notice of the King when the King was but a young prince, living in the shadow of an elder and much loved brother, Arthur, the boy expected to be King. Henry, the younger brother, was destined—so the father thought—not to sire a dynasty, but be a prince of the church. Thus, an aid and comfort to his elder brother's reign. My father told me as a boy how Henry VII planned this because he had made a long and painful study of our recent bloody history. His own wife's father, the fifth Edward, whose own personal motto *the Sun in Splendour* may have been more truthful if it had proclaimed him *the Setting Sun of the Plantagenets*, had put to death his own brother, George. Though rightly so: George, despite his elder brother's care for his estate, had constantly attempted to rob Edward of his crown.

And then there was the Queen's other uncle, Richard, also a King of England, but only after putting to death two tender boys, the Queen's own brothers—two boys with greater right than he to bear the crown of St. Edward.

Henry Tudor, the first King of that name, was a wiser man than the son who bore his name. My own father rebelled against the tyrant Richard because he frankly saw the then Duke of Richmond as the better man. Verily, he was greatly sickened by the abominable acts performed by King Richard.

Ah! My writings begin to wander, dwelling on things with little to do with what I describe.

I was speaking of how the great Cardinal first began his climb in the English court. My father told me that the Cardinal's first appointment was not to the father of our present King, but to his Lord Chancellor, Henry Deane, in 1501—eight years before our present King began his reign as a near-eighteen-year-old youth. Wolsey, in those early years, was one of the tutors of the King's second son. And as I revered my childhood tutor, so did Henry, King of England revere the Cardinal—for many long years of his reign.

And Charles, Duke of Suffolk—the other man trusted by the King. How do I explain the enormous influence this man had on our King? I suppose, in a sense and in many ways, you could say, with truth, the King wished to magnify the mirrored image of the Duke. Verily, the Duke was the elder of the King by at least seven whole years. When the King was only a youth and still but a Prince, it was well known that he greatly admired and looked up to Charles, who was raised close to the family of Henry VII.

Both men were of similar height and build, and enjoyed playing to the full at the role of a chivalrous knight. Even so, if the King saw himself as cutting an amorous figure with the ladies, it seemed to me the ladies themselves, in their heart of hearts, would rather have the extraordinarily handsome Duke instead of the King pay them his knightly attention. The Duke was a man who clearly had the best of his Irish ancestry, with his pitch-black hair, pale skin, deep blue eyes, and sensual mouth. Even when he was in his forties, the Duke was accustomed to having ladies all but swoon in his very presence.

By 1522, the Duke had been married to the Dowager Queen of France, Mary Rose, for about seven years. Like her brother, Mary had loved and admired the Duke (or Charles Brandon as he was then) from the time she was a very small girl. And this strong-willed and very beautiful woman achieved her lifelong desire to be his wife when he came to escort her, then the newly widowed Queen, back to England from the French court. But in the year 1522, the Duke of Suffolk appeared to be restless. Verily, the Duke had begun in earnest, again, his serious pursuit of nubile girls (one of which had once been an innocent Tudor princess, but now was his maturing wife). And the older the Duke became, the younger also became the girls he chose to pursue.

But never in my wildest nightmares did I dream that one of these young girls would one day be Anne. Even so, barely two days after Wolsey had viciously destroyed the young hopes of Anna and Henry Percy, I walked along the corridors of Hampton to recognise Anne's terrified voice. Her cry suddenly broke off, as if a hand quickly plugged its source. I instantly opened the door of a nearby chamber to find Anne struggling hard with a huge man; a man who had his hand placed over her mouth and his back towards me. As fortune would have it, due to Anne's frantic scuffles, he remained unaware of my entry into the room. So, without any further thought, I rushed over and gave his shoulder an almighty shove, causing him to lose grip of Anne and tumble violently to the ground.

Freed, Anna ran to me. I tightly encircled her in the safety of my arms; her slight body shook violently in the aftermath of shock. But I could not long console her because I now stared at a naked sword, glinting with candlelight, in the hand of the now standing man. I lifted my eyes to his face, and saw with even greater shock that the man I so violently tossed to the ground was none other than the third most powerful person in the land: the Duke of Suffolk.

"So, Wyatt?" the Duke asked, rocking himself and his sword slowly closer to us.

I wondered if I should reach for my dagger—but pushed the thought aside, knowing such an action would surely sign my death warrant.

"No!" Anne screamed. I quickly glanced at her, to see her eyes staring at the sword, and to that my own gaze returned. I attempted to reassure her by squeezing her shoulders. She sounded very close to breaking point, for her voice was shrill and quivering.

"No! I beg of you, no! My Grace! Wyatt is my cousin. He did not realise it was you. He thought only to protect me. Oh, please, please, my Lord Duke. I'm sorry if I offended you, but you frightened me so! Oh, please, Your Grace, just let us go!"

As she spoke, Anne pulled me slowly and steadily away from the now stationary Duke and towards the still open door, until we stood there ready to flee at any moment.

The Duke, with sword still drawn and pointed towards us, lifted his body somewhat from his fighting stance.

He stared at us for one long, dreadful moment, and then suddenly yelled.

"Go, then, you bloody slut. And take your worthless, accursed kinsman with you. But I promise you both, I will never forget or forgive this insult!"

With those words ringing loud in our ears, Anne and I hurriedly bowed, and ran as if the furies themselves were after our skins.

At last, we were far enough from the Duke to begin to feel somewhat safe and began to look around for somewhere private so we could converse without fear of being overheard. Soon, we found a room full of disused furniture and entered it.

Anne, looking like she was ready to collapse, flung herself down on the nearest bench, her body twisted in its distress. I could see she shivered, seemingly uncontrollably. Even so, I could not ignore my own feelings of panic.

"What, Anna, in God's good name, was that all about?" I shouted at her. I needed so badly to find an outlet for my apprehensions that it came out in a kind of anger, anger directed towards the fearful girl before me. I too felt full of great fears. Verily, I felt as frightened as I had ever felt in my brief life. It is not every day the greatest peer in the land promises you vengeance.

Anna raised her body until she sat with her head bowed over knees, as if ready to vomit. She then looked up at me with wide, dark eyes in an all too pale face.

"You saw. What do you usually call it, cousin? I only know but for you, Tom, the Duke would have dishonoured me by now. On the Holy wounds of Jesus, Tommy, I think this is the final straw… Hal has been sent home today… Did you know that, Tom? Wolsey and Northumberland schemed together to find that he had been precontracted elsewhere. May their souls rot in hell forever for such a tassel of lies! Hal was not—nor ever was—precontracted!"

Anne stood, then began to walk around the chamber, but still the torrent of words came flooding out.

"Perhaps in the past, Tom, a possibility of a contract may have been discussed, but there had never been any hand-fasting… how could there have been, when he swore to marry me? Yea, marry me!" Anne hiccupped, glanced quickly at me before continuing again.

"Tom… the Duke wished to gain by force what Hal would not take until we were truly wed. The Duke thought I would prove easy, just like my sister Mary… Dear Jesus, this has been the worst day of my life! Hal… By all the saints in Heaven! He was not even allowed to say farewell to me… Oh, Tom, they say Wolsey broke his spirit. Gentle Hal… Sweet Hal… My beloved… I will never forgive Wolsey for that! And do you know, can you guess, Tom, what Wolsey called me? An upstart! Aye!" Anna harshly laughed. "He said Hal was foolish for falling for an upstart! By God and all the saints in Heaven, I swear I will show him one day what this upstart can do. I swear to you, Tom, the day will come when I bring him down. And the King! I swear I will make him pay too!"

Anne returned, sitting back on the bench. On these final words she closed her eyes, and put her hands together, palm to palm, in front of her face, as if it was a prayer she made, rather than an oath for vengeance.

I went and knelt near her, taking her hand in mine.

"Yea, Anne, I heard about what happened... Verily, the whole place clamours with the tale. I am so very sorry, Anne."

I put her trembling hand against my cheek. She stayed silent, staring blankly into space, as if she had exhausted herself and could speak no more. I tried to return her to the present moment by asking her a question.

"I do not know what else to say, dear heart, other than I am truly sorry, Anne. But what of the King—how does he come into this?"

Anna's eyes focused back on me. She raised her free hand to rub her forehead, briefly closing her eyes tight, grimacing as if in physical pain. Anna looked back to me again and said: "Cousin Tom, his good Emissary, the bloody Duke of Suffolk, tells me that the King wishes to favour me, just like he favours Mary. So much so that he could not bear to see me marry Hal and live as his wife miles away from court. But when I told the Duke that I was an innocent maid, and I had no desire to ruin my reputation as Mary has done... Coz—you saw what solution he came to, so to get me quick to the King's bed—warm with body of my very own sister."

Anne got up from the bench then, taking her hand away from mine, and began pacing around the room.

"Oh, Anna. What are you going do?" I asked, watching her with great concern.

Anne stopped walking, and looked towards me. She appeared so haunted, as if in this darkened room the furies that I felt after us both just moments before had flung themselves onto her person. I myself began to shake for her barely suppressed agony.

"Go home, Tom... Father came and told me that I am to go home. Indeed, Simonette was packing my bags when I received the message that the Duke wished to see me about my troubles. I know better now about going anywhere unattended, but I really thought and hoped he had some comforting message from the King about Hal and I... I see now how stupid I was to think that."

She came back to lay her body upon the bench, and then stared

71

wide-eyed at the ceiling. I went back to her, sat beside her on the bench, clasping her hand firmly again.

"I know words are an empty thing, Anne, to heal a grief such as yours, but I truly understand, sweetheart, what you're feeling. What else can I say but to say again, and again, how sorry I am for all that has happened? If you feel like crying, Anna, I am here to comfort you. I am here to hold you. Please Anna, cry. Dearest girl… it will help you to cry."

Anna turned her head, looking at me with eyes so huge and dark with sorrow.

"Tom, I cannot cry. I am hurt so deeply, cousin, it goes beyond just simple tears; I feel like I bleed inside. Yea, I bleed inside. Tommy—'tis my heart that does the weeping."

When she said those words it was I who silently cried, my head bent over her too-clammy hand. Here she was, not yet sixteen, and there was I, just passed my nineteenth birthday, but both of us alike in that we were both denied the people whom we loved with all our utter beings.

Chapter 3

"That sometimes they put themselves in danger."

Thus, the next day Anne left the court and was gone from it for nearly three years. During that time, I visited her at Hever as much as I could, which, unfortunately, because of my commitments to the Court, was not as much as I would have desired. When I was able to get away, Anna would mostly want to ride with me and we would talk together whenever the going was slow, or, if the weather was too bad for riding, we simply stayed indoors with our lutes to play our songs to each other.

It struck me with each visit that Anne's spirit became wilder, and more tormented. It was as if this exile had not allowed her the opportunity for the healing she so badly needed. Indeed, even more, it struck me she had too much time to brood, thus her deep wound remained wide open, and now wept with malignancy.

Certainly I tried my best to salve what I could of her hurts. But my visits to Hever were infrequent at best. My duties at the court were increasingly demanding, and it was not often that I received permission to journey home to Allington. And whenever I did make the journey from Allington to Hever Castle, Anna had yet another new, vengeful song to sing to me.

Verily, this was a very bleak, dark period for us both.

Not long after Anna returned to Hever, I arrived home at my father's estate to find Elizabeth in the arms of a stable-hand. In the ensuing argument, Elizabeth utterly spat out her spleen at me, saying she found more pleasure with the attentions of uneducated villeins, than with the clumsy flumblings that I thought of as lovemaking.

I was so shocked by her actions and words that I quickly got back on my horse and rode straight over to Hever Castle. While I rode, I tried to make sense of the many cheerless thoughts going through my head. Yea, I knew Elizabeth did not enjoy my attempts at passion. I knew, and I suppose she did too, my efforts to love her were all a great act. That first night of our marriage was such a complete failure it had built up a high barrier between us, and I did not care enough to try to knock it down. I had given Anna my heart long ago. I had nothing left to give Elizabeth.

God's oath! I had not expected Elizabeth to be unfaithful to her marriage vows! Verily, I thought, Bess was a mother twice over, surely that should have been enough to occupy her without having to indulge herself with any man—as Bess claimed she did—who took her fancy. As I sifted further through all my thoughts, I found myself wondering about little Bess, the child who Elizabeth claimed was mine. I had never been able to detect any hint of family resemblance. I could not help but speculate whether some other man could have indeed fathered her. Verily, it all made me sick to my stomach.

Thus, Anne and I had nothing at this time to take much joy in. At least I tried to spend whatever free time I could with my broken-hearted girl, even if I was not sure if I helped her in any way. But what else could I do? I could only try my best to heal what I could, doubting constantly if she really healed at all.

Soothly, her riding showed how unstable she had become. Anne now had in her possession a black stallion by the name of Pegasus, a horse that was sixteen hands high if it was anything at all. Pegasus was one of George's horses, but he thought the stallion too wild and unpredictable to trust for the long journey to and from his college at Oxford where he now studied. And this was the horse that Anne chose to ride during the time of her exile.

When she was a child Anne often frightened me with her riding. Now I felt more terrified because it was clear she rode recklessly since she no longer cared whether she lived or died. Yea, when she was a child, my Anne was a lover of life. It made me so very afraid, during those long years of exile, to watch that love flicker like a candle placed near an open window, and almost be blown out.

★

In 1524 I was appointed Esquire to the body of Henry VIII, and Clerk to the Royal Jewels. My father, for many years and amongst other things, had been responsible for the upkeep of crown jewels, and thus brought into being this very important appointment. I felt very pleased. Many men at court had to wait until they were greybeards before they gained a position worth keeping, and here was I, not yet twenty-one, already making sure strides upon the stage that went by the name of the English court.

At the end of that same year, I found my good friends Francis Bryan and Henry Norris, both groomsmen of the King, engrossed in talk in a dimly lit corridor at Greenwich Palace. Curious, I went and joined them.

"By my faith, you two look as if you're plotting to overthrow the French."

Henry and Francis looked at me, then at one another and laughed.

"Nay, not the French, Tom. Rather we plot something closer to home," Harry said, grinning again at Francis.

"Closer to home? What can you mean?" I felt more curious than I had been when I first joined them.

"Harry, you'll have Tom distrust our loyalty to the King." Francis laid a hand on his shoulder.

"Nay—that never." I smiled at them both, thinking how long both of them had been attendants to the King. Indeed, Henry Norris had been with the King since they were both young lads. .

"If you wish to join this conspiracy, Tom, you'll need promise to assist us. We need all the help all our friends can give us."

"You best tell me then. I give no sworn oath unless I first know

75

what it entails."

Henry laughed.

"He does not trust us, Francis. We must look the part of proper scoundrels—when all we wish to do is serve well the King."

"Are we not all here for the same purpose? Harry, speak plain of what you do plan."

"You heard, Tom, that the King has kindly entrusted me to oversee one of the main festivities celebrating Christmas-tide? Francis has agreed to be my aid in this. What say you, Tom—will you also lend your hand in ensuring the success of these festivities?"

"Yea—of course. What have you planned, Harry?"

"A mock battle, taking place here at Greenwich over a period of divers days. On the tiltyard I plan to have built a sham castle of wood and other materials. Look here, Tom."

Henry passed to me a paper, roughly scrawled with a drawing of a small castle.

"The King drew this himself—now 'tis up to me to bring his drawing into being. I envision the Castle of Loyalty—Francis here named it—shall have three turrets stretched between two battlements, each battlement slitted with at least three lancet windows, and the flags of England rising above them. I've already asked the artisans to make ready a rampant lion to be fixed upon the gate. Within the castle, I shall place four ladies of our court under the protection of a captain and fifteen gentlemen. I hope one of those gentlemen will be you, Tom. What say you—are you party to this plot?"

"Why not—I can think of no other men presently at court whose company I'd rather be in than you two—proper scoundrels or not."

Thus I became part of Henry Norris' enterprise to entertain the King at Christmas-tide.

The castle, I must admit, seemed well made. Nevertheless, I think we who were within its protection spent much of our time being afeared that the castle—our only protection—would suddenly buckle under the constant onslaughts of assays against its outer shell.

Early in the morning of St. John the Evangelist Day, we sent out from the castle six of our men, armed with lances and on horseback. Thus, signalling the end of the ramming of the castle, ramming thinly disguised under the knightly name of a tilt. However, methinks our female companions found other, unflattering words for it, seeing how these ladies would scream in absolute terror whenever the castle was rocked or dented by the assault of yet another knight.

Our six comrades in arms made their emergence from the castle's outer shell and the next stage of this feigned battle began—for two ladies, clothed in stately gowns of damask, arrived on the scene, riding upon white palfreys and escorted by two supposedly ancient knights with long, silver beards. Sitting erect upon black steeds, the knights were dressed in rich cloaks suggestive of great nobility.

Queen Catherine now entered upon the spectacle. The Queen, as well, was very finely dressed in a gown adorned with costly jewels and cloaked in a heavy, purple garment of velvet. Though she looked every inch a Queen, no rich clothes could hide the fact that the Queen's beauty was no more. Though very short, Queen Catherine remained erect in stature, but was also very stout, looking every day and more of her forty years. I could not help reflecting and wondering at the feelings of the Queen. From the early, blissful days of her marriage to the King, the Queen always had an important part in these elaborate play acts. It was to be the same on this day, during this grand performance. Queen Catherine was here to listen to the petitions of these supposedly elderly knights. Yet, so much had now turned. Where once these performances were filled with the expectancy of youth, now youth fled, leaving in its place an empty, hopeless thing.

When near the Queen, the ladies and knights reigned in their horses and pages ran onto the grounds to hold fast the horses' reins. The two knights then dismounted and bowed to the Queen. The Queen then spoke in her strong, deep and vibrant voice, reaching all those who listened on this day.

"I have taken heed of your approach, my lords," she said to the men. "You appear to have travelled from afar. Tell me, good sirs, what is your desire? For what reasons have you journeyed here?"

One of the tall knights moved forthwith towards her, and knelt before her upon one well-shaped knee.

"Your gracious Queen," he said, his words muffled by his headgear. "Though we are hindered by the great disadvantage of age, my good fellow knight and I desire permission of your Grace to assail the defenders of the castle. We wish to reveal to you, gracious Queen, that strength of character, and attributes of good will and courage, are all that are needed to gain true and valiant victory."

The Queen and her ladies applauded these words of courage, coming so earnestly from the mouth of this knight, and gave him and his companion her permission to proceed with their desire. All of us then tried to act surprised when the knights tossed away their disguises revealing that they were none other than the King and the Duke of Suffolk—dressed richly in gold, silver and the deep purple of royal estate.

We, who had been left behind in the confines of the castle, now watched—from the high planks fastened behind the fake walls of the castle—a tournament unfold between our defenders and the King and Duke. Within minutes the contest was over. Indeed, the King demonstrated his usual standard by breaking at least seven spears.

On one of the final days, our great enjoyment of this great make-believe soured somewhat when, out of sheer boredom I believe, some defenders of the castle began throwing stones at the people standing outside the walls. Very soon, to the horror of us who wanted nothing of it, a real and somewhat bloody battle was taking place. Unfortunately, as was usual in this sort of situation, the only people to be really hurt were a few innocent bystanders.

★

78

Thus, 1524 came to a close, and 1525 began in earnest. And this was the year that saw Anna summoned back to court.

Anne had left a broken-hearted girl of fifteen—all her young faith about what life would bring her completely destroyed. She came back at eighteen, on the threshold of womanhood, utterly desirable. And with plans to use her desirability as a way to gain revenge. I had never stopped loving Anna, but this was one time in our long association when I came close to losing my patience with her, and thus was brought many times near to anger.

Alas, it was easy to see that the King had not lost his interest in her. But, for me, it was also easy to perceive that Anna had worked out the King's character during her time in exile. Therefore, she made him more intrigued and interested by appearing utterly disinterested in him. I did not believe for one moment that Anna knew or understood what danger she was putting herself in. So I devised a plan of my own to keep her safe. The King was not the only man to be wooing Anna… I likewise followed suit.

I reasoned that if my wooing resembled that of an Arthurian knight who chose to honour a lady with acts of chivalry and platonic devotion, (abiding by strict rules existing for hundreds of years— yea, ever since Eleanor of Aquitaine wedded England's second Henry) then the King, with his great love for role-playing, might also follow suit. Thus, I greatly hoped, Anne, for the moment, would be protected from the King's barely concealed lust.

Yea, I freely admit, my plan was rather mad, and probably ill thought out. But God help me! I could not sit by and do nothing.

Anna, who could remember well our childhood acting, gave away with an amused glint in her eyes that she saw through my act. I think she assumed that I was trying to help her by increasing the King's ardour through the rivalry of competition. To my eyes, Anne became more beautiful every day. It was an absolute torment and agony to pretend something that was not pretence.

Anne was at this time a Lady in Waiting to Catherine of Aragon. I thought the Queen a very gracious lady, for whom I once was given the pleasure and honour of composing poems. And I, despite all the conflicts the future would bring, always thought most highly of the Queen, believing with all my heart that this saintly woman was great and noble. Utterly undeserving of the terrible, most cruel future the fates held in store for her.

And what was the King, her husband, like? King Henry was now a man of thirty-five, a man very much in the midst of his prime. He was also a man who had, many years before, fallen out of love with his older wife, a woman rapidly aged by frequent child-bearing and the deep grief of losing all her children, bar one—the nine-year old Princess Mary.

Yea, I will admit the truth. Our King at thirty-five was a man nobly made. Indeed, Henry of England was a man among men. Taller by far than most men of his court, he was a man exceedingly vain about his presence, and with every reason to be. Red golden hair, bright blue eyes, athletic body, and skin so fair and clear that it was the envy of many a woman. Verily, England took great pride in its manly and seemingly courageous King. Almost as much as the King took pride in the image he himself presented to his Kingdom.

Sometimes I cannot help but thinking that the King's greatest love affair was with himself. Verily, so much so that it affected his prowess in the bedchamber. It must be hard to make love to a woman when you are so used to making love to yourself.

His courtship of Anne was very different to his usual, easy conquests, simply because she rebuffed him. And Anne's utter indifference to his kingly desires would have, I believe, shocked our poor King right down to his toenails. Never before had a subject—and a *woman* at that—rebuffed him. Anne was clever enough to realise that her apparent rejection of his advances was like putting a red flag to a bull, and she soon had this particular royal bull charging at that flag.

And it was not only the King who could not get enough of her company. Since Anne's return from Hever she had fast become a major influence at court. Verily, many of the ladies at court were trying desperately to follow her lead in everything. Indeed, in so many different directions that George and I could not help sharing our amusement with one another. Certainly, Anne only had to alter her dresses slightly for this alteration to become the latest fashion—very quickly copied by all the women at the court. Even Anna's favourite colours were seen everywhere.

However, I also could not help thinking that many of these mature, court ladies made utter fools of themselves when they attempted to copy Anne's lovely, fluid manner of dance. To watch her dance was to watch something truly unique and marvellous. But then dancing, from the time she was a little child, was always one of Anne's greatest gifts, and I felt it could never be copied to the soaring level she was able to achieve, and with such apparent, effortless grace.

Standing alongside George, I felt embarrassed for these older ladies when I watched them try to match and outdo Anne's movements upon the dance floor.

I turned and whispered to George.

"Can one expect a duck to be as graceful in the water as a swan? Nay, I say, and more: Anne has more grace in one fingertip than those other women have in their entire bodies."

George's eyes shone his amusement and he gave a brief laugh.

George knew, as did I, that Anna had made good use of her time away from court. Verily, it was during this time when she was "exiled" at Hever that she had found the time to experiment with her style of dance and dress. Indeed, it was now, when she re-emerged at the English court, that her father's decision to send her to France was showing its greatest benefits. For it was during this time abroad that Anne had absorbed her knowledge regarding fashion, and how it could be used to add to her attractions and hide what she wished not to show.

In all honesty, my cousin Anna, from the time she was a little girl, had been very self-conscious about her body's imperfections, especially that of a mole upon her neck and a tiny growth upon her right hand's fifth finger. Yea, she was very aware of these two defects. Aware, because whenever Uncle Boleyn was angry with her as a little child, he always brought up those minor blemishes, saying that no man would ever have her for his wife if he realised her body hid two marks of the devil. Verily, I remember to this very day one occasion when the little girl that Anne once was went completely white and sick-looking after her father had told her that the lump on her finger reminded him of a devil's teat. Something possessed by one of his followers so the Prince of Evil could come and suckle at their person.

Thus, by the time she returned to court Anna had thought of two ways to hide these physical flaws. Around her slender, beauteous neck—to cover up her pretty mole—she now took to wearing some sort of collar, whether it be simply of cloth or ribbon, or something that was made of precious metals and jewels.

And I discovered, only days after she returned to court, how Anna conspired to hide her misshapen finger. I entered her chamber to find Anna sitting in the window seat, her back to the afternoon sun, sewing together pieces of fabric. Seeing a stool next to the window seat, I went over to sit beside her.

Concentrating hard at her task, Anne gave me a fleeting glance and a brief but welcoming smile. For a few minutes, the only sound I could hear was the needle pushing its way through dense fabric. At length, I felt a need for Anna to do more than just momentarily acknowledge my presence.

"What are you sewing?" I asked.

Anna bit off the strand of cotton, and spread the black material out on her lap.

"Do you not see, Tom? I am making new sleeves for my gowns. Simonette told me of this old design—remembering a gown of her mother's. Let me show you."

Anne pulled the long and wide sleeve up her left arm; the material, cut in a point, draped over her fingers.

"See, Tom, does it not look elegant?"

"It suits you," I said, thinking that Anne's good taste ensured all her gowns suited her. But I could not help watching her as she lowered her arm. She bit her lower lip, her face tight in concentration, as she moved her hand backward and forth, and looked at it from all possible angles. I knew at that exact moment the reason why she had chosen to seize hold of this past fashion for the sleeves of her gowns.

But then Anna knew too well that the wooing of a king, such as Henry of England, meant always thinking hard on her strategy to do so—though for a reason I could but shudder at. Revenge had become the only reason for her life.

It so maddened me to watch this drama being enacted before my eyes. To see what Anne was doing and was determined to do.

Aye, within weeks of her return from Hever, Anne had the whole court buzzing around her. Alas, it was not only the court. It was too easy to see that the King was completely captivated by her, and could not get enough of her presence. I grew more uneasy hour by hour.

Nonetheless, if anyone understood what was really going on inside of her, it was I. Anna had not been stable in her actions since that dreadful day when she first left the court. Knowing that, and believing Anna was taking herself deeper and deeper beyond the point of saving, I could not help trying to make the King lose his interest in my cousin and my beloved. Indeed, I think I was in a temper to attempt anything.

An opportunity to do so came about one day when the King, the Duke of Suffolk, and my friend Francis Bryan were playing bowls together. An argument began about who had been the most recent victor. The King pointed with his hand bearing a ring— taken as a token from Anne recently—saying that it was his victory. It was completely clear to me that, when he looked me directly in the eye, he was speaking of other than the game we were playing. I glanced at the King, realising he was hinting about his wooing of Anne. I thought in a hurry, and remembered a locket I had taken recently from Anna as a jest. Taking it off from my neck, I bowed and then said to the King: "And if it may please your Grace, to give me leave to measure it, I hope the victory will be mine."

I then began to measure how far it was between the bowls and jack. The atmosphere was suddenly charged all around me. It was like the threat of a dark storm had come to foreshadow the bright day. The King plainly realised that the locket belonged to Anne— his face reddened with rage.

"I am deceived," the King shouted, in his high voice, heading off in the direction where we had only recently left Anna. Hurrying after the King, the Duke and Bryan strode away too.

I stood, now altogether alone, watching them march off into the distance—and as I watched I reflected I had doubtless ruined any chance I had to further advance myself at court. I sighed, thinking I would doubtless now be sent far away from these blessed shores of England. But if what I had done had achieved its purpose, if the King's interest in Anne was now destroyed, well then, I thought, my banishment would be well worth it.

Anne and I had arranged to meet at a certain hour in the gardens after dinner. In due course, it became time to meet her, and I strolled towards our designated meeting place.

Anne was already there, walking up and down as she often did when she was upset or angry. I sauntered over casually, sat on a nearby bench, crossed a leg over a knee, glanced around at the beautiful gardens surrounding me, and prepared myself to listen to her recriminations.

At length, she stopped her stalking and stared hard at me. Her eyes were brightly dark, almost like glittering jewels.

"How could you, Tom?" she snapped at me.

I jerked back—she sounded so angry. I was so unused to having her anger directed towards me that I felt like I had been suddenly slapped. I felt angry in turn, and spoke with bitterness in reply.

"How could I, Anne? Why ask that of me, when it should be

me asking, how can you continue playing this cat and mouse game with the King? Yea, I know that you wish to make him to fall in love with you so you can hurt him as he hurt you. But 'tis a mad, mad plan and you should stop—stop before you become any more hurt than what you've been already."

I arose from the bench, and went as to embrace her, but Anne backed away from my reaching grasp. Thus, putting down my hands and staying where I stood, I tried my hardest to make her see reason.

"Believe me, Anne, the King knows nothing of love, except the love of himself. Anna… Anna… I do not know what is happening to you. And I do not believe that you know what is happening to yourself. This is so unlike the girl I grew up with! Anna, how can you be so untrue to yourself?"

She moved closer to me and gestured angrily to her breast.

"I, Tom? Untrue to myself, cousin? You know, as George knows, that for the last three years I have been promising myself revenge. I could only be untrue to myself if I did any other than what I planned."

I stared at her. Surely Anna could not have changed so completely from the carefree and compassionate spirit I had come to love so early in our lives. I shook my head slowly, saying with utter solemnity: "Anna, I promise you will rue the day you decided on this course."

"Cousin, if I do, I do. I am willing to take the consequences for any action of mine. What I am not willing to do is to forgive or forget what Wolsey and the King did to Hal and I. All the dreams they so heartlessly destroyed. They deserve to suffer for what they did. And I promise you, cousin, I will not rest until they hurt as I am hurting. As I will always hurt!"

Anne stood white-faced before me, visibly trembling. I wanted so much to take her in my arms and kiss away everything afflicting her so. But I also knew, with a sudden sense of helplessness, that I had little power to help her.

I could only hope and pray she would heed my words.

"Anna! Anna! Can you not see you are on a road where you could destroy yourself?"

"And what if I am, cousin? I feel like Wolsey and the King have already destroyed everything that made my life worth living…"

She again looked hard at me, as if any affection she had for me had instantly been dealt a deathblow. Blinking away tears, my heart began to ache within my chest. I wished simply to disappear.

"Are you my keeper, Tom, that you worry so much about my concerns? You have told me much about your own problems at home. Look first to solving them, Tom, before you meddle again in my affairs."

With those final words still vibrating through the air, Anne spun away and ran from the garden, leaving me absolutely desolated and wretched.

Chapter 4

"That now are wild and do not remember."

ay swiftly followed day, and I soon found myself appointed to the company of Sir Thomas Cheney, a short and stocky man who was a long time friend and neighbour of my father. By the command of the King, Sir Thomas was being sent with a group of young courtiers to *François*, King of France. The reason for his mission was to congratulate the King on his recent release from the captivity of the Holy Roman Emperor, Charles V, as well as to offer the support and protection of England to a league formed to combat the actions of the Emperor.

I had expected this "exile"—though no one claimed it as such— from the time I had watched King Henry stalk from the bowling courts, his tall body pulsating with barely compressed anger. I felt very thankful (for my father's sake—if not my own) the King had seen fit to close his eyes to my insult, choosing to content himself with his decision to send me, for a time, away from his court and presence.

Perchance the King unknowingly did me a great service. It was spring—the weather simply as glorious as it could be in this season, the Channel crossing as smooth as one could wish it. Verily, the short voyage across such gentle seas was good for my lowered spirits. I felt almost happy again as I stood on the deck watching the sapphire coloured water lap and splash against the ship's bow, while behind us the churned up sea slithered like a snake in its death throes. This was my first voyage upon the seas. I felt somewhat astonished to find myself little affected by the movement of our small craft, especially since many of my companions had turned pale and ill looking at the first rock and sway of the ship.

Thus, by the time we disembarked on the sixth of April at Bordeaux, my faith in life had begun to return somewhat. At twenty-two, I was still young enough to take joy in the feel of the sea-kissed wind blowing against my face, the smell of the salt air, and the sight of sea birds spiralling up, higher and higher into the blue and often unclouded sky.

Most of the company forming our embassy were young men I had known since early youth; friends like Francis Bryan and Francis Weston. It began to feel to us all as if we had been suddenly freed from the strict dominion of our English court. While on our journey towards Cognac, we would often sing and jest to one another. Verily, on many an occasion Sir Thomas had to speak firmly to his young companions for instantaneously breaking loose from the group and racing their horses until they reached the next bend in the road before us.

Spring had begun its magic when we had left England; in France the spell appeared completed. It was so utterly enchanting—very, very green, with wildflowers everywhere. I remember that we would often stop our horses so to discreetly watch the peasants tending to their fields and livestock. The scenes we saw could easily be described as peaceful and homelike, except that when we were noticed, the peasants would act as if stricken with great panic, running fast to the nearest shelter. Many a place we noticed had the obvious signs that battle had been engaged there in recent times. Verily, many times in our journey we were confronted by the ruined remains of a homestead or village—clearly once full of human life, but now being reclaimed by nature.

The weather stayed warm, with sunlight making our fair skins tingle and glow. Without doubt, this lovely weather helped us to make good time and, thus, our very happy journey soon came to an end. Within two weeks of arriving at the southwestern seaport of Bordeaux we made our entry into the city of Cognac, where we knew King *François* resided.

As I have said, this was my first time abroad and my first experience of the French court. I remember when Anna first returned from France how enthusiastic she often was about her years at Queen Claude's court. Now I began to understand why. The French court was very different from the court I had left behind. During the days I was there, I felt so overwhelmed by each and every impression. The strongest impression made on me, however, was the impact made by *François* of France. In England, at court, I had seen many French charters, charters that would often include an image of the French King. Even so, meeting him in the flesh was a different matter entirely. Several years younger than our King Henry, *François* was similar to the English King in some ways, and very dissimilar in others. They were both men of comparable height, but our King was proud, and rightfully so, of his athletic, muscle-bound thighs. The French King's legs were skinny—verily, almost stick-like. I remember a story that one of his ancestors had gained the nickname of "Spider" for his ability to tangle unwary foes in his web. But I could not help wondering if another reason he was so named was because of this physical defect of terribly thin legs, a defect clearly passed down to his descendant.

The King of France also had a very strange face: an extremely long nose, dark, beady eyes set too close together, and a very full, sensual mouth. Sometimes, I thought, his facial expressions could only be described as leering—especially if an attractive, young woman stood near.

Nevertheless, when I met the King of France that spring, I met a man very much embittered by his imprisonment by Charles V, telling all and everyone how badly he was treated by the Holy Roman Emperor and how little stock had been taken for his Royal blood. King *François* had given up his own young sons as hostages to the Emperor to ensure his good behaviour and release. Condemning his two sons to live their young years as bleakly as he had lived since his defeat at Pavia. Sometimes the reasoning of kings defies all my attempts of understanding.

Thus, in this spring of 1525, much had reversed against *François* of France, the expected becoming increasingly uncertain. Not only had he given up his supposedly beloved heir *François*, and his second-born son Henri, as hostages for his freedom and "good behaviour," but the first Nobleman of his realm had, only a short time since, deserted from the ranks of loyal Frenchmen. This was Charles II, the *Duc de Bourbon*, who had gone over to the side of the Imperial Emperor. Verily, Bourbon had been very much the genius behind the "shaming" of the French King at Pavia. The breakaway of the *Duc de Bourbon* had happened just over a year before. The events that led up to it had caused much scandal and upset in the French court, and grim amusement in ours.

I have also seen many images representing this great *Duc*. If these images were true depictions of Charles, *Duc de Bourbon*, then I could not help thinking him far more handsome than his cousin *François*, King of France. The *Duc* possessed very heavy lidded, large eyes; eyes extremely soulful and expressive. He was also blessed with a very clear complexion, in addition to a well-defined mouth. Though his pictures clearly showed he had not escaped the long nose of his *Valois* ancestry, it could also be seen that this famous *Valois* feature appeared less pronounced in him than in some of his kin—kin such as the King's beloved sister: *Marguerite Valois*. A sometime moody man, occasionally inflicted with darkness of soul, the *Duc*, nonetheless, greatly loved his wife, the beautiful *Suzanna de Beaujeu*—an heiress of great estates, which added immensely to the wealth of the *Duc*. It was her tragic, early demise that put him upon the road that would lead him to turn traitor to his King. Before her death, the *Duc* was virtually undisputed King of most of central France. Indeed, the power that he wielded in the realm rivalled that of the King himself. After her death, he was not only a grieving widower but also facing a future where he could no longer claim possession to many of his former lands. This was despite the well-known fact that his dying wife and her own mother, the woman to whom these lands had originally belonged, had undoubtedly desired for the lands to stay within his wise and stable rule.

So, a savage struggle began between *Bourbon* and the Crown for
the supremacy of these lands. The King's mother now stepped onto
the stage to make matters even more complicated. Even though
François' mother was at least fourteen years the elder of *Bourbon*,
she had long loved the *Duc* from afar, and now deluded herself that
he would return her affections if it meant assuring his lands stayed
safe. The King's mother was completely certain that soon she would
achieve her desire of becoming the *Duc's* new wife, but she had
never stopped to consider that the *Duc* would put his heart before
his head. The King's mother sent a friend of the *Duc* with her
proposal of immediate marriage.

The *Duc* was horrified, and angrily said to the envoy: "I have
loved and lost the best woman in France. It defies all understanding
that you, my supposed friend, can actually stand there and offer
me marriage to a woman who can only be described as the worst
woman in the world."

So the chessboard was set, and the game began in earnest, but
the end of the game far outweighed the imaginings of any of
the players.

All of this I discovered in conversation with the French courtiers
during the evening banquets. It struck me that many of the court
grieved things that had come to such a past, and were torn between
the habit of love for their proud *Duc* and the hate that they were
now supposed to feel for him.

As well as to offer congratulations, our mission also had a more
delicate purpose. France, Venice, Milan, and the Vatican had formed
the Holy League of Cognac, attempting—vainly as it turned out—
to block the Imperial Emperor's hold on Italy. We had been also
sent abroad to ascertain whether this League would suit the purposes
of England, and whether England should support and protect it. It
did not take Sir Thomas long to come to his conclusions. Perhaps
I even assisted him to come quickly to some firm decisions about
the directions that should be taken, because on the first of May I

was commanded to his presence.

I found him in the rooms that had been allotted to us for our stay, sitting at a desk and busily engaged in writing letters.

"Tom. Good man! You wasted no time in getting here."

Sir Thomas arose from where he was sitting, and began to shuffle some of the papers on the table into order.

"Come here, Tom," he said, gesturing to a seat near his desk. "Come on, lad. Come and sit down, and I will tell you what is ado."

So I went and sat, and waited for him to speak. This he did while standing, looking at me with one hand behind his back.

"First, Tom, I must say I have been pleased with you. You have the makings of a true and useful diplomat. Not like those other, foolish lads I have been appointed nursemaid to. You, my lad, have not only kept your eyes and ears opened… you have also known when to keep your mouth shut. Your observations have been extremely valuable, and I believe that they would also find value with the Cardinal. So I am sending you home, Tom. I want you to go to the Cardinal and tell him all that you have told me. And give him these messages." He handed to me some sealed papers.

I felt embarrassed by his praise and attempted to hide my embarrassment by spoken words: "Sir Thomas, I thank you for your good opinion. I feel honoured that you think so well of me, but good Sir, I only thought to do as my father would do."

"Aye. Indeed, Tom, if that was your intention, then you have fulfilled your purpose with great success. Your father will be proud and pleased, young Wyatt, when I tell him how well you have pleased me."

I began feeling overcome with all this praise. Indeed, my cheeks felt as if they were becoming as red as the brightest sunset. Finally, I flustered out another reply and question: "Thank you, again, Sir Thomas. When do you want me to go?"

"Today, Tom. I need Wolsey to tell me how now to proceed, so be as quick as you possibly can."

So, I was sent briefly back home to England with messages for

Wolsey. Cardinal Wolsey came quickly to his recommendations and orders regarding what we should do. Indeed, within only days of arriving in England, I was despatched to France again. It was a good thing, indeed, that my stomach had proven to be the stomach of a sailor!

Sir Thomas acted quickly once he received these messages from the Cardinal. Thus, within days of my arrival back at Cognac, our mission's purpose had been fulfilled—verily, as much as possible—to everyone's satisfaction, England agreeing to protect the league. This was as far as our country could go, not only because France, our country's traditional foe, led the League but also because to do any other put in jeopardy English trade with the subjects of the Imperial Emperor.

Only a short time after the final documents were signed, we were told by Sir Thomas to begin our preparations for return to England.

But… I possessed no desire to return.

I felt still angry with Anne, and, no doubt, she with me. I could see no purpose for my presence in her company at court. For if I returned I knew it would be to court, and Anne was constantly there in the company of the King. I felt so utterly helpless, helpless to prevent her from destroying all what remained still good in her life. I knew if I returned I would only be opening myself up to further pain. I felt myself neither brave, nor strong enough for that yet.

So I went to Sir Thomas and gained his permission to depart from the company of my fellows, as well as gaining a letter of introduction and good conduct to aid me on my journey. I had told Sir Thomas that I greatly wished to visit Italy and partake, even if only for a short time, of everything that could be offered to me. This was true enough. Since my time at Cambridge, I had been a lover of all to do and could be learnt of Italy. Just as, so many years ago, Father Stephen had once been a lover of all things Greek. I had so longed for the opportunity to see, hear and smell the reality—

rather than experience its beauties second hand from books, or from the tales of people fortunate enough to experience the actuality of Italy for themselves.

Even so… there were other reasons why I went, and the constant ache where my heart lay was indeed the truer one. So I felt a pilgrimage to Rome in order—perhaps, I thought, this and time away from court would help to bring my aching heart to "stiller waters."

Thus, I gave to Sir Thomas messages for home—a letter for my father and also another one for George to explain this sudden change in my plans. Though it was only a brief explanation saying I wished to make a short visit to Rome since I found myself not many days' journey away. I then gathered up my belongings, ensured myself of a good horse, and began the journey towards Italy.

There is an old Italian saying, *per pium strade si va a Roma*, which literally means "many roads lead to Rome." The truth of this ancient saying I found out for myself when I travelled there in 1525. I also discovered how, in this glorious spring, travelling could be an experience open to much pleasure. Indeed, Rome had been the destination of so many, for so much of history, that the inns and roads along the way are inferior to none. Especially to the type of abode I had become accustomed to in my travels in England. I also felt so blessed with wonderful weather: blue skies for much of my journey, sun-filled days, making the going both swift and purposeful.

My duties at home were such that I knew my time would be brief and limited, so I went as quickly as I could to Rome. Sir Thomas had written an introduction to the English officials who made their work there, and they kindly invited me to stay with them during my visit.

During my first days there, I explored my new surroundings. There was so much to see and do that I could not help reflecting that I would be unable to enjoy to the full all that Rome had to offer.

However I did happen to spend a fair amount of my first day in Rome enjoying one building that had withstood the changes that the centuries had brought since its completion. The building of Santa Maria Rotunda had once been called the Pantheon, meaning the Temple of the Gods, and surviving to this day because in Anno Domini 130 the early Christians had adopted the building to be one of their own. It was a tremendous example of bygone Roman architecture. Frequently I had to remind myself to stop walking around the building like an overly awestruck boy and shut tight my mouth!

The Pantheon had an enormous vaulted roof, achieved through the ancient Roman understanding of how best to use wedged arches to fashion a huge, round and windowless hall. The only natural light came from a circular opening—seeming to me so small and far away—placed in the centre of the dome. This opening allowed just enough light in to bring alive the inside of the building. And the inside of the building, how absolutely glorious! Nay, one cannot help but be completely in awe of the genius of the ancient Romans. Having set out to make a temple to their own gods, they had somehow managed to give the future a building which confirmed the great glory of our Christian God, where all in Christendom could go to worship him. Verily, there was such a sense of calm and deep tranquillity within the Pantheon that I soon became lost in prayer and quiet communion; thinking over the direction my life now took me.

Though, I need be truthful, and admit that all my time was not spent in holy prayer and reflection.

The English officials that I had joined with would often spend their evenings at the banquets prepared by the papal court. I accepted their invitation to attend also, and met there an Italian courtesan who soon became my bed companion during my stay in Rome. Lucrezia made my stay in Rome memorable for other reasons than what I had originally planned. Indeed, lovely Lucrezia was a woman who it was extremely easy to come to care for; but it soon became time to return to England. Thus, after grateful thanks to my fellow Englishmen who had welcomed me into their company, and a more poignant farewell to Lucrezia, I began my trek back to England.

Book Three

Trustee estaba el Padre santo
Lleno de angustia y de pena
En Sant' Angel, su castillo,
De pechos sobre una almena,
La cabeza sin tiara,
De Suder y povo llena
Viendo a la reina del mundo
En poder de gente ujena.

Sad was the Holy Father
Filled with anguished and pain
In Sant' Angelo, his castle,
High in a turret,
Without the tiara on his head,
Covered with sweat and dust,
Seeing the queen of the world,
In the power of foreigners.

An opening stanza of a Spanish romance,
written at the time of the sack of Rome in 1527.

Chapter 1

"I would fain to know to what she has deserved."

ime went by, and my life in England was resumed once again—though if the pattern was beginning to change, the substance remained much the same.

Early in January of 1527, I decided to avoid the weather-battered roads that normally took me to Kent by travelling part of the way to my family's holdings by barge. When I made my way down to the river to hire a craft, I discovered Sir John Russell, an old family friend and neighbour, similarly engaged. So, it soon came about that we were the two main occupants of a barge starting us on our journey home to Kent.

Sir John, a very tall and lanky man, even though beginning to grey and peer at you through very short-sighted eyes, retained some essence of youth and vitality. I have a very good opinion of Sir John, and he of me, thus we soon fell into easy conversation.

"So, Tom, what good fortune has us meet upon the bank back there?" He waved his hand in the direction from whence we had just departed. "Though I have to admit that I had to think hard for a moment to place who you were. Verily, I found myself thinking in astonishment: *'Tis young Tom Wyatt!* God's oath, Tom! The years have flown too fast for me to keep tally!"

He paused for a moment to look closer at me.

"Methinks you look more the part of the man now, Thomas, and less the boy I once knew!" he concluded with a happy laugh, even if his face was full of unspoken strain and tension.

I raised my hand to my new beard, grinning up at him.

"I believe this hair upon my face has something to do with that…

But you, Sir John, you seem like you have just swallowed the kitchen cat and find yourself worst for it!" I smiled jokingly at him, knowing he would take the remark in the jesting spirit that it was said, although wondering to myself why he looked so worried.

He gazed again at me, and screwed his face in a grimace of disgust.

"I do not wonder that I look like that... and, by my faith, I have good cause, Tom, yea, very good cause..." he responded in a whisper, looking over his shoulder to make sure we were not being overheard by the barge-men.

"Oh? And what reason is that, Sir John?" I too lowered my voice.

"You understand, of course, that what is said between you and I stays only with you and I, and goes no further?"

"For certes! You have my oath on that, Sir John, my oath as a loyal subject of the Crown," I said quietly, wondering what was likely to be the cause of all the secrecy.

"Good. I would expect no less from Sir Henry Wyatt's son. Tom, 'tis like this: our good King Hal has commanded me to go to Italy, to parley with the Holy Father himself. It is a secret mission which the King feels necessary, but I am not too pleased to be the one chosen." He grunted his annoyance, and shifted his tall body upon the wooden plank that doubled as our seat.

"What a time, Wyatt, to trek to Rome, with thousands of cut-throat Spaniards between here and there, determined to get control of the papacy."

"I went to Italy myself, Sir John, not so many months ago," I said, thinking back with fondness to my time abroad.

"Oh? And was it to your taste?" Sir John's voice returned me to the present moment.

"Yea, very much so, Sir John. Indeed, good Sir, I have yearned to make a return ever since I came back home."

Sir John looked hard at me, laughed, and slapped his leg.

"That's very interesting, Thomas Wyatt. Very interesting indeed! Here I was thinking, Tom, that I would like a companion for this journey and there you are, my lad, someone known to me and with recent experience of Italy who expresses a desire to return... I have a question to ask you, young Master Wyatt! Tom, how would you like to come abroad with me and act as my equerry and companion?"

'Twas my turn to look hard at him. So many thoughts passed through my head, but the one demanding my most attention was the sudden desire to assent. At last, I laughed, and held out my hand to him.

"Why not? Why not indeed? And here is my hand on it, Sir John, and also the hand of your journey's companion."

"Good man!" he said, as he firmly clasped my hand and smiled broadly. "This has been a very fortunate meeting, Thomas!"

"Aye, it has at that, Sir John. But I need to return to my home to put my affairs in order and to obtain some gold for our travels."

"That is why I return to Kent also... Try not to be over-long about it, Tom. I leave for Dover at the close of the week."

Soon after that we came to the place where we would disembark from the barge. After finding some mounts to hire for our short trek home, we arranged a day to meet at a certain inn in Dover where we would begin our trek to Italy. Sir John and I then parted company for a brief time.

So it was, after our farewells, I began the short journey to Allington. In recent years I had not taken much pleasure in my infrequent homecomings, but this time was different. Elizabeth had been taken into service with the Queen and decided to remain at court, no doubt finding quick some man to keep her bed warm while I travelled to Kent. 'Twas the main reason why I had agreed to go with Sir John. I found it easier to avoid the many problems breaking apart our accursed marriage by travelling on frequent court business.

I had ventured down to Kent to ensure that the estate was running smoothly in the absence of my father and myself; but also to spend some time with my son. Tom was now a big lad of near seven, and always in some type of trouble. He was a boy who any father would be proud to own as his; tall and with a strong look of his grandfather. Verily, I have high expectations for young Tom's future.

Bess was also there to take pleasure in. She was now almost six, a tiny girl, with raven black hair. Even though I felt often inflicted with grave doubts about her parentage, Bess was a very easy child to love. Indeed, she often reminded me of the Anne I remembered from my childhood, being always full of questions and bubbling over with the excitement and ebullience of just being alive. Soothly, it seemed to me that little Bess just wished and needed to share her happiness with everyone.

How uncomplicated, I could not help thinking, are the joys of childhood! Thank God we have that brief time before all the care and grief of adult years descend on us!

I had three days with which I could indulge myself with my children. Verily, I almost felt drawn back to my own young days when I rode alongside these two youngsters. Tom and Elizabeth were, so obviously, deep in the midst of their first pleasure and excitement of having their own horse to love and ride.

Nonetheless, those three days passed quickly, and it was soon time to make my way to Dover to meet with Sir John as planned.

'Twas a very cold and early morning when I farewelled my home yet again. Despite the fact that I had told my children the previous evening that there was no need to do so, both Tom and Bess came to the courtyard to bid me a good and safe journey. It wrenched my heart to see them struggling so bravely with the threat of tears. Verily, I gathered Tom and Bess up in my arms, kissing and blessing them.

I also made a promise I would return as soon as I could, not knowing that almost a full year would pass before this promise could be kept.

Without further ado, I got onto my horse and rode away, feeling undeserving of the strong affection that Tom and Elizabeth evidently felt for me. Being the children of their mother, I had not looked, nor sought, for their loves. This visit to Allington had served to make me realise that there were two small children who looked to me as I still did my own father. It was enough to humble me, yet make me proud at the same time.

Thus, early in the year 1527 I journeyed with Sir John Russell to Italy, when the King sent him on a secret mission to Pope Clement.

Clement VII, formerly *Giulio de Medici*, was a bastard son of a brother of Lorenzo the Magnificent. An extremely ambitious man, Giulio became Pope late in 1523 despite the stigma of his bastardy. However, these years placed him in a very perilous and difficult situation.

When Clement first became Pope he quickly showed that his loyalty (if one can call his easily swayed support by that word) was completely given over to the side of France. This was despite the support of the Emperor Charles he had received in the past. Support which, indeed, had helped gain him the papacy.

The previous Pope, Leo X, had assured Charles V that he would support any move the Emperor made against France, if Imperial Emperor would promise to rid him of the troublemaker Martin Luther. However, all was changed when the Pope's cousin, Giulio, succeeded him.

Two years before, early in the year 1525 when I was still in England trying my hardest to save Anne from herself, France was entirely demoralised by its defeat by the Emperor's troops at Pavia. Even more demoralising to the French was the fact that this defeat included the capture of their King *François*.

Some people at the English court had compared Pavia to the Scot's crushing defeat at Flodden field. I personally thought that it did more damage than that. The fragile power balance on the Continent was tilted completely over to the side of the Imperial Emperor, and our uncertain world made more uncertain.

After this defeat at Pavia, Pope Clement desperately tried to change his colours by appearing to bow and scrape before the victor, the Imperial Emperor Charles. However, Emperor Charles no longer had trust for the Pope, thus wished to hold the Pope in the palm of his hand where he could ensure that the Pope danced completely to his will. Part of the result of all this was that now thousands and thousands of unpaid mercenaries, mostly soldiers who had been completely swayed by the Lutheran doctrines, were now scouring the Italian countryside as they made their way to *Roma*. These soldiers, led by the renegade French *Duc de Bourbon*, a man who believed himself wronged by his own king and so had gone into self-imposed exile, were robbing and raping as they moved steadily towards Rome. So, reader, you can understand why Sir John was not at all pleased to be given by our King a mission to the Holy City at this time.

Nonetheless, armed with the usual weapons, a safe conduct, and dressed in plain travelling garb, Sir John and I began making our way to Rome.

Chapter 2

"I was unhappy, and that I prove,
To love above my poor degree."

ast time, I savoured almost every moment of my journey to Italy. However, understandably, travelling to Rome this time felt more an experience of facing utter shambles. Most people, other than men-in-arms, were escaping from, rather than travelling to, the Holy City. Thus, Sir John and I, not long after we began our journey, decided that it was best and safer to take roads other than the main ones, especially after listening to the dreadful tales being told by other travellers.

We eventually arrived at the port of Civitas Vecchia, almost exactly a month after we had departed from the shores of England. By the time we arrived there, we were in great need of good horses, so I spent two full days searching for reasonable, and affordable, horseflesh.

We were very fortunate in that we were able to obtain the services of an Italian captain and his men, and, with their assistance, we soon found good mounts. This band of Italian soldiers even went so far as to offer to accompany us to Rome for our protection along the way. With gratitude, we readily agreed to this, also requesting that the Captain send one of his men post-haste to inform the papal court of our imminent arrival within the next two days. Thus, when we reached the outskirts of Rome, we were met by one of the Holy Father's grooms. He had for us, even for the captain and his men, a change of horses. And what horses! Such splendid horses! The groom told us with great Italian gusto that they were horses given to the Pope recently as gifts by the Turks, and were much valued by the Pope for their beauty and intelligence.

Sir John gave to me a long look, as if to say: *Take note of this Tom, and wonder what else can be in store for us.*

Indeed, we were soon to find out. We were swiftly escorted to comfortable lodgings: a two-room, stone building with a stable behind to house our mounts. These buildings, obviously owned by the Vatican and used to house "guests" of the Pope, were built on the *Via Aurelia Antica*, close to the *Villa of Belvedere*, and within easy walking distance from the court of the Vatican. Having now been received in the protection of the papacy, we gave our sincere thanks and farewells (and some well-earned gold coins) to the soldiers who had made the last leg of our journey to Rome so agreeable and untroubled.

Even I, who had embarked upon this journey with the idea I would gain some satisfaction from the excitement of travel, was thankful to be at last in Rome, safe and still in one piece. Verily, Sir John was still expressing to me his annoyance that the King had given him this task.

I could only sympathise with him. I too have enough liking for my skin to wish to stay in it without violence hastening the day of my death. Indeed, I freely admit it is not in my character to overly tempt the fates to rid me of my skin sooner than I would like. Nevertheless, the dominant memory of my recent visit to Italy was how much I had enjoyed my travels, and all the sights I had been able to see in the brief time available to me. I had no idea how the situation had changed with the passing of only a few months.

The Pope, we soon discovered, still resided at his papal residence at St. Peter's; resisting all attempts by his officials who would have him moved to the safety of the *Castel Sant' Angelo*, a fortified castle placed close to the Vatican.

The sound of gunfire constantly assaulted our ears (not real battle yet, but Roman citizens using this lull to practice and improve their aim). As well as gunfire, I had Sir John continually clamouring in my ear too. Sir John was, at this time, beginning to be not just annoyed with his superiors, but very angry—angry he was sent on a mission to Rome at such a topsy-turvy time.

Having presented our official papers to the papal representative and been told that the Pope would see us the following day, we decided to take the opportunity for respite and rest.

The first evening was spent in care of our horses. Then unpacking, and organising our belongings in the tiny rooms we had been given for our stay, though I also admit, compared to the many places we had slept in on the way, these rooms appeared to be the height of luxury. Verily, the building was snug and well built, and there were various pieces of well-made furniture in our apartment to make our stay more comfortable.

Before we knew it, the dark of evening had settled over our abode, and, as Sir John was utterly exhausted by the journey, we decided not to go in search of food, but eat what remained of our travel supplies. We were in no hurry to explore our new surroundings; Rome would still be there on the morrow. After eating, we took ourselves to our hastily arranged bedding, and laid ourselves down for an early night.

I awoke as morning broke, the sunlight peeking into the room via a partly opened window. I could tell by the loud snores almost trumpeting in my ears through the door-less next room—where a thin curtain slung across the entrance gave the illusion of privacy—that Sir Russell was still asleep there. I had lain out my sleeping pallet on the floor near the cooking hearth. Yesterday, on our arrival, I had lit there a fire, and stacked it well before night had finally taken over from day, thus had been able to revel in the fire's warmth which had done much to take the harsh chill off the February evening. Sir John's chamber had its own fireplace, which, when lit, had taken no time at all to warm his tiny space.

I am often astonished how the simple act of having a fire ablaze in a hearth will speedily give a neglected dwelling a sense of homeliness and heart.

Now fully awake, I decided to leave my older companion

continue his much-needed sleep while I went to look for fresh food with which to break our fast. I did not have to venture far. Verily, I had only to follow my nose to discover we were located near an inn with a bake house affixed to its rear. Very soon I was returning the way I had come, bearing "great gifts" back to our lodgings—freshly baked bread, soft cheese which looked fit to simply melt in your mouth, and a goatskin full of sweet wine.

Sir John was still abed when I arrived at the dwelling, so I put the food onto the table placed against the wall, and restocked the dying fire, putting a large pot of water fetched from the well outside our dwelling over the flame. Sir Russell and I had not washed since we first arrived in Civitas Vecchia, and I felt it was important that we groom ourselves, as best as was possible, before we paid our respects to the Pope. When the water had warmed, I stripped myself of my filthy and now stinking travelling clothes and washed myself with some soap that I had packed amongst my gear. I then trimmed my beard, and sorted out cleaner hose and the silken garments I had kept for our meeting with the Pope. I had recently bought myself a new green doublet in the latest style, stiffly quilted and slashed with scarlet silk at both arms. The final touch was a gold ring adorned with a hanging ruby, placed in the lobe of my right ear.

I felt completely refreshed by the end of my wash, and took the dirty water to the door to throw it out in the cobbled lane that led us out to the road. I then went back to the well, refilled the pot, and carried it back inside so Sir John could also wash when he awoke. When the water began to steam, I decided it was time to awake my companion. Thus, I went to his room, knocked hard on the wall, and entered. The knight of the realm was curled upon his bed, sound asleep with his arm flung across his face, as I had often seen my little lad and lassie sleep. I could not help smiling to myself that this aging man could remind me of a child—except the noise emitting from his person could not be described as anything childlike.

I went to his bed and gave his shoulder a hard and quick shake.

Sir John instantly awoke, confounded and bewildered by his surroundings. At last, as his eyes focused upon me, he visibly shook himself before he arose from his bedding. Sir John was dressed only in his dark hose and a white, drawstring shirt, and he now took the cloak from off his bed and put it around his thin shoulders.

"What hour in the morning is it, Tom?" he asked me drowsily.

"The sun has been up for two or more hours, Sir John. I have water prepared for you to wash in," I replied quietly in turn.

He straightened up his tall form, and pulled his cloak more around his scantily clothed body.

"Good thinking, Tom! I suppose 'tis best to tidy up."

I followed Sir John as he made his way into the next room. When he arrived at the fireplace he pulled the large pot of water away from the flame and then stripped, as I had done, and began to wash his face. He then looked up at me and asked: "Tom, can you do me the great favour and search amongst my gear for my shaving razor and towel?"

I returned to his chamber, and found his saddlebags flung casually to one side. I opened one of the bags and easily found Sir John's wash bag, in which was his razor and a piece of large towelling he used to dry his body when he washed. I decided that while I was there I might as well grab the clothes he would likely choose to wear for our meeting with the Pope. I had been his companion for over a month now, so possessed a firm idea of what his desires would be. So gathering his best hose, doublet and codpiece in my arms, I returned to the next room and put them on a chair near where Sir John was washing.

I next turned my attention to our morning meal. Drawing out my dagger from my belt, I cut up the fresh bread and cheese into more manageable chunks and put it all on a large wooden trencher for my knight and I to share. At last, my companion stood beside the fire clothed in all his fresh clothes. Now that he had cleansed himself, and clothed himself in his rich clothes, he looked more the acceptable picture of an English diplomat.

"I must say, Tom, that feels good, to rid myself of all that grime and filth." He walked over to stand across from me at the table.

"Aye, the last few days have been dust and more dust," I replied. "Come and eat, Sir John. The food is too good to waste."

Myself, I could wait no longer to begin my breakfast, so took up a piece of bread and folded it around a chunk of cheese. I began then to eat hungrily, enjoying to the full the taste of freshly made bread, and the moist, creamy taste of cheese.

Sir John gave a short laugh, moving quickly to take some food.

"Leave me some, Wyatt! You do not have to act as if you have starved upon the journey!"

Sir John smiled at me with an amused glint in his blue eyes.

Our appointment with the Holy Father was set for the first hour after midday, thus, Sir John and I felt we could linger a while and enjoy our meal in leisure.

We could hear the bells chiming the eleventh hour somewhere in the near distance, and were partaking of a second cup of wine when the door of our dwelling was loudly knocked upon.

I looked at Sir John, and he at me, wondering who it could be; then Sir John gestured with his head for me to attend to our caller.

I opened the door and stood suddenly transfixed, for before me bowed an Italian courtier, revealing behind him two utterly beautiful women, all dressed richly in garments that seemed to make our surroundings feel both colourless and shabby.

I recovered my voice, bowing deeply to our visitors, saying: "I am Thomas Wyatt, esquire and equerry of Sir John Russell. How can I be of service to you?"

Again, the man before me bowed back with a deep flourish, and replied: "Good morrow, *Signor*. I am *Michelangelo Oddo*, emissary of his most Holy Father, the Pope." The man paused, and looked over my shoulder into the humble room that was barred from him by my body.

"May we come in?" he asked, returning his attentions back to me.

The Italian spoke good and clear English, but I could not help wondering what his visit and the visit of these two beautiful women could mean. However, I nodded my assent and moved aside to allow our callers clear entrance to our abode.

The ladies closely passed me, and the sweet fragrance of perfume followed in their wake. Even close up these two women were nothing less than visions of loveliness. One girl—she must have been in her early twenties—was dark haired and had the most alluring dark eyes. Indeed, for a brief second of time, I could have imagined this girl to be my Anna, firmly entrenched into adulthood.

The other woman, her beautiful red hair carefully arranged around a well-shaped head, enhancing her clear, pale skin and large green eyes, seemed her elder by several years. I glanced at Sir John and saw he stared open mouthed at the red-haired woman. I hid a smile at the picture he must represent to our visitors.

The Italian bowed slightly to Sir John, giving him some sealed papers.

"I bring you the most sincere apologies from the Pope, Sir Russell. He will not be able to see you today as arranged. However, he sends, with his compliments, *Signora* Beatrice and *Signora* Angela to help you pass this day in comfort and great pleasure." Giving a short laugh, the courtier now winked at both of us. I glanced aside at the girls to see that they both had a fixed look on their face, as if their thoughts had swiftly taken their minds elsewhere.

The courtier briefly bowed again, and moved towards the door that he had just entered.

"I bid you gentlemen, for this day, farewell. Tomorrow I will come for you and take you to the most Holy Father. I also bid farewell to the two *Signoras*; remember that the Pope commands and expects you to make the stay of these Englishmen completely enjoyable and memorable."

With a final bow and flourish, he opened the door of our dwelling and went back into the outside world, leaving us with our two lovely, new companions. For a moment there was an uneasy silence, and then the red-haired woman laughed a high, melodic laugh and moved quickly towards Sir John.

"Our two Englishmen have been eating, Angela! But why only bread and cheese? Surely we Italians can offer more than that!" Even though she spoke English with a deep Roman accent, her words were easy to understand. Verily, the woman's voice was very charming and sweet.

I could see that Sir John was utterly beguiled by this "Italian Madonna" who was so close to him that he needed but reach out his hand a short distance to touch her. Now that the elder girl had made her claim, the other, younger girl, began to glide towards me. Closer up she appeared to strike a strong note of artificiality—as if she was, somehow, uncomfortable in her role of courtesan.

"Would you like to go to the best inn in all of Roma, *Signor*, and experience such food delights as you have never before encountered in your lives?" this girl now said, speaking also in English. Even though her voice was also accented, it was not as heavily so as her friend's was. The girl looked at me frankly, with large, dark eyes that seemed to be on the brink of tears. I had no problem in understanding what her eyes begged. I could see clearly that she desperately wished for me to agree to the suggestion that we direct ourselves to this inn.

I suppose she was afraid that our lusts for their fair bodies would win out over our already satisfied need for food, and soon she would find herself copulating in a strange place with an unknown man she had only just met.

We had eaten, but I could not ignore the pleading of the girl's eyes, thus I turned to my companion and said: "What say you, Sir John? Shall we let these fine ladies guide us to the best food in all of Rome?"

Sir John stirred from his gaze of the other fair Madonna, and glanced sourly at me.

"If that is what you want, Tom, then that is what we will do. I suppose the walk will give us an excuse to look at our surroundings."

The inn the girls spoke of was only a short distance from where we were staying; in fact, very near to the same inn where I had found our morning feast. Yea, the girl was right, it did have simply wonderful food: meat cooked in a kind of creamy sauce with some sort of string-like food that our companions assured was made of flour and water. Even though, during my last visit, I had eaten at many banquets I had never come across this wholesome and delightful dish before.

After we had eaten to the full, we agreed to allow the women to show us all they could of the glories of ancient Rome.

On reflection, I suppose that this decision may seem to many to be the height of lunacy, to indulge ourselves in a tour of a city which resembled, in some quarters, army barracks. But, good reader, you must remember that we had just trekked from England, frantically dodging through a rabble army on the move. At this moment, I think Sir John and myself felt the safest we had felt in weeks. Like the Pope, I could not believe the army of the *Duc de Bourbon* really meant to render this city—a city that had once given birth to the greatest Empire known in the history of man—any real and lasting harm.

Even preparing for a siege, Rome could not be called any other word but beautiful. Furthermore, I will take the risk of offending many of my own countrymen when I state what I truly believe: even London cannot hold a stick to the renown of Rome. In a way, walking around the city at such a time, when its streets were mostly emptied of the usual pilgrims and students, had the effect of making me even more aware and reflective of its wonders. More so since most of its citizens tended at this moment to keep within the safety of their own doors, and this helped to give us the impression that we had the city of Rome to ourselves.

Whilst the four of us strolled together amongst the many ruins I mused to myself about the destruction that man and time had wrought. I thought, here once upon a time long gone, men had laboured hard to make a beautiful city of marble. All that remained of their years of drawn-out labour were only tantalising remnants of what had once been the glory of an Empire. It made me more deeply aware that nothing in life is forever.

Even though I had for a short time visited Rome late in the year of 1525, I am somewhat chagrined to admit I had only skimmed the surface of its sights. When I arrived that first time, I was made quickly a member of a party of English officials who spent many of their evenings as guests of the papal court, freely indulging themselves at the nightly papal banquet and revel. Thus, during the days that followed, I had neither the energy nor the inclination to explore the many wonders to be seen of ancient Rome. Nay, to be utterly truthful, there is another reason for my lack of inclination. At the very first papal banquet I was taken to, I met a lovely Madonna—or, should I really say, a very lovely whore. She too reminded me so much in appearance of an older Anna. Verily, so much so that I was easily persuaded to part with a few gold coins to keep her as my bed companion during my stay. I must be more truthful when I admit that, apart from an occasional visit to a London brothel, when George would get me drunk enough to do so, I had little enough experience when it came to making love to women. 'Twas my time with Lucrezia that taught me otherwise. I suppose it was the only time in my life I succumbed purely to my body desires and learnt the true satisfaction there is to find in good lovemaking.

Remember, I was then a young man of barely twenty-two, away from home for the first time, and also away from a wife who welcomed me to her bed through duty only. Lucrezia, even though golden angels passed from my money belt to her, truly seemed to welcome me to her bed for other reasons. I must admit that I grew to care for her too. I recall my lovely Lucrezia telling me that it was a true joy to her to be entertaining a young man who took such simple pleasure in the normal, physical joining of a man and a woman. Rather than some corrupt, base and elderly Cardinal, whose senses could only be aroused by more and more perverted acts.

Truly, the poor girl had small scars on her private parts where the "Good Princes of the Church" had left their mark.

I often wondered when I returned to France and from there to England, what became of Lucrezia after my departure from Rome.

This time I had no desire for love games. Furthermore, "the French disease" currently raged throughout the Continent and I had no wish to join its numbers. And, to be even more candid, I have for long realised I am not a man who can freely engage in bed sports without having my heart somehow engaged. I suppose that is why I spend so much of my free time composing love songs for my lute, rather than indulging myself in the pursuit of fleshly desires. I had concluded, even at this early stage of my life, that if I cannot be with someone for whom I feel deeply for I would rather not be with anyone. My affection for Lucrezia taught me this: lust is akin to dust, barren and without true purpose. Moreover, I had not much liking for the taste it left in my mouth.

Thus, the girl who looked at me with such frightened eyes had nothing to fear from me—I was emotionally spent. Sir John and the woman with the red/gold hair were a different story. We returned to our lodgings by late afternoon. When I entered our dwelling, I went first to the fireplace to rebuild and re-light the fire that was long-hours dead. As the rooms were now fairly dark, John went around the building and lit the tapers set in holders upon the walls. Once I had finished my task, I turned my attention back to our female companions. Beatrice was taking a goblet of wine and smiling flirtingly at John. And my knight was being responsive, yea, very responsive indeed, to the charms of this Italian Madonna. A woman obviously more experienced in alluring and arousing a man than the woman set-aside for me.

So, what of her—what of Angela, the woman companion chosen for me by the papacy itself?

Angela stood near the table, with her back turned to me, and her head bent as if she simply wanted to disappear.

I decided to take pity on the girl. She was obviously finding the situation of being alone with two strange men too hard to bear. I went amongst my gear and brought out the lute I took when I travelled. Even though it was old and worn, it still had the ability to thrum the hearts and souls of those who listened when I played.

Sir John reclined upon a chair when I returned, with Beatrice, her arm looped around his neck, seated on his lap. He lifted up his head when he saw me return to the room with my lute in my hands, and laughed his bark of a laugh, saying: "Good thinking, Tom. Music to help speed us into the night, and maybe into other things as well."

My knight laughed again, as if he had made the best joke in all Christendom, but, though his companion laughed her appreciation, I noticed my companion's back had become even more rigid.

I found myself a stool and began experimenting with a few tunes, wondering which one was the best to put the poor girl at her ease. At length, with a sense of relief, I thought the music had already subtly changed the atmosphere in the room. Indeed, Angela gazed towards to me with a more reflective, less frightened look in her eyes. I smiled at her, and beckoned her to come closer to the fire, and where I was seated. For a moment the girl's eyes became somewhat glazed. Then, with a swift, fleeting look at her now embrace-locked friend, she moved slowly over to seat herself at my feet. We were both suddenly startled by the sound of Sir John laughing as he arose from the chair. I looked immediately at him, and saw that he had his arm over the shoulders of Beatrice and was leading her in the direction of his chamber. He saw my look and winked at me.

"I bid you good people farewell for this night. I think this night will bring us many pleasures unexpected from our meeting with the Pope. Goodnight, Tom! No need to keep to your playing, Tom lad. Perhaps 'tis time to give your fingers other work."

Sir John barked a final laugh, and then took Beatrice into his chamber, tugging the curtain closed behind him.

I then happened to look at the girl beside me. Tears rolled unchecked down her cheeks. For a few moments, I sat there, unsure what best to do. Finally, I put my lute carefully on the earthen floor, and went to kneel beside her.

"My dear girl, you really have nothing to fear from me!"

She laughed a bitter laugh, and wiped away her tears hurriedly with her hands, making her pale face dirty in the process.

"You are a man, *Signor*, and only a man would speak such foolishness! You tell me that I have nothing to fear from you! Do you call that nothing—what is happening in there?"

With those words she gestured her head in the direction of Sir John's chamber from where the clear sounds of lovemaking could now be clearly heard.

"But, surely, Angela, this is not the first time that you have acted the courtesan? Surely you must know the way the dice is thrown?"

I felt very confused and bewildered. She was obviously very upset by being here with me, but I could not bring myself to believe that an innocent would have been selected to make this day pleasurable for the "shunted to one side" English diplomats.

Angela's tears began to flow again; she then took in a deep breath and began to speak in a hoarse, tense voice. "*Si*, I know now how the dice is thrown, as *Signor* said, but yesterday, yesterday I did not. Oh for yesterday, when my heart was full, and I believed…"

She covered her face with her hands. Angela appeared an image of absolute misery.

"You speak in riddles, Angela. But believe me, dear *Signora*, when I say that you have nothing to fear from me. I have no desire to indulge myself with a woman I barely know, and awake with ashes in my mouth. Especially with a woman who obviously desires me not. Trust me; I tell you no falsehoods when I say that I take no pleasure from bed sports where there is no love or true affection…"

Angela looked at me for a long moment, her eyes shining with unspent tears. She reached out to touch me fleetingly on my arm.

"You are a good man. A very good man! Oh, *Signor*, I feel as if my heart breaks."

"That, mistress, in itself is not an uncommon affliction. Many of us have broken hearts. If you like, I will listen to your tale… It may help to distract us from what goes on in the other room."

I wryly smiled at her, reflecting as I did so that Sir John was noisy in other ways other than just sleep.

Angela looked hard at me, and then deeply sighed.

"What has happened is the punishment of the good God. Indeed, *Signor*, I am just a stupid woman who has found out to her cost where her stupidity has led her."

I threw some more tinder upon the diminishing fire, then turned back to her to ask: "And how are you stupid, my dear?"

She stayed silent for a short time, staring with fixed attention into the fire as it increased its vibrant energy. She then looked back at me, and spoke.

"I am *Angela Zabotto*, daughter of *Paolo Zabotto*; perhaps you have heard of him?"

I slowly shook my head in answer.

"My father is a goldsmith of Rome, a very good goldsmith." Angela paused, and swallowed, wiping away the tears flowing again from her eyes. "Though I am dead to my family—and deservedly so."

Angela shrugged, speaking bitterly: "And all because, *Signor*, I trusted the man I loved."

I began to suspect strongly what her story would be. I have heard it many times in my life at court, but I decided it was best to encourage her to speak and listen as if it was the first time I had listened to a woman's tale of betrayal. Verily, this is what she said:

"The man I love is a noble lord. He would often give to my father much work. Indeed, good *Signor*, that is how we first met, when I came into father's shop with his morning meal. My lord is such a handsome man, and I? I was young and foolish, *Signor*. I knew he would never marry me, but I told myself that I was content just to be his mistress and have his love. Now he has tired of me. And, oh, good Master, I am told I am nothing, and must do what is commanded of me to do."

Angela again stared sadly into the burning embers, but this time dry-eyed, as if speaking of her grief and sorrow had helped her, even if only a little, to be resigned to how her world had suddenly turned, becoming dark and ugly.

I took a new piece of wood, and began to stir the fire. I glanced back at Angela, who still silently stared into the fire.

"So he now wishes for you to turn whore?" I asked her softly.

"*Si.*" She glanced over to me, and shrugged again. "It must be so, *Signor*, though only yesterday morning I would have said otherwise. The Holy Father wished for girls who could speak English, and when my lord heard he told the Holy Father he knew of such a girl. I!" She laughed, and cried, wrapping her arms tightly around herself. "Yes, I! I who spent my childhood in London, in the street of goldsmiths near Saint Paolo's Cathedral."

She glanced nervously at the floor, back at the fire, and then over to me. 'Twas as if she felt there was simply nowhere to escape. "My father took his family to England when I was but a bambini. He was able to gain much work with his Italian craftsmanship, that by the time I was twelve we were able to return to Rome with our coffers full of golden angels. My father has worked hard to give his children a good life."

She lifted up her head, gazed at the ceiling, and laughed. Quickly, her hand covered her mouth before dropping back to her lap. Angela looked bright-eyed at me.

"And look how I have repaid him! But my punishment begins now! I expect, when I return to my lord, he will have given me to one of his friends to enjoy. *Signor*, I swear to you that, if it was not such a great sin, I think I would simply throw myself into the river Tiber, and make an end to this nightmare I have woken up to."

I enclosed her tense hand in mine.

"Why not go home, Angela? Wouldn't your family forgive you rather than see you dragged out of the river as a bloated corpse?"

"*Signor*, you do not know a proud, Italian father. I have brought much dishonour to his name, the daughter who he loved so much that no man was good enough for her husband. My father thought so highly of me he dowered me with gold works made with his own, so wonderfully gifted hands. No. I cannot go home. I must continue in the life that I have chosen for myself, and admit that it is the judgement of God. *Si, Signor,* this is the punishment for my stupidity. I cannot hide my face from the truth—all the blame for my misfortunes lies with me!"

I thought about the heartless, thoughtless man who had seduced her, and knew immediately where I would lay the blame.

I felt such a great sense of helplessness, but other than suggest that she return to her family, I did not know how to help her. Even suggesting a convent was out the question, as I did not have enough gold in my money pouch to dower her.

Suddenly I became aware that all had become silent in the next room, though not for long because too soon Sir John's snores began to escape from his room and echo into the room where I sat with Angela.

I wondered what to do. There remained a long night ahead of us, and I had been completely honest when I told her that I had no plans to seduce her. Yea, when I first saw her she struck me, in appearance, somewhat like Anne. But I have been that way before, when I lost myself to Lucrezia for a time. I then, painfully, had to come to terms with the way I deluded myself into thinking affection for another woman could ever bring me lasting solace from my grief of loving Anna, and having that love not returned. Thus, I picked up my lute again and began to strum softly a few more of my songs.

"*Signor* is a very good lute player!" Angela said with a small, tight smile.

I looked at her, and smiled.

"My lute is like a part of me. It speaks my feelings better than I can for myself. Why not take yourself to the bed over in the corner, Angela, and let my music lull you into sleep."

A shuttered look came across her face, and I could easily guess what she thought. I reached out to take up her hand again.

"Angela, I have spoken the truth to you! Be unafraid that I will force myself upon you… That is truly not my way."

Relief flooded over her features, and she reached to touch me.

"You are so good, *Signor*. Such a good man! I am sorry I made you feel that I did not trust you."

Angela released my hand, and gracefully arose from the stool where she sat, walking over to the bed I had made upon the floor the previous night. Fully clothed, she lay upon the pallet and pulled some blankets across her body.

I began to wonder where I was going to sleep, and then decided that it was not important. Verily, I felt in the mood to write some new song; meeting Angela made me sad, and sadness always opened the gateway within me to the creation of another poem or song. I took my writing gear from the bag I had placed close to the fire, taking on my lap a board on which to write. For a few moments, I just sat there thinking, before I was able to let my mind and fingers explore the vivid valleys and peaks of creativity. And my creativity, at this time, had much to do with my thoughts of Anne, seemingly so far away from me—body, heart, and soul.

Alas, poor man, what hap have I
That must forbear that I love best?
Never to live in quiet rest.

No wonder is though I complain,
Not without cause ye may be sure.
I seek for that I cannot attain,
Which is my mortal displeasure.

Alas, poor heart, as in this case
With pensive plaints thou art oppressed,
Unwise thou were to desire place
Whereas another is possessed.

Do what I can to ease thy smart
Thou wilt not let to love her still.
Hers and not mine I see thou art.
Let her do by thee as she will.

A careful carcass full of pain
Now hast thou left to mourn for thee:
The heart once gone, the body is slain.
That ever I saw her, woe is me.

Mine eye, alas, was cause of this,
Which her to see had never his fill.
To me that sight full bitter is
In recompense of my goodwill.

She that I serve all other above
Hath paid my hire as ye may see.
I was unhappy, and that I prove,
To love above my poor degree.

When I lose myself in poetry I tend to lose myself for hours, thus night soon was gone and morning had come again. Angela began to stir and I decided that I done as much on my new song as I could do, being now so very tired, body and soul. I arose, rather unsteadily, from off the floor where I had sat throughout the night, and leaned my lute carefully on the wall near the table. With a final, exhausted glance at all that I had written—during the hours I had forbade myself to sleep—I determined, for a time, I could do no more. Thus, I put my new "scribblings" amongst my writing gear, and packed it away for another, fresher time.

I glanced over to Angela to see that she was now awake, and watching me with speculative eyes.

"I bid you good morning, Angela. Did you sleep well?" I asked her.

"*Si*, I slept very well, *Signor*."

"Are you hungry, Angela? There is still some bread and cheese left from yesterday morn. You are very welcome to break your fast with me."

Angela made no reply to this but looked with confusion around the chamber, and then returned her gaze to me.

"*Signor* did not sleep last night?"

She sounded very bewildered. Angela now pulled herself up, until she sat upright amongst the blankets.

I walked over to her, squatted down beside her and said: "I did not feel the need for sleep. My mind was too restless, and so I chose to exercise it with the making of a new song."

We both then looked up as we were suddenly disturbed by the opening of the curtain to Sir John's chamber. Beatrice now came into the room, looking bemused and completely unlike the image of perfection she had presented yesterday. Her pale face appeared very drawn, with dark circles etched deeply under her eyes, and her deep, red hair shaken out of the elaborate style she wore when we first had met.

She glanced at Angela, still sitting on the bed pallet with her back leaning on a wall, and then at me beside her. Beatrice smiled.

"So, Angela, it was not as hard as you thought to go from one lover to the next?"

Angela deeply blushed, scowling at the other girl. I felt it time to say something before a serious catfight began.

"*Signora* Beatrice! Angela may be in my bed, but, I assure you, she and the bed have not had my company."

Beatrice stared at me, and then pealed out a laugh.

"The English *Signor* does not like women?" she asked with a giggle.

"*Signor* likes women very much," I replied good-naturedly. "But *Signor* likes to chose his own women, and not have them chosen for him."

Beatrice then frowned at Angela, and spoke again to her.

"Your master will not be pleased to hear you made no effort to please the Englishman!"

"*Signora* Beatrice, please stop trying to upset Angela." I spoke with annoyance, thinking the woman appeared determined to cause friction. "Angela pleased me very much. I would have been more insulted if she had chosen to play the wanton, when I wanted it not."

Again Beatrice stared at me.

"*Signor* is a strange man!"

"No!" Angela broke in. "*Signor* Thomas is a good man, with a very good heart."

Beatrice looked with another frown at Angela.

"Perhaps it would have been better if you had tried harder with your *good* man, Angela. Good men are few and far between. It is not likely you will be so lucky next time."

Angela's face became as if closed in, but then she shrugged her shoulders.

"What will be, will be. But last night I found a friend who listened to me, who even gave up his bed for me. Such a thing will help me keep hope in the future. Perchance, Beatrice, I will find other friends, but I will always remember *Signor* Tom who was my first friend."

Turning her gaze away from Beatrice, Angela beamed at me and held out her hand. I took it and kissed her fingertips, wishing so much that I could help her more. I then decided that it was pointless in becoming too upset in something I had so little control over.

I felt suddenly aware of my hunger, so I put her hand gently on the bed coverings, stood up, and returned to the table where the bread and cheese were placed. Angela arose from the bed, and strolled over to stand beside me. I smiled again at her, and she at me. I handed her some bread and cheese, and we began to eat as if famished.

Beatrice grunted her disapproval, but also moved to stand beside me, reaching out for some bread and beginning to eat as well.

"Would you ladies like some wine to help wash down the bread? I am afraid it is not as fresh as it was yesterday. I'm just about to pour myself some, so I can attend to your needs at the same time, if you would like?"

"*Si, Signor*. I am sure Beatrice would enjoy some wine. I would enjoy some myself. But, *Signor* Tom, let me attend to it. It is the least I can do to repay you for your great kindness of last night," replied Angela.

"You do not have to repay me, Angela, but if it would please you to do so, you are welcome to play hostess."

With another bright smile, she reached out to pull the tray of goblets towards us. After Angela had poured out the wine into three cups, she gave one to Beatrice, and then one to myself, and at last took a cup for herself.

I could hear some groans emerging from Sir John's bedchamber, and knew it meant that he was now awake. Indeed, within minutes he emerged from his chamber, appearing very bleary-eyed and drawn, dressed again in only his hose and loose shirt. When he saw Beatrice, he instantly revived, grinning like a boy as he clamoured up to her. But, when he went to embrace her, she deftly moved away from him. Sir John's face fell, and he looked as if he had just been hit.

"*Signor*," Beatrice now said through tight lips. "The gold was paid for only one night. I am tired. *Signor* Oddo will soon be here to take us back to the papal court. Indeed, *Signor*, enough gold was paid for me to have the freedom to choose who will be my next lover. And, *Signor*, I will be blunt: It will not be you."

Sir John furiously flushed, and then scowled. He looked over to me and said: "I will return to my bed, Tom. Let me know when these two Italian sluts have gone."

And with those words, Sir John returned from whence he had come, yanking the curtain closed behind him. I shrugged my shoulders at the women, feeling rather embarrassed and uncomfortable.

★

To our good fortune, it was as Beatrice said. *Signor* Oddo soon arrived to confirm the papal appointment for this day, and escort

Beatrice and Angela back from whence they had come. So, again, we prepared ourselves for this day's meeting with the Pope. Sir John seemed quieter than usual. I supposed the events of the previous day had dampened his spirits somewhat. However, once again dressed in his rich clothes, he appeared able to hide his personal disappointment behind the facade of a brilliant diplomat—verily, a confident man who had successfully performed countless missions for his King in a career lasting over twenty years.

Our mission to Rome was especially important. As well as bringing documents from the King that would authorise the release of a large amount of money to the Pope, we were here to urge the Pope to strengthen his resolve against the Emperor and resist any temptation to seek out a peaceful solution. For the moment, the League of Cognac had failed in its purpose to make the Emperor come to heel and the Pope was, understandably, becoming more nervous with every passing day. Especially since the Emperor's soldiers now almost sat on the Pope's doorstep, just waiting for the right moment to strike. Our King Henry was nervous too. If the Emperor gained the Pope, then it would be more difficult than ever to gain his desire for a divorce. Queen Catherine was Aunt to the Emperor Charles, and the Emperor—if it so suited him politically—was loyal to his family.

So we had our meeting with the Pope. The Pope was extremely thankful to receive the money from the English King, but was unsure as whether he should wait any longer before at last submitting to something which, with every passing day, seemed more and more inevitable. Already we had heard rumours the Pope was prepared to submit utterly to the will of the Emperor. At length, Sir John persuaded the Holy Father to allow us to make an appeal to Venice join the league, thus the Pope would win more money and more soldiers. As it would cost him nothing, but might gain him much, the Pope agreed to this proposal. Thus, on the twelfth of February, we began our journey to Venice.

However, when we entered the town of Narni, our first major

mishap of our journey occurred. Sir John was thrown from his horse, and fell in such a way that his leg broke beneath him.

For a few fast heartbeats after it happened, I remained stock still in a state of horror. Sir John had fainted from the shock of his injury, and for a dreadful moment I thought he lay dead. I soon ascertained that, though he clearly had serious injury, he was alive and in desperate need of a surgeon.

Thanks be to all the Saints in Heaven, some local inhabitants of the town soon came to investigate what was ado. So, with their assistance, I was able to take my unconscious knight to a nearby inn. The good villagers also found Sir John's frightened horse, and brought the stallion to me. I thanked them sincerely, giving them coin for all their troubles.

The innkeeper knew of a good and reliable surgeon, and sent one of his young kitchen boys to run to get the man's aid quickly. Sir John was beginning to revive, though moaning now in great pain.

At last, the surgeon arrived, accompanied by his assistant carrying the tools of their trade. I winced to see that one of the tools was a bloodied saw, and prayed quickly to God to be merciful to the man who had become my fast friend.

God heard my prayers. The break in Sir John's leg was a clean one and easily set. The doctor assured me that, though Sir John would need to rest and thus would be bed-bound for a time, he should heal and walk again. I breathed a sigh of relief. But now a new crop of troubles came forward to plague me. What were we to do about the mission to Venice?

For the moment, my duty was plain—stay with Sir John until I felt assured his life lay in no danger. I have heard countless woeful tales of a man dying for less than a broken leg. So for the next four days, I remained with him in Narni, in the same inn we had been brought to after his accident. During this time, Sir John coached me in what I would need to say to the Venetians, until he was able to assure me I would do well enough, insisting too that I continue on the journey and complete the mission we had set out to do. As Sir John realised that he was forced to remain bed-bound for many weeks, he also gave me permission and encouragement to spend some days in Florence before returning to Narni.

This was my first, truly important diplomatic exercise. I could not help but feel excited at the prospect that it was now up to me to persuade Venice to concede to our proposals. I soon discovered how difficult and frustrating this task would be.

In Venice the English ambassador, *Giovanni Casale*, assisted me. We spoke together in the Palazzo Ducale with the senators of Venice, trying desperately to convince them of the wisdom of our proposals. Eventually, they agreed to join the League if France desired it of them. I began feeling as if Casale and I had spent our time talking ourselves around in circles. Of course, the French would agree to this proposal. To do otherwise would be alike to cutting off their noses to spite their own faces. Thus, after much wasted debate and arguments, the Venetians promised to send aid to the Pope. Little did we realise that, back in Rome, the Pope had finally capitulated to the demands of the Emperor, and signed with him an armistice of eight months.

Thus, believing I had now achieved part of my mission's purpose, and with yet no realisation that the Pope's recent actions had made it already fruitless, Casale and I, early in March, decided to travel to Ferrara. Here we wished to gain the support of the Duke of Ferrara for the League, and gain his endorsement and aid. The sanction of the Duke was easily obtained. Verily, the Duke appeared totally outraged against what he saw as an insult to the whole of Italy, so was easily convinced to give lend his support to the league.

Casale now returned to Venice, but I, having fulfilled my mission for England, decided to best make my way back to Narni, passing through Bologna and Florence before returning to Sir John. At Bologna, the good Duke provided me with a safe conduct and a courier to accompany me on my journey, and so I departed from his court in full anticipation of all the excitements that I would soon enjoy in Florence. How was I to know these excitements would take the form of something grim and ugly?

Barely more than two days into my journey to Florence, I stopped at a small town to rest my horse and give the courier a chance for respite. Verily, the courier was a young lad of fifteen and the poor, ill-fed boy had been made much exhausted by our long hours in the saddle. I felt otherwise. Indeed, during my absences from England, I had fast developed an enjoyment for travel and the viewing of new sights, which gave me a great zest to continue my wanderings. So, having free time on my hands, but feeling too fidgety to sit still, I decided to explore my surroundings.

By the time I returned to the street to where I had found lodgings, the sun had lowered behind the hills edging the horizon, I found myself feeling very surprised, realising how long my feet had spent wandering through all the town's narrow, dusty streets. But my arrival in the inn was not meant to be, for as I came close to the inn's door someone clouted me from behind, and all went black.

Chapter 3

"And she me caught in her arms long and small."

I returned to consciousness, finding myself tightly tied up, lying on my back in a tent with a short, dark man dressed in the garb of a Spanish soldier bending over me.

"Buenas noches, Señor," he said, smiling gap-toothed at me.

I stared at him, trying desperately to make sense of what had happened while fighting strong waves of nausea seeking to draw me further under. At last, I felt able to speak.

"What in God's holy name is the meaning of all this?"

I struggled hard against my bonds.

"Señor was rather stupid. *Señor* made the mistake of leaving his papers behind when he went out for the afternoon… papers for Spanish friends to find and read. Now *Señor* is a guest of the Imperial Troops."

"You must be mad. I am on official business for the Pope."

The Spaniard spat loudly at that.

"That will not help you, *mi amigo*. We will soon make that dog pay for the insult he gave our Emperor."

I stopped moving, as my bonds were just getting tighter and tighter. I gulped down a couple of deep breaths, trying to keep myself calm. I gazed back at the soldier.

"What do you want of me?"

The Spaniard laughed. I thought it an ugly sound.

"Gold. *Señor* had very little gold, but his papers told us he is an important man to *los Ingleses*—important enough for a ransom of three thousand ducats. We have already allowed the Italian you travelled with to return home to his master, to demand fast payment of the ransom. All you need to hope is that we are not wrong about your value!"

Knowing that being thought important enough to ransom would be enough to save my skin from further harm, I could only briefly shake my head in assent. Reflecting as I did so that a ransom would probably break my family's back for many years.

"*Señor* is hungry, hey? *Señor* would like some food?"

My head aching, again I cautiously nodded, thinking a meal might help settle my queasy stomach.

"I will untie *Señor* now. *Señor* must realise that it is no use to escape. *Señor* has many good Spanish and German soldiers looking after him."

With those words the soldier cut the bonds that made me so helpless. I then sat up, shaking my body to rid myself feeling the kinks of the ropes, watching, as I did, my captor leave the confines of the tiny tent.

Imagine my surprise when it was not the Spaniard who returned but an Italian woman with plaited black hair, dressed in clothes that had seen better days—a woman big-bellied with child.

When she saw me, she almost dropped her basket of food. I too felt utterly astounded.

"*Tomas,*" she whispered, moving a quick step closer to me.

"Lucrezia," I likewise replied.

She fearfully glanced behind her, but seeing us still alone, she came closer to me, putting the basket on the ground.

"*Tomas.* How come you here?"

"I do not know, Lucrezia. All I remember is walking back to my lodgings. Some one must have been waiting for me..."

Lucrezia stayed quiet for a short time, clearly thinking, and then came even closer to put her hands on mine.

"Some Italian traitor must have realised who you were, and sold you to the Spaniards. I am so sorry, *Tomas.*"

We were both silent for a moment and then I began to perceive a way out of my predicament, but it all depended on this woman before me. I returned my gaze to her.

"Do you think you can help me escape, Lucrezia?"

She dropped my hands and backed away from me, fear etched deep onto her pale face. Furtively Lucrezia looked all around her.

"Oh, *Tomas*. Do not ask this of me. It would be too difficult. I am a Spaniard's woman now. I bear his child. He has promised to take me back to Spain with him. I cannot risk to make Juan angry."

"There must be a way you can help, Lucrezia, without the Spaniards knowing."

Lucrezia stared at me with those huge, dark eyes—eyes that were reminiscent of my dearly beloved girl back home. Coming back to take my hand, she looked around again, and squeezed my hand quickly.

"I go now, *Tomas*. Maybe I can help, but I can promise you nothing."

Lucrezia departed from the tent and I was left with a basket of stale bread, a flask of wine, and vile tasting meat.

While I ate what I could of this I looked around at my surroundings. The interior of the tent was lit by only one large candle. Thus, what I could see was very unformed and difficult to fully make out, yet the shadows cast by this one candle told me, without investigating further, that I was in space not much bigger than a few feet across in any direction. I got up from the straw where I was lying and walked slowly to the flap of the tent. What I saw when I lifted the flap was as the soldier said—a hoard of troops surrounded me. I wondered how I could possibly escape from this dreadful mess I now found myself in.

Several days later, the army began its march through the Italian countryside. I was securely tied to a mule, with two mounted guards on either side of me; thus, I was unable to do anything that would achieve my freedom.

I felt depressed by the turn of events, but not altogether hopeless. Carlo, the courier sent with me by the Duke of Ferrara, would have, by this time, raised the alarm about my forced absence. I knew that Sir John would not hesitate to use his influence, and the influence of others, to obtain my release. I only hoped that my release could be achieved without any gold having to be passed from hand to hand.

This particular army moved slowly over the Italian countryside. Indeed, it struck me that this rabble of soldiers appeared to possess very little discipline: just a body of men and their followers who seemed to be headed in the same direction.

I could not help remembering one of my father's tales from my boyhood. Harold, the last Saxon King of England, marched his army up near to Scotland and defeated one army seeking conquest of his Kingdom, before having to march his men back to England only to be defeated by another rival seeking conquest. Though defeat and death was at the end of this story, one could not help but feel a sense of pride that England could boast of such men in their history as this King Harold. I felt very sure that if an Englishman led this rabble of men surrounding me, it would have been an army to be proud of. Instead I watched a body of apparently disorganised groups going here, there and everywhere. However, despite the apparent slowness of its operation, we had still made good distance when the soldiers began to make camp again.

This time I was taken to an empty barn, the only remains of what had been obviously a homestead in former, more peaceful days. The soldiers, who had "escorted" me on my journey, now untied me, dropping the bonds on the earthen floor of the barn after unceremoniously shoving me deep inside. I inferred from the noise they now made on the outside that they had found a beam to ensure that the door remained firmly fixed until they chose to open it.

My enforced dwelling place had become completely dark when the noise of the door opening put me on guard. I relaxed when I saw Lucrezia, bearing a taper in one hand and a basket of food in the other, enter into my harsh abode. She closed the door behind her, walked over to where I was sitting, putting the taper in its holder down near us, and moved to pass to me the food from the basket.

"*Tomas*. We have not long, so please listen carefully."

I stopped eating, and stared at her. Hope was beginning to come alive in my chest. "The men who were guarding you are no longer camped outside. They have gone to the village to find drink and women. So, *Tomas*, if you are to escape, now is the time to do it."

"But how, Lucrezia?"

"*Tomas!* Please! There is no time for questions. Just listen, and I will tell you how I think you can do it. Most of the soldiers are gathered together to the left of this barn. There is a good chance, if you are careful, that you can get by the few soldiers camped on the other side. Many soldiers, including my *Juan*, have gone to the village for the night. Those who have stayed behind are too occupied with other things to pay much attention to the frightened Englishman imprisoned securely in this barn. And *Tomas*, it is a moonless night, so it is very dark outside, which is good because the night will hide you, but not so good in that you will have to move slowly and carefully, *Tomas*, if you are not to knock into something that will raise the alarm. Once you cross the river, you will know you begin to be safe. I have a small purse of gold in the basket to help get you away to safety. Oh, *Tomas*, for the love of God, and both our sakes, please don't raise the alarm!"

"Lucrezia. How can I ever thank you?"

She laughed grimly.

"*Tomas*—you can thank me by not getting caught. They will find the gold and wonder who it was that gave it to you. It would not be difficult to work out it was I. Oh, *Tomas*, I beg of you, for the sake of my unborn *bambino*, do not get caught!"

I took Lucrezia's hand. It felt so different from the hand of the woman who had once been my lover. The hand I held was now reddened and broken-nailed, and very, very thin. I raised it to my mouth, and kissed it gently before placing her shaking hand on my cheek.

"I promise you I will not get caught. But, my dear one, why do you risk so much for me?"

She laughed, and laid her free hand on my shoulder before lifting two fingers to caress my neck.

"No other man has ever written me a love song, *Tomas*. I am too much of a woman to ever forget that. But, *Tomas*, it will need to look like you overpowered me. We will use those ropes near the door to tie me up."

I grunted my disgust for this task, but could see the sense of it. So, the next few minutes were occupied ensuring that Lucrezia was well bound.

"Now, use my scarf to seal up my mouth!" Lucrezia said when I had finished with her bonds. I removed the red scarf from her dark hair. I looked down at it in my hands, and then at her.

"Hurry, *Tomas!*" she whispered.

"Aye, Lucrezia. I will hurry. But before I tie the scarf around your mouth, there is something I must do," and I bent my head and kissed her long and hard.

For a short moment, it seemed easy to forget where we were. For a short moment, it was like we had stepped back to that brief time when we had loved with all the abandonment of the very young. When we had finished our kiss, Lucrezia laughed a soft, gay laugh.

"Oh, *Tomas!*" she said, shaking her head and looking at me with amusement. "Goodbye my dear, my very dear English lover. But, *Tomas*, do not waste any more time. *You must go now!*"

"Yea! Farewell, *bella Lucrezia mia*. May our roads cross again so I can repay you what you truly deserve!" With a quick and final kiss, I tied the scarf around her mouth, bent and retrieved the small purse of gold hidden in the basket, and began to make my escape.

It was like Lucrezia had said. When I emerged from the barn I stepped out into a world seemingly black, except for some faint light emitted from a few stars breaking through the dense veil of evening clouds. Verily, I knew that the going was to be extremely difficult because it was almost impossible to see more than a few steps in front of me, especially as thick mist rose out from the cold earth at my feet. However, I knew if I hurried I would be more in danger of being caught and put at grave risk my delivering angel, Lucrezia, so I forced myself to ignore my strong sense of panic, and went to the right of the barn, moving steadily and purposeful into the night.

Travelling in this fashion made certain that I was able to avoid such areas that appeared to be encamped upon, but progress was so slow that I began to fear that all life had stopped still, and its movements would never start again.

Just before I reached the bank of the river, the wind strengthened, tearing apart the heavy veil of clouds. The extra light giving forth from the night sky allowed me to quicken my pace. Reaching the river, I began to breathe easier again. However, I knew there was a new problem to be faced and overcome during the river's crossing: I have proven to be a good sailor, but my ability to stay afloat, once in the water, had little to recommend it. I knew that if the water proved to be too deep it was likely I would drown, and I possessed no desire to go to my death in that dreadful fashion. So, after a brief prayer, I expeditiously began to follow the river, further away from where the Spaniards had made their camp.

At long last, I found myself able to make out the faint glimmer where the water came against a bank on the other side. Feeling that time now gave me no choice but to cross, I took my quaking courage firmly in hand, and began to wade across the river. Good fortune smiled on me; the water at its deepest point reached but to my chest. Thus, dripping wet and shivering with utter cold, I emerged safely onto the bank that took me closer to safety and freedom.

My good fortune continued; I soon came to a sleeping farmstead, and there I was able to steal a good horse, leaving behind more than his price in gold coin placed upon a tree stump in the field where I had found him.

Thus, I began to escape now in earnest, making my way swiftly along the roadways I had travelled, tied on an army pack mule, the previous day. Dawn was now approaching, and still no one was in pursuit, thus I slowed the horse to a steady canter and headed to the west and the dominions of Ferrara, where I could begin to feel safe once again.

By noon, my horse was completely spent, but I was able to exchange it for another mount in the town I had now reached. I was determined not to rest until I had arrived at the court of the Duke, and the men in this town assured me that I had not long to go before arriving there. Yea, even though it was beginning to grow dark when I saw the Duke's palace, it seemed but a short moment before I was at the palace where the Duke resided.

One of the first people to confront me, as is often the way of life, was none other than the lad who had been sent to accompany me on my travels. Carlos, cleaner and better dressed than I last remembered, greeted me first with great astonishment, but delight following next, and he took me fast to his lord. The Duke also appeared astonished at my quick escape, and told me the moves that had taken place in my brief absence to free me. As soon as he heard of my plight, my knight, the Duke informed me, had written to the *Duc of Bourbon* in an effort to gain my speedy deliverance. Indeed, even the Holy Father had commanded one of his officials to write and demand my release in the name of the papacy. I rested at the Duke's court for divers days, and then decided it was time to return to Sir John. The experiences I had just lived through had quenched my desire to see any more of the countryside of Italy. Indeed, I just wanted our mission to be over and to make our way back to England, and home. Yea, home, even if it meant facing up to the problems I had left there.

This time, the Duke sent two of his men in arms to accompany me back to Narni, commanding them to remain with the two Englishmen until their services where no longer needed. Sir John seemed very much recovered from his injury, and very relieved to see me and hear that I had been able to escape before a ransom needed to be paid. Sir John told me that we had one task left to do before we could begin our journey back to England. We must return to Rome and try yet again to persuade the Pope to stand strong and firm against the Emperor—despite what promises he had exchanged during this period of duress.

'Twas the end of April when we at length arrived back in Rome. The situation had become no better during our time away. Verily, it felt to me that events had come to such a pass that all out warfare could no longer be avoided.

Soldiers, who had recently gathered to protect Rome, had just days before our arrival been sent away in disgrace. During their time in Rome, these soldiers had caused the inhabitants of the city such terror that only the brave had dared to walk the streets—even in full daylight. The Romans had breathed a sigh of relief to see the backs of these brutal men gone, but now Rome was left to whatever defences it alone could raise. This defence seemed half-hearted in many quarters. The Pope had lost much of his popularity through the harsh taxes imposed to combat the Emperor. Verily, many Romans could see no difference between being under the thumb of the Vatican or the Imperialist government of the Emperor Charles.

Loud rumour was now rife that the *Duc of Bourbon* had received word of this state of affairs, and was beginning to march his soldiers steadily toward Rome. Thus, those Romans who supported the papacy were now busily engaged in preparing themselves for the unavoidable battle that was looming before their frightened eyes.

Indeed, within days of the arrival of Sir John and myself, *Bourbon* and his multitude of men began to make camp before the ancient walls of Rome. Within hours of their arrival, the sounds of savage battle began to vibrate throughout the streets of Rome.

Sir John and I could do no more. Indeed, all that we could hope for was that we could escape from the city with our skins intact. Verily, the month of May, I thought, was becoming fast an unlucky time for me, but even more unlucky, this time, for the ancient city of Rome.

Thus, escape we did, as the bells of Roma tolled out their panicked warning. Though escape proved a difficult feat to achieve; fog shrouded the lanes and streets of Rome, its series of dark, narrow, dust-filled alley ways twisting into a maze of courts and passages, dotted here and there, verily everywhere, by a church or fortress rising over our heads—emerging through thick fog—that hindered us at every turn. We, Sir John and myself, protected by the Italians by the Duke of Ferrara, desperately tried to make some sense of these bewildering and strange surroundings, hoping to be able to gain a quick way of escape. As good fortune would have it, one of the soldiers sent with us had been born in Rome. Verily, without his help, I dread to think what our fate would have been. In the heat of battle, it serves no purpose to cry "immunity!"

But God, and all his angels and saints, was on our side, and our good fortune held out. In the heat of battle there is also much confusion; thus, we were able to leave the poor city of Rome to its dreadful fate, and begin to make our long way back to England.

Book Four

"The chances most unhappy
That me betide in May!"

Chapter 1

July 1528

"In thin array after pleasant guise,
when her loose gown from shoulders did fall."

It was during the time Anne lay ill at Hever Castle that I returned again to our childhood home—greatly disenchanted with my life. My wife Bess I had come home to discover in bed with another of her base lovers. I dragged him out of my bed, pushed him out the room, and returned to my wife to engage her in the most horrible quarrel—verily, the worst of our marriage.

This time my usually restrained anger let loose, with the grave consequence I came away from her leaving her bruised, battered, and promising to make my life more miserable. And me? What did I feel? God's oath! My anger terrified me. I had never lain a hand on Bess in violence before, and I felt horrified to see what my anger had done. And I also knew only the lucky arrival in the room of our daughter (is she my daughter—how am I truly to ever know?) prevented me slipping into a more murderous rage when I confronted Bess. 'Twas enough to give me reason and cause to think for a very long time. Thus, not wanting to remain under the same roof as Elizabeth, I picked up my still unpacked travelling bags, got on my horse, and rode swiftly to Hever.

I had heard news of Anna from George, who I had seen days before at a London tavern. Anna had, only a short time ago, been sent away from court because the King feared her illness could be the plague or the sweating sickness and thus wished to protect himself from contagion. I, who truly loved her, felt afraid for her and resolved to be with her at this time. The discord I had left at my house only increased my determination to see Anna and make some attempt to renew myself in her presence.

I found it strange to ride my horse up those same tracks and lanes that had seen us running wild as children. I had only infrequently visited Hever Castle since I was sent to Cambridge University when I was thirteen.

Now in my twenty-fifth year, I could not help but feel that I had lived through so much since the time of my boyhood that I had become utterly world weary since those happier and simpler times.

Even though a summer's day, it was cold and wet, and riding had become swiftly a damp business. I greatly looked forward to the end of my journey and the warmth of a welcoming fire. Even so, I could not resist my urge to stop my horse on the crest of the hill overlooking the castle. From that distance, I found it as I remembered it, a small, charming, golden-stone castle, surrounded by a moat and high yew hedges. Aye, Hever—set amidst the green meadows of my childhood where I had numbered the flowers into thousands.

I wasted no more time, urging my horse into a gallop. Home! I was so near to home and my beloved Anne! At long last, now drenched to my skin, my horse's hoofs rattled loudly over the wooden drawbridge, and I arrived in the castle's courtyard. I slid off my exhausted mare only to find a heavily cloaked, silent groom had already come to take my horse's head. I thanked him, gave him a coin to care well for her needs, and walked swiftly towards the entrance of my former home, enormously concerned about what I would discover within.

Happily, to the delight of us both, Simonette was there to welcome me, and quickly reassure me that Anne's life was no longer threatened. All illness, she told me, thank the good Lord, had now passed from Hever. I had concluded this in any case as there had been no sign on the castle gate warning of contagion and Hever Castle lay wide open to all visitors. However, Anne had come down with a very bad dose of the sweating sickness, and was now low in spirits. Simonette felt that it was her malaise, rather than any lingering illness, which was affecting her recovery and subsequent return to full health.

Our initial greetings done, Simonette took me to the room that I had once shared with George, leaving me while I exchanged my wet garments for drier ones. Once I had done so, I left my old room to rejoin Simonette in the castle's Great Hall.

I found her seated by the main fireplace, in front of a spinning wheel sorting out the unspun wool. As soon as Simonette saw that I had returned, she stopped her work and stood, smiling to me brightly and holding out her hands for me to take. It struck me, as I spoke to Simonette, how young she must have been when she had taken over those mothering needs of our childhoods. Looking at her face, still so youthful, and her almost unchanged hair and figure, I found it hard to imagine that she must now be fast approaching her forties. Her hair still as deeply auburn as I remembered it from my last visit to Hever, her skin also seemed to be as clear and untouched by age as I recollected from my youth.

"Simonette," I said, "you grow more lovely with every passing year."

Simonette laughed softly.

"Oh, Master Tom! Your time in the Continent was well spent if you have learnt to be gallant. But, I know too well how time has sped. How could I not, when I remember the little lad I cared for and see him grown into the man before me... Yea, truly, time has gone too fast for me."

At last, after giving me another kiss and wiping away yet more tears, Simonette left me, so as to go and prepare Anne for her visitor.

Soon after Simonette's departure, I got up from the chair and wandered around the Great Hall, taking in all the changes. Rich tapestries hung on every large portion of available wall space and beautiful paintings were to be found in the smaller areas. I could see before me the clear evidence that the Boleyns had become wealthier than I remembered from my childhood.

Standing alone in this Great Hall, I tried to recapture some feeling of the magic that I recalled of Hever and my childhood. 'Twas all gone: the air I breathed still and ordinary, so much so I began to feel melancholy for a time forever vanished. Despite struggling with this feeling, my childhood home appeared much the same, though I thought it also appeared to be diminished, lacking some inner strength. I wandered to the nearby window. Outside, the weather was still bleak and miserable. The rain fell heavily, hitting in bursts against the thick glass, while the wind bowed tall trees as it howled around the castle.

I looked away, and a small painting hanging on a nearby wall, glowing with such colour that it seemed almost jewel-like, caught my eye. I went closer to heed that it was a painting of Saint Francis. It reminded me of other paintings I had seen during my brief time in Venice. I remembered these other paintings were the works of Giovanni Bellini, an artist of Venice whom I liked for the poetic mood he often captured in his paintings. Being a poet myself gave me a sense of fellow feeling with Bellini, whose skills were such he could render as if poems on canvas.

I went even closer to the painting, to see if the painting of St. Francis was in fact by him. I often find it strange the things bringing to the surface my true feelings; why I now felt bereft. As I looked away from the painting of this small Franciscan monk, it became crystal clear why the Great Hall seemed to me so utterly empty. Yea, I realised, as I waited for Simonette to return from Anne's room, what it lacked was the giant presence of Father Stephen. The Great Hall stayed empty of the boom of his voice and laughter. The good father had died... yea, he had died to the grief of us all, during my last year at Cambridge.

At length, Simonette came down the stairs to tell me that Anne was now ready to see me. I walked up the spiral stone staircase leading to Anne's chamber, wondering if I would find her more changed, and horribly afraid that I would. It had been two long years since we last had been together, and then we had fought with great bitterness over her relationship with the King.

Entering Anna's chamber, I felt surprised to find her out of bed and seated by a fire, though she was dressed in what was obviously her night attire with a shawl slung loosely over her shoulders. Her black hair was braided in one thick plait and fell down over one shoulder to her waist. She looked both very young and very mature, as if she had become an adult since last we had met but her body not yet caught up with the changes wrought by the two years now gone. On her lap she held her precious lute. Her hand, with its lovely tenuous and tapering fingers, was poised as if ready to pluck a note. I noticed some of her nails were badly chewed, something she had grown out of when last we had met but obviously taken up yet again. When Anne saw me she held out her free hand to me. I took it, concerned to find it even more fragile than usual.

"Dearest Tom!" she said. "I hoped and prayed that you would come!"

Her first words, spoken with such tremulous emotion, surprised me. They and the timbre of her voice suggested the fragility apparent in her body transcended to the spirit. I bent my head and looked deep into her eyes, trying to find the right words to reassure her.

"Why pray and hope for something bound to happen sooner or later? I am only grieved, Anna, that so much time had to pass before my duties on the Continent enabled me to come to you. And I suppose I must too admit to stupid pride."

I took her hand to my mouth and kissed it gently.

"Your hand is so cold, Anna," I told her, enclosing it in mine.

"*Froides mains, chaud amour, cher* Tommy," she replied with a quick smile.

I smiled back at her. "Yea, cold hands and warm heart. As it has been for always. How, dearest Anna, could you have ever doubted that I would come when I heard you were ailing?"

I noticed she had flushed at my kiss and again at my words, and seemed ready to shy away.

"What is it, Anna?" I asked, drawing up the nearby stool to be seated close to her. She bent her head towards the lute and held onto my hand tighter.

"Why should I not doubt, Tom? Even the King, who professes such great love for me, does not come." Anna sighed deeply and seemed to sink into dejection.

Oh my God, I prayed, *please don't tell me she has grown to love that heartless, vainglory-puffed bastard.*

"Anna, I am not the King! He would never come as long as he feared for his own safety or health. Forgive me, and I ask your pardon if I in any way offend, but my opinion of the King's love for you has not changed one small bit since last we spoke. Please, Anna, do not let us spend these first moments together in argument!"

At these words Anne raised my hand to her cheek, and looked at me beseechingly.

"Oh, Tommy! Please do not scold! I know now you were right… And I was so wrong. I was such a young, stupid fool! If only I could have known then what I know today. And now I am trapped! Trapped, Tom! And it is all a trap of my own making. Oh, Tommy! I cannot help but think that the evil I planned so long ago has now caught me in its clutches."

I looked at her to find her eyes were full of tears. My Anna, who never cried when we were children; even when her father beat her until her body was bruised and close to bleeding. Even when her heart broke at the loss of Henry Percy she had been dry eyed. Such hurts, she had said, go too deep for just simple tears.

"Tell me, Anna. Tell me everything," I said to her.

For a moment there was no sound in the room other than the occasional crackle of the feasting fire beside us.

Anne had lowered her head and seemed to be looking at her lute again; a few tears dropped from her eyes and lay upon its strings, as if raindrops beading rainbow dew onto grass.

In due course, she sighed, and spoke.

"Tom, I cannot escape from him. He will not let me escape from him. I am a deer, Tom, and the King is my hunter. He will not let me go until he has me where there will be no avoiding him, and then, if I fail to achieve my ends, if I prove to be weaker than him, Tommy, it can only be death, death, death!"

"Anne, what do you speak of?"

For a dreadful moment I felt she was touched with fever and thus hallucinated, though her hand lay cool and still in mine.

"I am not sure how best to explain… I only know that I feel inside. You must know that I would never have chosen the King in my heart. Indeed Tom, when I lost Hal I was so consumed with hatred for the King and Wolsey that I imagined myself a spider that would entrap the King and hurt him as he had hurt me. All I wanted was to make him feel what it was like to want something so badly, to know it is yours and then have it snatched out of your very hand… to see it destroyed forever. Now I find that I am not the spider, rather the fly, and I am entangled in this web where the biggest spider of all is lurking. Tom, you told me to put aside my foolish plan to hurt the King… Tommy, you were so right and I was so completely stupid and blind."

"But tell me, Anna, why do you think you cannot escape?"

"I tell you, Tom, it is because he will not let me escape. He holds the lives of everyone I love in his power, to do with as he wills. The only escape for me now is to become his Queen, which I fear means death for so many…" Anna replied so softly that I had to lower my head to hear her.

I looked at Anna and she at me. I took her other hand and felt how utterly cold she was, despite the blazing heat of the close-by fire.

"Anna, I find it so hard to understand you."

I felt confounded and frightened by her words. Her distressed eyes dropped from mine and turned to stare into the fire. For a long while there was silence in the room. Anne sat as one lost deep in inner turmoil. At long last, after what seemed an eternity, she sighed, turned back to me, and began to speak once more.

"Tommy, the King is a man who will not allow anyone to make a laughing stock of him. I have led him a chase that has been on public view to all. If I deny him his desire for me much longer, I fear his feeling for me will be turned into hatred. Yet... Oh, Tom... I also fear once he has his desire he will hate me because he will need to find someone to blame. Someone to blame for all the many troubles he has had over the *Great Matter* of trying to disentangle himself from his marriage to the Queen."

"Aye, Anna, but..." I began to say—only to see Anna lean towards me with a hand upraised to halt my speech.

"No, Tom—in this there are no buts. The King is never at fault; only his loyal subjects... Have you not ever noticed, Tom, how easy the King finds it to destroy a thing he has no further use for? I have. He gives me cause to notice every moment that we are together. Look how he treats the Queen, whom he now desires to remake the Dowager Princess of Wales. Poor Lady! I cannot help but feel pity. Her only crime is that she has never stopped loving the King. Now she fears so much for his soul she is willing to sacrifice all that is good in her earthly life to ensure that he—a man who wishes her dead—ends up not in hell.

Oh, what is the use of speaking of this any longer? Oh, Tommy! I fear in my heart that I am lost already. Even my father would see me destroyed rather than allow me to deny the King his great desire. Yea, Tom, my father sees I have it in my power to become England's Queen and give the King the son he would murder half the Kingdom for. I see beyond that and know what my fate will be if I fail in my promise to provide the King with his heir."

She stopped speaking for a moment, but my face must have revealed what I feared to put into words.

"Oh, Tom! Don't look so heartbroken, man! I shall do my best to save myself. I am not sure how, but maybe the fates will be good to me after all and bless my royal marriage with a first-born son."

"Please, Anna, no more… It frightens me so much to hear you talk of your royal marriage."

"If the truth is said, Tom, it frightens me too. But the die has been thrown—*jacta esta alea* as Julius Caesar said. There is no other choice but to continue until the game is won or lost."

I placed her hands between mine and raised them to my lips, our eyes locked together. It seemed as if we were the only people left living in the entire world. As I looked at her, I felt my heart fill with yearning. I loved her so much that it was hard to prevent myself from crying out to her…

Anna then deeply sighed as if she had at last come to some long-considered decision. She gently took her hands from mine and put her lute carefully down alongside her chair.

"Dear Tommy, I know that you have always loved me. More deeply than was ever good for you. I have always loved you too—as my dearest friend and cousin. Oh, Tom, sweet Tom… please kiss me! I do so want to feel the kiss of a man who loves me knowing me for what and who I am, not the kiss of a man who is enjoying the chase and now is so very eager to make the kill."

Anne placed her hands on my shoulders and put forward her face towards mine. We had kissed much in our lives together. As children we had kissed often in play, though as I grew older I had used every excuse to seek out her lips and dream that they were meant only for me; that she one day would desire me as much as I did her. This time it was no dream. I sat there broad awake and knew it for no dream. There was a hunger in Anna's lips that I had never experienced before—a blazing fire where before there had been no hint of heat. I began to feel like Joshua, at the moment when the blast from his horn stopped its reverberations before the citadel and the walls of Jericho commenced trembling, crumbling before his eyes, and he at last knew victory was his for the taking. I drew away from her and stood up. My senses were reeling. I badly needed time to take stock at this great change in her—of what it meant for me. When dreams begin to become tangible one no longer knows what is real and what is not.

Anne stood up too, her shawl quickly sliding off her body to the floor. I looked at her; her thin lawn shift hid but greatly suggested the body beneath. She was high- and small-breasted, with the smallest waist I had ever seen in a woman. Narrow hips and flat stomach. I looked away from her again, aware that my body was suddenly full of desire for her. I did not know what to do.

I heard her softly laugh—that lovely laugh that always seemed to ripple out of her.

"Oh, Tom! Dearest Tom." She raised her hands to the drawstrings of her shift, undid them, and allowed the garment to fall to the floor.

My Anna stood all-naked before me, her skin so white that the darkness of her body hair struck an extreme and bold contrast. She smiled shyly, but her eyes brimmed with invitation as she walked gracefully those few steps towards me. She put her arms around my neck, pressing her naked body ever so gently to mine.

"Tom," she said softly. "Oh, sweet, sweet Tom. My own loyal and darling Tom. My lovely boy; dearest of hearts, how like you this?"

In answer, I lifted her in my arms, (how light did she feel to me), and took Anna to the nearby bed.

And that was the only time that I ever made love to my beloved. I remember feeling astonished to find her yet a *virgo intacta*, but after the first gasp of pain, her body joined with mine to complete what she had begun.

She was not completely innocent. Her hands betrayed to me that they had, sometime and somewhere, learnt certain games of love. Indeed, her fingers caressed and touched as if she knew instinctively how to stir and excite me. As our bodies joined, her hands stroked my inner thighs, travelling upwards in widening circles to my groin, then, having reached there, going behind me to grip tight, with her two hands, my buttocks, drawing me deep, deeper inside her.

So slender was Anna's body I could easily feel the fine bones beneath her skin, while cupping her small, maidenly breasts in my eager hands. Her skin seemed so soft and tender that I feared to bruise her in my passion. But it was not only my passion... there was such a fire in Anne that I felt almost burnt in her heat. Verily, it took all my restraint to not loose myself in an early release. I had waited so long for this dream to happen that I wanted to hold on tight to the moment, just as I was holding tight to Anne, and never, ever let it or her go.

Anna moaned softly as I kissed, over and over, the soft spot between shoulder and neck and laughed wildly as my fingers loosened her plait, looping her long hair around my neck. Then I forgot her and me and became lost in the fusion of ecstasy that we created together.

That summer's day showed that the dream I carried of Anna was all I imagined it could and would be, and more.

I had bedded with women since I was seventeen, but none of them compared with Anne; and none ever would. There was such a sense of giving in her lovemaking that suddenly doors were opened within me that I never knew existed. Within those doors I discovered things free of the deception on which I had based my life—that I could find true happiness without her. This time I shared with Anna I knew to be my truth. The poems that I wrote suddenly breathed and sighed, shivered and trembled—the rhythm of the rhyme dictated by two young hearts beating fast, and, for once, in symmetry.

And in those long, emotion-laden moments, just after our lovemaking, it suddenly came home to me that Anna may have realised (and perhaps she did) how often I had stood by watching, wanting her, but had remained silent. Never, ever coming forward to speak to her of my desires. Perchance, George had told her how my heart had broken when my father refused to speak for me, saying Anne was destined for a greater match than the one she could gain with me. That wanting her was like a dog howling for the moon—

insisting that I marry elsewhere as decided by the family. Now Anne had given me freely a part of my desires. 'Twas not a dream. I could not believe it was not a dream, even though I held my dream, could feel my dream's naked, soft warmth right here, right here next to me.

As I continued to lay wakeful, with my sweet love nestled in the crook of my arm, I reflected it very likely that Anne had chosen to bestow upon me something she wished not to bestow on the King. Perhaps too, I thought, it had been Anne's great need to be loved and comforted, on a day when she felt herself so alone and afraid, that at long last had won her for me.

Anne soon began to stir in my arms and I looked down at her. Her eyes looked so wide with fright that I held onto her tighter.

"What is it, Anna?"

"Do you hate me very much, Tommy?" She whispered so quietly that I had to bend my head close to her to be able to hear.

I stared at her, saying with surprise, "Why, Anna, should I hate you?"

She stirred uneasily in the bed.

"Because I used you to rid me of a virginity which has burdened me over long. I am so sorry, Tom. I would not blame you if you hated me. But I rather it was you, if it could not be my sweet Hal, to be the first with me. Simonette told me, when I first began to become a woman, that your first man puts a brand upon you that you carry until the day you die. There is no way that I would have wanted my branding to be that of the King."

I could not help but laugh.

"I have been laying here thinking that may have been the reason for your sudden passion for me," I replied with a grimace. "But I do not hate you. I could never hate you Anna. I think I would accept any affection from you, on any terms, as long as you always thought well of me."

Anna began to sob as if her very heart was breaking.

"Oh, Anna, my lovely girl… I have never known you for such tears. What have I said to cause you so much grief?"

154

I cradled her in my arms as I would my little girl. Never had Anna struck me as she did that day as someone in great need of comfort; someone who needed to have all her hurts kissed better.

Anna took great gulps of air, wiping away the tears from her eyes. She reached up to caress my face.

"Tommy, Tommy. I do truly love you dearly, and I am glad that something about today helped me come to the decision to seduce you to my bed. You spoke of wanting me to think well of you; I was so afraid that *you* would not think well of *me*. Especially since this day must be the first, last, and only time that we can be true bed-mates."

"But, why Anna? Why? I know enough about a woman's body to know that you found pleasure with me. I know that I am wedded to another, though after all the events of the past few years, I no longer consider myself to be Bess' husband. Especially since it is you who I have loved and wanted since we were children. Now you have given me some of my lifelong dream—why should you say it is to end so soon? We can…"

"Tommy!" she said sharply, breaking into my imaginings.

"Were you not listening at all to me before? I belong to the King. I have no other choice but to belong to the King. I love you dearly, Tom. I love my brother George more than life itself. I love my sister; even to my father do I feel enough duty to ensure that he is not destroyed. The King's vengeance is a thing beyond measure."

"Do you think my family knows not of the vengeance of Kings?" I asked her.

"But yourself, Tom, you do not really know… You do not realise, Tommy, I have only one possible way to save the people I love, and myself. I must become Harry's Queen. And I must have his son. 'Tis so amusing, cousin. I could laugh, if it was a subject for laughter, at the plans I once made for revenge, Tom. We all would be safer if I had become his mistress in the beginning, like my sister did, thinking it was such a great honour to have the King thrusting between her legs. But my beginning with the King was when I was so busy with my plotting and my snares. Teasing him with half promises and rendezvous never kept, because I am a pure and modest maiden who greatly desires to be wed before she is bedded."

She sat up in the bed then, pulling up the blankets at the same time to cover her nakedness.

Looking at me, she said: "Now I have no choice but to go on with what I have begun. Can you not see, Tom? The King would destroy us all if I bow off at this point of the play. For this is what I believe this grand passion has become for him, some sort of make-believe play where he is the errant knight winning the pure maiden from his enemies. Perhaps, Tommy, he sees himself as a Tristan and me an Isoldein some sort of glorious love story where to achieve his desires he must sacrifice all. Who knows? I only begin to tremble when I ponder what will happen when he wakes up to the truth. I am but flesh and blood and not at all like the fantasy woman he imagines himself to be in love with."

"But surely, Anne, there must be a way you can break away from the King?"

"Tommy, believe me, even a nunnery would be no refuge for me any longer. Even if the King hadn't started to think about disbanding all England's religious orders, what I have heard him call those bloodsuckers of his kingdom! Rely on me, Tom; I know the King. I have no escape."

Anna came back to snuggle closer to me. I put my arm around her, reflecting on what Anna had said. For a long while we lay abed, both of us lost in our own reflections and fears.

I could not help thinking and hoping that Anne was wrong. Surely the King was not the complete monster she believed him to be. Yea, I knew he had the greatest vanity that could be found from here to the end of Christendom, but surely Anna was not even sixteen when he decided to break her heart, and he more than double that! Surely the King had enough man in him, enough honour, to give a young woman some kindness and so her freedom.

Suddenly a thought struck me—a thought that was both terrible and pleasing.

"Anna?"

She lifted up her head to look at me. Her eyes were big and luminous in her pale face.

"Yes, Tommy?"

"What happens if we have made a child today?" I asked her.

Anna flung herself deeper into her pillows, and looked up at the ceiling.

"I do not think that will happen, Tom. I have been sickening for a long while, even before I caught the sweat, and my courses have stopped. I do not think or believe my body is well enough to begin the making of a child. Even if I was, Tom, Simonette is wise regarding these matters. I tell you true, Tom, Mary would have left a litter of babies behind in France if Simonette had not accompanied me to the French court. I will ask her to prepare a potion for me to drink tonight."

I sat up abruptly in bed, dazed by her words.

"You are going to tell Simonette what happened here between us?"

Anne laughed up at me.

"Tom. Dear Tom. She knows. Indeed, 'twas Simonette who first put it in my mind to seduce you this afternoon… She knows everything about me, and she knows everything about the wooing of the King. Simonette also agrees with me that the only way to keep the King's desires burning is to keep on denying to him what he thinks he wants… Yet, Tommy, I too have desired the fulfilment allowed other women. It is so difficult for me, Tom. I am a normal woman deprived of a normal life. It has been so hard and painful, Tommy, when I think that only but for the King I would have been Hal's wife and a mother probably three or four times over. I worry that when the King gains his desires from me, my power over him will begin to wane… Indeed, I truly fear that once he has gained his desires the King will begin plotting my destruction."

I pulled back from her, saying crossly: "Oh, Anna. This is too much! You cannot be right about all this!"

"Aye, Tom, I feel in my blood that I am right. The King is enjoying the chase, but what is the end of the chase but to make the kill? That is another reason why I must become his Queen. 'Tis the only way I can ensure my survival at the end of the chase. Tommy, Tommy, sometimes it is so hard for me to resist the King's batterings on my virtue. Hal Percy, so very long ago, lit a fire in me that often seeks to consume me. Today it consumed us both... I am so sorry if it seems to you that I have used you for my own ends. I know I can trust you, Tom."

"Anna—my heart—I would die before I betrayed you."

"Aye—I know, Tom. Otherwise I could not trust you with my life—for if the King was to find out about today I fear that his anger would be so great that I shudder at the likely consequences. Of late I find it hard to think clearly, but still—there are in my heart things that I can hold on to. I almost died, did you not know, Tom, when I ailed with the sweat? The King sending to my bedside Doctor Butts, his second physician, but Simonette swears that she alone saved me."

Anne laughed, and rolled on her side towards me, resting her head upon my shoulder.

"Simonette tells me that she cut an apple into three, and wrote upon its pieces: *The father is uncreated*, *The father is incomprehensible*, and *The father is eternal,* and that, and that alone Simonette assures me, is what saved me when the fever was at its worst."

Again Anne shifted in the bed, now lying back amongst the pillows.

"You know, Tommy, it felt strange to be so ill. When I had the fever, it was like I was plagued by dreams, which were all so real. Aye... Tommy, I came very near death, but one thing kept me comforted as I felt death try to pull me into its final embrace. I have loved, and been loved, Tommy. Not by the King—what does he know of love? You know, Tom, sometimes I find myself so full of pity for him. The King has so much—yet so very little. But I… I've always known what it is to love and be loved."

I reached out and picked up a lock of her hair that was lying on the pillow, intertwining it loosely in my fingers before bringing it close to my face to breathe in its scent of rosewater. My heart constricted tight in my breast. I looked at her, swallowing my urge to cry.

I cleared my throat, and said: "Sweet love… my beloved— forevermore."

Eyes shining, Anna smiled at me tenderly.

"Loved by George, and Simonette, and Hal, and you—always you. Aye, suddenly it struck me as I lay there close to death that your love has been like a beacon that drew me always into a safe and secure harbour. Sweet Tom, you have never asked for anything from me, so let today make up for all I cannot ever give."

Laying back deeper into the pillows, she reached for my hand, holding it firmly in both of hers. 'Twas as if she took my oath, unsaid, to accept without complaint what she had given. What could I do? Yea, what else could I do but draw her closer into my arms and give her lips a lingering, tender kiss. Then I shut my eyes and tried to sleep.

I awoke in a strange bed—alone. If it was not for Anne's night attire flung untidily on the bed, I could have easily persuaded myself that the strange happenings of the night before were some illusion of my senses. I got out of the bed, wrapping the sheet around my body, and went in search of Anne. I found her seated in a corner of the room's partly recessed window seat, wrapped in a blanket, looking out at the break of day.

"Could you not sleep?" I asked her.

She looked at me, smiling shyly through a half veil of dark hair.

"Yea, Tom, I did sleep for a while. But then I awoke and my body reminded me of what I had done. It is very amusing, Tom, but I really had not expected that losing my virginity would be such a soul-shaking event. I feel so different, as if I had been reborn in some way. Even the dawn looks different today."

I sat near her, on the other side of the window seat, and brushed gently away with my hand the hair hiding her face.

"Did I hurt you too much?"

She laughed softly, tossing up her head so her hair fell away from her face. I saw tears glistening in her eyes, but they seemed to be tears of great emotion rather than tears of any great sadness.

"Dear Tommy, today my body tells me that you branded me well. But it was only what I asked for, so I have no complaint… I just did not expect to feel so brimming with all these feelings."

"What sort of feelings?" I asked her.

She reached out and took my hand.

"So many different feelings that it is hard to break into them and name them all."

"Why don't you try to, dearest? Try to for me."

Anne released my hand and looked out the window. I looked also, silently sharing with Anna the beauty before our eyes. Indeed, the sky, ablaze with so many different shades of pinks, promised so much for the new day. Her gaze returned to me.

"You want me to speak to you of my feelings, Tom… 'Tis true when I say they are many… For one, I feel regret, yet not regretful. 'Tis like I am grieving for a part of me that was all innocent, and now that is gone forever. Perhaps I am sad to farewell the girl and unsure if I welcome the woman. I cannot help but feeling, Tom, there is so much I will need to rediscover about myself that, at the moment, 'tis like I am on some perilous precipice where I am desperately trying to find my balance."

"I remember that the first time I bedded a woman I felt something akin to the way you are feeling," I replied, shifting further into the corner of the window seat. "Except I also felt cold and sick at heart… You do not feel like that, do you, Anna?"

She turned back towards me, briefly touched my cheek.

"No, of course not, Tom—nothing at all like that. How could I

160

feel cold and sick at heart when last night was so beautiful? Poor Tom, how sad your first time was such a sham. Especially after all the love and tenderness you gave to me last night. Indeed, I have always suspected that such a magnificent poet could not be other than a magnificent lover."

I bent over to kiss her, but she jerked her face away from mine, reaching out to put her hand over my mouth.

"No, Tom. I told you that last night would be the first and last time."

I shook my head, saying: "But I still find it hard to understand why. Oh, I listened to you last night, but we are far away from court; Hever is virtually empty. No one knows what goes on between these walls…"

"Tommy!" Anne broke in. "Please, for my sake, what is between us must return to what it was when you first came into my chamber. I am not strong. If you were to kiss me now I do not know if I would have the strength to keep it just to a kiss. Please try hard to understand what I feel; all these emotions I have within me, I need to keep bottled up inside of me, otherwise everything will be lost. Haven't you understood, Tommy? Last night was the first and only time that I can allow myself the freedom to give full reign to my heart's desire, and to the innocent girl I once was—to the girl Hal Percy loved. Aye, Tom, to survive this game I play with the King I have to turn myself into something other than what I truly am…"

Anna then turned half away from me, looking out again at the break of day.

I heard her then say, ever so softly: "Sometimes I think I am going mad… Sometimes, Tommy, I see clearly I really want to be Henry's Queen."

"Anne!"

She gazed at me and smiled strangely.

"I told you Tom—I am going mad!"

Anna laughed, a laugh so pealing out of her she soon became breathless. She then leaned over, grabbing both my hands.

"I'd make a good Queen, Tom. And I could give England the Prince it sorely needs."

I carefully disentangled my hands from hers, moving even deeper into the window box at the other end from her, totally aghast.

"Anna, I think you are right. You are going mad. Or perhaps you begin to believe all that the King tells you when he does his wooing. Aye, you would make a good Queen. But at what cost?"

Anne bent her head over her hands and remained silent for a long moment. Then she raised her face, looking at me again.

"At great cost, I know. But then all great enterprises are won only at great cost… England has been too long under the thumb of Rome. 'Tis time to see our country come into its own. By his efforts to make me Queen, the King begins to cut the ties to a corrupt power. Surely you realise what a mockery the papacy is?"

"Surely you realise that *all* power is corrupt, and a mockery of what it should be."

Anna moved over closer to me, taking my right hand in both of hers.

"Perhaps when I am Queen I can change that."

"Anne, Anna… 'Tis very unlikely a single person can change how the world is."

"But the world is changing, Tom. Martin Luther has taken the papal bull by the horns and turned it upside down…"

I broke into her argument.

"Anna, you mistake what I just said. Yea, the status quo is changing, but it does not change the fact that power taints all that it touches."

Anne removed her hands from mine, pulled the blanket tighter around her thin body, and gazed back out the window before gazing at me again.

"You are very cynical, Tom. I did not expect you to be so."

"You forget, Anna, about my imprisonment by the Emperor's troops, and my experiences in Rome, as well as having actually having met men who know this Martin Luther… These sorts of things do tend to make you rather less wide-eyed about the world around you. Anna, I don't want to argue any longer about something we will never agree about. All I really want to know is where we go from here."

"I told you, Tom. We go back to the way it was before. We make believe that last night was a fantasy that never really happened."

As she spoke, something snapped inside me and, without wanting to, I cried out loud in agony. Anna slid back over to my side of the window seat and held on tight to my body.

"Tom! What grieves you, Tom?"

At this point I was crying. I could not help but cry. My dream had become reality but it was a dream that seemed destined to quickly turn into a terrible nightmare. Anne also began to cry and speak at the same time.

"I greatly feared I may have been asking too much of you... I told Simonette so... Oh, dear God. What a horrible mess it all is... Tom, Tommy, please forgive me. I should have left it all alone. I have been selfish, so thoroughly selfish."

She rested her head on my chest and I could feel her silent tears soaking into the linen bed sheet I had wrapped around my body. I took one long and gulping breath, and tried my best to take back control of my shattered emotions.

"I love you, Anna. I have always loved you," I whispered to her, brushing my lips against her hair, breathing in its rose-water fragrance.

Anna lifted up her head at this and took my face between her hands.

"I know, Tom. I think I have always known, and took for granted your love from the time I could barely walk. Please believe me, Tom, when I say that I love you too. But our lives are not our own. We belong to our families. You are married. I do not believe that you would ever bring shame upon your kin by divorcing Elizabeth, especially when it would mean putting into doubt your own son's name. And I have told you that I cannot bring my own family to ruin…" Anne stood up then and began to walk a little way from me. She then turned back to face and talk to me again.

"Furthermore, I truly believe my father would kill me if I gave up a King to hold not even a knight in my hand. Do you not see how impossible it is for us? There is no choice for us but to go back to what once was… And is that really so hard? Oh, Tom! Can you not see? You, George, and I are tied by stronger bonds than those bonds forged between a man and woman in bed. Verily, I have always believed that our souls are securely and eternally joined by deeper bonds than those we shared yesterday.

"I truly believe, Tom, that last night changed not one jot of these realities. I believe with my soul and heart that last night served to make what really connects you and I only stronger. So much stronger, I see—even if you do not—that it would destroy you to continue for even one more day your hope of what cannot ever be. I could never forgive myself… that is something I cannot risk. Oh, Tom, I could never forgive myself if you destroyed yourself over something that could never be."

Yea, I had to admit the truth of her words. Our lives had never been our own. And something strange had seemed to happen while she spoke, and while I watched her. Call me fanciful if you will (and are not all poets fanciful?), but it seemed to me that the light of the sun now breaking through the bedchamber's window had filled the room with a strange mellow, diffused light. This light now appeared to centre upon Anne—creating a golden aura, completely delineating her slender form. Even most of the darkness of her hair had been robbed of its blackness to be given in its stead a crown of gold. Thus, it seemed to me that there stood before me a regal figure, robed like some Roman empress. I could not help but think that I had been given a distinct vision of what Anne was meant to be. That it was the Fates themselves who had chosen for her this impending regal role. Yea—and who am I to argue with the Fates?

Shaking myself out my musings, I returned my thoughts to those concerns of the present moment.

"Aye, Anna, I admit the truth of all that you have just said. But I have one request, Anne, just one. I want you to kiss me one last time. And not the kiss of life-long cousins… Anna, what I want is for you to kiss like you did so many times last night, and I promise that I will be strong enough for both of us to keep it to just a kiss; a farewell kiss, if you will. But a kiss that will always be to me another precious memory of this brief time we shared, even if it means naught to you."

"Tommy… My sweet Tom!" Anna laughed and lifted a hand to me. "Come here, and kiss me then."

I went over to her and took her in my arms. I looked deeply into her eyes and then joined my lips to hers. That last kiss lingered on for as long as I could maintain it. Indeed, what stopped it and made me pull away from her was the awareness that my senses were demanding to continue in such a way as I promised her I would not. She was right: the longer I had hold of her, the harder it was to give up my dream.

Anna, after I had released her from my embrace, crumpled down, kneeling on the floor.

With her tears flowing unchecked, she looked up at me and said: "Tommy, you have made this so hard."

I laughed wryly, and went back to sit at the window seat. I wanted to get as much distance between us as I could.

"I am glad I've made this hard for you. At least I can take the consolation with me that things could have been so much different if we had been born other than what we are."

Standing up with unsteady movements, Anna gazed at me ardently, her dark eyes huge and shining with tears yet unshed.

"Yes, Tom, I do believe now that you are right. Perhaps if our lives were different… who can tell? But, Tom… I think I am very tired now. Tommy, I beg you to leave me… return to your room. We will see each other later, but at this moment I wish—and beg— the favour of being by myself."

I came over to her and kissed her gently on the forehead.

"Yea, Anna, I too wish to be alone… Come to your bed and try to go back to sleep. You truly are looking much too wan for my liking. I will dress as quietly and go as quickly as I can."

Anna appeared to me to be close to fainting, so I again picked her up and carried her to the bed—this time for different reasons. Desire had now completely gone from me to be replaced by the heaviness of utter sadness—sadness threatening to have me again in tears. I carefully placed Anne on the bed, covering up her slight body with the bedclothes. I kissed her tenderly—though chastely— on her lips, her eyes remaining shut as if she had already gone fast to sleep in my arms. Gathering up my clothes, I retired to the other side of the room and dressed myself as hurriedly and silently as I could.

Chapter 2

She wept and wrung her hands withal.
The tears fell in my neck.
She turned her face and let it fall,
Scarcely therewith could speak,
Alas the while!

I reflected, as I descended the stone staircase from Anne's bedchamber, on how eerie and empty Hever Castle seemed. 'Twas often the case that a dwelling emptied of most of its usual inhabitants when a member of the household had serious illness such as the sweat, leaving only a few servants to care for the one sick. This appeared to be the situation here at this time.

Last night had been like Anna and I were the only two people left in the world. In a sense this feeling still lingered. Indeed, going down those cold, stone stairs I felt more alone than I had ever been in my life.

I arrived at the chamber where I used to sleep as a boy, and went inside. There I sat on the edge of the bed, bent my head, and howled out my grief until I had no more tears left to cry.

So much had gone wrong in my personal life in recent times. Besides the happenings of the day before, I also found myself thinking about the way my marriage had gone from bad to worse over the years.

"*Dum spiro, spero,*" Father Stephen often said to us when we were children. And so it was—I had breathed and I had hoped. But now last night had opened me up in such a way that the door to years of pent up emotions remained left wide open. Now I had to face up to what was true of life and make some hard decisions.

So, where do I go from here? Anne was right when she said there was no normal future for us. She had steered herself on a course that left little room for me. Back to my wife? No. Things had come to such a pass that I realised I could never go back to my wife. There had never been any love between us. Even when Elizabeth bore my children into the world it was as if she had martyred herself in some way. My wife had never forgiven me for this marriage that had been forced upon her. That it had been forced upon me too seemed to make not one jot of difference to her. No. I could never go back to Elizabeth. The violence of our last argument showed too clearly the direction that our marriage was heading. I was beginning to find it far too easy to hate her—and hate, I knew, would destroy us both.

So, where to from here?

I had been recently told of a position in Calais that was soon to be made available. I had not really wished to return so soon to the Continent, but it offered me a kind of solution. After what had happened between Anna and myself, I knew that I could no longer stay in England and watch the King's pursuit of Anne. My father had given his house a reputation for loyalty to the Tudors. I could neither distress him nor break his heart by giving him a son who was other than loyal too.

So my marriage was over, even though there would be no divorce. Anne was again right. My son Tom was the apple of my eye. I could and would do nothing that would put into doubt his future. And what had happened between Anne and I was also over. Perhaps I would one day find a woman to heal this rent ripping apart my heart. I doubted it, but I could not bear to think that, at twenty-five, I was doomed to spend my life alone, unable to ever release myself from the cords binding me to Anna. Thus, utterly spent from all the recent happenings, I lay on the bed and tried my best to sleep.

I was awoken by bright sunlight streaming through my chamber's window and landing directly on my face. The harshness of the light and the position of the sun made it known to me that it was now late in the afternoon. My stomach then reminded that I had not eaten since noon the previous day. My nose informed me that I badly needed a wash. Idly debating which of my needs were greater, I at last reached the decision that, as water and bowl were readily available in my chamber, it would be best to clean myself up as best as I could. Especially as I have known since I was a young boy that both Anna and Simonette have very delicate noses that were easily offended by too obvious smells.

After I washed and dressed in a change of clothes, I went to the kitchen, like George and I had often done as hungry, growing boys. Stopping still in my tracks when I saw before me Simonette dressed in a faded and shabby garment—obviously her working dress.

I could scarcely believe even now that the events of the night before had taken place virtually on Simonette's suggestion. Simonette turned from the task she was engaged in and saw me.

"Master Tom?" she said, smiling with a touch of amusement. "You look like you have seen a spectre."

I moved towards her and kissed her quickly on the brow, whispering for her ears alone: "Simonette, I do not know if I should curse you or thank you."

She reached out to touch my hand, saying quietly: "I would be very sad if you ever had cause to curse me, Master Tom."

She stood there looking at me with candid eyes; a suggestion of a slight smile touched her lips.

"I just cannot understand how Anne and you could be so contriving," I responded, looking away from her with a deep frown.

"Oh, Master Tom! How can you say such a thing? Especially when it was yourself I thought of first when I decided my girl should know of true bed love at least once before she is wed to the King. I dearly love my young lady. My poor young lass. She is the daughter I always wanted. It grieves me so that her heart is still broken over the Lord Percy. She tells me often that she would rather have been Hal's Countess than have the promise of being Henry's Queen.

Do not blame me, Tom. I only tried to do the best for my dear children. Truly, Master Tom, you should realise, my dear, if Anna is like my daughter, then you and George are like my own sons. I know how you feel about Anna. Tom, try to think of it this way: at least now you were given something of what you have always yearned for."

I stared at Simonette, disbelieving what my ears had just heard. "You know? How…?"

"Tom… Tom… My dear young Master. Your eyes have never lied to me. Verily, your face gives away many of your thoughts and what is best kept secret. I have known you had given your heart to my Lady ever since you were twelve and you cried yourself asleep when you heard Anne and I were to go to France. You must try to school your face, Master Tom—for your own safety, if not for my Lady's."

There was nothing much I could say to this. I had long known myself to be a man who found it hard to not show his heart upon his sleeve. So I shrugged my shoulders and wryly smiled at Simonette. She took my arm and led me into the kitchen.

"What would you like to break your fast with, my dear?" she asked me.

"Is the bread as nice as it used to be when I was a lad?"

Simonette shook her head at this and laughed.

"Tom! Surely, at your age, you must realise that nothing will ever taste again like you remember from your childhood?"

I sighed deeply.

"Yea. Not only taste, Simonette, but once you have lost the innocence of childhood, all becomes soured and embittered by many dark emotions."

"Poor Tom! Life has treated both Anne and you so unkindly when it has come to being fortunate in love. But joy is still there to be found. One only needs to stop searching for joy for it to find you."

"I am not sure if I understand what you mean, *chère bonne*. I am too soon out of bed for that type of obscure philosophy." I laughed, and laid my hand lightly on her shoulder. "I do know my stomach aches with lack of food, so I am willing to eat whatever you lay in front of me."

Thus, Simonette bustled around the kitchen, preparing a tray of victuals to eat. After a short time, she came back carrying a heavy tray laden with bread, beef, cheese, and ale.

"I shall take this up to my Lady Anne's room. I know you would want to break your fast with her," she said as she walked past, heading in the direction of Anne's bedchamber.

I felt rather stunned by this. I was not sure if I wished at all to break my fast with Anne. My feelings were all still so raw and tender. However, as I knew that sooner or later I would have to face Anne, I soon followed after Simonette's fast-retreating form.

Anne was still abed, but now wearing a shift and fully awake. She sat up amongst her pillows, her lower body completely covered by the bed's fur coverings. Simonette had placed the tray upon her bed and was now busily attending to the room's huge fireplace.

When Anna saw me her face lit up and she said brightly, "Simonette tells me that you have just woken up too. Is it not strange to wake and find that you have slept the entire morning away?"

I went over to kiss her gently on the forehead, and whispered softly, "Good lovemaking often makes one sleep more soundly than you are used to."

Anna deeply blushed, and then laughed.

"Dear Tom. So now you have told me the secret for a sleepful night. What else have you to tell me?"

"Nothing, except that I am starving! Shall we break bread together?" I asked her, taking a loaf off the tray for her to tear what she would. Thus, we both were on her huge bed (so huge that Anne's thin frame appeared to be almost lost in it) breaking our fast together.

For many, many heartbeats we just sat there eating, but then I became abruptly aware that Anne was studying me carefully, so I looked at her, and smiled.

"You have seen me eat before, Anna, so there must be another reason why you look at me so closely. Have I crumbs upon my face?"

"Nay, Tom," Anne replied, laughing. She then reached out to touch my cheek ever so gently. So gently that I could easily imagine her fingertips into butterflies, brushing against my face. "You are in bad need of a shave, but that is not what I was thinking."

"What then, my dark Lady?"

"Dark Lady? You have never called me that before, sweet cousin Tom," Anne responded.

My eyes lingered on her, and I gave a slight smile.

"You do not know how many times I have called you that, my lovely dark Lady—but never aloud. Only softly to myself, in long hours of the night when I could not sleep; when only I could hear… But, Anna, I think my dark Lady avoids the question I have asked her."

Anne pushed the tray with its demolished food away from us, and quickly got out of the bed. Simonette had left us to our breakfast, so we were all alone. Anna was wearing the same lawn shift that she had worn only minutes before we had become lovers. I turned my eyes away from her, feeling so utterly wretched for all that could not be.

When I looked for Anne again, I saw she had put on a heavy, green velvet dressing gown, richly embroidered at sleeve and collar, and had seated herself near the fire. Anna held her lute in her hands. Except for the fact that her long, black hair was now completely unloosed, she reminded me so much of how she looked when I first had entered her chamber the previous day.

I walked over to her, and squatted beside her, putting my hand over hers.

"Anna, you *are* avoiding the question," I repeated. She raised her free hand to the side of her face and smiled at me ironically. The gesture and smile reminded me so much of George.

"Tom, perchance some things are better left unsaid." Anne spoke barely above a whisper.

"Anne, you know how much I hate that—to be left dangling like a fish on a line. Cannot you leave me to judge for myself?" I asked of her crossly.

Anne laughed, and squeezed my hand gently.

"How little we really change from children. George and I used to love to see your frustration when we would not let you into our secrets. Though we loved you too much to do it too often."

"Yea, Anne, that I well remember. But still you avoid giving me an answer to my question."

"Oh, Tom, what can I say? Why must you make me say it? Does it make you any happier that I was just thinking… thinking that this is what it would have been like, if we had wed? You and I eating together in complete companionship. But, I do not wish to rub salt into your wounds. We spoke all that we will ever speak on that matter last night… So, now that you have the answer, Tom, does it make you content to know it?"

I remained silent. There was no ready, easy answer I could give her.

Anne then shook my hand, and gaily said: "Where is your lute, cousin? I so wish to hear you play, Tom."

"My lute is still packed amongst my gear. Why not play to me, Anna, since you have your own lute right there upon your lap?"

"All right then, cousin Tom. A song for a song… but if your fingers cannot make music, your voice still can. Sing, Tom; sing as I play."

"Oh, Anne! My voice cannot compare to yours. I will sing only if you do so too."

She laughed again.

"It seems you strike the better bargain, coz. What song then?" she asked, as she began to tune her lute.

"What about Greensleeves?" I now asked her, smiling teasingly at her.

Anne looked up at me with bewildered eyes.

173

"But surely George…" she began.

"Yea, George wrote in one of his letters that the King composed the words of this song for you, putting it to one of the old tunes," I finished for her. "But, I think it is the best of his songs, and I have a strange hankering for us to sing it together."

Anne laughed, and then played the opening chords.

Thus, Anne and I sang:

Alas, my love you do me wrong,
To cast me off discourteously
For I have loved you so long
Delighting in your company.

Greensleeves, was all my joy,
Greensleeves, was my heart's delight,
Greensleeves was my heart of gold,
And who, but my lady Greensleeves.

I stopped at the end of this chorus, laying my hand on hers to stop her playing.

"Who would have thought that our King could be so inspired by my dark Lady's green sleeves?"

Anne raised her thin eyebrows, and looked at me slightly askew.

"Tom, I do believe you mock the King's passion for me!"

"Where you are concerned, Anna, I will mock anything in this life that seems not good enough to give you what you truly deserve."

Anne's eyes widened at that and glazed over with tears.

"Oh, Tom," she now said, her voice choked by tears, "let us finish the song before you make me believe that I still have a heart to break."

Anne's fingers again strummed the opening chords, and we sang together these concluding verses:

My men were clothed all in green,
And they did ever wait on thee
All this was gallant to be seen,
And yet thou wouldst not love me

> Greensleeves, was all my joy,
> Greensleeves was my heart's delight,
> Greensleeves, was my heart of gold
> And who, but my lady Greensleeves?
>
> Thou couldst desire no earthly thing,
> But still thou hadst it rarely,
> Thy music still to play and sing,
> And yet thou wouldst not love me.
>
> Greensleeves, was all my joy,
> Greensleeves, was my heart's delight,
> Greensleeves, was my heart of gold,
> Who but, my lady Greensleeves?

Anne then put her fingers on her lute strings to quieten its final vibrations. We sat there for a few moments, close together, in a silence that seemed to tremble with so much that would always be left unspoken.

At length, she reached down to gently stroke my cheek.

"Yea, dear Tom. I agree with you—Greensleeves is the best of the King's songs… But I believe—and always will—that your songs are written with more and truer sincerity," she said.

I smiled sadly up at her, and held out my hands.

"Pass me your lute, Anne. I will sing to you one of my *sincere* songs."

Anna gave into my hands her lute, and I sang to her this song:

> And wilt thou leave me thus?
> Say nay, say nay, for shame,
> To save me from the blame
> Of all the grief and grame.
> And wilt thou leave thus?
> Say nay, say nay!

And wilt thou leave me thus,
That hath loved thee so long,
In wealth and woe among?
And is thy heart so strong
As for to leave me thus?
Say nay, say nay!

And wilt thou leave me thus,
That hath given thee my heart,
Never for to depart,
Neither for pain nor smart?
And wilt thou leave me thus?
Say nay, say nay!

And wilt thou leave me thus?
And have no more pity
Of him that loveth thee?
Alas, thy cruelty!

And wilt thou leave me thus?
Say nay, say nay!

I looked up at Anne to find that she had drawn up her knees to her chest, bowing her dark head over them, and was crying silently. My dark Lady seemed to me so broken that I regretted instantly my "essay" in sincerity. I put her lute gently on the floor and moved to embrace her. Her body was rigid in my arms, and I greatly feared the harm my song may have done.

"Forgive me, Anna," I said to her, my chin upon her dark head. "Some songs go beyond and deeper than what the singer truly desires."

Anne gently pushed me away and stood up. She walked over to the stone fireplace, blackened by countless years of fires, and gazed down upon the burning wood.

Anna then turned around, saying: "Why ask for forgiveness when you speak only the truth? I am cruel. Yesterday showed to me how cruel I have grown… I used you. Yea, I used you like I have used, in recent times, so many, for my own selfish ends… Years ago, when we had that horrible argument, you told me that I was untrue to myself. Tom, sometimes I look into the mirror and see some terrible stranger. Only when I am with you or George do I feel that I return to what I really am. Otherwise, it is like I have told you before. I am caged, Tom. Caged by what the King wants me to be. And worse, I sicken myself by all the corruption I have allowed to flower within me. You said something to me yesterday that has preyed on my mind ever since. Power taints all that it touches, you said. Yea, cousin, I am tainted as a piece of meat left too long in the summer's heat."

I stood up from my kneeling position and went to Anna, gathering her in my arms.

"My darling girl, speak no more. Your words frighten me so. I am such an ungrateful wretch! You freely bestowed upon me the gift of yourself, and I stand here like a spoilt child who cries for more and more! Oh, Anne! My lovely, darling Anna! I do love you so! But, I swear to you, that no more shall I hurt you by asking for more than you can give. I swear to you, that my desire for you will be locked away forever; still my love you will always have!"

"You truly *can* forgive me, Tom?" she asked, raising her tear-stained face from my chest. I bent my head, and kissed her softly on the lips.

"Yea, sweetheart. Forgiven, and one day surely blessed. You have given to me a part of my dream; a dream I would never have believed could come true. But the dream comes at a cost, Anna. I do not believe that I can stay in England and watch… I cannot, cannot watch… Anna, you must understand that! I will return to the Continent as soon as I am able."

Anne gently removed herself from my arms, pulling her loosened dressing gown firmer around her too-slender body.

"I understand, Tom… And that may be for the best… I too feel full of regrets for what cannot be. Perhaps it would be better not to

177

prod our hurts any more than we need to."

"Yea, Anne," I replied, trying so hard not to break down again. "I think it would be best, until time heals what it can, to see each other as little as possible."

Suddenly, Simonette rushed into the room interrupted our conversation.

"Lady Anne! Master Tom! Lord George is here!" she called to us.

Almost as soon as she said this, George came into the room, his thick, blonde hair wind blown all around his head. He looked both saddle-sore and weary.

"George!" Anne cried, rushing over to fling herself into his arms, bursting into fresh tears. Simonette then glanced over to me with a question in her eyes. I signalled her with my eyes to depart and leave the three of us to deal—as best we could—with the problems of our grown-up lives. Simonette was always good at receiving unsaid messages. Thus, with a final concerned glance at the three of us, she quietly left Anne's chamber.

"Anne! What is to do? Have you and Tom been disagreeing again?" George now said, looking over Anne's head, to search, worryingly, for me. Catching his gaze, I shook my head, walking up close to my cousins to put a hand on both of them.

"Nay, George," I replied to him. "Anne and I are just so very pleased to see you."

"Yea," he said, gently removing Anne's face from his chest so as to wipe away lovingly with his bare hand the tears flowing down her cheeks. A concerned and bewildered expression became fixed upon his face. "So pleased that my sister completely soaks and no doubt ruins my new silken doublet with her tears."

George's voice had become thick, as if Anne's uncontrolled grief was threatening to bring him to tears too.

Anne broke away from him then and wiped her face hurriedly on her long sleeves.

I am very sorry, George," Anna quietly said, in a voice that showed she still struggled with the seesawing of her emotions. "I did not mean to greet you so."

Anna hurried away from him, stopping when she stood again near the fireplace. She had her back turned towards us, her head bowed as if staring into the dying fire.

George looked long at her, and then looked hard at me. I could easily see that he was gravely suspicious of something, but was bewildered by what to be suspicious of. He lifted an eyebrow up at me, as he often would do when curious and wanting an answer to a riddle. I shrugged my shoulders in return and walked over to stand by Anne, turning back to face George.

"I have been telling Anna of my plans to leave England soon. I am afraid it made her sad."

I hoped, in desperation, that he would accept this explanation and not go searching for deeper reasons. George's head tossed back in surprise.

"But, Tom! You have hardly been in England during the last two years. Surely 'tis time for you to stay at home for a while, rather than go back abroad!"

"Aye, George. I know. But travelling often gives you the taste for more travel. Only a week ago, when I came to court to pay my respects to their Majesties, I spoke to Lord Henry, who was about to take on duties in Calais. The good Lordship told me that he was going for the King, and I asked if I could accompany him. He welcomed the suggestion, so back to the Continent I go!"

Actually, my conversation with this ambassador had been all in great jest, and I only had remembered it when I struggled with my torments after leaving Anne's chamber. Now I spoke of it, trying to distract George's attention away from the true cause for his sister's tears. I could well imagine Lord Henry's astonishment when I presented myself in the near future as his companion for the journey.

"No wonder my sister cries. Both of us have missed you so much, Tom. Letters are one thing, coz, but the flesh and blood person is a different matter entirely. I have ridden hard this day because I wanted yours and Anne's company, and now I find my best friend plans to depart again when he has just returned to us! But why, Tom? Why?"

"Oh, for a lot of reasons, George. Mainly, I suppose, because I can no longer pretend that the problems with my marriage are solvable. I have decided to separate forever from Elizabeth, George."

He deeply sighed.

"I am sorry that things have come to such a pass, Tom, but I am not surprised to hear it. 'Tis bad enough to be joined in holy wedlock to a shrew, as I am, let alone a woman who is determined to play harlot while her master's back is turned," he said.

"And not only when my back is turned, George. I cannot help but believing that Elizabeth has deliberately set out to destroy this mockery of a marriage from the beginning... No matter; if that had been her intention, she has now achieved her ends. And if there is another cause, I no longer care. All I wish is to never see the woman again in this life."

Anne had listened silently while I spoke to George. She now came to me and took my arm gently.

"Alas, poor Tom!" she said, and then reached out a hand to her brother, who clasped it firmly in his. "Poor George! And poor me! Life has dealt us bad cards when it comes to love. But at least we are blessed in one thing; the three of us still have each other."

"Yea, sister. But now part of the trio has decided to absent himself again." George released his sister's hand, and turned his head to glance at me in an almost chiding manner.

"George!" I put my right hand firmly on his shoulder and said, "Both of you know that if you have need of me, all that is required is a message and I will come. All going well—Calais is only but a short journey away. In any case, George, you too are committed to working for the Crown, and, no doubt, will also be sent away from court to serve best the interests of the King."

Anne laughed then and we both looked at her.

"Now I am to be made doubly sad! Not only Tom to abscond from my life, but George too!"

Both George and I bellowed at the same moment: "Never…" then looked at each other and burst out laughing.

George then pulled up a red-velvet covered stool and sat down on it.

"Yea. 'Tis pointless to upset ourselves over something which is unavoidable."

I sat back upon the rushes on the floor near him and looked at the fire. Seeing its great need to be replenished, I picked up some firewood and tossed it in. I looked up at George.

"We three carry the imprint of one another on each of our souls. So what if our bodies linger only briefly together? Anne told me— only hours ago—we three are bound together by stronger ties than any bonds our bodies can create. The love and good fellowship which we three share is like an oasis that we can come to during the hard moments of our lives, so to refresh and make ourselves anew."

Anne then knelt on the floor near the two of us and held out a hand. George and I each took one of her fragile, delicate hands in one of our own hands, callused by much hard riding and made strong by the virtue of our manly estate. I then turned to George and we clasped together our free hands. We looked long at one another, smiling and tightening our grip on each other's hands.

"Yea," George said, and his voice was thick with the strength of his emotions. "We have much in life to be thankful for."

"Aye. As long as we have each other, we will surely withstand all the dire twists and turns that might befall us in the future," Anne softly replied. Her grip on my hand again increased, and my eyes gazed into hers. There was so much that had been left unsaid between us three, but then, what comes from the heart is often said without the use of simple, spoken words.

"I feel we should take a cup of wine and drink to our lifelong fellowship," I then said, releasing their hands after a final, gently increased pressure. I walked over to a small, roughly hewed oak table placed near the chamber's window where a ceramic flask of wine and some silver goblets had been put.

I filled up three goblets, taking up two to pass to Anne and George. I then took up my goblet and returned to my cousins.

"To loving fellowship," I said.

"To loving fellowship!" Anne and George responded together, smiling broadly.

And so we touched goblets, and drank the wine.

"So, verily," George said, breaking into the drawn-out, heavy silence that had developed between us—a silence which, nonetheless, spoke strongly to us of our deep and abiding friendship. "I do not know about you, my two good people, but I have ridden hard this day and have not eaten since early morn. Excuse me while I leave you both for a few minutes so I can go and find myself some food."

George then walked over to the small table, placed his empty goblet down near the jug of wine, and then went out the door.

Thus, Anne and I were left alone for a few moments. Anne breathed in deeply, and sighed. She looked at me with eyes shining with unshed tears, and asked: "Do you think I should tell George what has really happened here, between you and I?"

I turned my head to glance out the window above the window seat. I could see by the diminishing light that the lovely summer's day was rapidly passing us by. The light coming into the room reminded me of the surf upon a beach being drawn back into the sea. One moment the light was strong, the next moment weakened. The moment after that the wave of light was strong again, but not as strong, and, in the next breath, the light entering the room was further weakened. And so the pattern would be continued, until darkness in the end took dominion. I could not help reflecting that there was a pattern to all natural things and this pattern was continued even into our own lives.

I then turned my attention back to Anne, to answer her question with a question: "Do you want to tell George?"

Anne put her hand on my arm.

"Tom, I tell George everything. I have always. You, of all people, should know that."

"Yea, Anna. I know. But grant me the favour of not telling him until I leave England."

Anna looked hard at me, and then took my hands in both of hers.

"You do not want George to know, do you?"

"Anna!" I broke away from her, and walked back to the table to replenish my cup. I turned back to her, and furiously said: "What is there to know, Anna? You have spent hours telling me how that part of our lives is all finished. Why tell George when there is nothing... nothing at all to say?"

Anne bowed her head, and was silent for a moment; she then, with a great air of sadness, nodded.

"You are right. There is nothing for George to know. Only you and I will ever know what really happened."

"Thank you, Anne. I know you hate having secrets from George... I too, find it a very new experience. No doubt, one day, he will put together the bits and pieces that made no sense to him this day... But, Anne, I now... I, at this moment... I am too unsure and confused... I think I can come to terms with all this better, Anne, if George does not look at me with pity."

"But Tom, George would nev..." But at this point Anne had to break our conversation, because we could hear George's deep voice singing, becoming closer and louder with every passing second.

George entered into the chamber carrying two lutes: his own and mine. Simonette followed swiftly after him, again bearing a tray loaded with food, this time two cooked fowl and more fresh bread and cheese.

"It seems today that I have been taken back to the days when you three were in the nursery," Simonette now said. "Here am I, ensuring that your stomachs stay full! My lady Anne! Why are you still out of your bed? Back there at once, *chère belle*, before I grow cross."

"Oh, Simonette, my brother and Tom are here!"

"My dear, dear lady! As if they would care if you were abed or not! I did not say that they were to go, but you need all your rest, and they can talk or sing to you while you are resting."

"Yea, Anne. We will come and sit near you by your bed," George said in support of our nurse. Anne did appear to be worn out again, so I took her arm and gradually led her back to her rumpled bed. When she had walked those few steps, and had almost reached her destination, her body began to sway and I sensed her utter weariness, so I picked her up again in my arms, her head nestling into my chest, and carried her those few remaining steps to the bed.

"Oh, Tom," she said, laughing softly, as I gently placed her slender form on her bed covers, "I could have walked myself."

I smiled at her, pulling some of the bed covers over her, and took up the breakfast tray, which we had left before. I turned around, still holding the tray, to see George watching me with a strange glint in his eyes. *God have mercy!* I thought. *I think he begins to put together the true pieces of the puzzle!* But then George quickly lowered his eyes, and when, a few moments later, he glanced up again, it was as if he had shuttered away all his thoughts, pushing them into the far recesses of his mind. Simonette put the new tray of food onto Anne's bed, and took the other tray from my hands.

"I will leave you three to enjoy your meal in peace," Simonette said as she passed George and I, before going out the chamber's door.

George was still holding both our lutes as Simonette left the room. He slowly walked from where he was to pass over my lute to me.

"Come, Tom," he said, as I took the lute from him. "This is what I have dreamt of since you wrote to me that you planned to return to England. The three of us together, playing music like we used to."

I smiled at him.

"Yea, cousin. Many a time I would dream that dream too."

Thus, we walked together to Anne's bed, pulling up two stools, and began to tune our instruments. I glanced at Anne to discover that she was lying amongst her pillows, smiling lovingly at us both. I smiled back at her, and then placed my instrument on the floor.

"Perhaps it would be better to eat first, and play with full stomachs. You said before, George, that you have not eaten since early morn."

George nodded in reply, and put his instrument alongside mine.

"Aye. Let us eat, and talk, and keep the greater pleasure for the last." He arose from his stool and walked over to sit on the edge of his sister's bed, reaching over to pull apart a fowl. He passed to me a leg, and then offered the other leg to his sister. Anne shook her head slightly and said, "Nay, brother. I have no appetite for meat."

"Come, sister," George said, taking Anne's right hand in his free hand. He then placed the fowl leg in her hand and closed her fingers firmly around it. "I insist you eat something, Nan. How do you expect to put some flesh back on your bones if you will not eat?"

"Am I an infant that everyone needs to fuss over me? Tom will tell you, George, that I have already eaten well this day."

But, on reflection, I could remember her eating little, though picking much.

"Nay, Anne. I cannot tell George that you have eaten well this day, because you have not. I agree with George; you are a shadow of what you should be. Eat, Anna. You need to eat to regain your strength."

"*Jesu!*" Anne exclaimed, pulling herself up so she was sitting upright. "You both win! But just wait until I become strong again! We will see, then, who will be the winner of the arguments!" Anne, after an impish smile at both of us, began to chew upon the fowl's leg in her hand.

Thus, while we all ate, we spoke together. George restarted the conversation by saying: "I must tell you, Anne, the King grows more fond of those manuscripts of mine. You made the right decision to give them to him, so he could study them well."

"What manuscripts are those?" I asked.

185

Anne lifted her head from eating, and answered: "'Tis a long story, Tom."

I laughed. "You know how I like long stories, Anna. Can you not share this one with me?"

"If you must know, Tom, it all began when one of the Queen's ladies entangled herself badly in a mess of politics and love. Good fortune, it now seems, has now decided to smile kindly at her. And me too, I suppose…"

"But you spoke of manuscripts?" I was beginning to feel very bewildered.

"What my sister speaks so cryptically about, Tom, is this: Anne was able, by her quick thinking, to save two of the Queen's attendants from the threat of certain destruction. And she even risked herself in so doing."

"Oh, George! Do not make too much out of so little! I believe that I have a good understanding of the King. I never thought, for one moment, that there was much chance of making him angry at me."

I looked at both of them.

"I am confused! What have books to do with all this?"

"My cousin Tom, 'tis like this." Anne turned to face me. "I have in my company a certain lady who has recently been betrothed. This lady is secretly of the Lutheran persuasion; thus, she often has in her possession books, which can only be described as illicit reading. Her beloved, in jest, took away from her one of these books; no doubt thinking it was some romantic fable he could tease her with. But when he read it, he became so taken with this book that he took it everywhere with him. Fool that he is, he even took it to the royal chapel. My friend came to me in tears. It seems that she had somehow become aware that Wolsey had taken notice of her lover's great idiocy, and was making moves to tighten a net around him. George had recently given to me his copy to read, and, as I read it, I could not help thinking that it contained certain sentiments that would easily gain the sympathy of the King. Thus, when my dear friend told me of her troubles, I decided to take matters into my own hands and gave to the King two of George's books."

"And how many sleepless nights I have suffered since!" George exclaimed, with a laugh.

Anna turned to her brother.

"Oh, George! I told you to trust me. Have I misread the King's character yet?"

"Nay, Anne. But the tide runs with you. What will happen when the tide turns against you? That is my greatest fear."

"Fear not, brother. I will have to make a gross mistake for that to happen. And, George, I do not plan to make that sort of mistake."

"You are so confident, Anne. I feel that you almost mock the fates, my sister. I hope that the fates will not decide to put you in your place."

Anne stuck her tongue out at George before pealing with laughter.

"Why do you laugh?" I asked her.

Anna gazed first at me and then at George.

"Because I believe we are all too serious… Either I am meant to be Queen, or I am not meant to be Queen. Let us wait, and see… and speak of other matters." Anne tossed her meatless bone onto the platter placed on the bed. She then flung herself upon the pillows, and stared up at the ceiling.

George and I looked at each other; we knew, without having to say one word to the other, that Anne, despite her attempt at gaiety, had, for some reason, been swept away by a wave of sudden remorse, and was vastly in need of our comfort.

"Have you eaten enough, Tom?" George muttered under-breath to me.

"Yea, I have had my full," I likewise replied.

"Cousin, let us then play our lutes, and sing to each other our new songs."

Anne rolled over to her side, and leaned her face on a hand.

"Cannot we have some of our old songs? So many of the new

tunes speak of only pain and heartache."

When she said that I remembered the conversation I had only hours before. I had spoken of my regret to Simonette that things could not remain as we remembered them from our childhood. What had she said to me? Yea—verily—I remembered her words.

Thus, I turned to Anne and said: "There is joy still to be found in our music, Anne; only you must not go seeking it, but let the joy find you."

Anne wiped away some tears from her eyes with a free hand.

"How that brings to my mind dear Father Stephen! Do you remember, Tom, how he would often say to us as children, that true happiness could be found by not concerning overmuch with your own happiness, but by always seeking out the best ways for the happiness of others?"

"Yea, Anna. He was a very godly man." I paused for a moment to look at Anna and smile. "Now George and I will wash our hands, and play to you our songs."

So, that is what we did. My kinsman and I went over to the jug and basin placed on a square table near her bed, and washed and dried our hands. Then we played our lutes until the twilight moments of the day at length diminished, and the room became darkened by the night. And George and I found when we lit the candles around the bed that Anne had drifted into a deep slumber.

Chapter 3

1528–1532

Patience, though I have not
The thing that I require,
I must of force, god wot,
Forbear my most desire;
For no ways can I find
To sail against the wind.

I left Hever Castle the next day, accompanied by no one, as George had made the decision to stay and try his best to cheer his still ailing sister. Within a week I sailed for Calais, leaving England and my heart behind.

My cousin George told me, the night before I left Hever, that he truly believed God had chosen Anne to lead the King away from the great evil of the papacy and take him and England back to the road of righteousness. George, I found to my great dismay and concern, had become very much a Lutheran during my time abroad, and we argued through the night about the rights and wrongs of what I could not help but see as a terrible calamity for the three of us. At last, we concluded that we would never agree, so it was best to allow the other his own opinions. George, though, did admit to being sometimes plagued at night by many doubts and fears.

My new duties in Calais were immense, but still they did not keep me so busy that I remained unaware of the happenings back home. Verily, with a constant flow of letters from George and my father, I often felt better informed than when I resided in England!

Not long after I settled into my new life in Calais, I heard that

Anne was now returned to court, though George wrote that she never fully regained the physical strength she had lost. He wrote worryingly that she pushed herself so much that George feared she would soon have a new and worse collapse. The only outward show of her body's weakness, however, was that her temper would suddenly flare with apparent little reason, leaving some poor mortal singed in its wake.

When Anne eventually became Queen, many of the common people detested her because they saw her as the young hussy who had heartlessly used her youth to turn the King away from his older and more steadfast wife. Verily, Anne, they believed, was the shameless usurper—whore some called her—of a well beloved and sainted Queen. George wrote to me, in one of his many letters, how Anne still attended to the Queen even though it was now obvious to many at the court, what direction the tide took both of them. Indeed, the young woman the King wished to make his Queen would often play a game of chess with the older woman who had held right to that title for close to twenty years. George described one such scene so vividly that I felt I watched the same scene as he…

The Queen shifted the chess piece, and peering short-sightedly across at Anne, now puckered up her brow in concentration. With the final moments of daylight ebbing, a servant went around the room lighting candles in the Queen's chamber. Waiting for the much younger woman to make her move, Catherine of Aragon— her Queen's mask seemingly undisturbed—straightened her back and lifted her chin, rubbing the side of her face where her Spanish gable chafed her skin… Anne's chair backed the long windows. Two hours ago, when the game first started, sunlight shone bright upon the Queen, making her grey eyes water and squint in protest. But she hadn't uttered a word of complaint. Rather, the game had been played with every iota of immense skill she could muster. Anne too played as if the game's true meaning went beyond just a simple game. Verily, all watching knew the high stakes between these two women.

Hearing pieces click upon the board, the Queen dropped her gaze from studying the dark-haired girl, seeing her snatch a piece from the board. Dark eyes shining in triumph, Anne held the Queen's king in her open palm. Catherine of Aragon's composure broke.

"You are not satisfied with just the King; you mean to have all," she snapped.

Yea. All who listened knew what the Queen meant—Anne held out for the crown.

Poor Queen Catherine! The Queen was not only very beloved by the common people—I was also one of those who were often torn with conflicting loyalties. As I heard one of my friends say, so will I say also: "Queen Catherine was beloved as if she was of the blood royal of England."

Nonetheless, I do not believe that Anne was the complete cause of the final collapse of the King's marriage. Yea, the King did fancy himself in love with Anne, but years before, when she was still a young child in her nursery at Hever Castle, he had already spoken to many at court of his doubts regarding his marriage to the good Queen Catherine.

My father told me one time in conversation how, as long ago as 1514, King Harry had flirted with the idea of getting rid of his Spanish wife. This was after his final falling out with Ferdinand, that old fox of Aragon, who also happened to be his wife's father. Nonetheless, in 1514 Catherine was discovered to be again with child so the idea of a divorce was put aside, to eventually re-surface in 1528, when ten long years had gone by without the Queen showing any more sign of child-bearing. This could be hardly surprising, since it was also well known that the King and Queen very rarely co-habited with one another as husband and wife.

Furthermore, by this time King Henry had convinced himself that his marriage with Catherine had been cursed right from the start, taking as his proof a text in Leviticus, which said if a man married his brother's widow their marriage would bear no fruit. True to his character, the King completely closed his eyes to the fact that there was a text in Deuteronomy that said a man *should* marry his brother's widow, so to raise up living children in his dead brother's name.

Yea. Events were rapidly on the move in England, moving swiftly to their final outcome. One only had look at what was happening to Cardinal Wolsey to realise how much change was in the air. Many years ago, when her heart was breaking over the loss of Hal Percy, Anne had sworn to me that one day she would bring the great Cardinal down. Letters from home made it clear that moves were now afoot in England to make that threat into an actuality. When Wolsey returned from France in the summer of 1527, Anne had tilted the power balance completely over in her favour. No longer would Henry sign Wolsey's charters without first reading them for himself. No longer would the King receive Wolsey into his company without first acquiring the approval of that *upstart* Anne Boleyn. Clearly, the writing, for the Great Cardinal, was on the wall! However, nothing is ever that simple. The King still had need of the man who had virtually ruled England during those early years when the King was but a youth.

I gathered from my father's letters that Wolsey was very uncertain if the King's arguments regarding the validity of his marriage would hold much water when tested out in an ecclesiastical court. The Cardinal himself made it very clear that he did not fancy the prospect of Anne as the future Queen of England and, understanding how Anne felt about him, who could blame him!

The Cardinal pointed out to the King that if he were to decide on a political marriage—for instance deciding to marry a Princess of royal blood rather than insisting to marry for "love"—it would make achieving this divorce so much easier.

The King was flabbergasted and enraged by this argument;

instead of making him change his stand regarding the divorce, it made him more determined than ever to triumph over all the obstacles that could be put his way.

George also wrote to tell me that Anne was making good use of the frequent separations of the King and Wolsey, using these absences to further the ever-widening gulf between them. My cousin went on to say, in this particular letter, that the nobles of the land, especially the Dukes of Suffolk and Norfolk, were delighted in what they saw happening between the King and the Cardinal. Thus, they did all that they could to encourage and assist Anne in her endeavours to bring the mighty Cardinal down.

This was no surprise to me.

The powerful nobles of the land had long resented Wolsey's influence over the King. *The King and I*, usually spoken by the Cardinal to foreign dignitaries in the Latin, *ego et rex menus*, had been said so frequently by the Cardinal over the years that it had now become a common saying. Verily, I remember well a season at court when it was much quoted by one and all. However, this authority of the Cardinal annoyed those who believed that the authority should belong only to them. Indeed, all the nobility of England whole-heartedly believed that the power the King gave Wolsey was the right of one of their own ranks, rather than one they sarcastically called "the butcher's son"—since rumour at court claimed him as such.

'Twas also clear, in these years when so much was changing, that Wolsey no longer was held in any esteem by the common people; indeed, whatever love or respect they had for him had long since flown. It was very easy to see the reasons for England's disenchantment with Wolsey. The people of England perceived that the problems that afflicted the land, especially the constant threat to the much needed trade with The Netherlands, trade which had brought prosperity and livelihood to so many, was very much due to the incompetence of the Cardinal. It surprised me to think how very few laid the blame upon the King.

Seeing his power rapidly slipping away from him, Wolsey desperately tried to gain the acceptance of Anne, but she heeded him not. In his great fear, the Cardinal then made the biggest mistake of his worldly ambitions. (Though, who knows? Perhaps his actions simply showed a man whose sleeping conscience had awoken and now looked uneasily on the events of the last few years.) Wolsey turned against the wishes of his King, and began to seek ways of supporting Catherine, her nephew the Emperor, and the wishes of Rome.

Anne discovered this turn-around, and became terrified of disaster, which would cause her fragile pack of cards to come tumbling down.

Anne's own fear made her speak angrily to the King: "I have lost my youth and reputation for my love of you, Harry. Yet you will do nothing against Wolsey, who insists in trying to find more and more ways to destroy me. I can bear no more of this! Harry, either you must choose between having me as your wife and Queen, or continue in your favour of Wolsey. I will leave you, Harry. I swear to you, I will leave you, if you do not make up your mind and resolve to bring the Cardinal down!"

The King made his choice, and Cardinal Wolsey was arrested. I cannot help but wonder if it was just an act of fate that the man who was sent to take him in custody was none other than the Earl of Northumberland—once known as Hal Percy. Aye—Hal Percy, once the beloved boy of Anne Boleyn's youth.

Thus, preparations were made to send Wolsey for trial, but before the Cardinal need be fight for his life, preserving all that he had gained in the service to the King, death came and took him to face a more eternal judgement. Perhaps truth is starker when death looms vividly before your eyes.

Yea it must be so, because the Cardinal's final words, as he lay on his bed a-dying, were: "If I had served God as diligently as I have done my King, He would not have given me over in my grey hairs."

So the great Cardinal died; a mighty tree felled by a mere slip of a girl. And the loud sound of his fall made the whole land sit up and take notice

Was revenge sweet, my Anna?

I think not. I think now you began to truly taste the feast that your plot had led you to. And it was vile, utterly vile and spoiled. Like a decaying apple full of creatures of the earth. But, Anne, you were right when you told me that once begun there was no drawing back. Especially now that you had begun to truly love the King. Yea, it was obvious to me, who knew you better than you now knew yourself, that you were indeed caught in a trap of your own making. Thus, does fate make a mockery out of the plans and hopes of us poor mortals!

But, even though I admit to the truth that Anne was wrong to do what she did, still I lay the blame on the King. Anne loved Hal Percy, perhaps too much. When he was ripped so violently from her life, she felt she had no other reason to live but to plan revenge. She was too young to suffer such a broken heart and come away whole. If only the King could have left well enough alone, we all could have been spared much suffering.

Yea, I love Anna more than I can ever hope to express. Even my poems are but an echo of what I truly feel. But, I believe I could have been content in my life to simply see my girl happy. I had no prior claim on her. My heart had always been freely given. With no expectation, aye, no expectation at all, that she would ever love me like I did her.

The King, with little thought and with care only for his lust, destroyed whatever happiness we all could have had from life. I blame him and only him for all the tragedy that was to befall us.

One other who also lay the blame upon the King, for *his Great Matter*, and cared not to hide it from him, was his youngest sister, Mary the Duchess of Suffolk, Dowager Queen of France.

At the end of Easter 1531, I heard from George how the Duchess had insulted Anne by expressing her amazement, in front of the entire court, that her brother the King would look so low for a wife.

As the Duchess left the confines of Whitehall, the servants of Anne and the Duchess continued the slanging match. A fight then broke out between these attendants, with the grim result that one man lay dead before the horrified eyes of the court.

The household of the Duke and Duchess Suffolk was, for several long months, somewhat in disgrace over this bloody mishap. Matters, however, began to return to a semblance of normality when the Duke made the King a promise to keep his men—and his wife— under tighter rein.

However, the threat of violence still lingered as if taking the shape of storm clouds gathering force, darkening the sky. It came to the ears of Thomas Cromwell and, through him, to the ears of the King, that certain servants of the Duke had sworn to wreak revenge at the earliest opportunity.

When the King heard this he went quickly to his sister and her husband, demanding that they and their household bow to the inevitable and pay proper respect to the woman he planned to make his Queen.

Not only was George, as one of the attendants to the King, witness to this meeting, but my father also wrote to me an account of it, so I can easily reconstruct how this meeting took its form. Imagine, reader, this scene: Two towering men, and a tall and slender woman—a woman who was overly slender because of illness taking its relentless course in its destruction of her body. The three stood close together in a dark library, made even darker by the near-black wood panelling, and the fact that the only source of any sunlight was a narrow window set high up in the wall. In a huge fireplace a fire burns with hungry heat, giving to the room's winter pale occupants a curious, reddish glow.

"So, Henry," said the woman, tossing her head slightly, "you think you can come here, to my own home, and tell me how I should conduct myself."

"I am your King, Mary, and you are subject to me just as the lowest of my subjects."

Mary frowned at her brother, and gestured to him with impatience.

"Henry, you forget the blood that flows in your veins also flows in mine!"

The other man, who so far had stood by silently, jumped into the conversation. "Mary, you forget yourself!"

Angrily, the woman spun around to confront him. "Who are you to tell me that I forget myself?"

The man stood up taller, loudly saying: "Lady, I am your husband!"

The woman grimly laughed, raising both her hands to place them on her slim hips.

"My Lord, 'tis so amusing that you remember that now. Do you only remember that you have a wife when it is convenient to do so?" Pausing slightly but not waiting for an answer, the woman continued: "Let me say that today I find it convenient to forget I have a husband. Keep your overly large nose out this, Suffolk! This matter concerns not you, but is only between my royal brother and myself."

Her brother laughed, and looked around the room. Suddenly he espied a flask of wine, with an empty goblet beside it. He moved briskly—more briskly and gracefully than expected for such a huge and tall man—across to the table and poured himself a drink. He turned back to his sister before raising it to his mouth to drink.

"Yea, Mary, you too are a Tudor. But I would have thought you, of all people, would support me in this."

Mary looked at him sadly, saying: "Brother, 'tis because I am a Tudor that I do not support you. I believe you to be so wrong, Henry—so very, very wrong."

"Woman!" The taller man straightened his form so he towered over the woman even more.

"Who are you to say the rights and wrongs of this matter? 'Tis I, by Divine Providence, who is the King here. Surely 'tis I, not you, who is to say what is, or is not right."

Mary looked at her brother for a long moment before replying quietly and sadly: "But, brother, in this you are not right, and my conscience would not rest easy if I were to do other than what I am doing now."

The King took a deep breath, as if to control an urge to lash out. His voice, when next he spoke, stayed soft, but behind it was a strong promise of a storm, if things were not soon decided his way.

"Mary, you reason this matter like one of your sex. I will try to be patient with you."

Mary smiled slightly to herself, turning her face to hide her amusement from her brother.

"I will try hard to remember that you do not have the skills to dismember and make logical decisions."

Mary now raised a hand to her mouth, as if stifling an urge to laugh.

"Firstly, Mary, you have not made long years of study, like I have, to discover why my so-called marriage to Catherine has been cursed with such a lack of living sons…"

Mary turned back to face her brother with a harsh laugh.

"Long years of study!" she mocked. "Long years of study just to affix the blame of the loss of your sons on something other than yourself! Have you never thought, brother, that the fault for your lack of sons lays not with Catherine, but with you?"

The King stirred, beginning to swell with rage. Mary reached out a hand to him, palm facing him, but not touching. She then said: "Stop! Henry, do not become angry, but wait and hear me speak."

The man before her stared at his sister; clearly it was only the great regard and affection he had for her which prevented the storm, which he held uneasily within his chest, to at last break loose and overwhelm them all.

"I will listen, sister, but be warned—even you can go too far!"

"Perhaps my words were too ill-composed to be said, but they are true nevertheless." The man before her began to move in agitation. "No! You have not yet heard me out. Please listen to me, Harry! If there is a cause for the loss of your children, I believe it lies not only with you, but also with all the Tudors. Think, my brother. How many children did our parents have? Eight, was it not? And how many lived to be full-grown? Only three... Arthur, I count not. My earliest memories, yea, even before I could put voice to my thoughts, are of a sickly, forever-ailing elder brother. And fifteen is too young to regard as full grown; he died still only a boy."

Seeing her brother starting to stir in anger again, Mary touched him gently on his arm. "Aye, brother, I know your thoughts regarding Arthur, but let us at least agree to differ. And Harry, of the three who lived to be full grown—what of us? Have not the three of us buried more babes than our hearts could expect to cope with? Look at Margaret. She lost baby after baby before she was blessed with her two sons. Then there is you; to the kingdom's great unhappiness, we all know how fate has dealt with you.

"And I?" Mary became for a moment silent, closing her eyes tightly as if she was suddenly struck inwardly with a great pain. She opened her deep blue eyes, and looked sadly at her brother. "And I? I too have watched most of my babes sicken and die before my eyes. Aye—lost too many of my children not to wonder why. Look at your nephew—my son... he is too alike to Arthur. He has no strength to withstand further illness. 'Tis not Catherine's fault your sons died. Our blood is bad, brother."

The King turned his glance from his sister, and muttered as if only to himself: "Am I, then, not a man like other men, sister?"

"Yea, Henry, you are a man like other men. But you are a Tudor, and we Tudors are bad breeders. Look at our grandmother Elizabeth of York. Was she not one of twelve children who grew to adulthood? I believe that was because her mother was not royal, nor interbred so her blood ran thinly in her veins. There is something wrong with us. There must be something wrong with us!"

"Mary! You forget that with another woman I have sired a son who has lived to be weaned!"

"Yea, brother—a boy who reminds me so much of our poor brother Arthur… and my own boy. He will not make old bones nor live to have hair upon his face, this son of yours."

"Mary, you go too far! What do you desire of me? To doom my only living son to death, even in words? Mary, I cannot believe this of you! 'Tis as if you wish to see me bleed to death before your very eyes!"

"Is the truth really so hard to bear, Harry?"

The King stood even taller, puffing out his chest, slowly saying in a voice vibrating with feeling: "I see it not as truth, but the ramblings of a poor woman who deludes herself that she knows better than those who are more equipped than she to decipher what is truth or untruth."

Mary shook her head, laughing softly with sarcasm.

"I may be a poor woman, brother, but I know well enough when a man wishes to rid himself of one woman to make way for another. Is this not what this is really about, Henry? You wish to get for yourself a new and younger wife?"

The King spoke again very slowly, as if he wished for his message to be completely understood, leaving no room for misunderstanding.

"Catherine has never been my wife. Our supposed marriage was a sin against God!"

Mary looked at her brother as if she wished to see into his soul and see for herself what he truly believed.

"Harry, how can you say that? Do you not realise that one of the best things that you have ever done for England was to marry Catherine? And you forget, brother, she is Queen anointed. She belongs to England, just as surely as you do…"

The King shook his head, saying bitterly in reply: "Do you not realise Catherine has failed England. I have no heir..."

"Yea, you do." Saying these words, Mary went to her brother and put her hands on both his arms. "Oh, Harry, dear brother, you do have a heir—your daughter Mary! She is all the heir you will ever need! Can you not see what a child she is? She is Tudor all over."

"A girl child!" The King grunted in disgust, looking away from his sister as if he wished not to discuss the matter any further, but his sister shook him to gain his full attention again.

"A Tudor girl child, whose worth is twice more than any other man who is not Tudor."

The Duke, who had been listening in silence and in great fear to this royal debate, now stirred.

"I do not have to stay and listen to this!"

Mary turned to her husband.

"No one invited you to stay, Charles. I said before, and I will say it again: this matter concerns only the King and myself. You, of all people, have no part in it."

His eyes blazing, Suffolk then turned smart on his heel, and left the room, banging the door loudly behind him. The King glanced over at the now shut door, frowning slightly, and then returned his eyes, deep blue like hers, to his sister.

"Should you speak to him like that? Suffolk's a prideful man, you must know, and he is still your husband, Mary."

The woman shrugged very slender shoulders, and went over to the fireplace. She studied the dying embers for a moment, and then turned to face the King.

"I care not for his pride. And he has betrayed me too many times for me to take much note of my marriage vows... But, I repeat to you, brother: what of your daughter Mary?"

"Aye! What of Mary, sister? She is but full cousin to the Emperor. Be it, Mary, your desire to see England under his dominion one day? Be that so, I tell you, sister, 'tis not mine!"

"Brother, cannot you see that would only happen if you continue as you are doing now? If you remain determined to travel in the same direction you are moving in now, it will happen, even as you say. But, Harry… I know my small namesake well. She idolises you, and would only wish to emulate you, Harry, if given half a chance… Take her under your wing, brother, and you could mould her to the shape and form of a great monarch…"

"But she is female, and must be subservient to any man she weds."

"Not necessarily so, Henry. Make sure that Mary understands that she must be Queen Regnant, and any man she marries must always remain her subject and be given only very little power… You have, if it pleases God, many long years left to you, brother— many years in which to prepare the ground for Mary. Choose well her husband, and make her into a Queen that all England will be proud to own. And, brother, have you not thought that Mary could give you grandsons?"

The King suddenly pulled up his form, shouting, "Sister, 'tis not grandsons I want, but sons! Can you not understand that I want no other man to sire England's Prince but I?"

Mary's face lost all its animation, to become expressionless.

"Aye, Harry, you are a man like other men. Verily, it always, always comes back to this: your need to prove your manhood by siring sons!"

With a swift stride, the King moved towards her, slapping her hard across the face. Recovering from his blow, Mary raised her hand to her bruising cheek. She looked bright-eyed with unshed tears at her brother, and smiled ever so faintly.

"Yea, my dear brother, yet another way that men have to demonstrate their manhood."

The man before her blushed deeply, now appearing shame-faced. He sputtered out: "I did not mean to strike you, Mary!"

The Princess Royal of England and Dowager Queen of France moved over to her brother, embracing him lovingly. For a few minutes she leant her throbbing cheek upon his silken doublet.

"Yea. I know, Harry. I know," Mary comforted, reaching up to gently caress his face, and wipe away the tears falling from his eyes.

"Our Tudor tempers are hard to keep under tight rein. Perhaps we both have said enough on this matter, brother. I am so tired... so very tired," Mary now said, as she moved away from him to look sadly down at the dying embers in the fireplace.

"But you *must* understand this, Harry." Mary turned her attentions away from her thoughts, and back to the humbled man before her. For a brief instant in time, the King had vanished, leaving a very worried, utterly human man before her.

"I love Catherine. From the time I was a little girl of five, she has been like an elder sister to me. More so, Harry, with our own mother gone, I often as a child looked to Catherine to take her place. I cannot and will not accept another woman in Catherine's place. I simply cannot. Not while my true sister still suffers and lives. I am sick, Harry. I feel death stalking my every move. I will do nothing, I swear to you, Harry, nothing, which I feel could endanger my very soul..."

"Be it as you say, sister." The man stirred, and straightened up his tall frame, taking back, as it were, the cloak of Kingship upon his broad shoulders once more. "I will let you keep to your conscience, Mary. All I ask of you is to keep your sentiments to yourself."

Mary shrugged her shoulders.

"I have spoken my mind to you, Harry. That, for the moment, is enough. I can rest easier now. But, I am very weary. My brother, if you will please excuse me, I will send Suffolk back to attend you. All I want now is to go up to my chambers to rest."

With that she deeply curtsied in her brother's direction. The King then went quickly over to her so to help raise her visibly trembling body. He kissed twice the cheek he had bruised.

"Yea, go sweetheart; go and rest."

Suffolk was said, by George and other reliable informers, to have shuddered with horror as this battle of Royal wills was enacted before his frightened eyes, and within his very home. Later, after the King had departed from their house, the Duke begged his ailing wife to keep her feelings under strong control, otherwise all would be lost for their house. The Suffolks owed great debts to the Crown.

I sympathised immensely with the Duchess, and could understand why she did what she did. Indeed, she only did what she felt right. Mary loved Catherine greatly; indeed, was namesake to her only living child. She grieved that things had come to such a pass as this, and also grieved for Catherine when all her sons had died. Mary too had borne sons into the world, only to see them quickly snatched, by death, out from her arms—many of them before they were weaned. The Tudor Princess and former Queen of France, though sickening with the illness that would kill her all too soon, was, nevertheless, still determined not to bend too much to the will of her brother. A brother who appeared to be so hell bent on his own destruction.

Verily, it seemed to me, even though I heard all this second hand from George and my other sources, that the ailing Duchess had appointed herself Catherine's avenging angel. So angry was she that Catherine had been tossed aside like a worn out shoe.

And discarded, Catherine was. On July the eleventh, 1531, Anne and the King packed all their personal belongings and left Windsor and Catherine for Anne's favourite royal residence: Greenwich—the palace where Anne could take much pleasure in the nearby sea. Catherine of Aragon was not informed of this move, but discovered it to her immense sorrow the following day, when it became clear to all that the King planned not to return.

Catherine wasted no time in sending a courier with a letter for the King. In it she expressed her great grief that the King had not even come to say goodbye to her.

Poor Catherine! Ever since she was a frightened, lonely widow of sixteen, Henry, the new heir to the throne of England, had been like a shining beacon where all else was darkness. Even if the beacon was but the promise that one day they would be man and wife, and, thus, the eventual King and Queen of England.

Sometimes the pattern of life takes us in a complete circle. After her first husband—Prince Arthur—died, the Spanish Princess was severely pushed aside by the first Tudor monarch, and had to wait many a long year before her knight and King came to take her from the darkness and back into the light of day.

Now the fairy tale was ended. This was no tale from the pages of *Le Morte D'Arthur*, but the true story of people of flesh and blood, with all the despair and agony poor mortals like ourselves have inherited since the time that Eden became lost to us. For it was that same knight who now forced her back into the darkness. But this time, any hope of earthly happiness for her was utterly shattered and destroyed.

The King made this even more obvious by the stinging letter he sent her in reply to her message of regret that he had left her in such a manner. The King wrote to her in his dispatch that it was a pack of lies to claim that she came to him a virgin from her marriage to his brother Arthur, thus, Rome had no authority to disallow him his divorce. She must, from hence forth, regard herself as the Dowager Princess of Wales, and no longer as his wife. And, as she only had the relationship of that of a sister-in-law to him, Catherine was, in future, to keep her nose out of his concerns, and stop complaining to the whole world how she had been wronged. The King ended this message to his former wife by daring her to prove that she had been indeed a virgin when he had married her more than twenty long years ago. Catherine was then separated from the Princess Mary, her beloved daughter—the only child of her supposed marriage to the King to survive both birth and infancy. A daughter Catherine never saw again.

In the end, the King commanded to take her household to the royal estate of More. Thus concluded Catherine of Aragon's union with the King.

Book Five

1532–1533

Some tyme I fled the fyre that me brent,
By sea, by land, by water and by wynd,
And now I follow the coles that be quent
From Dover to Calais against my mynde,
Lo! how desire is both strong and spent!
And he may see that whilom was so blinde;
And all his labour now he laugh to scorn
Mashed in the breers that erst was all to torne.

Chapter 1

"And she also to use newfangleness."

ate in the year 1532 we received messages in Calais from England, telling us to make preparations to ready ourselves for the arrival of the King and the Lady Marquess of Pembroke—a lady I once had simply known as my cousin: Anne Boleyn.

I was commanded to return to England, so to prepare the way from that end. I did all the duties expected of me, but in the back of my mind (or did it originate from my beating heart?) there was a kind of painful pulse, constantly crying out: *Anne! Anna! Anna my love!* I thought my years of absence from her company would cure and heal me of this love, this passion that had done its best to torment me throughout life. I tried to tell myself that I no longer cared; the fire was dead, the passion had blazed bright but was now spent. I tried to convince myself through my poetry, that this was truth. But my heart knew otherwise.

> *For to love her for looks lovely*
> *My heart was set in thought right firmly,*
> *Trusting by truth to have had redressed.*
> *But she hath made another promise*
> *And hath given me leave full honestly.*
> *Yet do I not rejoice it greatly*
> *For on my faith I loved so surely.*
> *But reason will that I do cease*
> *For to love her.*
> *Since that in love the pains been deadly,*
> *Methinks it best that readily*

I do return to my first address,
For at this time too great is the press
And perils appear too abundantly
For to love her.

Once my duties were complete I sailed back to Calais to assist with the final preparations needed for this very important royal visit. At length, the day arrived, and, with my heart in my throat, I strived desperately to ready myself for the arrival of the woman whose complete love was all I had ever truly wanted in this life.

Anne and the King arrived as the bells rang out the tenth hour on the morning of the eleventh of October. I was one of the party who went down to the Port of Calais to welcome the King and the woman he wished to marry. The day was one of those magical days when sun and wind unite to make one tingle with the elation of being alive. Even so, there was little I could take true joy in.

It had been obviously an excellent crossing for the King and his party, because they all disembarked in extremely high spirits.

I made my greetings to the King and his bastard son, the Duke of Richmond, before I was suddenly face to face with the new Marquess of Pembroke—Anne, my dark Lady. The woman to whom I had, so long ago, given all that I had to give of love.

I took her hand and bowed over it, saying as I did the customary greeting, and then looked her in the face. The last time I had seen Anne this close was the day after we, for that first and only time, had been lovers. During the time since, as we had done whenever separated by life, we had sent messages to each other through George, but we had kept to our bargain of seeing one another only from the safety of distance. Thus, during my brief visits to England and court, I had made no effort to seek her out. I wanted only to give myself the opportunity to heal, and come to terms with what would never be.

I felt shocked at what five years had done to Anna. It was not that she had aged so much—though she was now twenty-five—but her fragility had increased to such a point that I could not help thinking that her outer flesh was being slowly burnt away by all the battles she had fought during these last five years.

"Verily, cousin Tom, 'tis as bad as all that?" Anne asked, laughing at me.

Obviously my face had given away some of my thoughts. I mentally shook myself, thinking as I did that her appearance of greater fragility only served to increase her semblance of loveliness.

"No, my Lady. 'Tis only when last we met you were at the close of girlhood. Now I have the pleasure to meet the lovely woman for the first time."

"Gallant, as always, dear Tom." And with those words she left me to continue along the line of other Calais officials come hither to welcome the royal party. Soon, I watched the King and Anne as they were both led to waiting horses for their journey to the castle, realising for the first time that one of the ladies riding alongside Anne was my cousin Mary. In recent years, Mary—who now had two children—and I rarely crossed paths. *Perchance*, I thought, *here in Calais we might meet and speak—enjoy some moments remembering the past.*

Making my own slow way back by foot, I passed the Duke of Suffolk, surrounded by his men. The Duke cast me a hawkish glance as I gave him a hurried bow. Quickening my pace back to the castle, I found myself plotting ways to avoid the Duke during his stay.

For the next few days I stayed busy attending to my various daily duties. Thus, I could only see Anne when the castle's household sat down to dinner and, of course, the dais was too far from mine for us to be able to engage in conversation. Not that we could have sat side by side; Anna had gone far beyond the simple fare of talking in such a place with one like I. A few days after the royal party's arrival, the King and his attendants left for Sandyfield to meet with *François* of France. This was the main reason for King Henry's visit to these shores: to gain the French King's support for the annulment of his marriage to Catherine of Aragon. King Henry also hoped to gain *François'* assurances that he would use his influence with the Pope to help our King achieve his desire for a new wife. While King Henry went to parley with the French King, as no French noble woman of suitable rank had agreed to accompany the French King to meet with Anne, she remained at Calais with the Duke of Richmond.

Not long after the King departed Calais, I received a young boy in my chamber, with a message from my Lady requesting the enjoyment of my music. I took my lute out from its wrappings, made a quick check to see if it was properly tuned, then followed the page to Anne's apartments.

I was not surprised when I came near to her rooms to hear the sounds of Anne's own music coming through the closed doors. For a few heartbeats, I stood and listened. Anne's playing had never sounded better. Verily, there seemed to me a far greater depth in her music, a depth not apparent the last time we played together.

I entered the room to find Anne, with her little dog Purkoy curled up at her feet, attended by several ladies and, to my great surprise, also the Duke of Richmond. Why was I so surprised to see him present, and apparently in good spirits, here in Anne chambers? To be utterly truthful, I felt surprised because I would have thought that the young Duke could have no liking to pay court to the woman his father, the King, hoped would provide him and England with a true heir. 'Twas well known that King Henry had made moves, beginning with giving his bastard son the titles that had once belonged to his father, before becoming King of England, to have his only living son recognised as a solution to the Tudor succession.

As I moved into the chamber, Anne saw me and stopped her playing. She smiled brightly, and then turned to her attendants and the Duke.

"Now your Grace and good people, you will hear such music

which is fit to be heard by the ears of angels."

I kissed her hand in greeting.

"Yours or mine?" I asked her in a voice meant only for her ears. Anna laughed.

"Both of ours," she replied, laughing again. Yet I thought I could see a heavy sadness shadowing her eyes.

Thus, for the next hour we forgot about our audience, and played our lutes together as we had done often since our childhoods. In due course, after playing many, many songs with meaning to us, a string on my lute broke, and I halted to make repairs. Anne then ceased her playing too. The Duke and all the other attendants broke out in loud applause.

Some called out "Bravo!" and asked for us to play more.

We both looked at each other in amusement and then turned to our audience, bowing slightly. Gazing at me, Anna laughed. It did my heart good to see her happier than when I had first entered the room. It did my heart good just to be thus so near.

"Enough, my good people," Anne said to those listening. "My fingers are out of practice and they ache now from all the playing. Excuse me, your Grace, if I take this time to converse with my cousin Wyatt." With that, she gave her lute to one of her ladies, curtsying slightly in the direction of the Duke, and stood. She then held out a hand to me.

"Come, my cousin Tom. Give your lute to Madge, and come over to the window so you can tell me what you know of home."

I took her hand, giving my lute to the girl Anna gestured to, a girl I recognised as another of our many relations. We walked, hand in hand, closely followed by several of Anne's attendants, and even closer by Anne's dog, to the enormous window at the end of the room that looked down upon the port of Calais. Dropping hands, Anne and I stood, with Purkoy yawning and scratching between us, looking out at the vivid blueness of the sea and sky—there seemed to be no end or beginning to either one or the other. And while we stood there, gazing out to this vastness of the seemingly infinite, we talked of things less complicated by the power struggles affecting our daily lives within the world in which we lived.

Trying hard to ignore those attendants who, we could not avoid noticing, were trying their best to listen to what we said, Anna imparted to me, as gently as she could, sad and tragic news from home. Simonette had swiftly sickened of a fever and, just as quickly, died. Peacefully and without much pain, Anna told me, with brimming tears lighting up her dark eyes. We both were silent, sharing together the grief we felt for the loss of this genuine godsend, that truly magnificent woman who had been the real maternal force of our younger years. I took Anna's hand in mine, though circumstances dictated that it was only for a brief moment, and looked back out at the sea.

"I wish I could have been there. I cannot believe that I will never see Simonette again. Never again in this life…"

Blinking away my own tears, I felt myself suddenly filled by the memory of a golden summer afternoon. I could see it all so clearly, aye, so very clearly… Shaded by a tree from our favourite oak grove—her skirts spread out on the ground like the outstretched petals of a daisy—Simonette cradled upon her lap Anna, fast asleep, index finger popped into mouth, while helping Mary read her hornbook. And not far from her loving care, two small boys played sword fights with one another…

By and by, we put aside our common grief and went on to talk of other things. Anna told me the reasons why the King raised her to a noble rank in her own right. He wished to make her feel secure concerning his efforts to make her Queen, and know that if a child came before the wedding it would forever be protected by the rank Anna now held in her own right. Anne then spoke about her sister Mary. Anne sighed and frowned, saying she wished now she had not brought Mary to Calais. Mary spent almost every moment in her new lover's chamber, embarrassing and disappointing Anna with her uncaring behaviour. Anna also shared with me recent news of

George, who was with the Duke of Norfolk at the court of the Pope on a mission for the King regarding "His Great Matter." George's marriage was also going from bad to worse. Still there was no sign of an heir, nor did Jane ever show any hint of being with child. Other events had consoled George somewhat; his mistress had recently given him a very welcomed son, even if born on the wrong side of the blanket.

After conversing long about this and other homely things held close to our hearts, Anna looked to me and said: "Tom, I need to ask a boon of you."

I glanced at her, lifting an eyebrow. So surprised was I that a rising star such as Anne, Marquess of Pembroke, could ask an ordinary court official such as me for a favour.

"Aye, Anna?"

She smiled. "This is something I wouldn't ask just anyone— but I know you would do it so well."

"You have made me curious—what's this something I would do well?"

"Help me entertain the French King when he arrives at Calais."

"Entertain King *François*? Whatever do you mean, Anna?"

But even as I asked the question, I didn't doubt for one moment that she already had a firm idea on what she wanted.

"I had in mind to arrange a revel based on the hunt of the white hind. It would do me a great service if you could think hard on it, so to compose one of your beautiful sonnets for this performance."

I laughed, bowing to her.

"How can I refuse, Anna, when you but honour me? I will attempt to do my best to compose something suitable."

Alas, too soon we realised that it was time to part. Indeed, the darkening of the skies outside the chamber's window told us that it would be soon time to prepare for the evening revel. Thus, I kissed her hand again and took my leave.

Sometimes, it seems to me, even with the best intentions, a poet cannot prevent his hand from writing other that what he planned. That is what happened as I tried to write the sonnet Anne had asked of me. What appeared on the paper had suddenly materialised from deep inside of me, something deeply personal, something that I doubted I would enjoy sharing with one and all:

Who so list to hunt, I know where is an hind,
But as for me, helas, I may no more:
The vayne travail hath wearied me sore.
I am of them that farthest commeth behind;
Yet may I by no means my wearied mind
Draw from the deer, but as she fleeth afore,
Fainting I follow. I leve of therefore,
Sins in a net I seek to hold the wind.
Who list her hunt, I put him out of doubt,
As well as I may spend his time in vain:
And, graven with Diamonds, in letters plain
There is written her fairer neck round about:
Noli me tangere, *for Caesar's I am;*

And wild for to hold, though I seem tame.

"Yea, touch me not," Anna had said to me long ago, "for I belong to the King." Aye—to the King! Nay. I could not give this sonnet to Anna. Carefully I folded it, over and over again, and put it into the box where I keep all my songs for my dark Lady

The kings of France and England arrived in Calais on the twenty-fifth of October. Anne remained within the castle walls while the English welcomed *François* in grand style. Nevertheless, *François* sent to Anne a costly present, a large diamond rumoured to have a value of more than three thousand pounds.

While Henry Tudor was busy welcoming his brother king into his domain, Anne oversaw the preparations for the royal banquet fixed for the Sunday evening, and putting the final touches to the entertainments prepared for the French King. In the castle had been readied a great room, decorated with cloth of silver and many gold garlands of precious gems hanging upon the walls. The tableware was to be gold plate, and the feast prepared was a mixture of popular French and English dishes favoured by both kings. However, Anna was not with us when we ate what we could of this seemingly endless array of food. Verily, it was not until after we had finished eating the final course that Anne and her ladies—one of them her sister Mary—emerged from her rooms, all of them masked. Gold and silver seemed to be the colours for this night's work, for Anne and her six attendants were fantastically apparelled in loose overdresses of gold and silver cloth. I applauded loud with the court as they arrived on the dance floor.

Each lady chose a French nobleman to begin the evening's dance with. *François* was himself escorted out onto the dance floor by Anne, and there they danced several dances. At least three of the dances were arranged to music composed by a well-known royal hand.

King Henry, I could not help but notice, was puffed up with pride, as he watched his future bride dance with such utter grace and charm, making such a lovely picture as she partnered the French King. At last, Henry could hold himself back no longer. He went amongst the lady dancers and removed their masks, so the fair beauty of these ladies could astonish the French King and his court.

Anne, now unmasked and laughing, escorted the French King away from the floor where the dancing still continued. I watched them for many minutes as they spoke together, alone in a tiny alcove, and found myself wishing that I could hear what was said. But I could see that the French King took pleasure in her company. Verily, one time his laughter made all eyes turn towards them.

"Prithee tell, coz, do you think like I—that my sister has more in common with kings than us poor mortals denied access to Olympia? Hear me, Tom! How well I remember our childhood tutor's tales!"

I spun around to face the person by my side.

"Mary!"

We embraced, but Mary broke away, looking towards the alcove where her sister still spoke to the French King.

"Better not be seen overlong with me in your arms, Tom. You may do your self a great disservice. I hear tell from my friends that the French King calls me the 'greatest whore in Christendom.' I care not. He may have been my first lover, but he won't be my last. I am no longer a young damsel; my marriage and late widowhood take me far enough away from my father's dominion to now bed men of my own choice and desire. In truth, Tom, I have discovered a widow has more choice to live life the way they want, being no longer a wife or maid restricted by family. And I no longer believe that honey drips from the mouths of princes."

I looked towards the alcove.

"I wish Anna would not believe…"

"Aye. I know. But I admit Harry seems far more smitten than when he took me to his bed. My sister tells me she has not had the joy of the King's lovemaking. May I wish her more pleasure in his bed than what I gained as the king's mistress. Tom, I best go. If I linger much longer in your company, I will say things I rather not. And I know you would rather not hear them. I bid you goodnight, Tom."

I took her hand.

"Fare ye well, Mary. I am glad we met this night," I said.

"I am glad of it too! But if you wish to meet with me again, Tom, do not look for me in Anne's company. I have decided it best that I stay away from court. Its heat has burnt me more than once; 'tis not to my liking to place myself in danger of more hurt. Verily, Tom, I am but a simple woman—happiest when with my children and friends. I do not need all this,"—Mary waved her hand towards the dancing courtiers—"but it seems my sister does. Fare well, Tom."

After kissing me, Mary went towards the door taking her back to the private chambers of the castle guests. Thinking, I watched her. Mary's loose gold and silver gown shimmered and glittered bright in candlelight, but dulled as she moved deeper into the shadows. I felt I gazed at some beauteous moth, which knew not to dance too close to the flame. That was the last I saw of Mary in Calais.

Soon, it became time for the French King to return to his kingdom. King Henry went with many of his courtiers to bid farewell at the border that divided French territory from English. Once the farewells had been done, matters were put under way to get us back to England.

I too decided to return to England. More and more during the past year I had grown homesick for what I had left behind in Kent. I had been away from home far too long. There lived a young lad at Allington who was growing fast into a stranger, a boy who had been too long without a father, as too had been little Bess. Also, being with Anne—even but briefly—had made me realise how much I had truly missed her. And how truly empty I had been without those short moments in her company.

So, I gained permission from the King to resign from my duties at Calais, and return with the court to England. Thus, we all boarded the English galleons and sailed for home. And, what a crossing that was! Within hours of leaving port, a violent storm blew up, seemingly from nowhere. I had chosen to travel on one of the first galleons to leave for Dover. 'Twas very providential for us that our galleon only received the tail-end of the storm, but I saw from the deck of my craft that many of the other vessels were forced back to take shelter again at Calais.

Amongst those ships was the one carrying the King and Anne.

Chapter 2

"How like you this?"

Early in the year of 1533, I returned for a brief visit to Calais to tie up my affairs unravelled by the sudden decision to depart for England. I had made many good friends while abroad; I wished to see them, and I abided with them when I received a messenger carrying a sealed message from my cousin George. When I opened the letter I found, to my amazement, that George had written to inform me that Anne had secretly married the King on the twenty-fifth of January. George's messenger went on to tell me that his master had attended the early morning wedding, as did the bride's parents. How Uncle Boleyn must have felt! Father-in-law to the King no less.

I came home again at the beginning of February. My father was gravely ill and had sent a servant to me to request my presence at home. I arrived at Allington to find my father out of immediate danger, but still very sick and weak.

I spent as much time as I could in his bedchamber, keeping him company, and often he would talk to me regarding what had been happening at court. Of course, being in Calais for much of the last five years, I was not ill informed, especially since both George and my father had been in contact with me throughout that time with their constant letters.

However, there was a lot of information one hesitated to commit to paper, fearing that the information could land in hands other than for whom it was intended. Thus, being face to face with my father for long periods gave him the opportunity to impart all that he feared to communicate through his letters. My father, as a member of the Privy Council, had a perspective on these events that went deeper than the norm.

Since the King's marriage to Anne, great moves were now afoot to ensure its legality. Our King now attempted to remove England from the absolute power of the papacy. Furthermore, Parliament had brought into force a new statute that declared that England had the right to decide its own laws, and therefore had the right to solve for itself the kind of problems now confronting it. Verily, it was even concluded by Parliament that England would no longer recognise any other higher earthly power but that found in its own dominions.

At the end of February I felt assured that my father was recovered enough to be left, for a short time, in the care of his trusted servants. I greatly desired the occasion to visit my cousins, and see for myself how Anna and George were faring in their new status at court. Anne and the King were at this time staying at Greenwich palace, which Anne now regarded as her home. It was a cold time for travelling, but I arrived at Greenwich within a day of leaving Allington. As I got off my horse a man grabbed me from behind. I turned, putting my hand quick upon my sword, only to find myself facing George. He had grown a beard since last we met, but his eyes were still as brightly blue as ever.

"George!" I said, embracing him hard for a short moment before releasing him to look at him more closely. We had grown to be men of similar height and build. Indeed, if it was not for the fact that George was so fair and I of a darker hue, I believe others could easily take us for brothers.

George gripped my arms.

"Tom! 'Tis so good to see you, coz! You should have sent word to the court that you were coming. Anne and I would have laid out the red carpet for you ourselves."

I laughed, and embraced him again.

"No need for the red carpet, coz. Your presence is all the

welcome I desire. But, I did not know if I would be able to come, George. My father's sickness has been swinging, backward and forth like a pendulum. One moment better and the next worse again. But he has been improving for the last two weeks, so here I am!"

"Glad I am to hear your father improves. He is too good a man for the court to lose.

"What am I thinking of, cousin? Here we are standing out in this freezing weather when we could be inside talking and drinking hot mead."

With that, George quickly summoned a groom to attend to my horse, first taking off my saddlebags to pass them on to me, and then escorting me inside. Soon he took me into rooms that were obviously his chambers, for I could see his cherished lute leaning against the wall, near the chamber's large window.

"Gil," George called, to be answered by a young lad of about twelve rushing in from the connecting room.

The lad gave a quick, curious glance to me and then bowed at George saying: "Aye, my Lord?"

"We need warm drinks and food, my lad. Do you think you can arrange that for us?"

"Of course, my Lord."

"Good boy. And when you have done that I want you to prepare a bed in my chamber for my cousin, Squire Wyatt, to sleep in while he is here at Greenwich."

"Aye, my Lord." With those words the boy bowed and departed out the door we had just entered.

"Put your gear down anywhere, Tom." George gestured with his hand around his large chamber. "And sit yourself down. We have so much to talk about that we better be assured of some comfort."

I did as he told me, finding two stools near a roaring fire. There I sat, and waited for George to follow and be likewise seated before beginning to speak.

"Thank you, George. I am very happy that you wish to share

your chambers with me. It brings back so many happy memories of when we were boys. But, I hope my presence in your rooms will not cause trouble with your wife."

George barked out a sort of laugh and shook his head.

"You know—or should know, Tom—how it is between Jane and me. I would be amused, if it was issue for amusement, that we both lacked any fortune in the marriage stakes. We have shared so much from boyhood, but, do not take what I say wrongly, Tom; that is one thing I would have wished not to have shared with you... Jane stays in her chambers and I in mine. Verily, Tom, we see each other only when it is unavoidable. So, you being here in my rooms presents no complication."

I looked at George, and reached over to grip his hand.

"To declare that I am sorry about you and Jane goes without saying, George."

"And I likewise about your marriage," George replied, squeezing my hand quickly before releasing it. "But at least you got a son and heir out of Elizabeth before she turned slut behind your back..."

"Forgive me for asking, coz..." I glanced worryingly at George, being unsure how he would take this question. However, I had often wondered as to the reasons behind the failure of his marriage. "But, George, is Jane... well, does Jane... Cousin, you must know what I am trying to ask. Does she do as the mother of my son did often, and does still, so I believe?"

George looked at me and raised an eyebrow.

"Tom, do you think I would still be with her if she dared turn whore? Barren I can forgive, especially as I am as much the cause as she, not having any liking for her bed—but catch her with another man and I would get rid of her as quick you would say *Jack be Nimble, Jack be quick*. Verily, at least a great deal more quickly than the King replaced his Queen."

"Let us change the subject, George. I am sure you are like me: there are other topics I'd rather speak of than waste my breath about marriages that are not marriages. In any case, I never wrote to thank you for your message at the beginning of this year. Even though, I must admit, it came as such a shock to hear that Anne and the King were at last wed. Tell me, cousin, what came to pass to make for such a move?"

George gazed at me with surprise.

"Cannot you guess?"

"You know I have never been good at guessing games, George. Tell me the answer to the riddle, George, or I may be tempted to wrestle it out of you."

George laughed, perhaps remembering back to our childhood when he would tease me by making me guess what his secret was until I could not take it any more and would wrestle him until he at long last told me.

At last, he stopped laughing long enough to say: "My sister— your cousin Anne—is with child. And has been since December."

I stared at him, feeling my face go red with shock and embarrassment.

"What! Do you mean…?"

"Yea. When the storm returned the royal ship to Calais, my sister gave the King what he had wanted ever since he first saw her. But what good that has done both of them I do not know."

"Whatever can you mean, George?"

"The King's passion for Anne is over. Perhaps the wait was too long… Perhaps the first time had them, instead of ascending to the mountaintop, grovelling in the dirt. Who can tell? I only know that both Anne and the King had the foulest tempers by the time they returned to England… and she refuses to talk to me about it." George paused, and considered me sadly. "I think, Tom, that if the King was a less prideful man, if they both could admit to making a grand mistake; if a child had not been made that night, then there would have been no marriage…"

"So Anne has not found any happiness with her marriage to the King?" I asked.

"Oh, she is happy enough about the coming child. You know,

as I do, that Anne has always wanted a dozen children. But, aye, she wishes that things could be better between the King and her..."
He contemplated me for a very long time, so long that I became bewildered as to what he could be thinking.

Then he softly said: "I thank God that my sister has, in her life, been blessed with one day of true love."

'Twas my turn to contemplate George. He lifted an eyebrow at me and I realised with a sense of shock that Anna's and my secret had never been a secret from George,

"So, you knew?" I hoarsely whispered, clearing my throat. It felt as if I drowned in a tidal wave of repressed emotion. I looked away from him to the window close by. It was completely grey outside, and I thanked my stars that I had arrived when I did. Snow looked very close at hand. Using my sleeve, I wiped my eyes, glancing back at George.

"So, you knew." And I deeply sighed.

"It was not hard to guess, Tom. How could I not guess, especially with Anne and you both looking like you had just trespassed where you should not. But, who am I to say nay? I know, Tom, how you love my sister. I have always known.

"Where is that Gil? Surely obtaining food and drink would not take him all this time?"

George then got off his stool and went to the door, looking out.

"Ah... Here comes the good lad now. The food looks good, Gil, but hurry boy; I am starving!"

George came away from the door, closely followed by Gil carrying a loaded tray.

"Bring it over to the fire," George commanded. Gil placed the tray on a small table between us, and turned back to face George.

"I am sorry I have been gone so long, my Lord. But you should have heard the foul temper of the Master Cook! It was hard to get from him what I needed."

"'Tis no matter, Gil, the wait has been well worth it. Could you organise my cousin's gear and bed now, lad?"

"Of course, my Lord. I will get the bedding from the next chamber."

Gil bowed slightly to us both, grabbed hold onto my saddlebags, and went back into the room from which he had first emerged.

For the next hour George and I devoured the food that Gil had provided, conversing of other subjects that were safe to be overheard.

I felt not overly surprised that George knew about Anna and me. I suppose I always suspected he discerned the truth behind our uneasiness on that long ago summer's day. But, I also suspected that he knew, as I did, that such a matter needed to be left secret and seemingly forgot. Especially now that Anne was wife to the King.

Eventually we had eaten all that there was to eat and I began to feel restless to see Anna. This desire I mentioned to George, who then got up and said he would take me immediately to her. Thus, without further ado, we went out of his chambers in search of her. It did not take us long to find her: Anna sat in her chambers, listening to a young man of no more than twenty sing and play his lute. When we were announced, the exquisite music came to a halt and Anne arose from where she was sitting.

"Sweet cousin," she said, holding out both her hands to me. I hurried over to her and took her hands, bowing over them. Anna then turned to the minstrel.

"Go now, Marc. Tell my Chamberlain that I am well pleased with you. I will have you join my company. My brother, the Lord Rochford, will go with you, to tell him that I have said for you to be provided with suitable livery. You do not mind, do you George?"

Her brother smiled at her, and shook his head.

"Nay, sister. I will attend to it."

The minstrel bowed deeply, gave his thanks to her, and departed swiftly with George from the room.

Anne turned back her attention to me; she had kept hold of one of my hands and now led me over to a superbly carved harpsichord.

"Tell me, Tom, what do you think of this?" she asked.

I looked at it, sat down, and began to play. Indeed, I began to feel enraptured by the wonderful sounds it made.

Anne's happy laugh reminded me of why I was truly here, and I turned back to her.

"The instrument is simply splendid, Anne."

"It was a present from the King. The King is very generous, Tom. He even managed to find me sun-kissed apples in the dead of winter. He tells me that such desires means that I am with child."

With that remark Anne laughed again, and walked back to her chair. I stood for the moment at the harpsichord, completely transfixed by her words, and looked around at the roomful of people. It seemed to me that they all had stopped what they were doing. Verily, the household stayed silent, as if they had heard every word that had been said and now absorbed the implications. 'Twas like the motion of time had stopped for one long moment, and now stood as if frozen. But then I felt it swing back into action, and people suddenly returned to what they had been doing just before these words had been said.

I returned to where Anne was sitting to find that George had rejoined us also.

I took her hand from her lap, and quietly said: "So, dearest Anna, you are with child?"

Anne smiled brightly and gave my hand a slight squeeze before freeing herself from my clasp.

"Yea, Tom. And not with just any child, cousin. Verily, I feel in my heart this child I carry is to be a very special child."

I smiled at her, and replied with a laugh: "All mothers feel like that about their children. Especially when the child is their first."

"Yea. But not all mothers can feel that they bear a child who will one day be the glory of all England—even the heavens tell me so, Tom. I remember well the comet last year…"

Anne laughed, and George and I could but join in her laughter. Her hand then reached to touch my sleeve.

"Do you doubt me, Tom?"

For a moment, I enclosed her hand in mine, and smiled.

"What is there to doubt? Perhaps one day I will say to you that you have been proved right... My father once told me a tale about William of Normandy, who became the first William of England. His mother also felt that the child she bore would one day be great, and we know that history proved her all too right. God, perchance, gives knowledge to mothers denied to us lesser mortals."

I winked at George, and he smiled at me in return, but I could not help thinking that Anna's disappointment would be great if the babe proved to be a girl. However, after so many long years of waiting to be a mother, Anna appeared ecstatic to find herself with child. I would say nothing to darken her happiness.

"Tell me of your wedding, Anne. George's letter only gave me the barest details."

Anna's smile became subdued.

"Oh, Tom. It was not as I hoped it would be. I so wished to have my marriage with the King celebrated in full light of day at Westminster, but had to be content with being wed before the break of dawn at Whitehall... No matter, what is done is done."

"I could not help being astonished how events, when they began to move, moved so fast."

Anne placed both hands on her belly and said: "Why astonished, Tom? Surely you know that the King would not risk this child to be born out of wedlock. He has enough of bastard slips... There is no child with more right than the babe I have here to sit one day upon the throne of England.

George laid his hand on Anne's shoulder.

"Tell Tom how the King tricked the priest into marrying you."

Anne laughed again, her eyes lighting up as she looked from George to me.

"I think it was the funniest play-acting I have ever seen! The poor priest wished to see the licence before he proceeded with the ceremony. My husband, the King, assured him that the licence could be found amongst his private papers, but to send for them would cause rumours to fly and secrecy thus destroyed. The poor man had no choice but to marry us; he could not very well call his own King a liar!"

I picked up Anne's hand again.

"Anna, I have not had the chance to pass on my best wishes. Believe me when I say that I hope this marriage brings you every joy."

She placed her free hand back on her belly.

"In September I will have my joy. That is all I wish for now."

Anna arose from her chair, gently freeing her hand from mine, and walked back to the harpsichord. She began to play a slow piece of music—a piece that sounded like a lament.

I gazed at George and he at me; without having to speak one word, I knew he the same thought was in his mind, all our joys depended on what September would bring.

★

By the twenty-third of May, 1533, the ground had been prepared sufficiently for the King's marriage to Catherine to be, at long last, declared null and void. Thus the King's true and only wife was a girl who had once been my goodly playmate. Aye, unbelievably, that playmate had grown up to be Queen Anne of England.

Thus, all was put in motion for the coronation of our new Queen.

My father was still too ill to take part. This being the case, despite feeling cast down and ill at ease, I agreed to take on his duties of Chief Ewer. If I had any real choice in the matter I think I would have chosen to stay at Allington. I possessed many misgivings about Anne's marriage to the King.

Indeed, even at the beginning everything did not go smoothly. The King had been extremely annoyed to hear the barge that had been made ready for Anne had once been the royal barge of Catherine of Aragon. Anne had the former Queen's insignia removed to make way for her own: a crowned, white falcon (it was so in Anne's character to choose for herself a falcon!) with Tudor roses growing on the ground near its talons.

It soon became well known around the court that the King did not take his anger directly out on his pregnant wife. Rather he spoke harshly to Anne's Chamberlain, saying that there had been other barges available, barges that could have easily been made ready for the coronation of his new Queen. I could not help thinking that it brooked no good about his true feelings toward his wife. Nonetheless, this was still the barge used on the twenty-ninth of May, when Anne, looking completely ethereal in a gown of silver cloth, with her long black hair altogether loose and threaded here and there with the sparkle of diamonds, was rowed in great triumph to the Tower from Greenwich Palace.

All down the Thames, other similar barges escorted Anne's (or Catherine's) barge, also done up in the highest style, belonging as they did to the high nobility of the land.

Hundreds and hundreds of common folk were there also. But it was too easy to see who they supported in the "King's Great Matter." Here and there, I heard cries of "Nan Bullen, goggle-eyed whore!" but, other than those sorts of remarks, the crowds remained silent—a silence that but spoke far too loud their disapproval.

Joyful music helped to distract from this ominous note to the coronation. And there was music everywhere, from the music played aboard the barges to the music heard in the streets of London.

At last, the royal barge finished its slow journey and Anne arrived at the Tower, all its cannon firing their noisy, ear-hurting welcome. The sound of the Tower's cannon was echoed further afield—ships docked in the Thames also saluted the importance of this day by firing their guns, as did the cannons at Limehouse.

After the Tower's Constable and his Lieutenant greeted Anna and her attendants, the Constable escorted my cousin to the King. I noticed that Anne held in her hands a golden purse, which she now passed on to one of her ladies. The King frowned when he

saw this, but he came and put his hands—sparkling with jewels—
on either side of her swollen belly; bending to brush his lips for a
second to hers.

I, who closely watched all this, could not help reflecting that it
was as if the King said to all: "But for this child growing within this
belly you would not be here!"

The King took Anne's arm and began walking with her.

"How liked you the look of London?"

"My sovereign husband, I liked the city well enough—but I
saw a great many caps on heads, and heard but few tongues."

The King and his yet uncrowned Queen entered the refurbished
apartments at Westminster; the great chamber and dining room
had been specially rebuilt for these celebrations.

★

I sank my eager teeth in the soft manchet loaf, my mouth watering
for more. Casting my gaze around the dining room, I again took in
the decorations. Like all things King Henry commanded of his
servants, no expense or talent had been spared. On the chamber's
brightly coloured walls not only suspended a long, wooden frieze,
painstakingly carved and gilded with gold, depicting Bacchus and
his followers—an over-abundance of playful putti acting the part
of their audience—but also costly silk wall-hangings of royal
emblems. Everywhere I looked proclaimed this new chamber a
majestic place of wonder.

Next to me, George made a pile of rose petals, gathering them
from the thick layer strewn—intermingled with sweet smelling
herbs—across the table. Paying closer attention, I smiled to see
that he had formed a pattern of Tudor roses from the petals. I
thought he shaped a pretty design, adding greatly to the gold thread
embroidering the white damask.

Seeing me watching him, George gave an abashed laugh,
sweeping his hand over the petals. When he removed his hand, his
fashioning lay no more, but the weight of his hand had left behind

on the damask the colour of the deepest rose petal. The area in front of George now appeared streaked with blood. Not knowing why, I shivered, my heart growing cold and heavy in my chest. I took another bite from my bread.

Freed from my duties for the night, George and I sat amongst handpicked friends of the King and Anne. I was included for the most part because of my close relationship to Anne (how close, it goes without saying; I prayed for Anne's sake that the King will never, ever come to suspect). Near us, on the dais, set twelve steps higher than the four tables for guests, the royal couple relaxed for the evening—the King at his most hale and genial. That night we, the company of the royal couple, all enjoyed an elaborate meal; each course announced by a fanfare from one of the ten minstrels playing either trumpet, pipe, harp or lute.

Swallowing the last mouthful of loaf, I reached to take up a small cherry tart from the dish loaded with an assortment of fruit tarts, ignoring the fact my stomach groaned at the thought of more food. Tonight I had strived to quieten my fears by eating much and drinking deep. Dish followed yet another dish: steamed sole, roasted swan, huge sides of beef, succulent pork, venison covered with flaky pastry (one of the King's favourite dishes) sweetmeats, and then various deserts. The King's kitchens had left no room for complaint.

All through the long night I had closely watched Anna. Maybe because of her pregnancy or nervousness (perchance a combination of both), Anne ate little of the feast set before her. Rather she sat there bright eyed, drinking in everything with her eyes as if she could barely believe the events taking place. I found myself taking yet another tart to settle my unease.

★

The following day, the King and Anne spent resting up for the ceremonies on the morrow as well as seeing to the needs of the young men who would be knighted in honour of their new Queen's coronation.

Saturday arrived, with its flawless, blue-skied weather, to see all the court, either on horseback or in litters, gathered together to witness the making of a Queen. Because of Anne's goodly belly, holding all the King's hopes, a comfortable litter had been prepared for her, pulled by two white palfreys—above all picked out for this day not only for their gentleness, but also because of their training to not be startled by large crowds.

For the occasion of her coronation, Anne wore a pure white gown and mantle, both of which were trimmed with ermine. A canopy of silver cloth was carried over her litter, held by four knights of the realm, who themselves were clothed in scarlet robes. Her litter and horses, all covered with silver cloth, completed the picture she wanted aimed towards perfection. Though if Anna was striving to achieve an image of purity, I must be truthful and say her swollen belly added a wrong and jarring note.

In a comfortable litter, provided for several elderly noblewomen, rode the Dowager Duchess of Norfolk, dressed also in scarlet— the bright sunlight glittering the coronet of gold upon her head. The old lady had taken the place of her daughter-in-law, who had refused, despite her relationship of aunt to Anne, to have anything to do with a coronation replacing a very living Queen Catherine with Anne, the concubine and usurper. The Duchess of Suffolk also refused her brother's invitation to attend this day, though she used her ill health as the excuse. Even so, it was plain to those of us who lived our lives around the English court that the Duchess would have refused to attend even if she had not been sickening.

Nevertheless, despite the disapproval of many, from the ranks of nobility down to that of commoner, the whole day was full of bright colour and pageantry. Magnificent and priceless tapestries were hung along many of the main streets of London, and red wine flowed as if without end from many of its fountains.

As soon as Anne arrived at Westminster she was given food and drink; with a smile of gratitude she swiftly passed the refreshments to her attendants. Anna then left by a side door to go to Whitehall to spend the rest of the evening in the company of the King. The next day, Sunday, the first of June, was the grand finale: my cousin's crowning. On this day, Anne wore a long train the colour of royalty: purple velvet.

I could not help remembering—my eyes filling with tears I quickly blinked away—that early morning so many years ago, after we had made love for the first and only time. Then I had a vision of Anna as some sort of regal figure. I could hardly believe, even as I watched it happen before my own eyes, that it was all coming true.

The Archbishop of Canterbury, Cranmer, who had done so much to make this day possible since his appointment, anointed Anne's hands and breast with warmed holy oil. Solemnly, he placed the crown upon her head—the heavy St. Edward's crown. *Too heavy for my Anna? Oh how that question gnawed away at me.* At last, the symbols of royalty were placed in her outstretched hands; Cranmer placed the jewel encrusted sceptre in one thin hand and in her other the golden orb, dulled to seem greenish-blue in the haze of candlelight and ornamented round its middle by blood-red rubies and sapphire gems. Even from where I stood—quite a fair distance away—I could see several of Anne's nails were badly chewed. Suddenly I felt deafened with the roars of the people within the confines of Westminster, and I added my own voice—trembling with emotion—to the deluge of sound.

Anne. Anna. My beloved. My dark lady. Now the anointed Queen of all England. Queen Consort to King Henry.

The die was cast, she had once said. Aye, the game, for the moment, was won. All she needed now was to have the Prince all England prayed for and the game would be forever won.

King Harry took no part in the proceedings, but I heard that he watched closely from a screened gallery. The King would have had no cause for complaint. Anne—the girl whom Wolsey had once called foolish and an upstart—struck everybody that day in Westminster as a woman foreordained to be Queen.

I returned after the day of the coronation to my father's home for an extended stay. He was still very much bedridden and thus unable, as yet, to look after all his affairs. Despite the distance separating us from the court, I still managed to keep myself closely informed about events happening there. Despite everything that had gone before, eventuating in Anne's coronation, the King was still determined to have his new wife and Queen recognised by the papacy. George was sent again abroad; this time to Lyons, where he was one of the party of English diplomats who had gone with the Duke of Norfolk to parley with the Pope. England was still trying desperately to avoid a complete schism with Rome. However, Pope Clement's hand was forced by the pressure of the Imperial Emperor—who was the old Queen's nephew—to threaten to excommunicate the King if he did not take back Catherine of Aragon as his Queen and wife. The force of this excommunication was promised for September.

Not long after all this occurred at Lyons, my father insisted I leave his sickroom and visit the court, even if but for a short time. He felt it was important that the King forget not his loyal servants by the name of Wyatt.

While at court, I was immensely delighted to see George, who had just arrived home back from the Continent. My cousin had been sent briefly back to England so to be able to receive further instructions from the King about how he desired that they should proceed. When we spoke together, George told me of this threatened excommunication and these new demands of the Pope. When I heard all his news I could not help but laugh. As if a King who was lacking heirs would put away a wife who was due that same month to correct that very situation. However, George told me that, understandably, the English party was badly shaken by this threatened excommunication, as was, similarly, myself and most of the court. Verily, George's uncle, the very Catholic Duke of Norfolk, had taken it so badly that he had fallen down in a dead faint.

We at court were not the only ones to be shaken up by the news. All of England wondered what would happen next. For myself, I was astonished to find that the King, instead of raging loudly as he usually did, took the news as if he was more than half expecting it. Without delay, George was sent on his way back to France with a message from the King for the Duke of Norfolk to bring the English party home. Even if the King appeared to us at court to have expected this development, it was easy to see that it still worried him greatly that things had come to such a pass.

George, when he arrived home again, stayed at court to give Anne the support she needed during the final months of her pregnancy. Soon August of 1533 had come to its end, and it was September. The time was drawing near for Anne to give birth. I could not help feeling like the spouse myself (yea, if only I was!), experiencing more concern than what I had felt when Beth had brought her own children into the world. I was so worried that Anne's fragile frame might not survive the tortures of childbirth. It was easy to see that the final stages of pregnancy had been an absolute trial for her. Every time I saw her she seemed to have grown more grey and gaunt, while her belly grew and became huge. Thus, every day I lit a candle to the Madonna and prayed hard for my dark Lady's safe delivery.

At last, on the eighth of September, I received a messenger from George that informed me that at 3 o'clock, in the afternoon of the previous day, Anne was safely delivered of a daughter. A daughter! Yea, verily, how does fate laugh upon all our hopes!

I could well imagine what the King's feelings were at this time. All had been prepared for the birth of a son. Anne's lying-in-bed had once formed part of a French prince's ransom; a magnificent bed meant to welcome into the world the new Prince of England. Indeed, so much did our King believe in the birth of his *son* that it was well known two names had been put forward for the new prince: Edward and Henry. So sure had been the King, aided in his beliefs by the confident predictions of stargazers and the like, that the proclamations told all about the birth of a Prince. (I found out later, Anna herself had to alter the *Prince* to *Princess* before the proclamations were sent out.) Poor little lass—how unwelcome must she be.

But it was the child's mother who I was most concerned for. It was the mother who I loved, and have always loved. What if the King decided to blame her for this all too natural mishap?

Already it was obvious that there were gigantic cracks in Anne's marriage to the King. It was common knowledge that he had, uncaring for Anna's feelings, taken a mistress during the last months of Anne's pregnancy, even though Anne was sick and ailing. It was the main reason that George had chosen to remain at court with Anne. When Anne had discovered this affair she had gone straight to the King to confront him. This was when she was more than seven months with child—six months after her marriage in January. I think it says much about their relationship at this time that the King had told her to shut her eyes, do as her betters had done, and endure. And Anne, being Anne, refused to talk to the King for days.

George's messenger told me that the baby was to be called Elizabeth, named after the King's mother, Elizabeth of York. It was also the name of Anne's own mother, but that was of lesser importance. Nonetheless, despite the obvious and great disappointment felt by the new parents, a magnificent christening was put under way to baptise England's Princess Elizabeth, with the baby's own godfather, Cardinal Cranmer, baptising her. King Henry put on his brave face that day; he carried his new daughter around as if she was the most precious thing in the world. I suppose it may not have all been pretence. It had been a long time since he had held a baby of his born in wedlock. Verily, a healthy and living baby—even if only a girl.

If September had been the month that the King had been promised his much-wanted son, September was also the month that the King

237

faced the prospect of a very dreaded excommunication. If he was less than delighted with the birth of a daughter, I am sure it pleased the King that the Pope had somewhat relented and postponed the excommunication until November.

Stephen Gardiner, who had only recently been an ambassador at the French court, had stayed behind at Lyons when the rest of the party had been recalled. Now he was joined by another diplomat, Edmund Bonner, who had in his hand a document prepared months before in anticipation of these events—a document calling for an appeal to the General Council.

The Pope (accompanied by his two mistresses) was now with the French King in Marseilles, so it was to here that the two Englishmen went to meet with him. The meeting was a failure from start to finish. Pope Clement refused to give King Harry his appeal and refused to back away from the threat of excommunication. In all of this, our own King felt badly let down by the French King. *François* had promised to support King Henry but, on this occasion, had appeared to the English diplomats to be more interested in pandering to the Pope's desires; thus, gaining a better settlement for the marriage of his second son *Henri* to the Pope's niece *Catherine Medici*. When King Harry heard of this, he went into one of his more violent rages, verbally abusing the French King in the presence of his entire court. The King's rage was also witnessed by visiting French officials.

These officials lost no time in informing their King about what the English King had said, and the mood in which he had said it. *François'* usual even temper was shaken by these outbursts, and he replied angrily that Henry had done just about everything the wrong way. Rather than handle the matter delicately, as *François* would have done, King Henry had angered Rome with one transgression after another.

"As I study to win the Pope, ye study to lose him. Yea, ye have marred all," *François* angrily said to Gardiner.

It frightened many people in England that such things had come to pass. My poor ailing father muttered that an excommunicated King virtually meant an excommunicated kingdom, and he thanked God that He had seen fit to take my mother into His eternal care before this day. My mother, my father believed, would have had a broken heart over all that was happening and was bound yet to happen. In the worst scenario imaginable, we could all be plunged into a civil war or have another Christian king attempt to battle England's king to the death, bringing all our country to bloody war.

Thus, Parliament moved swiftly to prepare itself for all possibilities; stating that if the Pope made any move to denounce the kingdom, then all monies to Rome would immediately cease and be given over to the King for defence of his realm.

'Twas not only events over the seas that caused us great concerns. Not long after the baby Princess' birth, the situation with a woman who called herself "The Nun of Kent" reached crisis point, resulting in this woman's arrest and trial. Elizabeth Barton claimed to be a visionary, and said she had received messages from God to condemn the actions of the King. She promised that if he married Anne, he would be dead within six months of doing so. God, she said, was very displeased with the "infidel prince" of England, and King Henry would have to be prepared to face divine vengeance if he insisted in casting aside Catherine to marry Anne.

However, at her trial the Nun confessed to being involved in a conspiracy to overthrow the monarchy of Henry Tudor. Elizabeth Barton had tried to draw powerful figures into this conspiracy. Verily, she had even sent messages to Catherine, now Dowager Princess of Wales, and her daughter Mary, but Catherine wisely decided that she would have none of this plot, and her daughter followed suit—unlike Bishop Fisher, who had believed so strongly in this woman's visions that he had written to the Spanish Emperor encouraging him to invade England.

From what I gathered from the gossip at court, her trial ran wild with savage emotions. Many people there often cried out: "Burn her! Burn the witch!"

However, there were other people who had begun to regard the poor, misguided woman as some kind of saint; saying that she was like an English Saint Bridget or a Saint Catherine of Sienna. Thus, the King, wisely in this case, moved very carefully, though the woman was eventually burnt at the stake.

Not long after this mad woman's arrest and execution, George and I followed Anne into her chambers after an afternoon spent at the hunt.

Coming into her rooms, we saw her standing still, looking down at an opened book placed on a small table. Anne's usually clear brow puckered up into a frown, and it was clear that something she saw in the book worried her.

When George and I approached her, she glanced at us, and lifted up her eyebrows.

"George and Tom, look what I've found here."

Anna gestured to the book. It suddenly struck me that she had no wish or desire to touch it. She laughed, lifting up her chin.

"So, I see some kind soul wishes to provide me some light reading material."

Going to the table, I picked up the tiny manuscript, to see that it was none other than the Book of Oracles, the ramblings of the so-called Nun of Kent. It had been left open to the page predicting Anne's eventual death by fire—the death already suffered by Elizabeth Barton not long after Anne's marriage to the King.

"And what do you say, Tom? Should I be afraid?" Anne asked me. She stood there before me, looking down at her hands placed together, palm to palm.

"Nay. If I remember rightly, this book also predicted that the King would be dead six months after divorcing Catherine. Well, Anne, six months have come and gone, and the King is still hale and hearty."

Anna sat on a stool with her head tilted to one side. Her dark eyes, so very pained, hinted that she wished to be somewhere, anywhere other than where she now found herself. For an instant,

I remembered the young deer we had hunted down in the forest only an hour before. When it had collapsed from exhaustion, finally run to ground by the dogs, it had looked at me with the same expression I now saw in Anna's eyes.

In a voice suggesting she but spoke the thoughts going through her own head, Anna said to no one in particular: "I wonder if the person who left this book here was the same person who left this book in my chambers before I married the King. I suppose it must be so."

"This is not the first time you have seen this rubbish?" I asked her, holding out the book to her.

"Nay, Tom. You remember, George, when I found another book, twin to this one?" She turned to look at George.

"Yea. I remember." George came and took the book roughly from my hands. "And as I did then, I do now."

With a savageness so unlike him, George tossed the book into the fire. We all watched silently as the flames began to take a firm hold on it. The parchment turned brown, then black, and at last began to turn to ash before our eyes.

Anne let out a great sigh, and I glanced over to her to see she had wrapped her arms around her body, as if she suddenly had grown very cold.

George, too, had looked up at her sigh. He now moved over to her and put his arm around her thin shoulders.

"Do you remember what you said when you first saw that accursed book?"

Anne leaned on him in a kind of half embrace. It reminded me so much of when they were children, and how Anne would seek out her comfort by being close as she could to him.

"My brave words, George?" she replied, looking up at him with half a smile.

"Yea, your very brave words. Were they not to the effect that no matter what the future would bring, you would not turn one bit from the course set before your eyes?"

"You remember my words better than I do, George. But I was big-bellied with Elizabeth. Knowing that the near future held in store my child, thinking my daughter would be my son… it made me braver than I feel now."

She sounded so sad that I too tried my best to comfort her.

"Take heart, Anna. That book is worthy only to feed a fire. 'Twas written only with the intention to do what it is doing now: destroy your peace of mind. Surely, you realise, Anna, that is the only reason why it was placed where you would see it?"

Anne looked at me fleetingly, and nodded.

"That I well know, Tom. 'Tis painful that I am hated so. 'Tis strange, coz, so very, very strange. The first time I saw that book, I laughed. Even more when George threw it, as he did now, into the fire. But now sometimes I find it so hard to shake off this sense of impending doom…"

And Ann began to cry. George put both his arms around her, saying quietly: "Nan, please don't. I hate it when you weep."

Of all the bad timing, Jane, George's wife, chose this moment to come into the room. Jane was a stern-face young woman, with little to recommend as regards to her appearance. When she saw Anne in her husband's arms, her face screwed up in a grimace of deep jealously.

Even so, she soon recovered herself, and curtsied.

"Madam. The Chamberlain has asked me to tell you that the King, your husband, wishes you to attend him."

The way Jane uttered the words *your husband* instantly made me focus more of my attention onto her. Jane's eyes were fixed on George with a look speaking of anger and jealously—even hate. It reminded me how my wife Bess sometimes gazed at me.

"I must not let him see that I have been crying. I cry too much, he says."

Anna quickly went over to the bowl of water placed in her room, and splashed water all over her face. "Can you please help me get ready, Jane?"

242

"Of course, my Grace." Jane looked away from her husband and again curtsied, following Anne as she went into the next room, the Queen's bedchamber.

George's eyes followed his sister, and then looked piteously at me. I had noticed all the time I had watched Jane that George had taken not one jot of notice of his wife. I could understand that. We both had more important things to worry us than the care of Jane's spiteful feelings.

"What can we do?" he asked.

"There is nothing much we can do, but try to be always there for her," I replied.

And that we always tried to be.

Chapter 3

"But all is turned, thorough my gentleness,
into a strange fashion of forsaking."

In January 1534, three months after the birth of Elizabeth, Anne was overjoyed to find herself again with child. With Elizabeth's birth, discovering no true fulfilment in her marriage to the King, Anna realised being a mother would allow her another kind of fulfilment. Thus, the thought of another child so soon filled her with considerable delight. Verily, Anna often said to me after Elizabeth's birth, that children were the world's greatest consolation for every grief that life could bring. Yea, that she was to have yet another child made Anna very happy.

Being so happy made Anne desire the happiness of others, and the first person she thought of was her stepdaughter, the seventeen-year-old Lady Mary.

Lady Mary was now with her new sister's household and very unhappy (understandably) at where the events of the past years had led her. Thus, Anne told me she was determined to do her best to make things up with her, even going so far as to say that, if Mary would meet her half way, she would not have to walk behind her at court, but rather walk alongside her as her near equal. Thus, at the end of March, Anne with her household, which included me at this time, came down from the court to visit her daughter Elizabeth at Hatfield.

On our arrival, Anne, who understood how strongly Mary felt about her, made no effort at first to converse with the newly usurped Princess, who was now forced by the King to be at the beck and call of her new sister's household. Rather, Anna expressed her hope to me that by going slowly she would achieve a more lasting and satisfactory solution for all concerned.

Verily, for a long time now, Anna had suffered terrible confusion and indecision about what to do regarding the state of "war" that presently existed between herself and the Lady Mary. I know for certes, being in Anne's and George's confidences, that Anne carried around a great deal of guilt on Mary's behalf. Indeed, more than anything else at this time, when she was so full of hope for the future, Anne wished to make things better between them.

The next morning after our arrival, a morning that began bright and sunny, promising (so falsely as events soon proved) a joyful beginning for our stay, started with an early Mass. This Mass saw the attendance of both Anne and her stepdaughter Mary. When the service was over, Mary arose and made a brief curtsy to the altar, close by to where Anne was kneeling, then in silence departed from the chapel. Anne, deep in prayer with her dark head bent, remained unaware of her stepdaughter's departure. However, one of Anne's ladies had taken notice of her curtsy and mistook it for a curtsy to her Queen, and did not hesitate to comment on it to Anne soon after the service. When Anne heard that Mary had so honoured her in the chapel she clapped her hands, overjoyed. Now Anna hoped she could achieve the solution she desired to end this very bitter situation.

Thus, Anne sent one of her ladies to Mary, to verbally tell her this message: "The Queen salutes your Grace with much affection and craves pardon, understanding that at your parting from the oratory you made a curtsy to her, which if she had seen, she would have answered with the like. She desires that this may be an entrance of friendly correspondence, which her Grace shall find completely to be embraced on her part."

The Lady Mary was enraged by this olive branch now offered to her by the Queen. Saying that she knew of only one Queen, meaning her mother, and that her Lady mother, the Queen, could have sent her no such message since not only was the Queen forbidden to communicate with her daughter but she was simply too far away to send this type of communication. The Lady Mary even went on to say that any friend of Anne Boleyn was no friend of hers, and she would no longer waste any more of her time speaking to one so mistakenly loyal to Anne.

Thus ended that very brief interview.

I could see Anna was hurt, embarrassed, and extremely angry when her lady brought back the Lady Mary's message.

I stood by in an alcove, warming myself with the sunlight coming through its windows, and watched Anne as she stalked up and down her chamber. My cousin was wringing her hands and looking utterly white with indignation.

Suddenly she stopped stock still, crying out to all of us in the room: "One day, I shall bring down that girl's high spirits." Abruptly the room lost the sway of the sunlit day and seemed to be overcast with grey. I could not stop myself from trembling; 'twas as if someone had just walked over my grave.

I lived thereafter, day by day, in more great fear of what the future would bring.

All Anne's hopes for reconciliation with the lady Mary had been shattered by these events. Verily, Anne was made instantly depressed, and deeply so, by this incident. Even when she played with her baby daughter one could detect the sudden change in her spirits.

We left Hatfield not long afterwards, but 'twas a different journey back to court than the one we had experienced in going. Then Anna had reminded me of Anne of old: very gay, sparkling with health and good spirits. Now she rode with her head bowed in silence and took no notice of the beauties of the world around her. Leaving her small daughter behind had not helped. Anna told me it had broken her heart when the King had insisted on the baby Princess having an establishment of her own. Of course, Anna understood that it was healthier for her to be away from court. Knowing this had made the separation a little easier for Anna to deal with, but it was hard for any new mother who had just had her arms filled to have them made empty again. Verily, before the move of the Princess to her own establishment at Hatfield, Anne greatly annoyed the King by spending every possible moment with her daughter. Even if was just to place the tiny girl on a cushion, to watch her kick and gurgle in the way that any healthy infant would.

At long last, we arrived back at Greenwich. Anne looked dreadful at this stage, grey-faced and haggard. I could not prevent myself from moving through the members of her household, so to go near her, hoping that my presence would lend some sort of moral support.

When I arrived at her side, I whispered to her: "What ails you, Anne?"

Anne looked at me with frightened eyes, but said nothing. 'Twas as if she was greatly afeared to tell me what afflicted her. She turned to her ladies and asked to be taken with haste to her chambers.

Later, that same night, one of Anna's ladies told that the Queen had miscarried of her new baby.

The King was at this time at Hampton, whilst we had returned to Greenwich. A messenger was sent posthaste to him, but the King came not and the messenger returned to us empty handed.

The King's silence said so many things.

Almost a week passed and I requested and was given permission to go and see Anna. If I had been shocked when I had seen her in Calais more than a year ago, I was more shocked now. She was still very much abed. Her skin had taken on a yellowish hue and one could clearly see the fine bones etched beneath the thin surface. She looked like she had aged ten years or more since I last lay eyes on her. Days before I had heard from George—who had come to be by her side even if the King chose to remain at Hampton—that she had lost a great amount of blood. Indeed, the bleeding had been so uncontrollable at one stage, her doctors feared for her life.

247

When Anna saw me, she held out her hand for me to take.

Years ago I had told her that her hand was cold; today it was dry and felt hot with fever. Her ladies, so used to seeing me in conversation with Anna, were far enough away from us that we could talk without restraint.

Thus, I was not too surprised to hear her softly say: "Sweet Tom, always here for me when the King comes not near."

"Yea, dear heart. That I will be for always," I vowed to her in a whisper.

Her eyes shone with tears and she turned her head away from me, closing her eyes. For a moment I thought she had gone to sleep, but then I saw the tears running down her face. I could see from her expression that she was struggling hard to control herself. I tried to find some words of comfort. Some words to help stop the flow of tears.

"There will be other babies, Anna," I at last said. Next thinking savagely to myself, *What empty words of comfort were these?*

It did not surprise me greatly when I heard her say: "Oh, Tom! You cannot begin to understand." Anne turned her dark head to gaze at me again.

I sighed, and squeezed her hand.

"Anna, you do me wrong. Forgive me my words. Sometimes, even with the best of intentions, I say things that I wish I could call back. Tell me all that ails you, dear heart. All I want is to be able to help you, to be here for you. Let me, Anna, try my best to understand."

She wiped away her tears, grimacing as she said: "Tommy, you are a man. You mean well, I know, but just like a man you say that there will be other babies. Even George said those same words to me yesterday morning before he left to return to the court. Only a woman could understand how much this baby meant to me. Only two weeks ago I felt it quicken inside of me for the first time and I rejoiced, Tom, thinking that my child was growing and living within me. Now it has been cast out of my body, perfect in every way except that it was far too early for my little one to be born. I dared not tell the King that it was his Prince. Oh, God! Oh, dear God! What care I for that? The babe was my son—my baby son. And he is dead! Dead! Oh, Tom, I have lost him. My little boy, Tom!"

With those final words, she crumbled before my eyes and began to cry out loud; so loud that all her ladies came rushing over to her. One of them took me aside firmly leading me to the chamber's door.

"Go now. Our poor Queen needs time to rest and grieve in peace."

So I left, my body shaking for all the misery that I had just left behind.

I acknowledge that my own history as a husband is nothing to speak of. I acknowledge that to maintain good sympathy between husband and wife is rarely an easy thing. But in the early days, when I tried to do all that I could to encourage the growth of sympathy, if it could not be love between Elizabeth and I, I would never had treated Bess like the King now treated Anne. I remember that for both Elizabeth's babies I was home to greet their births. Even when I began to harbour grave misgivings about my wife. Verily, I am sure of the first being mine, as he was conceived that first dreadful night, but the girl? Not long after the birth of my son Tom, I had begun to suspect that Elizabeth had taken to playing harlot in my absences.

But I will speak no more of my own doomed marriage.

My dearest Anna lay sick and the King made his feelings plain by staying firm at Hampton palace.

Not long after my first visit to Anne's sickbed, one of her ladies came and told me that Anne requested that I come again to her chambers with my lute. So I took my lute out of its case and followed Anna's woman back to the Queen's chamber. Anne sat up in her bed, cradling tightly her own instrument. As I entered the chamber, she gazed agitated at me.

"I cannot play, Tom. My fingers... Oh, Tom, my fingers refuse to do as I tell them," she said, her dark brown eyes looking bright and enormous, still feverish in her too-thin face.

The woman, once she led me to Anna, retired to the other side of the room where she sat down, picking up some discarded sewing. This elderly woman was the only other person in Anne's bedchamber. Thus, as the woman was seated far enough away from us, Anna and I had another opportunity to talk freely.

"Dear heart, of course you can still play. 'Tis just that you're so weak at the moment. Let me take your lute and put it back on its stand. Then I will come back and let my fingers and voice do what they will for you."

So I took her lute gently from her hands, handing her mine in its stead, and carried it over to the window where there stood a stand for it. I returned to Anna to find her cradling my lute as she had hers, like a newborn child. I stared at her, my heart cold with fear. What if the events of the past week had broken her in a way that was irreversible? I tried to break the mood by speaking with a cheerfulness I did not feel.

"I have a new song for you, Anna. 'Tis a tune from Ireland, and I have no doubt that you will enjoy it."

I took my lute carefully out of her arms, tuning it before I began playing this merry melody I had recently learnt to amuse my son. Tom loved music but as yet had little success in the making of it himself. It was one of those songs that had been composed by an Irishman to make fun of others of his race. Thus, it was full of insights that rang true and could not help but amuse. Especially since Anne and I both have Irish blood running through our veins.

When I finished my song I looked closely at Anne, her eyes were still bright, but now it seemed the brightness of amusement. I began to relax. Perhaps Anna could be healed of this new grief.

"You must promise to teach me that song, Tom. When Elizabeth is older I will play it for her."

"When you are well I plan to teach you many new songs. I might even teach you some of my own new songs, but only if you promise to be a good girl and get better as quick as you can."

Her smile disappeared and she looked again the very sick Anne that she had been minutes ago.

"Oh, Tom. Don't speak to me as if I am a child. My life is so full of adult problems that I can never feel myself a child again. Cousin, if you would know the truth, sometimes I think that it would have been better if I had died when Elizabeth was born." She said this very quietly, in a voice suggesting she struggled, with great difficulty, not to cry again.

"Anna! Sweetheart! What an utterly dreadful thing to say!"

"I tell you, Tom, 'tis only the truth. If I had not had grown to love my little girl, I could easily have let myself die when I bore my dead boy into the world. But I do so love my beautiful Elizabeth. More than I could ever have imagined possible. I cannot, and will not, leave her alone in this world with only a father who curses her every time he sees her, curses my sweet daughter just for being born not the Prince he desired!"

I laid my hand upon hers, gripped hard upon the bed's coverlet.

"You only speak like this because you are sick. When you are better you will see things in a different light."

"Nay, Tom. I speak like this because I know the King, and I know my husband no longer has any care for me."

"But…" I tried to say something to reassure her, but Anne quickly broke in.

"Tom! You do not need to find falsehoods to explain how the King deals with me. I have long known and faced up to the truth! The King's great love is no more. And I like not that I am only the vessel for his royal seed—a breeding mare he services, not even hiding that he finds the chore distasteful. Harry does not care that I am flesh and blood and hurt. Sweet Jesus, Tom! My life is agony!"

I had felt my face redden with her confidences, but, nevertheless, I felt also comforted that Anna was so close to me that she could freely express her most private thoughts. I glanced over to Anne's lady, to find that the old woman had gone to sleep in front of the fire. We were then completely alone, thus I felt able to ask her something that had long bewildered me.

"Anne, why, after wanting your love all those long years, did the King stop loving you?"

She looked silently at me for a long moment, and then whispered: "I believe, Tom, that his feelings for me started to change when he began to believe that I came to him not a virgin. I told you long ago that you branded me well. Never did I realise that the branding would be suspected by the King."

I could not believe what I just heard, but finally sputtered, "Oh, Anne! Sweetheart! What can I say?"

"There is nothing to say, dearest Tom. All of this is of my own doing and making… But, Tom, if I have regrets, you are not one of them. Long ago you showed me what it was to truly love. The memory of that one day of love, of how it should be between a man and a woman, is all that I have to sustain me when the King ruts himself upon my body. Your face, Tom!"

Anne hysterically laughed, and then hiccupped in her attempt to stop laughing.

"Tommy! Your face! Here you are thirty, and still you blush like a boy! Oh, Tom! I am so sorry for having burdened you so! But you are the only one I can speak of such matters to. Dearest Tom, we have made ourselves too sad; let us see if your lute can cheer us up again!"

So, nothing more to say, I played to make us forget all that saddened our hearts.

Another week passed and Anne was well enough to travel by litter to Hampton. In all, more than two weeks had passed since her miscarriage. Those of us who had cared for her during this time could not avoid the stark reality that she had received no personal message from the King since then.

Anne was extremely pale and drawn, still very much the convalescent; thus, we took the journey slowly and with many rests, hoping not to tire her unduly. However, too soon we arrived at Hampton. Anne's ladies assisted their Queen out from her litter. I could see that Anna had spent the last leg of the journey making what repairs she could to her haggard appearance. In my opinion, the heavy, white powder only worsened her look of illness. Anne shook away the helping hands of her attendants; forcing herself to walk upright and erect up the flight of stairs that led into Hampton Palace. I followed Anne from a distance, and wondered what welcome we would have from the King.

It did not take us long to discover that the King was nowhere to be found. Indeed, the King's Chamberlain soon informed us that the King was out hunting with members of his court. Anne seemed to be relieved; more than that, it was if a terrible weight had just been taken off her shoulders, and she retired, for the moment, to her chambers.

I gained Anna's Chamberlain's permission to leave the Queen's company, and went to seek out George. He had returned to Hampton after he had assured himself that his sister's life was no longer in imminent danger. He had felt it was important that there be someone in the King's household who served best the Queen's interests.

I found my cousin in his chambers, sitting with his lute near the fireplace, strumming and humming to himself.

"Tom!" he said, stopping his playing when he saw me enter his rooms.

I walked over to where he sat near a window, and pulled up a stool to sit near him.

"You have led me such a search, cousin! I did not expect to discover you here, all alone in your chambers. If it was not that I found Giles running his errands for you, and got out of him where to find you, I think I would be still looking high and low for you."

George's fingers strummed idly again at his lute, and then gazed bleakly up at me.

"I had no wish this day to pander myself to the King and his court. How is my sister, Tom? Will she return soon?"

"Did you not hear that we were coming here? Anne is back in her chambers now."

"What!" George jumped up from his chair.

"Yea… We have been back an hour or more. Anne is resting, before she need face the King."

George sat back down, and the bleakness returned to his face.

"Face the King… Aye, things have come to such a pass that my sister need fear to face the King…" George put his lute on the floor. He seemed very depressed, and I wondered what other grim happening had taken place during our absence.

"Anne does not feel herself very secure." I sighed, and picked up from the floor George's lute and began to slowly play the Irish melody that had lightened Anne's spirits.

George touched the strings and said: "Peace, Tom. I find I cannot take any joy in music today."

He then tilted head to look up at the ceiling, and raised both hands to cover his face.

"Sweet Jesus, what am I to do?" he moaned under his hands.

I got off the stool, putting aside George's lute, and went to kneel near my cousin. I lay my hand on his arm and asked, "George! Tell me, cousin, what can it be that so troubles you?"

He took his hands away from his face and looked down at me. His blue eyes were extremely bright as if tears hung there, ready to flow loose.

"My sister loses her babe and almost loses her life, and what does the King do? Come to her side to comfort and console her? No! Does he send a message of love and sympathy? No! What does he do when my sister is near death? What else does the King do but find another woman to favour with his clumsy bed sports. Yea, Tom! Yea! That is what the King has done while my dearest sister is sickened with the loss of their son. Tom, I think I begin to detest the King." He had harshly only whispered those final words, but I still stood up and looked around to ensure that we were safely alone.

"Oh, George. We must tell Anne before some other person does. She is so sick and hurt, that if the wrong person blabs, I feel she will lose her reason completely."

"Aye, Tom." George stood up from his stool, and walked over to his bed to take up his cloak. "You are right, 'tis best we two tell Anne."

But we were too late. Some person had taken much pleasure in gleefully informing their sick Queen about the King's new mistress. Thus, Anne had rushed to angrily confront the King, now returned from hunting, with the result that they had the worst argument of their marriage. The King had ended this interview by violently pushing away his very fragile and ill wife and saying as he left the room: "You have reason to be content with what I have done for you, and I would not do it again if the thing was to begin again. Consider, woman, where you have come."

George and I arrived in time to pick up the fragmented pieces of a woman whom we both so loved.

Chapter 4

"Busily seeking continual change."

The King and Anne were very good at play-acting. Thus, it appeared to those who were not close to them that their marriage swiftly returned to normal. The King would say to all and sundry that Anne was the best of wives, while she searched long and hard for more gifts that would be pleasing to the King, her husband.

But long months would pass before there was any sign of a new baby.

George and I remained close to court, both of us very concerned for Anne's well being. Her sudden bouts of hysteria, which I remembered so well from her breakdown over Hal, as well as make her fresh enemies, often threatened to destroy any chance she had of reclaiming the King's shallow affections. Though the making or breaking of the King's marriage was not the only event I had any concern in. My own life too had its share of drama.

'Twas not long after Anne's miscarriage that I was walking through some alleyways of London at dusk. Suddenly, I turned a corner to be confronted by some drunken, brawling men-at-arms. Seeing that one of the men was someone I knew, a guard who I sometimes spoke to at Greenwich, I went up closer to break them apart. Another man suddenly appeared on the scene. He must have thought I wished join the foray, because, before I knew what was happening, I had a man crouched before me, snarling and with a glinting dagger in his hand. I fast drew out my own dagger—wishing desperately that I had kept myself out of this predicament—and was soon engaged in fighting for my very life.

The man immediately went for my throat. I bent back my upper body as far I could from his fast approaching knife, and stepped to the side. I then swung my own dagger up, to feel it go into the soft flesh of his belly. Frightened, I yanked the weapon out. Blood spurted out all over me, and I dropped my dagger in disgust. The man crumbled before me, emitting a scream that would have done justice to a fury straight from Hades, and I watched helplessly with shock as his life's blood poured out of his body, into the dirt and mud at my feet.

Holy mother of God, I thought. *I never meant to kill the man!* The noise of the brawling and sudden death had brought more men running to see the fun, including a troop of Sergeants of London. One of them came up to me; standing over the newly-dead man; he bent and turned the body face up.

"Look who we have here! 'Tis Black Jack!" he cried to his mates, casting a wary glance at me.

I began to think frantically: a friend of the man I killed? What if he decided to seek revenge? And here was I, with my dagger lying on the ground, too far for me now to reach without drawing their attention. I cursed myself for being the biggest fool born under God's Heaven. Why did I ever see fit to leave my lodgings this evening? More importantly, why did I leave my sword behind? The only weapon left to me was my tongue, so I began, in earnest, to use it.

"By all the Saints in Heaven I did not mean for this to happen! I tell you, it was an accident, if it was anything! The man came at me with a knife. What else could I do but defend myself?"

The man straightened his form and wiped his bloody hands upon his tunic.

"That sounds like Jack—fight first, ask questions after. But he is dead, and you are alive, so needs be that you may have to pay some penalty for being the winner of this fight."

"What in God's good name do you mean?" I asked him, feeling like the situation was worsening with every new moment.

The man shook his head, and pointed at the still form at our feet.

"There is a dead man, mister, and though the City of London will always have a place for dead men, I am a Sergeant of London who tries hard to do his duty. And my duty now tells me 'tis best that you are taken to the Fleet, and let my superiors decide what best to do with you. But fear not; Jack was well known to us. Drink always gave him an evil temper, and many a man will thank God at his just passing. But justice needs to be done, so we will have you as our guest, but rest yourself easy. I swear to you, good sir, you'll not regret giving yourself freely over to our care. I doubt your visit at Fleet will be a long one, of that I can assure you. Jack was no friend of ours."

The man before me was an easy man to be reassured by. Thus, without further ado, I allowed myself to be taken to the Fleet— feeling certain that my status at court would, in any case, make certain that my stay in the gaol would be a short one.

This proved to be the case, and I,—with less coin in my pocket but somewhat wiser about concerning myself in brawls where I had no business—was soon on my way back to Kent and home.

In June, my increasing estimation in the King's eyes was proved furthermore by his granting to me, for my lifetime, the command in time of war of all the able-bodied men of the counties of Kent. The King even went so far as to approve my request that I have a small band of men dressed in my own livery.

My climb upon the ladder continued even higher the following year, for at the beginning of that year I was made High Steward of the West Malling in Kent. And then, the most glorious honour of all: I at last gained my knighthood at Easter.

After my knighthood, I returned to my home, and it was not until the summer of 1535 that I was commanded by the King to accompany the court on a progress to Severn and then down to Hampshire. When I made my return to court, I was relieved to find that Anne was somewhat restored to the King's favour. Verily, when the King and Anne were together it seemed to me that this progress was for other reasons than the official one given. It was as if they had selected this time to rediscover each other and make anew their tottering relationship. Indeed, sometimes the King and Anne were as merry as when they were first courting.

Verily, the whole progress had with it a feeling of a happy holiday. But then, perhaps this too was easy to understand; Anne and the King were engaged in pursuits that they both enjoyed to the full: riding and hawking in the best possible weather. Aye, this was a joyful and restful time for us all. It did not even seem that the King was overly concerned about dealing with state business.

In September though, we stopped for a while at Winchester, where Anne watched with much delight the consecration of not only Hugh Latimer, but two other of her favourite clerics as Bishops. Anne had told me, so long ago, that she saw the King's passion for her as a way for the new religion to take deeper roots in England. Much of her time as Queen she spent ensuring that this would indeed be the case.

After the consecration of the Bishops, the court went to stay at Wolf Hall, the family home of the Seymour family. The King spent some of his time there dealing with the official business that had proven to be unavoidable, but still the holiday feeling lingered on. Around Wolf Hall were wondrous hunting woods, and many of our days there were spent, either on foot or on horse, hunting after all sorts of wild game.

Anne and I enjoyed these days to the full, but the King came not, and I wondered what matter of importance could be keeping him from the hunt.

Little did we know that the King had found other game to pursue without having to venture out of doors. And, perchance, the pursuing was not only on the part of the King.

One day, while we were chasing our quarry, the weather began to take a nasty turn. Most of the party that had gone to hunt with the Queen decided, after looking at the grim, grey clouds coming fast over the far horizon, to back up their tracks to where they had first set out not long before.

I rode my horse alongside Anne's, and we, not caring for the increasing strength of the wind or the darkening of the sky, allowed our horses to move slowly along the paths that took us back to Wolf Hall. Soon we were far behind the rest of the company.

Anne was dressed this day all in green. No longer in masculine attire as I remembered from our youth and childhood, but upon her dark hair (tightly plaited around her head, and thus in no danger of escaping) she wore an over-large cap—a cap I would swear to have seen upon the head of the King only days before.

Despite the rain beginning now to drizzle, and the skies that became more and more dismal, we had no sense of hurry, no urge to make quick our return. Verily, Anna and I had ridden our horses in our youth and childhoods in worse weather than this. Thus, we were content to allow our horses to choose the speed that they would like to trot. This leisurely ride also gave us an opportunity to talk together, an opportunity fast becoming something of a rarity, so difficult was it to gain a moment of privacy in our hectic lives at court.

"See how swiftly the rabbits run!" Anna said, laughing, gesturing her head slightly not to the ground but to the retreating backs of the courtiers, as Urien, her wolfhound, began to sniff out the nearby foxholes.

I laughed with her, but noticed that we indeed were being fast left far behind. Inside of me began to grow a surge of warmth and contentment.

Hold still this moment. Hold on tight to it. Treasure it. Remember it. As you will always treasure and remember that other summer's day when you thought you had gained part of your heart's desire. So much has turned and changed since that day became but a cherished memory. Verily, 'tis not often now that you are so utterly alone with her—this woman beside you who has always held your heart.

I looked at Anna, held onto her vision of loveliness with my eyes, and said: "Do you remember how many times you and I came home to Hever completely drenched from our rides together, Anne?" Being thus alone with my beloved, I could not help but feel very nostalgic for other times long past, even Urien made me remember Pluto, Uncle Boleyn's long dead wolfhound, a dog so loved by his youngest daughter.

That daughter glanced at me, and smiled.

"Yea, Tom. I remember. And I remember how dear Simonette would scold us dreadfully, and make us take off our wet clothes, and threaten that we would be forbidden our horses if we came home so wet again."

"But she never did," I said with a laugh.

"Nay. She never did." Anne glanced at me again, but this time appeared both sad and reflective before beginning to speak again.

"I think Simonette knew that riding gave to me an outlet for this wild spirit of mine. Tom, you are so very lucky not be cursed with a foul temper!" She had been speaking with her eyes directed towards the track before us, but at these final words she looked wildly across at me.

I gazed at her again, and smiled to reassure her.

"I never noticed it when you were a child."

"Nay, Tom, as child there hardly ever was a reason to lose such control upon myself. Verily, when I was a child, Simonette, Father Stephen, my brother and sister, and you too, Tom, surrounded me with much love. It little prepared me not for the world that I was one day to face."

"But, if it was not for that love, Anne, what wells of joy could we look back on now? Verily, my dearest dark Lady, when I look back on our childhoods, I remember such a golden time. It is like the landscape you have left behind is filled with blessed sunlight, where everywhere you look is full of beloved things, even if the landscape you have before you is dark and unknown. I take so much satisfaction, Anna, that our beginnings were so lacking in unhappiness."

"Yea, Tom. Perchance you have the right of it. But I know that my beginnings prepared me not for disappointment and despair. And when those two things struck me down in my life, well, Tom, you know—if anyone knows—how it shaped and twisted me... I would wish, and do pray for Elizabeth, that she is wiser than I, and makes not the same mistakes as her mother."

Suddenly, it was as if the courtiers racing ahead had realised that the Queen was being left further and further behind. A group of them now swung back and began to return fast to us.

I sighed. So brief a time!

Anne gazed long at me and smiled, such a tender and loving smile that my heart caught in my throat.

Calling, "Urien!" she turned her eyes from me and moved her horse to swiftly meet up with the approaching courtiers. I stayed back, to linger, and watch her safely from a distance.

I thanked God for the rain. It did much to hide the tears now falling from my eyes.

I returned to Wolf Hall, sometime after the rest of the royal party, to discover the place in something of an uproar. It appeared that the King had been unaware of the Queen's early and unexpected arrival. The Queen then had discovered him embracing and kissing the quarry he had been pursuing during her absence. When the Queen had entered into the room, the two parties had guiltily separated from each other. Anne, it was said, spoke not one word, but turned upon her heel and returned hence to her chambers.

It astonished me utterly to hear who this quarry was. Where

once the King's vision had been enraptured by the sight of a very young falcon flying high and free, so much so that he brooked at nothing to capture it and make it his alone, now his vision remained land bound. The woman who now interested him was alike to Anne as a falcon is to a field mouse.

Jane Seymour was the eldest child of the house. Indeed, the woman must have been at least twenty-seven, thus well past her youth and not much younger than Anna. And, as for her looks! I think the King had begun to lose his eyesight! Jane was so fair and whey-faced that she seemed completely colourless. Even her eyes were such a faded blue that those "windows to the soul" were not worth a second glance. Aye, not to me at least, who had long gloried in my beloved's bright and bold beauty.

More opposite to Anne you could not get, and perhaps that is where the attraction lay. Yea, demure and utterly plain, Jane had caught the King's eye.

But Anne was still his wife, and very, very attractive on this day. I could easily imagine that it was the sight of her, when she had interrupted his tender moment with Jane, that had stopped the King from going any further with his new *lady-love*. Yea, the sight of Anna, so vividly and dazzlingly dressed in green, somewhat damp from being caught out of doors in the light rainfall, and cheekily wearing his own cap upon her head, would have made him take better stock of the situation. As it would any man with red blood flowing through his veins.

But I can honestly only speculate, even though I know that things were very different between the King and Anne after this day. Perhaps it was the guilt, or the fact that, for once, Anne had not savagely lashed him with her tongue, as she would have done in days past, or perchance, a mixture of all these things. For the moment, the King seemingly forgot the Lady Jane to lust after his own wife.

Anne plainly welcomed the King's attentions. Since her miscarriage the previous year the King's passion had been much on the wane, and she was obviously relieved that, for whatever reasons, he now frequented her bed. Thus, by the time the royal progress had drawn to its close, Anne knew herself to be again with child. And all of us who loved Anne, prayed hard that all would go right for her this time.

But bad omens haunted the land.

December had been a bad time in the county of Kent; half the crop harvests of many counties had been lost and now the spectre of famine loomed before many peasants' eyes. It was often said, even by those who should have known better, that this was the judgement of God upon the marriage of the King. Thus, this state of affairs did nothing to improve the feelings of the common people towards his chosen Queen. Verily, the King's executions of Bishop Fisher, Sir Thomas More, and the holy Carthusian monks only served to increase the people's hatred of her. It seemed to me that Anna was increasingly made the King's scapegoat for his own wrong doings.

January came, and Anne, though not having an easy time of it again, began to feel secure in her new pregnancy. And a death now came to make her feel even more secure.

Catherine of Aragon, pushed from bad abode to worse, took her final breath. Some said it was poison, sent by Anne's own hand. But I know my Anna, and speak the truth when I say nay. It was not Anne. But I know what killed the poor, noble lady. Catherine's tender heart was broken by the callous acts of the King and she wished no longer to live. For a long while she had been sickening, and she was made even sicker and more invalid by the fact that Kimbolton Castle, where Catherine was forced to make her final home, was damp throughout, being situated on the Fens, and in a dreadful state of disrepair. For a long while, knowing that this illness was likely to be her last one, Catherine of Aragon had begged sight of her daughter Mary, and the King heeded her not.

Still the poor Lady died loving him, saying, in her final letter: "I make this vow, that mine eyes desire you above all things."

Yea! Poor Catherine!

She died loving a man not fully realising that this man was no more. The King had been killed by his own selfish lust: lust for power and lust for things of the flesh. Yea, the Henry who she loved was long dead himself.

And how did the King act when he heard of this lady's death?

"God be praised," he cried to all his court. "We are freed at last of the harridan. No longer do we have to live in fear of war!"

The King believed that Catherine, fearing that her daughter's rights were in danger of being lost forever, had written to her nephew the Emperor and begged him not to hesitate to make use of his armies, if that was what it required, so to protect his cousin Mary's birthright.

Anne also was pleased to see the end of Catherine. As Catherine was afeared for her daughter Mary, so was Anne for her own daughter Elizabeth. Anna knew that as long as Catherine lived the party resolute against her would have a backbone difficult to break. But now all was different. With Catherine gone there was no one to claim that there was one who had greater right to sit by the side of the King. Thus, Anne was the only Queen in the land, the King's undisputable wife. The child within her would be born without the doubt that had shadowed over the birth of Elizabeth.

So great, indeed, was the relief of the King that he ruled that a banquet, followed by much dancing, would take place upon that same evening. And when that evening came, Anne and the King arrived upon the scene dressed all in yellow; verily, all in yellow that is except for the white feather in the silken cap of the King. Their little girl, clothed alike to her parents in a silken dress of yellow gold, also attended this night's festivities. Elizabeth arrived soon after the banquet in the arms of her governess, Anne Shelton, who was the Queen's own aunt. Anne had been right; when big-bellied with her first child, she told me that her child was to be something very special.

Verily, Elizabeth was a child born to be taken notice of. Even though only two, Elizabeth seemed to all to be an exceptionally bright and intelligent child. Indeed, the infant girl no longer talked nonsense, as other young children of that age often do, but spoke good and clear sentences. The King made much of his little girl this night. Verily, the King took the child from lady Shelton and carried Elizabeth around the room to show her to all his court—taking much delight every time he snatched off her silken cap to display to the invited dignitaries her beautiful golden red hair so much alike to the hair of his own youth. The little girl laughed in his arms, and looked with adoration up at the gigantic man who was her father. And I could not help to wonder what the future had in store for this tiny child, this girl child who had been born into the royal house of Tudor.

I glanced at Anne, who stood only a short distance from me, to see her looking on with obvious maternal pride; but then, as I watched, I saw her grimace with pain and close her eyes, as if in prayer, with her hands on either side of her belly.

Remembering her last miscarriage, I moved swiftly towards her in fright.

"Anna!" I whispered to her.

She opened her eyes, and saw me there before her. I suppose the alarm in my face must have told her what I feared, for she smiled reassuringly at me.

"'Tis alright, Tom. Truly—nothing ails me. I but prayed to God to forgive my happiness. Look at me! Many people say that yellow is the colour that the royals of Spain wear in mourning. I know otherwise! Oh, Tom! That a poor woman must die before I could be so happy! What if God punishes me…?"

I thought through my memories to find words to comfort her, and found there words of a priest long dead.

"Remember, Anna, how Father Stephen told us that God is like a good blacksmith, and during our lives he shapes us into the metal best suited for his purposes? Think not on the punishment of God;

that is not his way. Think only that we must face and deal with life as best as we are able."

Anne smiled at me again, and went as to touch me, but then suddenly looked around her, obviously remembering that all the court surrounded us.

"Thank you, dear Tom. You always know what to say to best comfort me. I am full of strange fancies, but women with child often are." She laughed softly, but her dark eyes were sad and full of melancholy. Her eyes returned to reflect on me again, and she said, "Father Stephen also spoke that our life's shaping is through the gift of suffering... that both joy and suffering go hand in hand. Tom, do think I have suffered enough? Do you think that God will wish for me to suffer more than what I already have done?"

I looked at her, and wished we were truly alone. I just wished to take her in my arms and protect her from any further hurt. But I felt I had to answer her question the best way that I was able.

"Dearest Anna. You know as I do that true joy in this world is but a brief, fleeting thing, a glimpse we are given through the doors of Heaven but a glimpse soon gone. Oh, Anne! What can I say? As long as we live and breathe there will be pain..."

Our brief conversation was suddenly broken into by the arrival of the Queen's maid, Madge Shelton, who curtsied to the Queen and said: "Your Grace, the King desires your company."

I bowed to Anne, and took her too frail hand to kiss it tenderly.

"I am grateful to have had this opportunity to speak to my Queen."

Anne smiled her farewell, and then turned to follow Madge.

I watched her as she went to where the King now stood, and decided that I had had enough of this evening's entertainments. Thus, I made my departure to my London lodgings.

The old Queen was buried with little fuss. Death at last won the King his victory, to have her assume the title of Dowager Princess of Wales. But, then, the piteous lady was now past caring.

After the funeral of the old Queen—or, I should say, Dowager Princess—the King continued his celebrations at Greenwich by arranging a joust. As usual, the King was one of the participants, and was enjoying himself to the full in the competition of manly pursuits. But, at the end of the day, the King was galloping his horse in the tiltyard when his huge, black stallion suddenly stumbled. The destrier fell heavily, throwing the King head first onto the ground. Many of us watching now rushed forward in unison, seeking to go first to his aid.

When I had arrived at the side of the King, I found Henry Norris there before me. Norris was frantically trying to remove the King's armour. I knelt beside him so to help him. I looked at Henry Norris, and felt his great fear and love for the King had driven him close to breaking point. I gently removed the King's helmet from Henry Norris' shaking hands; indeed, his hands were shaking so much that I greatly feared the King's headgear would slip from his grasp and cause more injury. Poor Norris was repeating softly, in what seemed almost akin to a cry: "My Liege! My Liege! My Liege!"

I put down the helmet to one side, and began to attend to the King's chest plate. Other Equerries of the King's body now gathered around the King, removing, piece by piece, his near hundredweight of armour.

With his helmet removed, we all could see that the King was bleeding profusely from a head wound. Verily, his forehead was much bruised and already swollen. But the King, though deeply unconscious, was obviously very much alive, for his heart beat strong and steady. All who attended him thus began to breathe a little easier.

Now that the King's armour was stripped from his body, we were able to lift his enormous form on the waiting stretcher, and carried him indoors. Doctor Butts, the King's second physician, now walked alongside us, muttering loudly to everyone his immense concern.

The King was an extremely heavy man, and, despite the fact

that there were four of us bearing the weight of the stretcher, my arms began to feel stretched to their full capacity. I glanced around myself, to see how much further we needed to go, when I saw the Duke of Norfolk suddenly break away from the horde of courtiers following us and head in the direction of Anne's chambers. Anna had felt unwell this day, and had chosen to remain inside with her attendants.

In that same instant, I felt my skin prickle in fright and premonition of doom so near I could almost touch it.

My God! Dear God! I thought. *He must be going to tell Anna. Sweet Jesus! How will he tell her? What will he tell her?*

Norfolk had a reputation for being blunt and to the point; and he, despite the fact he was her uncle, had little love for Anne. Verily, Anna regarded him as her greatest foe.

I looked quickly around, and saw a face I knew.

"Francis!" I cried, and gained his attention. "Take my pole, I beg of you. I can bear its weight no more."

Francis came at once to my succour, and took the pole from my now trembling hands.

After being released from my burden, I began to race after the Duke of Norfolk.

Within minutes I entered into the chambers of the Queen, now fast on the heels of Norfolk, to hear the bloody idiot Duke announce: "Madam! The King is dead!"

Anne was seated on a chair near the fire. It happened so quickly that I could do nothing to stop it. When she heard the Duke's foolish words, Anne, heavily pregnant, at once stood up. Too hastily, because, when she arose in panic, Anna lost her balance and fell with a resounding thud to the floor.

"No! God in Heaven, no!" I cried, and rushed over to her.

Her maids fluttered around her in fright, while poor Anne both cried and said hysterically: "The King is dead? The King is dead? I am done for. My poor babes are done for! Sweet Jesus! What am I to do?"

"Have you hurt yourself, my Queen? Have you any pain?" I asked her, trying to lift her as gently as I could from the floor. The Duke, I could not help but notice, had disappeared from the room. As if he realised, now too late, what his ill spent words had put at risk. Or, I found myself wondering, had he meant for this to happen?

"Oh, Tom! Tom! The King is dead. What will happen to my poor, unprotected babes?"

"Anne! Anna! Please listen to me! The King is *not* dead. He is indeed injured, but I am not feared for him. He is strong, and will surely recover. But what of you? Dearest girl! Have you hurt yourself?"

The woman before me looked so white that she appeared like a ghost. So great, indeed, had been her fright.

"Harry is not dead?" she said, visibly beginning to shake.

"No, Anna," I repeated. "The King is not dead!"

"Oh, Tom. I feel so sick!"

And she looked it too. I gestured to her women to come and help me, so we could take her into her bedchamber. When we had helped her stand upright, we began to escort her to her bed, but Anne suddenly shut her eyes and became even paler.

Fearing in my heart that she was only short seconds away from a complete collapse, I threw discretion to the winds and picked her too frail body up in my arms. Despite the swelling of her belly, Anne seemed not much heavier than I remembered from that last time I held her so, near eight long years ago. Her ladies tuttered their great disapproval of my behaviour, but then saw that their Queen had completely fainted in my arms. It was I who now began to feel sick.

"Someone go and get the doctor! Where, in God's good name, is the midwife?" I yelled at those useless women who surrounded me, but did nothing but get in my way.

Thus, with further ado, I carried my beloved girl to her bed.

Chapter 5

"Thanked be fortune, it hath be otherwise."

ays later, and because she fought so hard against it, in great pain and agony Anne miscarried the King's child, his son. Some say it would have been her saviour. I say otherwise: the baby was her doom.

How could it be otherwise? The boy-child she gave premature birth to was deformed, with an over-large head and a stump where there should be an arm. The King—now up and about after his head injury, but shorter of temper than usual—was horrified, verily, sickened, when he was told of this. Deformed babies are believed by many to be the sign of the evil one and powerful witchcraft, and it was his own wife who had borne this monster within her, claiming it was flesh of his flesh.

Perchance, I can understand—a little—the King's first horrified reaction. He told Anne that she would bear no more sons to him— saying, as he left his distraught wife, "I will speak to you more of this when you are up from this place."

And he henceforth escaped from the birthing-chamber, with its sickly smell of blood, and the shuttered-in pathos of dark, hopeless despair.

Such dreadful horror from hell must have a cause. But the cause must never be fixed at the King's door.

It was not long after this that the King was heard to say that his passion for Anne had been caused by witchcraft. Thus, there was no recourse now but to rid himself of the witch who had put him under such a spell. I cannot say I understand why this catastrophe happened, but I know it was no witchcraft. I have always known in my deepest heart that Anna's relationship with the King was doomed from the start.

But there is always a lull before every storm. And for a time, those of us who stood steadfast to the Queen deluded ourselves into hoping that all could and would right itself one day.

Anne had many loyal and loving friends, friends who all did their best to comfort her during this most terrible time. When she had physically recovered from her miscarriage, we, including George, Henry Norris, Francis Weston, and myself (as much as discretion allowed), would all gather in her chamber and try our hardest to distract her from her grief. And she was grieving, not only for the baby—though it had been best for the poor thing to be born dead before its time—but for the final death knell upon her marriage. Anne knew the Lord Cromwell had made the King aware how, with Catherine now dead, he had but to rid himself of her and he would be free to gain for himself a *bona fide* marriage. And a new marriage would give the King yet another opportunity for siring his longed for Prince.

Once upon a time, so many long years ago, Anne had no love for the King, but with the passing of year upon year her feelings for him had become changed from hate into pity, and then to something akin to love. Perverse, indeed, are the winds of human life. And, as Anne grew to love him, so did the King's feelings for her change into something alike to hate. Hatred exposed to all close to them after the dead, deformed boy had been born.

Yea, there was so much for Anne to grieve for. Not least the fact that she felt herself increasingly swept away to where none could save her.

My beloved girl attempted to forget all that afflicted her by losing herself in the creation of new dances, dances that Anna would dance for us in her chambers. Sometimes, as I watched her, I was swept back into the far reaches of my memories. There she was, in a bright, sunlit room, a woman in a heavy golden dress, with her ebony hair flowing loose, past her tiny waist, whirling, always whirling around the room. And I? My heart would stand painfully heavy and still, remembering the innocent and happy child that Anna once was. None the less, where before the tiny child had danced to music she alone could hear, this time it was Marc Smeaton or myself who made the music, while Anne danced her latest dance with her ladies and some of the King's own gentlemen.

Marc, though lowly born, being the son of a carpenter, was a vastly talented young man, especially when it came to playing upon the virginals. He had been now in Anne's service for close to three years, and it often struck me that he was often jealous of the other gentlemen who had greater claim upon the attentions of the Queen. Anne was aware that his feelings for her were greater than were sensible. (But who is ever sensible when it comes to love?) Anna tried her best to remind him of his place, and stop the poor lad from deluding himself that he had a claim upon her closer affections.

Verily, one time when I was with the Queen at Greenwich, we noticed Marc eyes upon us with an expression on his face that could be only described as lovelorn. Anna shrugged her shoulders at me, and gave a wry smile.

"I suppose I must deal with this?"

"Yea. Perhaps 'tis best that you do. Poor Marc looks a picture of absolute misery."

So Anne walked over to the window embrasure where he stood, and said to him: "Marc, why so sad? Tell me what afflicts you, and perhaps I can offer you some solution to your trouble."

Marc glanced at Anne with his too pretty eyes, and blushed.

"Your Grace, please do not disturb yourself on my account."

"But I cannot have my servants looking so glum and unhappy. Surely you can tell me the cause?"

"It matters not, my Queen."

Anne looked sadly at him, and touched him lightly on the front of his doublet.

"Then let me tell you what afflicts you so. I know your life at court is not always easy, Marc. How can it be when you have been brought up to be a gentleman, but know that for you the status of gentleman is forever beyond your grasp. Poor Marc Smeaton! You would wish for my friendship, like I have with my cousin Sir Thomas here, but know that your low station grants not that desire."

"No, no, Madam," Marc replied stuttering. "A look satisfies me, and thus you fare me well."

"Yea, Marc. I understand. All life is not as we would hope or want it to be."

Anne gave a final sad smile to Marc, and returned to where I was standing to resume our conversation.

"Poor lad! He was taken from his family because of his talents, and raised here at court. Thus, he is neither one thing nor another. I am pleased that dear George has made something of a friend with him."

I could see that Anne forgot Marc at the mention of George's name, and she smiled gently at her private thoughts. If it was at all possible, these tragic days had only served to strengthen the bonds that bound them to one another. George rarely left her side now.

It was clear that George's dislike of the King had increased with every wrong done against his sister. I could not avoid my own thought that George was often unwise in his remarks concerning the King. Verily, sometimes his behaviour could only be described as downright petty, which surprised me greatly because George was rarely, even when we were children, ever petty. He mocked the King's dress, and his attempts at poetry, but worse of all George lashed out at the King's treatment of Anne in the bedchamber. It appeared to me that Anne, unwisely in this case, had shared some of the confidences with George as she had with me. Though he would speak only of these matters when he was alone with me; nevertheless, it made me very nervous. One never knows where a spy may be lurking.

My cousin loved his sister so much—perhaps too much to be truly understood by this carnal world—and it was evident that he was breaking his heart over where these events had led her. I felt, too, that his spirit was further darkened with guilt that he had encouraged her in those early days to pursue the King. Thus, George now thought himself partly responsible for his younger sister's dire and tragic predicament. It was also very clear to me, who loved them both, that Anne and George were struck by the same fever, living their lives frantically as if their next breath might, in fact, be their very last.

Verily, as George appeared to be throwing discretion to the wind by speaking his thoughts aloud to me, so likewise appeared his sister. I remember one time in special when I heard Anne speak to Henry Norris who often formed part of the company that surrounded and supported the Queen. Anne went up to him and said, "Henry, do you not think it was time that you were wed? Five long years have you been lacking a wife, and my own cousin Madge grows paler and paler every day from her devotion to you. Why wait any longer? Why not wed the poor girl and put her out of her misery?"

I saw Norris glance with surprise at Anne, and heard him reply: "Madam. You should know that my heart has been long given to another."

Anne stared at him, and then laughed as suddenly struck mad. She raised her hand to the side of her face, and said: "Oh, Harry, you look for dead men shoes, for if anything was to happen to the King, you would look to have me!"

Harry openly stared at the Queen, and began sputtering: "No, Madam. That is not what I meant! If I have any thoughts of that kind, I swear to you, my Grace, I would deserve to end my life here and now on the executioner's block."

But Anne laughed again, and walked away before he could make further reply, leaving poor Henry standing alone. He looked completely dumbfounded by both her actions and words.

I went up to him, and put my hand upon his sleeve.

"Take no notice of her. I cannot believe the Queen knows truly what she has been saying."

Henry turned to me.

"Yea, Tom, that I already realise. The Queen is a good woman, who feels herself totally rejected by the King, her husband. But, Tom, what if she was heard—what would the King think or do?"

He glanced around the room, and I glanced around the room too, to be abruptly made aware that people were watching us closely. A chill crept over my skin and I knew what it was like to be a trapped hare aware the hungry fox would in any second pounce upon.

Henry looked panic-struck at me.

"Tom! What should I do?"

I thought hard, and came to a kind of solution.

"'Tis best to snap this in the bud before it becomes any worse. Go now to the Queen's Almoner; swear to him what you and I know true: the Queen's a good woman. The King will believe your oath, even if he is tempted to use her words as a way to seek reprisal."

"I suppose there is nothing else I can do to help protect my Lady Queen. Yea, Tom, I will do as you say."

Henry then rushed out the chamber in search of the Queen's Almoner.

But these matters were difficult to smooth over so simply, especially when the King was willing to believe every evil of his Queen. Thus, when the King heard of the fracas that had taken place in Anne's chambers, he made his anger known to all the court.

Anne was frightened enough of where the future was taking her, now she was driven to an act of sheer desperation. Anna called for her daughter Elizabeth to be brought to her, and then took the child into the gardens. The King was engaged in a meeting of the Privy Council, and Anne knew in her heart of hearts that it was her future that would be discussed this day.

Thus, she went to an open window, where she could clearly see the King, and entreated him to forgive her for the sake of their child. The King just stared at her, and then turned his back on his now weeping wife. Elizabeth too began to cry, and Anne, not wishing to distress her young child any further, decided she could no more. Anna returned, with her still crying daughter, to her chambers.

Chapter 6

"It was no dream, I lay broad waking."

The weather remained hot that last week in April, but the atmosphere at court seemed as icy as the coldest winter's day. Since Anne's last miscarriage in January, the King's attitude to her had grown more and more hostile. The only time they now talked was when the King could no longer avoid the duty of doing so.

And it was in the closing days of April, George sought me out, *incognito*, at my London lodgings. My cousin entered my room, after the barest suggestion of a knock, while I was busily engaged writing my latest poetry. I was delighted to see him and rushed, after flinging aside my papers, from my chair to embrace him as he entered my chamber. I then quickly cleared away the pile of books and pages of scribblings from my spare chair and sat my clearly exhausted cousin down in it. I returned to sit in the chair that directly faced him.

"Thomas," George bent forward, looking closely at me as he spoke, "I had to come to see you… I am so worried, Tom."

"About what, George?" I asked, though I had strong and grave suspicions of what worried him. I too was extremely worried for what I easily guessed were the same reasons that had driven my cousin to my door. Verily, this was confirmed by George's next words.

"There are moves afoot. I am not sure but… I think the King has now a plan to rid himself of Anne. I am so frightened for her, Tom."

I got up and walked over to my small window. There I looked

out at the brightness of the day. The pleasant spring scene I beheld before my eyes mocked the fears that began to clamour for expression within me. I turned back to George.

"Are you sure, George?"

"Yea... I believe so. Did you know that Marc Smeaton has disappeared? Three days ago... dear Jesus... was it only three days ago? I feel I have lived an eternity since I became afeared about the true cause for his absence. Three days ago, Tom, Marc told one of my servants that he had been invited for dinner at Cromwell's house, and that is the last thing we know of him."

George too arose from his seat and began to stalk up and down in my chamber; this made me even more concerned. George rarely—and only under very extreme conditions—displayed the same nervous energy that sustained his sister. At length, he turned back to me.

"Cromwell is up to something, Tom. I feel it like I have never felt anything before. I know I am being followed by one of his spies."

I started at that, and George smiled reassuringly at me.

"Do you think I would be stupid enough to come here with the fellow following my lead? (I shook my head at that.) I had one of my most trusted men distract him and then went out the servant's entrance in disguise. I would enjoy this cat and mouse game, Tom, if Anne's future did not weigh so heavily in the balance."

George smiled wryly after these final words, and I similarly laughed, knowing what he meant. We had occasionally, as young youths, disguised ourselves to explore the darker side of London.

"Have you any idea of what the plot could be?" I asked.

He shook his head slightly, and returned to his chair, leaning his head against his hand as he did always when he was thinking.

"I wish I knew, Tom... By all the saints, I wish I knew. At the moment, it is like I am fighting shadows. Anne will no longer talk sense to me about what is happening. I never knew her so unwilling to go into battle for herself. She believes her doom looms before her and will only talk to me of that. Anna has even asked her priest to care for Elizabeth, when she is no longer here to care for her daughter herself."

At this George crumbled and tears began to run down his cheeks to soak into his beard. As quickly as he had begun to cry, his body straightened savagely, and he jumped out of the chair shouting: "God rot the King!"

At that I went from the window, and opened my door and looked out, thanking all the saints I could think of that the corridor outside of my chamber was completely empty of people. I closed my door and went to George, gripped his shoulders firmly, shook him and said: "George, be very careful, man; there are spies enough without you giving them something to run home to their masters about."

George looked at me and sighed deeply.

"I am sorry, Tom. We are all living on our nerves at court. The black clouds have gathered. We only now wait for the storm to begin. If only I knew what type of storm it will be, I would know then what weapons to fight it with."

We were both silent for a moment. I knew exactly how George was feeling. I too was churning inside with so many dark thoughts and fears.

Finally, I turned back to George to ask him: "In what ways could the King end his marriage to Anne?"

George went and sat back down on the chair. He leaned his head back on top of the chair and looked up at the ceiling.

"Tom, my greatest fear is that he may accuse her of adultery," he whispered so quietly that I could barely comprehend what he was saying.

"What!" I rushed over to him to be more near to hear.

He sat up, glancing at me, and then looked down at his feet.

"He wishes to rid himself of a marriage that all parliament recognised and declared valid. He wishes to rid himself of a Queen anointed. I believe the King also wants to make sure of revenge… Thomas, I have thought hard on this and have concluded that to accuse Anne of adultery would be one sure way of achieving all his ends. You know, as I know… 'tis treason for a Queen to be found guilty of adultery."

"But surely he would require evidence. As you say, Anne is a crowned and anointed Queen of England, George. The King could not put away his marriage to Anne without convincing proof."

"Yea, Tom, I know. But during these last months I have been wondering how it could be done. Tom, my sister is too friendly with those men she has around her. 'Tis all in innocence. Verily, you and I have long known that Anne has always preferred a man's friendship to that of a woman's. Who knows, Tom, perhaps it is because she grew up so close to us. But, nonetheless, I believe a plot such as we fear could make much of these friendships."

"How do you mean, George?"

"I can easily think of two examples, Tom. You recall how Anne thoughtlessly said to Norris about waiting for dead men's shoes? That was really stupid of my sister, but you know what mood she has been in since her last miscarriage. But I was also there recently when she was teasing Weston about not loving his wife, and you know what the fool said? He told Anne, in the presence of many, that he loved her better than he did his wife or mistress. Of course Anne tried to quickly turn the subject to something else, but it was said; and worst, Tom, it was heard."

"God's oath, George… What a bloody idiot! But surely they must have solid truth, not some ill conceived flattery that had got out of hand?"

"Truth, Tom? Tell me, what is truth? A man who is tortured until he would sell his soul to the devil, does he speak the truth or does he make known what others wish for him to make known? Where, Tom, oh where in God's good name is Marc Smeaton?"

I could see now another reason why he was here today. His thoughts regarding the disappearance of Marc must have driven him to distraction. But now it was not only George who trembled at what he could not see. I too could feel an abyss opening rapidly at my feet.

I am a fanciful man, I freely and without hesitation admit, but there has long been an image or waking dream in my mind that I feel now such a powerful urge to describe. I see in this vision a music room where Anne, George, and I are making music, like we often did when we were children. One of us—in this waking vision 'tis I—stands slightly apart from the other two, holding the paper on which the sonnet is written, and sings while the other two play upon their lutes. There is an open door to this room. Out of this door you can see on one side a large glass window lighting up a hint of corridor, but through the door, and into this chamber, there also invades a shadow, a shadow which is dark and threatening, touching all three of us. But it mostly blackens, having blocked out the bright sunlight, the seated forms of Anna and George. This shadow has the unmistakable shape of the King. I felt I was seeing within myself some type of premonition.

I mentally shook myself and returned back from my vision to that of this world. George was now looking out my window.

"Do you think that is what's happening, George? That they have Marc somewhere and are torturing him?" I quietly asked him.

George turned around to look at me once more. Never have I seen him look like he did that day—like a man who is haunted by things that are too terrible to even express.

"Yea, Tom. That is what I greatly fear."

"But why Smeaton?"

"Because he is a commoner, thus 'tis easier to do with him what they will. Because he is close to my sister… Alas, Tom, because he is the weak link in the circle of men who love Anna. Remember, Tom, that a classic tactic of war is to discover the weak link and use it for your own ends… Do you remember when we were boys, Tom, and Anne was sent to France? Do you remember how we could only stand by, too helpless to stop it? I feel now exactly how I felt then. Bloody, bloody helpless!"

"Aye," I answered him. "I remember too well that time. I also remember that we were only children then; now we are no longer boys but grown men. Surely that changes matters this time... Surely we are no longer helpless?"

George looked at me with agonised eyes.

"In this, we are."

Since my thirteenth year, it has long seemed to me that my life had been a long battle against things I could not change. That I remained as powerless to change the currents of my life as a drop of water is powerless to change the direction of the currents of the sea. God's oath! If there was anything that I wished to change most, it was the direction that these currents were now taking us!

I then remembered back to my childhood, when Father Stephen would tell us that life in this world was a series of battles, shaping us, forming us to the glory of God. Perhaps... But, there comes a point when you feel you can battle no more, when all you want to do is curl yourself up like a hedgehog, protecting yourself from any further hurts. If it was not for the fact that I felt I had to remain steadfast and be ready to do battle for my girl, I believe, at this point, I would have easily turned hedgehog.

I invited George to stay with me the night. He readily accepted my invitation. Verily, it struck me that he needed the comfort of my company. Certainly I needed the comfort of his. We went together to the local tavern to eat a simple meal of beef, cheese, and fresh bread. While we ate we spoke no more about the events at court; rather we dwelt long upon our boyhoods, remembering only humorous times. Like the time when we had climbed up an old oak tree to shake down the autumn leaves on the dozing form of our good priest, and he had woken up to shake his fist at us before splitting his sides with laughter.

It was as if we wished to escape through happy memories the immense unhappiness we saw looming before our eyes.

I have always been fortunate in my friends, but especially in my long friendship with George. Though our adult lives had often separated us, we, even so, had been always aware that if one ever needed the other that need would instantly be answered. Thus, there we sat talking, lost in times long gone, taking no note that evening was fast drawing to a close and soon it would be time for the sun to make a beginning to a new day. Never could I have realised that this evening and morning in George's company would be the final time that I would ever spend with my life's long boon companion.

So dawn came and we parted. Yea, we parted not knowing it was to be forever. Yea, verily, forever out of each other's lives. Though I was not to know that yet, and for the moment I no longer faced my fears—since I returned to my lodgings to sleep the day away.

Perchance that was for the best; at least I was totally unaware for one last day the grief about to break upon us all. That day, the day I slept until late afternoon, was May the first. Anne always loved May. Especially the first day of May, a day often spent by all England in merriment and dancing, as most likely it had been spent since the dawn of our history.

I was not there to witness the events as they happened, so I write of them as my father told them to me.

On this day a tournament had been arranged; both Anne and the King attended, but the King not for long. Anne tried her hardest to be her old gay self on that day, even though the King sat by her side glum and stern. Anne had long withstood her unhappy marriage by losing herself in the attentions of courtiers who offered her platonic and courtly love.

It was the same on this day, Anne encouraging those who competed in the tournament by gay but innocent flirtations. But on this day the King seemed ready to seize on any of her behaviour and make it appear the act of an evil woman. Thus, when she dropped her handkerchief as a token to one of the competitors, Henry stormed off, never to be seen by Anne again. The arrests began to happen promptly after this event. First Henry Norris, a man who had been with the King since they were both youths at the beginning of the Royal Henry's reign.

George had wondered to me where Marc Smeaton had disappeared. I found out later that poor Smeaton had been incarcerated in the Tower since leaving Cromwell's company.

But, I knew nothing of this yet. After I had awoken after noon on the first of May, I returned to polishing up my work of the previous day. I wanted to finish this work quickly because it was meant as a birthday gift for Anne, even though her birthday had already come and gone in early April. I found it hard to believe that the little girl I had climbed up trees and raced with was now a full-grown woman of twenty-nine.

This work of mine kept me busy all of that day and well into the night. In the end my mind began to play tricks upon my tired hand and I decided it would be best to put my poetry aside to the following day. So I went to sleep, and being so tired I slept until after the tenth hour of the following day. After waking, I decided to go and break my fast at the same tavern where George and I had gone not even two days before.

I found the place in a sheer uproar, and soon discovered the cause. Many voices told me, to my horror and dismay, Anne had been arrested and would be taken to the Tower as soon as the tide permitted. I left the tavern without having eaten, and set off as quickly as I could to court. I wanted to find George and discover from him the best course now to take.

I soon arrived at Greenwich, and went in search of my cousin. Thinking that he might be in his chambers, I went there first. I entered his chambers to discover within George's servant Gil seated at the sunlit window seat, sobbing with all his might. I began to sense myself starting to fall dizzily through the abyss that I had felt opening only days before.

"Gil... where is your Lord?" I asked the obviously grief-stricken boy, feeling terrified of what his answer would be. George could have easily taken leave of his senses, considering the state he was in when he visited me, and decided to take on the King and all when he heard his sister had been arrested.

Gil looked at me with red brimmed eyes, his nose running fast in sympathy.

"Oh, Sir Thomas. They have taken my good Master away," he blurted out.

I stared at him.

"Why, Gil? Why?" I asked him, feeling now worse than just simply frightened.

"I do not know, Sir Tom. I do not know," he answered, breaking out in fresh tears.

Utterly desperate, I left George's chamber in great haste. *Where to now?* I asked myself. I remembered it was likely that Anne would be separated from her loyal attendants, so decided to go in hunt of them. The whole of Greenwich was in complete disorder, with people walking around looking stunned and frightened. But I could see no one whom I knew would be able to give me the answers that I badly needed.

At last, not knowing what else to do, I went to Anne's chambers. I knew already she was gone from that place, but I hoped to discover within her chambers one of those who I sought. Anna's rooms were no longer guarded. I supposed the same guards who had ensured her security while Queen were now ensuring her security as prisoner. Therefore, without further thought, I burst into her rooms, never realising who I would find within.

"So, 'tis you Wyatt," the Duke of Suffolk said, having turned away from searching in Anne's writing cabinet. I swallowed in fright. The last person I would have chosen to see on this day would have been the King; the next person I possessed no desire to meet reclined there right in front of me. I decided to try to make the best of it and bluff it out, if I could.

"My Lord Duke. I am looking for my cousin, the Lord George Rochford."

"Are you indeed, Wyatt? Oh, I forgot. 'Tis 'Sir Wyatt' now."

The Duke sat there smugly smiling at me.

"No matter, your Grace. Can you not tell where my cousin is?"

"Boleyn you mean? Why, Sir Wyatt, I believe he too awaits the tide which will take him and his sister to the Tower."

I began to feel dizzy with all the fears bounding in my head.

"But, whatever for? The Queen has done nothing wrong. As is true of Lord George. My cousin is loyal to the King."

The Duke laughed; it was an ugly laugh—more than that, it was an evil laugh.

"Loyal? Loyal to the King, hey Wyatt? Funny sort of loyalty I would call it which has this so called *Lord* rutting between the Queen's legs."

I felt my mouth open in shock. I moved towards the Duke and said: "You are mad—mad! Lord Boleyn and the Queen are brother and sister. 'Tis plain evil what you dare suggest!"

The Duke now arose from his chair, standing upright in anger.

"You forget yourself, Wyatt. Remember, knight, that you speak to a Prince of the land. Yea, George Boleyn committed incest with his sister, our so-called Queen. Now, what of you, Sir Wyatt— what of you?"

I chose to ignore his question, and return to what we spoke just seconds before.

"But 'tis not true! I tell you, your Grace! 'Tis simply not true! My cousin, the Lord Boleyn, and her Grace the Queen are brother and sister, bound through love and honour only."

"Honour?" the Duke grunted and barked out a short laugh. "Anne, soon to be Queen of nothing, knows nothing of honour. Rather she is a bitch in heat who allowed the whole pack around her to service her until she was red and raw."

I moved even closer to the Duke, so angry was I now that I could easily have grabbed him and tossed him to the ground. Just as I had done years ago, not realising who he was, but this time with more deadly intent.

"How dare you speak like that of Anna!"

"Oh, 'tis *Anna*, say you Wyatt?" The Duke taunted, speaking slow and soft.

"Now tell me, knight, were you one of the pack which serviced the great whore's lust?"

I just stood there, staring at the Duke, thinking what would happen if they found out about that day so long ago. Surely that may make all these lies now seem true. At last, I regained hold on my trembling emotions and, remembering what George spoken of truth but days ago, said to the Duke: "I perceive, my Grace, that truth no longer means anything. That it is falsehood upon falsehood that now determines our destiny. Tell me, your Grace, are you enjoying all this? Has your need for revenge now been satisfied?"

Suddenly, without realising how I came to this knowledge, it had come to me the Duke's enjoyment of this day's events was deeply rooted in a time long since passed.

A door opened in my mind and I saw, as if I had indeed seen them with my own two eyes, a frightened youth and near to fainting girl facing an angry man who held a sword pointed at the boy as if to plunge. But it was now (so many years later that I had almost forgot) that the Duke's weapon, more painful than that long ago sword which had its existence only in the physical world, was plunged deep within my very spirit. The Duke's next words affirmed what I forthwith believed.

"Not quite, Wyatt, not quite. I did not enjoy being denied my pleasure that day long ago. Nor did I enjoy being shoved by you to the ground like a lowly menial. If the King had not fancied himself in love for the first time in his life, I am sure I would not have had to wait as long as I have waited to see that slut brought down low. Now what to do with you? What to do with you."

All of a sudden he went to the next room and yelled: "Guard!"

With the result that a guard suddenly appeared out of seemingly nowhere, and stood to attention, awaiting his command.

The Duke now moved away from me, saying to the guard: "This man is under arrest. Take him to my captain and say that he is to be taken to the Tower as soon as the tides permit."

I gave one last, lingering look at the Duke, trying to say with my eyes that he broke me not. But then the guard pulled at my arm, and began to lead me away. Thus, that night, in the closing hours of the second day of May, I was ferried to the Tower.

Book Six

Sir,

Your grace's displeasure, and my imprisonment, are things so strange unto me, as what to write, or what to excuse, I am altogether ignorant. Whereas you send unto me (willing me to confess a truth, and so obtain your favour) by such an one whom you know to be mine ancient and professed enemy: I no sooner received this message by him, than I rightly conceived your meaning; and if, as you say, confessing a truth indeed may procure my safety, I shall with all willingness and duty perform your command.

But let not your grace ever imagine that your poor wife will ever be brought to acknowledge a fault, where not so much as a thought thereof preceded. And to speak a truth, never prince had wife more loyal in all duty, and in all true affection, than you have found in Anne Boleyn, with which name and place could willingly have contented myself, if God, and your grace's pleasure had been so pleased. Neither did I at any time so far forget myself in my exaltation, or received queenship, but that I always looked for such an alteration as now I find; for the ground of my preferment being on no surer foundation than your grace's fancy, the least alteration, I knew, was fit and sufficient to draw that fancy to some other subject. You have chosen me, from a low estate, to be your queen and companion, far beyond my desert or desire. If then you found me worthy of such honour, good your grace, let not any light fancy, or bad counsel of mine enemies, withdraw your princely favour from me; neither let that stain, that unworthy stain of a disloyal heart towards your good grace, ever cast so foul a blot on your most dutiful wife, and the infant princess your daughter: try me, good king, but let me have a lawful trial, and let not my sworn enemies sit as my accusers and judges; yea, let me receive an open trial, for my truth shall fear no open shame; then shall you see, either mine innocency cleared, your suspicion and conscience satisfied, the ignominy and slander of the world stopped, or my guilt openly declared. So that whatsoever God or you may determine of me, your grace may be freed from an open censure; and mine offence being so lawfully proved, your grace is at liberty, both before God and man, not only to execute worthy punishment on me as an unlawful wife, but to follow your affection already settled on that party, for whose sake I am now as I am, whose name I could some good while since have pointed unto: your grace being not ignorant of my suspicion therein.

But if you have already determined of me, and that only my death, but an infamous slander must bring you the enjoying of your desired happiness; then I desire of God, that he will pardon your great sin therein, and likewise mine enemies, the instruments thereof: and that he will not call you to a strict account for your unprincely and cruel usage of me, at his general judgment-seat, where both you and myself must shortly appear, and in whose judgment, I doubt not (whatsoever the world may think of me), mine innocence shall be openly known, and sufficiently cleared.

My last and only request shall be, that myself may only bear the burthen of your grace's displeasure, and that it may not touch the innocent souls of those poor gentlemen, who, as I understand, are likewise in straight imprisonment for my sake. If ever I have found favour in your sight; if ever the name of Anne Boleyn hath been pleasing to your ears, then let me obtain this request; and I will so leave to trouble your grace any further, with mine earnest prayers to the Trinity to have your grace in his good keeping, and to direct you in all your actions.

From my doleful Prison, the Tower, this 6th of May.

Your most Loyal and ever Faithful Wife,
Anne Boleyn

Chapter 1

"Commend me to his Majesty and tell him that he hath ever been constant in his career of advancing me, from private gentlewoman he made me Marchioness, from Marchioness a Queen and now that hath left no higher degree of honour he gives my innocency the crown of martyrdom."

My last experience of the Tower had been shared by both Anne and George; a time of celebration (*Celebration? Rather the final build-up to all our heartbreaks!*) when Anne was crowned Queen. This time I was rowed underneath Traitor's gate, and taken without ceremony to a small cell in Bell's Tower. This time I was a prisoner, rather than a feted guest of the King. After they had closed the door on me, I sat upon the only piece of furniture—a sagging bed cot, which had clearly seen better days—and tried desperately to banish my feelings of panic. I was not so much worried for myself. In recent years my relationship with Anne had been as discreet and circumspect as I could make it—for the protection of my battered heart if for no other reason. Of course I was her kinsman, thus was granted greater familiarity than the average courtier... but since that day in July, almost eight years ago, I had been rarely left alone with her.

These thoughts led me to think how they could accuse George. Yea, he was often in her company; with both their marriages failures they often sought the support and comfort of the other.

But incest?

I never realised that evil was such a thing that one could touch, but the very thought of that hideous accusation made me almost feel I could almost reach out and hold evil in my hands. I wondered if Anne knew? Oh, God, if she knew that George was thus accused, she would completely give up on herself and lose herself in hysteria.

My thoughts kept me from any sleep that night, though the discomfort of my surroundings also did not encourage any attempts at rest. The worst thing was that I remained alone with my imagination. All through the night, I fought to control its dark conjurings, becoming darker and darker as the hours slowly moved toward dawn. Thus, I felt totally exhausted and even more fearful when the first rays of dawn finally broke through my prison window.

I found to my great surprise that when imprisoned in the Tower you are not unaware of all that is happening without and within its walls. Verily, a prisoner gets to hear so many, different things. Tower guards almost made it a part of their daily job to keep their "guests" informed about all that was happening in the outside the world; as well as what was happening to those in the Tower.

I had heard from the guards who brought in my meals, men who took great pleasure to convey to me this type of information, that Anna's courage had completely deserted her when she had arrived at Traitor's gate. My poor girl! When she saw Traitor's gate looming before her, Anna had crumbled to her knees, crying out to God and all who could hear her that she was innocent of all she was accused of. The guards also told me how Anna feared the King meant for her to be shut away in some dark, rat-infested dungeon. However, the Tower's Constable, Master Kingston, the same man who had welcomed her three years before in happier circumstances, was able to assure her that she would be housed in the same apartments that Anne had used during her coronation.

Yea, the guards kept me informed daily of everything that was happening to my poor Anna. And if I did not have these sources of information provided by the guards, there was also the information provided by my own father.

At the end of the third day I began to be afeared that none of my kin actually knew that I was here, imprisoned in this ill lit and, worst, damp cell. Indeed, I began to think that maybe the Duke of

Suffolk had planned for me to just simply disappear. It had happened before, I knew, so why not to me? However, late in the morning of the fourth day of my imprisonment, my door was opened, not to admit my daily supply of food, but my father struggling to carry into my cell a large saddlebag. I felt overjoyed to see him, and I rushed over to embrace him in my arms.

"Thomas, my lad, what fix have you got yourself into this time?" he asked, just like he would ask me when I was a youth entangled in some scrape and gone to him in hope that he would get me quick out of my trouble.

I laughed, leading him over to seat him on my bed. It was so good and such a relief to see again someone whom I loved. I took his hand and kept it in mine.

"Dear father, you always did tell me to watch my tongue when I spoke to my betters. But I do not recant any word of what I said to that bastard Duke... Even now do I wish I could ram my knuckles down his filthy mouth."

My father gave a short grim laugh and shook his head.

"Those words will not gain you release from this place. Do your poor old father a favour, Tom: try your best to get out of this appalling mess in one piece. I have been so worried about you, my lad."

I sat beside him.

"I am sorry that you have been worried, father. But I am not sorry, nor will I ever be sorry, for my words to Suffolk! But tell me, I beg of you, father, what is happening at court?"

My father looked at me and gave a brief smile.

"You are a very fortunate man, Tom. I cannot help feeling so very grateful that you are liked by most people—even if only for your poetry. More importantly, Tom, you are liked by our Master Cromwell. If you were not, my son, then you too could have been one of those ill-fated men facing charges of committing adultery with the Queen. Verily, Cromwell has already written to me a letter assuring me that he will do everything in his power to save your skin. I wrote back to him only yesterday, thanking him and pledging to him our family's eternal support."

I deeply sighed, and rubbed my forehead with my hand. My head so ached with all the thoughts passing through it.

"'Tis all so completely mad, father... Mad! Mad! Mad! And that they accuse Anne and George..."

"Aye, I know, Thomas. But they were helped with that madness, my son. George is a good man; liked and respected by many people. I have always been proud to count him as one of our kin. It is a shame that the one person who should be closest to him hates him so much that she now contrives for his death."

"Who do you mean, Father?" I asked him, though I was beginning to have firm suspicions of whom he referred to.

"That vixen who calls herself his wife. She was the one to give the Privy Council the basis for that vile slander."

"Jane," I said sighing. "I never realised that Jane could be so capable of such wickedness."

"Aye, that she is, Tom. I cannot think of a better way to describe the hussy. Aye, Tom, Jane is a very wicked woman, and poor George is in the Tower because of that woman's wickedness," my father responded with a grimace of disgust.

"Who else have they charged, father? I know of only George, but the good Duke gloated that there were to be others." I put my hand on his arm. "Please tell me, father, who else have they accused?"

My father looked at me with very bleak eyes, as if he was deeply afeared of what my reaction would be. At length he said: "Young Francis Weston, Brereton, and Henry Norris. All good and gallant men. May the good God have mercy on them all!"

I felt stunned. All these men were my good friends, and had been so for many, many long years. Verily, they were all Anne's good friends too—men who had stayed loyal to her when others would not. Yea, often we had been together in Anne's chambers, either making music or talking of new books just read. Certainly the talk with Anne sometimes took on an edge of flirtation, but all in innocence. All in innocence! By God's holy word, I swear to you that these men thought only to comfort Anne, not to bed with her. One name that my father mentioned shocked me more than all the others.

"I am finding all this so hard to comprehend, father, so very, very hard. Most of all, I cannot believe that they have accused Henry Norris. He has been with the King since they were both young lads. If the King had one true friend in the entire world, I always believed it to be Henry Norris."

"Aye," my father said with a deep sigh. "Such is the danger of being loyal to a King such as ours. Every moment, even when you think you are safe, there is a chance that our Master will turn on you, and make you into a scapegoat for his own ends. Even if you believed yourself to be his friend! His father was a better man, and I loved him and supported him unfailingly in the days even when he was not my King... Tom, I cannot help recalling what Sir Thomas More said of this second Tudor, this son of the King I so loved. Sir Thomas said that if his head would give our King a new Castle in France, then off his shoulders it would roll. 'Tis strange and tragic, Tom, that More's head rolled to make Anne Queen in truth. Now I am afraid that the King craves a new wife, and other heads need to roll before he can gain this new desire."

My heart stopped still in my chest, and I felt my eyes fill with tears. I had tried so hard these last few days to avoid facing what the end would be. Now I could avoid it no more.

"There is nothing to be done to save them?" I hoarsely asked him, struggling to control all my emotions of despair and feelings of hopelessness.

My father bowed his head over his hands, as if praying for guidance. He then turned to me.

"Thomas, all that can be done will be done. I know Weston's family hopes to offer to pay a ransom for his life. He is such a godly man that the King may heed their cries for mercy. I have spoken to no man who believes for a moment that these accusations are anything but what they are: a pack of falsehoods to rid the King of Anne. The King is good at believing what he would to make his conscience rest easier. I have heard him say that he would not be surprised to find that Anne had betrayed him with a hundred men. As if a Queen, completely surrounded by the court, could hide that sort of behaviour… Yea, our King Henry is good at seeing only what he would."

"Have you heard anything about Anne and George, father? I have heard so many conflicting things from the guards that it is hard to know what to believe and what to not take any notice of."

"Yea. In this place that I can well believe. You can rest easy about Anne and George for the moment, Tom. They are well, and are more comfortably placed than you, my son. But I take comfort from the fact that you are here, in this dismal cell. Placed here, I do truly believe, gives you more chance of escaping the foul wind that blows up above. You know that Anne has even been given the same rooms which she used when she had her coronation?"

"Yea, the guards here have told me that is where Anne now abides. But, that foul wind you spoke of just before, Father, do you not realise any foul wind that blows at George and Anne also blows at me too? Oh, my good sire, I have no desire to escape whatever destiny has in store for them. Verily, I want to share with them whatever lies ahead."

My father looked at me with very frightened eyes, and put his arm tightly around my shoulders.

"Son! Son! Son! I understand how you feel and I admire your loyalty to your cousins, but what of your close family? I am an old, sick man with only one son. Is it too much to ask…Tom, your mother, God keep her blessed soul, is long dead. She is the only woman I ever loved. You and your sister are all I have left of her. It would destroy me, Thomas, to see you go to your death like this. And what of your own son? You must realise young Tom idolises you. Fifteen is an age when boys begin to steer themselves in the direction manhood will take them. Can you not imagine what it would do to him if his father goes to a bloody, traitor's death? I am having enough trouble as it is keeping the boy calm; knowing that you are placed here has made Tommy want to storm the Tower walls all by himself. If you cannot think of me, Tom, think hard about your son. He needs a father more than a grandsire."

I stayed silent for a long moment, pulled this way and that way. At length, I inhaled a deep breath and said: "I have spent my whole life thinking of others, father ... I suppose 'tis too late to change a habit of a lifetime."

My father put his arm around my shoulders and hugged me gently. My father was the best of men, and I, even despite everything that was rapidly collapsing around me, could only be thankful that we had grown closer over the years.

"Good lad, I am glad you see sense. There will be blood spilled enough before the month of May comes to a close, without your own blood adding to the flow. Just keep yourself low and I will get you out of here as soon as I can.

"Tom, I must go. The guard has been more than generous with the time allotted me. I have given them coin to care well for your needs, so things should be soon improved in here for the better. I have also taken the liberty of going to your London lodgings and gathering up some of your clothes and belongings. I believe you will find all that you need to keep up with your scribblings."

My father got off the bed and went back to the door, grabbing the bag and bringing it to me.

"Thank you, father. I must look and smell like something out of a cess-pit."

My father grunted out a harsh laugh.

"You do at that. You do at that, my dear son. Did you know that your sister attends the Queen?"

"Margaret's here too? Oh, what happy news, father, that someone of our blood supports Anne in this dreadful time."

"Aye. I thought the news would make you smile.'

We embraced again, and he departed, saying as he went that he would be back as soon as he could. When I was alone I opened up the bag; inside were several changes of clothes, books, writing tools and the unfinished work that I had meant as a present for Anne.

I took it out of the bag and looked at it. So near completion. Would Anne ever get to see it now? I wondered if it was possible to finish it here and send it to her somehow. I picked out some writing tools, ink, and paper and settled myself back on the bed to try to make an end to what I had begun only days ago. And this is what I wrote:

My sweet, alas, forget me not,
That am your own full sure possessed;
And for my own part, as well yet wot,
I cannot swerve from my behest.
Since that my life lieth in your lot,
At this my poor and just behest
Forget me not.

Yet wot how sure that I am tried,
My meaning clean, devoid of blot.
Yours is the proof: ye have me tried
And in me, sweet, ye found no spot.
If all my wealth and health is the good,
That of my life doth knit the knot,
Forget me not.

For yours I am and will be still
Although daily you see me not.
Seek for to save that ye may spill
Since of my life ye hold the shot.
Then grant me this for my goodwill,
Which is but the right, as God it wot:
Forget me not.

Consider how I am your thrall
To serve you both in cold and hot.
My fault's for thinking naught at all,
In prison strong though I should rot.
Then in your ears let pity fall
And, lest I perish in your lot,
Forget me not.

So it was finished.

I did not think it was the greatest of my poems. I was not entirely sure if Anne would or could understand all that I meant to say in it. I was not even certain I could find a safe means of sending the poem to her. But to be just able to send this message to her—to let her know, for perhaps the last time, that my faith in her and love for her would be forever steadfast. One last message to her. One last message to my dark Lady. One last message to my love.

Oh, God, surely there must be a way of escape for her. The King is a man. Surely he is not so completely devoid of pity. Only in January, she was carrying his child in her body. Surely the King must now realise that the miscarriage and deformed babe was no fault of hers, rather something which was utterly tragic to them both. The Duke of Norfolk had said she had miscarried of her saviour. Alright then, perhaps if the boy had been born alive and whole, he would have been the saviour of their disintegrating marriage, but, verily, a woman who is beset by such a dreadful tragedy does not deserve to lose her life because of it. There must be a way of escape. There must be! And with that thought in my mind, I tried my best to sleep.

I soon realised that there was to be no escape. The first trials took place at Westminster Hall on the twelfth of May. These were the trials of Smeaton, Weston, Norris, and Brereton. Of all these men, only Smeaton admitted to having had intercourse with the Queen. I could not help to feel but great pity for Mark. He was a young man of twenty-three, greatly gifted, whose gifts had led him high, and now so low. I knew, again from my guards, that since the day he was first imprisoned in the Tower, he had been denied the simple solaces naturally given to us who were better born. Indeed, I had been told that he was kept in irons. I suppose to ensure that his spirits remained broken.

My good friends Weston, Norris, and Brereton were also found guilty of having had carnal knowledge of Anne. All of them would be executed on the seventeenth of May, five days from their trials. *(I find it so hard to keep going on with the recounting of all these memories. If I did not write this narrative in remembrance and love of them who were murdered from this world, I think I could speak no more.)*

Weston's family's offer of a ransom of 100,000 marks for his life was ignored. He, too, would be executed. The frantic efforts made by Weston's family to save his life made many people look askew at the head of the Boleyn family.

Many of the court, who knew him not, expressed their shock and disgust regarding how Thomas Boleyn, now Earl of Wiltshire, could act as if nothing out of the ordinary was happening. Here was his only son and youngest daughter facing certain death and still he went out hunting with the King. They said Anne's mother, who had grown closer to her daughter and son in recent years, would no longer speak to him or be in the same room as her husband. I was not surprised when I heard all this. I who knew him, just remembered back to my childhood; when I first began to grow aware that Uncle Boleyn cared for nothing in life but his own advancement.

Anne and George were to be tried on the fifteenth of May, separately, in the confines of the Tower. Their father had offered to take his place as one of their judges, but common decency prevailed and he was told his presence on the bench would not be required. Amongst the seventy-six judges was Anne's uncle, the Duke of Norfolk, and the Duke of Suffolk; both men who, for their own personal reasons, intensely disliked Anne, and, thus, wanted to get rid of her. Also amongst the judges was a man who, so many years ago, had loved Anne: Hal Percy, the present Earl of Northumberland.

My father was one of the many spectators at Anne's and George's trials. So, through his observant eyes, I have a clear picture of the events as they happened.

Anne, I was told, had taken great care with her appearance on the day of her trial. Indeed, she entered the chambers with her attendants as a Queen, and this was the presence she maintained throughout this most dreadful day. Verily, at that moment and during every moment of her trial, there was no trace of the hysteria that had afflicted her much of her adult life, as when she arrived at the Tower.

The charges that Anna faced were abominable. Saying that out of malice to the King, her husband, she had seduced five men, including her own brother, to her bed.

My father told me the dates would have had old wives counting on their fingers, discovering that five dates given were during the early stages of Anne's last, doomed pregnancy—a time when most wise wives abstain from intercourse for fear of causing an end to a new pregnancy. Considering how much of Anne's future had depended on the life and health of that unborn child, I thought to myself that the charges grew more and more absurd with every passing moment. One date given was within two weeks of her having given birth to Elizabeth. No woman in her right mind deliberately sets out to seek lovers at a time when her body is still unhealed from the birth of a child. Anne may have been, through the circumstances of her life and grief and despair, unstable at times, but never was she one who could be described as foolish.

And if this was not a trial for her life, it could easily have been a stage for comedy. Amongst the many absurd accusations that came out during her trial was one claiming that Marc Smeaton hid in a closet, and was brought out by one of Anne's ladies when the Queen asked for her nightly marmalade. I could not help but laugh when my father told me this. The men who put this case together must have been grabbing at straws when they thought that one up.

Anne maintained her calm composure during the whole of her trial. Yea, she had given Weston and Smeaton gifts of money, and so forth, but never had she given them the gift of her body. And it was the same with the other men accused; they were never, ever, her lovers. George, she said, of course was often in her chamber. But as he was also her brother, Anna went on to say, surely they could converse together without having evil being thought of them. Anne strongly refuted the accusation that she had plotted with her alleged lovers the King's death, or that she had promised herself in marriage to any of them.

Even though all her arguments were clear, and struck most of the people watching as being said by a woman who was completely innocent of the charges laid against her, they held no weight against the sworn evidence presented to the court. Therefore, Anne was found guilty and sentenced by her uncle to be either burnt or beheaded—to be decided at the discretion of our merciful King.

Still Anna remained calm, though she was heard to say quietly to herself: "Oh, God, you know if I have merited this death."

I feel that Anne had known what to expect ever since the morning of her arrest, thus the verdict came as no shock to her. But it came as a great shock to one other. Hal Percy, Earl and a grown man for many years—a judge upon this day at this great mockery and sham of a trial. The man who had once gazed at Anna with such complete adoration as her voice blended with his. Aye—Hal, the young man who had loved Anne in a time when all our lives were lived in innocence. The Earl of Northumberland could no longer take one moment more. He collapsed, and was carried out in a dead faint from the room. When my father told me this, I could not help but wonder how Anne felt, as she watched them carry out this utterly broken man, the shattered shell of a man who hid within him a boy whom she had never stopped remembering with tender love. Taken from her life for the last and final time. I can but guess.

As to the feelings of Hal Percy? To condemn to death the woman who once had been the young girl racing her horse with his, across the green meadows of long ago. Laughing with him, singing with him, and just being with him because they were so much in love. Giving him, for such a brief but unforgettable season, joy and happiness… I have a better idea of how he felt. I too have never stopped loving Anna. *Oh, Anna. My lovely girl! If only our lives could have been so different! Ah—how my heart tears…*

Thus, the verdict had come down, and Anne was asked if she had anything more to say. This is what Anna said to the men who had sentenced her to die:

"I am ready for death." Anna took a deep breath, and looked at those people around her. "I regret that of innocent persons. I have always been a faithful wife to the King. My only sin against the King has been my jealousy and lack of humility. I think you know well the reason why you have condemned me to be other than that which led you to this judgement. What I regret most deeply is that men who were innocent and loyal to the King must lose their lives because of me."

Anne paused, and was seen to swallow hard—as if all the emotions within her were attempting to choke her. She then quickly regained hold of her composure, lifted her head high, and concluded her speech.

"I willingly give up my titles to the King who gave them."

Anne, now finished, curtsied with great dignity, and left the courtroom, accompanied by the Tower's Constable and her ladies. The royal executioner also followed her, the axe in his hands symbolically turned towards her. My father told me that even though she had verbally given up her titles, no one present at the court could see her as anything other than a Queen of great nobility.

Even the King was heard to say, after he was told of her behaviour and words this day, "Yea. She has always had a stout heart."

Aye, indeed, all those who had listened to her final speech could not fail to be moved in some way. Verily, even the Duke of Norfolk,

Anne's uncle, was moved unto tears. When my father told me this, I could barely bring myself to believe that the Duke had broken down. For a long time now, it had appeared to all that the Duke of Norfolk had deeply resented—some even went so far as to say hated—his niece, the Queen. The Duke had seen Anna's support of the protestant faith a betrayal not only to God but also to her family.

I have never stopped wondering if he had meant for her to miscarry of her babe; how else can you explain his strange actions on that tragic day in January?

Anne. My dearest Anna. Now condemned to die so savagely. My brave, lovely white falcon, soon to be freed forever from the mews entangling her in the climbing, Tudor rose. Aye—my wild, white falcon had found that the climbing Tudor rose was thorned to rip and tear. To rip and tear to death.

But, to lose Anna so! Ah, how does my heart bleed! And it will never stop bleeding. Not while I still breathe and live!

There is still one trial to recount, one more trial to finish this day's work. When the Duke of Norfolk regained his composure, his nephew George was brought in. It was now George's turn to answer the charge of incest with his sister.

My cousin George also impressed all who saw him that day by his calmness, and his ability to refute all the charges that were laid against him. The feeling in court ran high that he should be acquitted. But then Cromwell handed him a paper, telling him not to read it aloud. George took the paper from Cromwell, glanced down at it, and then looked hard at Cromwell.

My father said that he saw George smile slightly, as if he was amused at something that only he himself knew. Then he caused the whole room to raise itself in an uproar by disobeying Cromwell, and reading out the document he had in his hand. A document stating that Anne had spoken of the King's frequent attacks of impotence and his lack of "vigour" in the bedchamber. No wonder George smiled as he read out that document! To be given, by Cromwell no less, a weapon for revenge against the King for his slanders against his beloved sister.

My father made me laugh through my tears when he told me that Cromwell was jumping up and down, going completely red with anger, as George read out these words. But George just kept on speaking, and gently smiling. It was as if he said: *"I am no longer the puppet of any man, be he King or knave."*

However, when he handed back the document to Cromwell, George faced his judges and said: "I deny utterly that the Queen and myself ever spoke of such matters…" George then gently smiled again.

"I will not create suspicion in a manner likely to prejudice the issue the King might have from a second marriage."

Cromwell then jumped back to face George yet again.

"And what of the issue that the King got from this marriage? Could not the Princess Elizabeth be not the daughter of the King, but rather a child born out of an incestuous union between brother and sister?" Cromwell asked of George.

George, now looking white with anger, answered clearly, in a voice vibrating with rage: "I refuse to consider, even for one moment, such a vile and untrue accusation."

George so impressed the court this day that the opinion was still running strong that he should be acquitted. But then Cromwell pulled out from his pocket a letter written by George's wife; a letter stating that she had witnessed Anne and George in acts of incest. Jane and Bess! What a pair we were married to. Thus, George's fate was now assured.

The Duke of Norfolk, an uncle who had grown to love him even if he had very little regard for his sister, now read out the sentence condemning George to the most dreadful death imaginable: George was to be hanged, drawn, and quartered. George was silent, after his most horrible sentence was read out, with his head tilted to one side as if lost in thought. Now that the fates had been accomplished on this day, he could only hope to be given the mercy of having his sentence commuted to a simple beheading.

My God! My dear God! Why have you abandoned them! What have Anne and George ever done to deserve such savage, bloody deaths? Oh, why do I blame God? This evil does not rest with God. Once upon a time, a long time ago when we were children, I remember Father Stephen telling us a story of a Demogorgon, a most hateful god who indulged himself in vindictive acts of destruction. Never had I realised until now that this demon went by yet another name: Henry the Eighth of England.

During this visit, when my father recounted to me all that had gone on in court that day, he also told me that I no longer had anything to fear regarding being summoned to court as one of the accused. Verily, Cromwell had made the point of coming up to my father after my cousin's trials to tell him that the King had no misgivings about my innocence, and that my relations with the Queen had always been beyond reproach.

How little they really knew!

I looked at my father when he was telling me all this, and realised what a weight he had carried on his shoulders during his previous visits. My father struck me now as a man suddenly made free of all fears. But, on this day, I was in no state to rejoice with him the promise of my eventual release. Anne and George were condemned to die—and to die very, very soon. That is all that I could think of. Verily, I wished my father to be gone from me so I could better despair in peace. Through my mind ran deep, dark melancholy. *Oh death! Come to me, grim dancer. I but need to reach out my hand, to join my dance with yours. Oh, if only I was free, to join my dance with yours.*

I think now that my father knew my mood, and desired somehow to console me. He stayed by me as long as he could, telling me of this and that, paying no mind that I was attending little to his words. One thing he did say penetrated my sluggish consciousness. My father spoke of how public feeling was now swinging to Anne's favour. The ordinary people were not unaware that their King was seriously wooing another lady. Indeed, every night since Anne's arrest, the King's barge was seen rowing down to where this lady resided, and noises of merriment and music were clearly heard until the early hours of the morning. The trials had been such a sham, and so utterly contrived, that the feelings of most people—even some people who were once Anne's enemies—were now running high for Anne and against the King.

Perhaps, I thought, this might force the King, who cared much for his subjects' regard of him, to find another solution, other than the death of an innocent woman and innocent men, for the dissolvement of his marriage. Perhaps, he might decide to banish all those now condemned to die from his kingdom. Perhaps, I began to lose my mind with dreams and hopes.

Days sped by, and all was readied for the executions.

Chapter 2

Oh death rock me asleep,
Bring me on my quiet rest,
Let pass my very guiltless ghost
Out of my careful breast.
Ring out the doleful knell,
Let its sound my death tell;
For I must die,
There is no remedy,
For now I die…
Defiled is my name full sore
Through cruel spite and false report,
That I may say for evermore,
Farewell to joy, adieu comfort.
For wrongfully you judge of me
Unto my fame a mortal wound,
Say what ye list, it may not be,
Ye seek for that shall not be found.
—Anne Boleyn

"The bell tower showed me such sight
That in my head sticks day and night;
There did I learn out of a grate,
For all valour, glory or might,
That yet circa Regna tonat."

he nineteenth day of May, 1536, is a date forever scarred upon my memory; for this was the day that I watched them murder Anna from my prison window. For days past I had watched the carpenters build the high scaffold (verily, the noise of its erection forbade sleep for all who resided in the Tower) and knew that it was meant for my beloved.

Already, two days before, I had watched in horror as they killed my friends Henry Norris, Francis Weston, and Will Brereton. How I had cursed at first the fact that my cell's window overlooked the place where they were to be executed. There I could not escape my feeling of obligation, being honour bound to watch every second of their executions; so to be witness to their martyrdoms.

Then the day before his sister's death, George, my greatest life-long friend and kinsman, was slain before my very eyes, our good and gentle King allowing him the mercy of a quick death by beheading rather than being hanged, drawn, and quartered.

I will write now what my cousin said to the crowd before he died:

"Trust in God, and not in the vanities of the world; for if I had so done I think I would not have found myself here before you condemned to die."

Dear George! Now are you forever gone from my earthly life. Now I must wait for my own death before I can walk by your side again.

My dear friends and cousin all went bravely to their deaths. But, as each of their lives came to a savage abrupt end, I felt my own youth spill out of me as the blood spilled out of their severed necks, and I knew now that I would never, ever again feel young. And with their deaths, I felt myself approach, again and again and again, a little closer to my own death.

I had heard that Anna's execution was set for the ninth hour of the morning, but that time had come and gone with the scaffold still not finished. Then at the eleventh hour, all was suddenly quiet in the courtyard underneath my window, and I knew that the final preparations were underway for my dark Lady's doom.

As the Tower bell struck twelve, the invited witnesses (imagine how I felt when I saw that one of the witnesses was none other than the Duke of Suffolk—I suppose he came to gloat at this inglorious end to Anna's life) gathered around to watch Anna's last earthly moments. I was unable to see her until she had climbed up the steps to the high platform.

When Anna reached the top I saw her stand perfectly still, looking upwards to the sky. It was a lovely spring day, this nineteenth day of May: blue skies, though with a scattering of white clouds streaked in one part of the heavens. I tried to follow the direction where Anna was looking and I believe I saw what she saw. In the sky those scattered clouds had a strange appearance, making me think of a staircase. Verily, the more my eyes took in this illusion formed by the clouds on this day, the more I could not escape the sensation of being drawn deeper and deeper into the vivid blue sky.

Suddenly I was swept back twenty years or more, to an unexpected shower on glorious spring day, when a little girl danced in the rain and then talked gaily of her death, imagining her journey to Heaven.

"You know, Tommy, when I die I will go up a staircase just like that," she had said, "and maybe when all earthly breath has gone out from me, God will let me become a small part of the air all around us."

Anne's words from our childhoods pounded in my ears with the increasing roar of my heart. Did my girl remember that day too? I believe with all my heart and soul that Anna did, as she halted on the scaffold on this last day of her life and looked up at the sky where a cloudly staircase became visible in the firmament.

But actions on the stage below me broke into my memories, for her attendants (one of them my own sister Margaret) now moved forward to take off Anna's dark-grey damask cloak, revealing beneath it an under-dress of deep crimson. The Swordsman from Calais, dressed all in black, with his face hidden from Anna by the black mask upon his face, came to kneel at her feet. I heard him speak in French these words: "Madame, I crave your Majesty's pardon for I am ordered to do my duty."

I could barely hear Anna make her reply, though it sounded to me like the usual, customary one of "'willingly.'"

I saw her then give to the executioner his fee to ensure herself of a swift, clean death.

Anna turned and looked behind her, her eyes frantically searching the walls of the prison. And with that physic connection that had always bound us to one another, I knew that what she so desperately sought was a face she knew so well: my face. My heart stood still in my chest, and I prayed to God to please let her eyes find what she so franticly sought, to let her eyes find mine. But God chose to not answer my prayer, for Anna found me not.

Anna moved, appearing to me as a vision of bright loveliness (verily, I had never seen her look so serenely beautiful) towards the rails to make her final address. Initially her voice was soft, the only sign of her nervousness, but, none the less, I could still hear her words.

"Good Christian people—I am come hither to die, for according to the law, and by law, I am judged to die, and therefore will speak nothing against it. I come hither to accuse no man, nor speak anything of that whereof I am accused and condemned to die. But I prayed God to save the King, and send him long to reign over you—for a gentler nor merciful prince there was never; and to me he was ever a good, a gentle and sovereign lord. And if any person will meddle with my cause, I require them to judge the best. And thus I take my leave of the world, and of you all, and I heartily desire you all to pray for me."

It struck me, as I struggled to hear every word of her speech, that there could be few women who would be intelligent and strong minded enough to be able to say, without actually saying anything, how harshly the King had dealt with her.

Her ladies, all of them crying hard by this stage, now returned to her. One passed to her a white linen cap, which Anna slowly and solemnly took from her. She stood there for a few seconds seemingly caressing the linen as if she wanted to capture, for one last, lingering moment, the simple sense of touch. Anna then came back to the present moment with a visible start and turned around, giving Margaret her scarf, which Margaret was to use as Anna's blindfold, and a small, gold-bound prayer book—a prayer book, I discovered later, Anna had left for me to keep as remembrance of her (as if I would ever need anything to remind me of my dark Lady).

Anna next removed from her head a pearl encrusted coif, showing briefly that her hair had been tightly plaited around her head, replacing the coif with the simpler white cap.

Margaret now came behind Anne to tie the scarf around her eyes. Blinded, Anna put out both arms in front of her, as if trying to gain sense of her bearings. Anna looked so frail and helpless that my already aching, bleeding heart began to break beyond hope of ever being made whole again.

The executioner now moved towards her and spoke: "Madame, I beg you now to kneel, and say your prayers."

Guided by Margaret to the block, my Anna knelt and, characteristically, fussed nervously with her dress around her feet.

Suddenly her back straightened and Anna raised both her hands to the sky, saying: "To Jesus Christ I commit my soul! Oh, Lord, have mercy on me. To Christ I commend my soul. Jesus, receive my soul!"

At the finish of the prayer, Anna lowered her arms and gripped her hands tightly on either side of the block. I saw the Headsman mutter something to his assistant, with the result that the assistant quickly passed to him his sword, which had been hidden from Anna's eyes behind a bale of straw placed on the platform.

Before I knew it, the wind carried to my ears the sound of a hiss as the blade cut through the air. And I watched, with a sense of deep disbelief, as the sword caused Anna's head to fall off her shoulders, and saw it bounce and roll on the ground. Anna's body was now but a vessel gushing forth a fountain of blood.

I could watch no more. Indeed, I had watched too much. I felt like my guts had been savagely wretched from out my body. Verily, I collapsed and was violently sick on the floor of my prison chamber.

Epilogue

What death is worse than this?
When my delight,
My weal, my joy, my bliss
Is from my sight
Both day and night,
My life, alas, I miss.
For though I seem alive
My heart is hence.
Thus, bootless for strive
Out of presence
Of my defence,
Toward my death I drive.
Heartless, alas, what man
May long endure?
Alas, how live I then?
Since no rescue
May me assure,
My life I may well ban.
Thus, doth my torment go
In deadly dread.
Alas, who might live so,
Alive as dead,
Alive to lead
A deadly life in woe?

ays passed as if I lay in deepest fog. I cannot even remember food or drink passing my lips. My only next, clear memory is of my father, when he arrived in my prison cell, coming through my dungeon door as if frightened of what he would find within. Without a word, my father took me in his arms and there I cried… I cried until there were no tears left for me to cry. Anne once said that it was her heart that wept… my heart… this heart breaking afresh with every beat with grief… It hurt so much, aye, my heart hurt so much that every living moment was an agony.

At length, my father gently shook me, saying as he did so: "Come on, Tom, I know… Oh, my poor boy, I know, but my lad, there is nothing more we can do for them. Let us get your things together."

He went from me, and began gathering up some of my possessions. He turned to face me, speaking each word slowly as if he doubted my full understanding.

"I have come to take you home, my son."

In due course, he was able to escort me out of Bell Tower, back into the world I had left what seemed to me so very long ago. Indeed, it felt to me as if an eternity had passed since the day of my arrest.

★

The mirror in my chamber tells me that I am an old man now. My once dark hair is thick with grey. Lines, not there before, bite deep into my face. Yea, all youth has flown from me. Anne, George, and my dead friends have all taken it with them.

I know what I saw from out the grate of my prison's cell will remain with me until the day I die. Day and night the smell and vision of blood comes to sicken me. Day and night my aching heart, lying bleeding and broken in my chest, reminds me of all that I have lost. Especially of my loss of Anna. Yea, especially my loss of the woman I loved.

Anne. My beloved Anna. You, Anna, haunt me.

Yesterday, I looked into my bedroom's mirror and it seemed to me that I could see you. Aye, see you, Anna! There you stood, clearly there behind me, your hair unloosed, its fine, ebony tresses streaming down your back, smiling as only you could smile. Then you beckoned to me, and I turned swiftly to find myself yet alone.

It was the same when I sat by the evening fire. The red and gold embers revealed to me your laughing face. I think I go mad with grief. Anne… Anna… My dark Lady love. 'Tis all finished.

> *Farewell my lute,*
> *this is the last*
> *Labour that thou and I shall waste,*
> *For ended is what we began,*
> *Now is the song both sung and past.*
> *My lute be still, for I have done.*

THOMAS WYATT'S BIOGRAPHICAL DETAILS

Born 1503 at Allington Castle, in Kent, Thomas Wyatt was the eldest son of Sir Henry Wyatt, a loyal Partisan and supporter of the first Tudor king. Some scholars believe Allington Castle, the family estate at Kent, may have been given by Henry Tudor to Henry Wyatt as a reward for his support—given even before Henry Tudor became King, and leading to Henry Wyatt's imprisonment during the reign of England's third Richard. [i]

The early years of Thomas Wyatt have been mostly lost to the pages of known history. However, we do know the young Thomas Wyatt spent some years as a scholar of Cambridge's St. John's College, beginning his stay there in 1516 during his fourteenth year. In 1520, when he was seventeen, he was married to Lady Elizabeth Cobham. After bearing him two children—Thomas and Bess—Elizabeth was discovered by Thomas to be a woman of loose morals. Lady Elizabeth made the gross "sin" of being unfaithful to her wedded spouse, resulting in the separation of Tom and Elizabeth as husband and wife. [ii] But divorce, because of the times in which they lived, remained out of the question.

As well as being one of the best metaphysical poets of the Tudor era, Thomas Wyatt became an important and useful civil servant of the Tudor government, beginning his diplomatic career in 1525 when he formed one of the party which accompanied Sir Thomas Chene's embassy to France.

In 1527, Thomas was captured by Spanish troops while on an English mission to Pope Clement VII. However, Wyatt managed to escape (which, I believe, aptly demonstrates his resourcefulness) before his family had to raise and pay a ransom.

During the years 1528 to 1532 he served the King as Marshal of Calais. The year after, 1533, Thomas deputised in place of his father at the coronation of Anne Boleyn, [iii] then five months pregnant with the King's child. This was a child destined to grow up to be one of England's greatest and best loved monarchs—indeed, in my eyes, England's greatest monarch—Elizabeth the First. Yet it was

Elizabeth's birth that caused her mother such disaster.

Thomas' involvement as one of the officials (Chief Ewer) at Anne Boleyn's coronation, when he took the place of his sick father, must have left him feeling rather odd and ill at ease. [iv] It is clear from his poetry that Tom was an extremely sensitive and romantic man; and it is well known to people interested in this period that it is likely Thomas wooed Anne during her first years at court. It has also been often suggested that some of his love poetry could have been directed to Anne Boleyn. This suggestion has always cried loudly to my imagination, and I believed for a long time before beginning this novel that his poem "Dear heart, how like you this?" would make a good basis for an intriguing book.

There is a story that Wyatt told the King at a Privy Council meeting "the truth" regarding his relationship with Anne Boleyn, saying that the King could not marry a woman who had already been bedded by one of the King's Servants—meaning Wyatt himself. [v] As Wyatt was an Esquire to the body of Henry VIII, I find it hard to believe he would have been so foolish as to make such a confession. Indeed, surely this would have meant that Thomas would have been one of the men to be executed along with Anne in 1536 when the King finally convinced himself that his grand passion was the result of some type of witchcraft. Remember, one of the men (Francis Dereham) to be executed with Catherine Howard was a lover she had prior to her marriage to Henry the Eighth.

However, this is not to say that I claim that my novel is a true interpretation of events as they happened; rather I have used these events to create a fictional love story that is conceived around people who were once flesh and blood. Herodotus wrote (many, many long centuries ago): "Many things do not happen as they ought; most things do not happen at all. It is for the conscientious historian to correct these defects." Historians in those ancient times had a much easier employment than do our present day historians! Let me just say here that I have not written this book as an historian, but simply as a writer, and, I hope, a conscientious writer at that.

Nevertheless, these following facts are safely documented and helped give me a structure to flesh my imaginings around: Anne and Thomas did form some sort of strong bond at an early stage in their lives. Indeed, some of Anne's last thoughts had to do with Tom. This, I believe, one can safely assume, since at her execution she passed to one of the women assisting, her own treasured prayer book which was to be given to Tom after her death. [vi] Anne and her brother George did have an especially close relationship but, like the Thomas Wyatt I have created, I do not accept incest ever came into it. Rather it was a relationship strengthened and made strong by common loves and interests.

Wyatt was imprisoned in 1536, during the same month that saw the arrest of Anne and her alleged lovers. Some historians even claim that his arrest took place the day after the arrest of Anne. The Lisle Papers, a series of documents written by people who lived during this period, make a strong insinuation that his arrest was the result of his involvement with the Queen. Furthermore, a letter written by John Husee to the Viscount Lisle seems to imply that Husee had high expectations that Thomas' execution would shortly follow the others. [vii] Thomas himself said five years later, when he was again arrested, this earlier imprisonment had been due to the interference of the Duke of Suffolk, the brother-in-law of Henry the Eighth and described as the King's "alter ego." [viii]

It is interesting to speculate on the reasons behind these arrests; obviously there was little love lost between the Duke and Wyatt.

After his brief detention in the Tower in 1536, Thomas Wyatt was given over to the supervision of his father, who gratefully took Thomas back to the place of his birth 33 years before. This period of disgrace was short because the King soon relented and forgave Wyatt for the alleged wrong. It seems that the King may have felt some guilt on Wyatt's behalf because Wyatt was then made Steward of Conisborough Castle. Wyatt died in 1542 after catching a fever in service to his King. [ix]

REFERENCES

I have put the books used as references for this novel in categories; for example, books used in relation to Anne Boleyn will be grouped simply under the title ANNE BOLEYN, and so forth.

ANNE BOLEYN

Antonia Fraser; *The six wives of Henry VIII*; Arrow Books, 1998.

Retha M. Warnicke; *The Rise and Fall of Anne Boleyn*; Cambridge University Press; Cambridge; 1989.

E.W. Ives; *Anne Boleyn*; Basil Blackwell; U.K.; 1986.

Hester Chapman; *The Challenge of Anne Boleyn*; U.S.A, 1974

Marie Louise Bruce; *Anne Boleyn*; Collins, London, 1972.

Norah Loft; *Anne Boleyn*; G.B.; 1979

J. Ridley; *The life and times of Mary Tudor*; G. Weiden Field and Nicholson, 1973

J.J. Scarisbrick; *Henry the Eighth*; University Press, Berkley & Los Angeles, 1968.

Francis Hackett; *Henry the Eighth*; The Reprint society, this Edition 1946.

Robert Lacey; *The life and times of Henry VIII*; General Editor: Antonia Fraser; George Weidenfeld and Niclolson and Book Club, London; 1972

Neville Williams; *Elizabeth I*; Cardinal, London, 1975.

Jasper Ridley; *Statesman and Saint*; The Viking Press, N.Y. 1982.

Alison Weir, *Henry VIII, King and Court*, Random House, 2001.

SIR THOMAS WYATT

Kenneth Muir; *Life and letters of Sir Thomas Wyatt*; Liverpool University Press, Liverpool, 1963.

Patricia Thompson; *Wyatt, the critical heritage*; Routledge and K. Paul, Publishers, London, 1974.

Stephen Merriam Foley; *Sir Thomas Wyatt*; Twayne Publishers, Boston, 1990.

Collected Poems of Thomas Wyatt; edited by Kenneth Muir, Routledge & Kegan Paul, London and Henley, 1949.

Patricia Thompson; *Sir Thomas Wyatt and his background*; Routledge and Kegan Paul, London, 1964.

General editor: Christopher Ricks; *Sir Thomas Wyatt, the complete Poems*; Penguin books; 1978.

Lisle Letters; edited by Muriel St. Clare Byrne, selected and arranged by Bridget Boland, The Folio Press, London, 1983.

ROME (1523 to 1528)

Benvenuto Cellini; *The Autobiography of Benvenuto Cellini*; translated and with an introduction by George Bull, Penguin Books, 1956.

Hugh Ross Williamson; *Catherine de' Medici*; The Viking Press, N.Y.; 1973.

Christopher Hollis; *The Papacy*; Weidenfeld and Niclolson, London, 1964.

Andre Chastel; *The Sack of Rome, 1527*; Translated from the French by Beth Archer; The A.W. Mellon Lectures in fine Arts, 1983, U.K.

Christopher Hibbert; *Rome; the biography of a city*; Penguin books, 1985.

TUDOR ENGLAND

Roger Hart; *English life in Tudor times*; Wayland Publishers; London; 1972.

FRANCE

Desmond Seward; *Prince of the Renaissance;* Constable and Company; London; 1973.

MISCELLANEOUS

W.D. Rouse, translator; *Great Dialogues of Plato*; The New American Library; New York; 1956

Notes

(i)   Muir (editor); Collected poems of Sir Thomas Wyatt; p. ix

(ii)   *Ibid*

(iii) *Ibid*

(iv)   *Ibid*, p. x

(v)   *Ibid*

(vi)   Patricia Thomson, *Wyatt, the critical heritage*; p. 47

(vii) Muriel St. Clare Byrne, editor); selected and arranged by Bridget Byrne; *Lisle letters*; London; 1983; p. 165

(viii) J.J. Scarisbrick; *Henry VIII*; p. 52.

(ix)   Christopher Ricks (General Editor); *Sir Thomas Wyatt; The complete poems*; p. 31.

We hope you enjoyed this book.

Other titles from Metropolis Ink

Fiction

Zarathustra / Walter Stewart

Point of Honor / Douglas de Bono

Cold Logic / C. J. R. Casewit

Laylek's Song / Timothy VanSlyke

The Logan Factor / Vincent Scuro

The Reckoning / John McLain

Roma / Helen Duberstein

Time Suspended / Lori Avocato

The Day of the Nefilim / D. L. Major

A Change of Heart / Jermaine Watkins

Non-fiction

God Makes Sex Great!
Dr. Renier Holtzhausen & Professor Hennie Stander

How to Promote Your Home Business
John McLain

For information about these and other titles,
visit our web site at *www.metropolisink.com*.

METROPOLIS INK

Printed in the United States
1294600002B/73-75

9 780958 054355